Victoria

Victoria

SAMI MICHAEL

Translated from the Hebrew by

Dalya Bilu

MACMILLAN

First published 1995 by Macmillan

an imprint of Macmillan General Books
Cavaye Place London SW10 9PG
and Basingstoke

Associated companies throughout the world

ISBN 0-333-64396-8

First published in Hebrew 1993 by Am Oved, Tel Aviv

1 3 5 7 9 8 6 4 2

A CIP catalogue record for this book is available from the British Library

Typeset by CentraCet Limited, Cambridge
Printed by Mackays of Chatham plc, Kent

Victoria

1

Never before had she dared to go so far from home without a male escort. The swells of the surging river rocked the raft bridge beneath her until it seemed about to slip its moorings and be carried off by the muddy current. When the green flag was raised on the tower on the opposite bank, stopping the flow of traffic behind her and leaving the vehicle lane briefly free, a sense of release verging on abandon caused the packed crowd of pedestrians to spill into the road that had confined it, from which it jostled back onto the pavement only when it heard the first honk of a car coming toward it.

Victoria had not dared step down from the pavement. Anxious to get off the heaving platform of a bridge, the drivers of the automobiles stampeded the panicky horses pulling wagons and carriages and forced their coachmen to descend and grab their bridles while running alongside them. Victoria heard the hoofbeats, the slapping of bare feet, and the pants of the wagon drivers, saw the rearing heads of the horses and the white foam running from their muzzles, and could barely keep from joining in the flight. A fresh wave of dizziness swept over her, drenching her with sweat beneath her black silk kerchief. The river boomed against the rafts.

Few of the people on the bridge needed to reach the other side. Most were out for the excitement of being there—and indeed, a taut sense of impending disaster hung in the air. The rafts were not strong enough to withstand the raging water for long.

It seemed to Victoria that she was the only lone woman on the bridge. Not that she had intended to cross it. Before setting out she had donned the kerchief, covered her face with a black veil, and put a second veil over it to hide her tears. But she had never thought there would be so many people. She had pictured the bridge with nothing on it, like the laundry lines on empty roofs. The solitary birds that perched there, heads nestled in their feathers as if trying to decide whether to spread their wings and fly or to fold them and plummet earthward, had always intrigued her. She had never seen one take the plunge. But she had heard of people who did.

Several men, having noticed that she was alone, had grabbed at her under cover of the crush. One thrust practised fingers curved like meathooks into her buttocks. "Did I give it to her!" she heard him hoarsely tell his companion. She felt a stab of pain, but the crowd was too dense to escape the roaming hands.

Most of all, she feared the river that was her destination.

More eager fingers plucked at her. She thought it best to do nothing; turning on her assailants would only encourage them. Someone jammed his loins against her rear. A surge of people fleeing a frightened horse swept him away from her. Out of the corner of her eye she saw him grin. And a Jew too, damn him! Did Rafael do such things too? The answer was obvious. The whomp of her rear when he slapped it drove him delirious, and sometimes, after an encounter with a woman as wild as himself, he turned up covered with scratches and bruises like an animal stepping out of the brush. Why expect him to keep his hands in his pockets? She cursed him again with fresh tears. Her body that ached from the pinches of strangers longed for the fiery sting of desire that only he could arouse in her. He's dying, she told herself, you mustn't think of such things. Perhaps he had died already; if not yesterday, then today. Or tomorrow for sure. Stronger men than him had coughed their lungs out until there was nothing left. Someone as thin as himself was barely a snack for so ravenous a disease.

She felt helpless. She had set out to drown herself in the river, and now every bit of her passionately craved the caresses of a dying adulterer. The motion of the crowd prevented her from stopping against the railing to think. What would she do when she reached the end of the bridge?

From the moment the car that took Rafael to the Lebanese mountains disappeared in the dust of the desert there had been no end of questions and of nasty answers supplied by Victoria's mother Najia. Although he had always kept out of her way, Najia had hated Rafael since he was a boy. She had loathed all the families living around the courtyard and kept her distance from them.

Of Victoria's father Izuri, an arrogant titan who delighted in his role of chief potentate and breadwinner, Najia had been afraid as is a mediocre pupil of a strict teacher. Izuri had built up the family business—in which his older brother Yehuda, an observant Jew with a beard, had been too sickly to shoulder his share—by dint of hard, honest work. His other brother Eliyahu had never cared for the drudgery of it, and when he was caught with his hand in the till, Izuri and Yehuda dissolved their partnership with him and helped him to open a small book-bindery. Whenever he made a bit of money he rented a country cabin and spent his time there with Najia's brother, Dahood the zither player, running through his cash in the company of whores. Eventually he returned home to the courtyard, eyes blazing in a haggard face. Before every Passover, and sometimes closer to Shavu'ot, he went bankrupt and had to flee his creditors. In punishment for his attempted embezzlement he had been made to give up the large room that adjoined the sunlit quarters occupied by Victoria's family and to move with his wife and children to a windowless ground-floor alcove whose only door was a jute curtain. Long ago, when Michal, the three men's mother, ran a flourishing sewing shop that made uniforms for the Turkish army, it had served as a storeroom for fabric.

And Eliyahu had not reached bottom yet, though Izuri and Yehuda continued to show mercy when they discovered him in cahoots with the night watchman to steal some expensive bolts of silk. This time too he took his medicine and moved his family into the basement, where his children went as hungry as the mice. They froze in winter and were choked out into the open by the summer heat, blinking their eyes in the burning sun. And yet they bore with their disgrace, coming and going from their shelter like aliens in a hostile land.

One day, to the astonishment of all the women and children, Rafael stepped out of the dim basement in a strange get-up. His head was bare and his metallically gleaming hair was parted in the middle like that of the German advisers hired by the Ottoman government. Instead of his usual camel-wool cloak and striped tunic, he wore a short jacket with tight trousers that fitted his slender limbs snugly, made with the same white linen from which Grandmother Michal had recently sewn herself funeral shrouds. The pockets of this suit were not on the inside like an honest Jew's, but on the outside where anyone could poke about in them.

Ordinarily, the young women in the courtyard would have howled with laughter at the sight of the shiny walking stick that Rafael brandished. Now, however, they stared wonderingly, and a few ran unconscious hands over their groins even though he was not even a man yet. Next, despite the fact that it was an ordinary weekday, Rafael demanded to have his main meal served in the shaded arcade of the courtyard on a table scrubbed and set with polished silver, then dumped it in the rubbish upon discovering an odd stain on the rim of a plate brought by his mother. Everyone expected him to be struck down by lightning, but when his brother Asher boldly protested and one of his sisters let out a shriek, he marched them both to the middle of the courtyard and made them stand there in barefoot silence, beneath the blazing sun and his own baleful eye.

A hush descended on the courtyard, which was always noisy with women and small children. Najia stopped in her tracks with the broken bits of a china bowl that she was about to bring to the fix-it man whose cries she had heard in the street, her eyes glued to Rafael's white suit. Grandmother Michal, who was sitting on her little carpet by the second-floor railing, summoned Rafael up to her. She was not your ordinary old crone who is shunted off to some stool in a corner for wanting to live too long. The whole street still remembered the days of her glory and called her clan Beit-Michal, the House of Michal. Even Yehuda deferred to her and insisted that she be treated with reverence. And so when she called for Rafael, it was so quiet that you could hear the flies buzz. She and her grandson conversed in low tones, after which the boy descended the narrow stairs with bright eyes. Victoria and Miriam, Yehuda's daughter, were standing next to each other. Both were about ten years old, and Victoria felt something powerful pass over her and noticed that Miriam did too. In those days "love" was considered an improper word even between a husband and his wife, but as she stood there with her shoulder brushing Miriam's on the worn floor tiles of the ancient courtyard that had known many births and sudden deaths, and in which Grandmother Michal herself had been raised and had watched her three infant sons crawl, Victoria realized that she had ripened into a woman.

All this while Asher and his sister baked barefoot in the sun. Najia stood behind Victoria and Miriam, looking more like an unwanted servant than the wife of the pillar of the courtyard. The lines of her palms were grimy with kitchen smoke, her slippers were torn, she wore a ragged dress, and her small, pretty eyes had a dark, hunted look. The beauty of the building was Yehuda's wife and Miriam's mother, buxom, light-skinned Aziza. The more Yehuda pored over his religious books, his silvery beard giving him a spiritual look that raised him above the trifles of the courtyard, the more Aziza enjoyed the pleasures of life. She had a laugh that was too easy and infectious for a decent woman, loved risqué jokes, and served meals that were a delight to look at. The household was convinced that her frail, kindly husband would have given up the ghost long ago if not for all the rich food that she fed him.

Najia's table was slovenly by comparison. Its silver was bent and she always burned the meat. Sometimes too she left the clothes hanging on the line until Izuri's shirts tore in the wind or a grasping neighbour stole the children's cloaks. Izuri, who liked to dress well, would clap his head in despair on Sabbath eves and go off to synagogue in clothes sour from sweat. Whereas Aziza's embroidered sheets had an aroma of soap and sun, Najia's linens looked as tattered and untidy as if a family of mice had just romped in them.

When Yehuda first fell ill, no one gave him long to live. For months his groans gave the neighbours no peace. He prayed to God to put an end to his suffering, and even Aziza was so nauseated by it that she took to throwing up on the roof. All sympathized and praised her devotion to the saintly patient in his rank-smelling bed. Only Najia was unimpressed. Some thought the prophetic smile that played over her lips in those days was a sign of being punchdrunk from life's blows—first, her father's, might he rest in peace; then her brother Dahood the zither player's; and finally, her husband's. Others considered it oracular.

In the meantime, while Yehuda bore with his pain, Aziza's stomach began to swell. Although Najia never said so in so many words, she hinted broadly that her husband was to blame. And yet despite the snide comments, Aziza displayed her belly proudly and—long, fruitless years after the arrival of her son Ezra—gave birth to Miriam. Najia made no attempt to hide her aversion for the baby, who was delivered in the same month as her own daughter Victoria, but no amount of gossip could cloud the blissful look that Aziza went around with. Sometimes indeed, even in the middle of the marketplace, Aziza forgot herself, bared both of her plump white breasts, and let the two little girls suck on their bounty together. They were raised like twins, and the older they became, the stronger grew the tie between them and the more quarrels and teenage crushes it survived. Both smilingly denied that this was because they were half-sisters, and both went on loving each other to a ripe old age.

On the day that Najia stood behind the two girls as they watched Rafael descend the stairs from his grandmother's carpet, she was already as weathered as a Bedouin. Grandmother

Michal, who suffered from her son Izuri's unhappy marriage, considered his match with Najia to have been the mistake of her life. And yet in a house that Eliyahu regularly fled for the arms of his mistresses and in which Yehuda sank ever deeper into his holy books, Izuri's unkempt bed was like a busy warren. With the fall of night he would ease himself down on its stiff mattress and bellow shamelessly for Najia, imperious tones issuing from his great cavity of a chest until, half-grumbling and half-fearful, she dragged her dirty feet to him.

Now, as Rafael headed back down to the courtyard, Najia listened mournfully to the vanishing cries of the fix-it man, not only because her broken vase would not be mended, but because she liked to watch tinkers at their work. She could stare at the sparks from a knife grinder's wheel for hours on end, and having grasped that all she had witnessed was Rafael's precocious passage to manhood, she wrote him off as a young profligate best steered clear of.

Just as some hidden property in her goaded Izuri's passion, so her body proved fertile ground for his seed. Whereas Aziza gave birth to Ezra and Miriam and ceased having children for good, Najia, who would live through two world wars and die in Israel, had eighteen of them. Ten perished in infancy, while the others grew up to be healthy and strong.

Michal was not happy with a single one of her grandchildren. In the last century her family had been wealthy and had even boasted a chief rabbi, and for years she had indulged in the dream of a future renaissance. And yet she had never expected much from her granddaughters, and it was with a sort of resignation that she now accepted the reality of Rafael's Western clothes. The one grandchild she had a soft spot for was Victoria, whose busy hands kept trying to make amends for her mother's ineptness, and while Victoria never responded to her grandmother's warmth, it was enough to make Najia treat her as a hated rival. Although Victoria wept and denied it, Najia insisted not only that her grandmother preferred her because she fawned on her, but also that she played the coquette with her father, baring her knees as seductively in front of him as if they were a pair of young breasts. Twice Najia spilled hot oil on her daughter, and twice too, steaming tea—each time, of course, accidentally. She was too much of a butterfingers to be accused of dropping anything on purpose, but when no one was looking, her incontinent hands sometimes lashed Victoria's face with a rough sprig of herbs while the child was helping in the kitchen.

In the end, it was Rafael who saved Eliyahu's family from starvation. He was the only reason that there was enough to eat, and while his father was off having revels he clothed all his sisters and promised each one of them that she would not have to die a virgin for lack of a proper dowry.

2

Victoria sat in the kitchen doorway, slicing stems of okra in the stupefying heat. Its sticky hairs stung her fingers. "What do you think he does every night in that theeayter?" she whispered.

Miriam flapped the bottom of her dress to fan her sweaty thighs. "He undresses women like Rahma Afsa in his imagination and wonders how he can fuck them. Oh, wouldn't I like to lay my head on his shoulder and soap his balls slowly while he bathes in the big basin!"

Victoria reddened. "Shhh!" she said. "They'll hear you!"

Sixty years later, she did not think of those days as unhappy ones. In fact, she nostalgically remembered them as the best and happiest of her life. The deep feeling between her and Miriam protected them both from the hostile incursions of the adult world. Like most girls, they were raised to obey their fathers and brothers blindly. Even Miriam, who was Aziza's pride and joy, could expect a cuff from her brother Ezra if she didn't do his bidding fast enough. And yet without being aware of it, Victoria projected her father's proud authority already as a child. As was the case in those days, her femininity awoke early and wild horses galloped through her dreams.

Families lived so crowded together that there was little to separate adults from children. For half the year all made their beds on the roof, one mattress touching another. At night both sexes bedded down beneath the stars and the moon, and Victoria and Miriam saw much and heard everything. Balky women were raped amid curses, while others yielded with the docility of dumb beasts. Slender girls screeched with pain and hefty wives swatted off scrawny husbands with disdain. Some were tigers who lay in wait for their prey, dripping venom when they arose unsated, and others shook the roof and all its sleepers when they encountered tigers like themselves. Nothing, however, excited Victoria more than the passionate cooing of the doves. As she imagined them dipping in silky whispers, bathing in caresses of rose-water, and spreading the fragrant pollen of the palm trees in the spring air, her hands stole to her budding breasts and fondled them gently.

Whenever she went up to the roof, she kept her eyes from straying to the forbidden rooftop of the Nunu family next door. Father and daughter would be lying there nonchalantly, attended by a bevy of silent servants, the subject of avid rumours in the narrow streets below. Victoria preferred to look at the lower roof between them, where Rafael made his bed far from his brothers and parents. Even when he slept, he kept to himself. A year had passed since his first emergence from the basement in his astounding suit, and now all were talking about a great war of Armageddon that might hasten the arrival of the Messiah. Meanwhile, he was already supporting his family from his father's business. Every evening he went to the mysterious place that everyone called "the theeayter", though no one knew what it was, and sometimes he returned home through the dark streets in the early hours of the dawn. Izuri looked on in reproachful silence. A Jew who did not fear demons, ghosts and the Turkish constabulary could hardly be counted on to fear God. And as if to confirm his uncle's premonitions, Rafael stopped going with the other men to synagogue not only on weekdays, but on holidays too. Coming home early from work, he would quickly wash and sit down to a leisurely supper without asking the Lord's blessing, after which he donned his suit and set out, graced by a bowtie and his ornate walking stick, at an hour when most folk were turning in.

Victoria looked down on his empty mattress from the upper roof and tried picturing the theeayter. She imagined it as a huge, steamy pool of the sort reserved for important people in the public baths, from which rose a column of scent and fragrant soap bubbles. Bare buttocks and testicles gleamed through its vapours, while the face of the water was rippled by eerie laughter like that coming from the house of Abdallah and Nuna Nunu. Darkly uttered words fluttered like moths and flesh slid off flesh with the loud, titillating smack of the netted fish on the banks of the Tigris. Victoria felt her throat tighten and a shiver run down her. The pleasure was so great that she felt ashamed to look up at the stars.

It was more or less agreed upon among the three fathers that, when the time came, Rafael would take either Victoria or Miriam for his wife. Yehuda, Miriam's father, made no secret of his fondness for the bright youngster, whose religious laxness he conveniently overlooked; Aziza exulted in his rakish appearance and honoured his silences, which harboured a masculine strength; their son Ezra, who would one day shake off the dust of the neighbourhood to become the owner of a fashionable pharmacy on El-Rashid Street, worshipped his older cousin; and so Victoria was sure that the choice would fall on Miriam—especially since, besides being disliked by Najia, Rafael was suspected by Izuri of challenging his preeminence. A cold wall rose higher between them day by day.

Miriam glanced at the bowl that was filling up with beheaded okra and said:

"You don't actually fuck in the theeayter, you just work up an appetite. They get drunk and go to Kilachia. Just think of it—a whole neighbourhood full of cafés and restaurants with no one living there but whores! Rahma Afsa works there. My father is like a candle without a wick, and my mother is like the fire beneath a pot. She goes all the time to Jamila. I even heard Jamila teaching her how to pee. It's something else. Come on, let's leave this cruddy okra and go up to the roof. No one's there. I'll show you how to do it."

Victoria glanced at her mother, who had dozed off open-mouthed in the hallway with her latest baby sleeping at her breast. Flies lapped at the droplets on her dark bore. Victoria felt goose pimples at the thought of all kinds of strange things coming out of there: bugs, and torn stockings, and watermelon peels, and curses, and dirty kinks of hair.

"Come on," urged her cousin.

"No," she balked.

Miriam sighed but explained anyway. "You have to pee and stop all at once, then pee some more and stop again. It's called making-the-deer-run-between-your-legs."

Toward evening Victoria went up to the roof to spread the mattresses out to air from the day's heat. She kneeled by the tin balustrade facing the Nunus and let her urine run out onto the rooftop, but no deer ran between her legs. With a smile, she forgave Miriam her imagination.

Rafael did not come home that night. In the morning there was more talk of the great war that would consume even the grass in the fields. Asher stood on the middle roof beside his brother's empty mattress and began to say something, then thought better of it. Najia welcomed the rising sun with her soothsayer's smile and hurried to bring Izuri his morning tea. She moved about energetically and refused all help from Victoria, whom she treated as if she were sick and needed rest.

Victoria wanted to be alone and went off to squat in the kitchen. Since the day it was built no one had bothered to scrub its walls, which were black from the smoke of thousands of cooking fires. There was something magical about this darkness with its invisible ceiling, unbrightened by any window or source of light. The children liked to pretend that the entire room was a tall chimney leading to the world of the dead, but even the real chimney had never been found and no one could say how the smoke escaped. Once, years ago, Victoria, Miriam, and the other children had watched Rafael try to solve the mystery. They sat sucking the tart juice of some lemons they had mushed and made holes in for straws while Rafael poked unsuccessfully at the ceiling with a long pole. Only when he mounted the stalwart shoulders of Miriam's brother Ezra did the pole appear to strike home. There was a cry as all quickly fled their tense post in the kitchen doorway—through which, pursued by Rafael, rushed a headless monster dragging its long black hair on the floor. Bruised from his fall on the stone ovens, Rafael kicked at it and shouted, "You moron, you nearly killed me," while Ezra frantically sought to shake off decades of sooty, greasy spider webs. Yet though Rafael soon returned with a kerosene lantern, the kitchen retained its secrets even after the avalanche and the chimney was never discovered.

As chief provider of the clan, Izuri enjoyed the right to live with his family in the room with the glass-paned windows, which also entitled Najia to the stove nearest the doorway—a privilege, however, like others both in and out of the kitchen, that she did nothing to exercise. Year by year she was shouldered aside by young daughters-in-law until she reached the last stove at the kitchen's dark end, which was where Victoria had found a haven this morning. Gradually, she began to make out her mother in the darkness. "The little bastard flew the coop," Najia said to her, her voice coarsened by its own sensuality. "Why expect him to be any different from his father? He's left his family to starve and gone whoring. That hunchback, Ma'atuk Nunu, is a better man than he is. You just remember what your mother told you."

Ma'atuk Nunu was Abdallah's son and Nuna's brother. The two families lived next door to each other, one roof facing the other. The Nunus' roof had an opening through which grew a tall date palm, the only tree on the street. Abdallah Nunu was so proud of it that a person might have thought he had planned his whole house around it. In the summer its great fronds shaded the white mosquito nets and swayed in the wind like a band of merry drunks.

Most of the rooms in the Nunus' house were empty. Ma'atuk was born after the beautiful Nuna, with a crooked spine and six fingers on each hand, and Abdallah was so aghast that he did not even pay the confined mother a visit. Already as a child Ma'atuk stayed at home because the boys in the neighbourhood made fun of the hump growing on his back. Worse yet, Abdallah's sister Hannah accused Ma'atuk's mother of bewitching her. It was no accident, she claimed, that she had lost her husband in the sixth month of pregnancy and that her own son Ilias was an epileptic. Not that Abdallah Nunu needed to be egged on by his sister. Two birth defects in a single child were more than enough for a wealthy cattle dealer who liked to entertain and give dinner parties, and he banished his wife and son to a rented room at the far end of the neighbourhood, where they struggled to get by. And yet instead of reverting to his old hospitality, he now proceeded to spend all his time cultivating the beautiful Nuna in blissful and forbidden solitude.

Nuna was rarely seen out-of-doors. At the age of ten she was wearing pearls, rouging her lips with French lipstick, and putting on eye make-up. But since Abdallah Nuna and Grandmother Michal's houses were two oases of affluence in a wilderness of indigence, and the poor looked up to whomever God smiled down on, none of the other families on the street ever dreamed of pointing an accusing finger at the Nunus. All the girls in the neighbourhood envied her. Her name rang like bells on their tongues. By the time she was twelve she had become such a recluse that she was never seen any more. It was even said that she had died of a sudden illness, a surmise confuted twice a week by Abdallah's jovial appearance on a white mule with red tassels and green beads. It did not even seem strange when he rejected all the feelers of the matchmakers, since someone like Nuna was clearly meant for high station. And so, when the Nunus' servants broke into ululations of joy at the news that a bridegroom had been found, the whole street was beside itself; yet great was the consternation on the night of Nuna's wedding, when the groom—a total stranger who reputedly come from a distant port, and according to some, from as far off as India—cut as sorry a figure beside his bride on their raised platform as the lowliest water carrier who toted cans from the river. The band, the hundreds of candles, the grand carpets—all seemed to have paralyzed him. Nuna did not even glance his way. Not a heart but was moved by her innocent laughter. The men got drunk and the women went home with a feeling of having been cheated.

Soon after, Najia began ascending to the roof and spying on the neighbours' courtyard. Her brother Dahood the zither player took this as one more sign of her being addled and advised forgiving her for her sinful thoughts. Not so Victoria. Once her father had taken her with the other children of the household to a tent of magic mirrors belonging to a travelling circus, and though all had howled with laughter at their monstrous images, she alone had noticed that the mirrors' depravity did not totally distort the truth. If you were a dwarf, they did not turn you into a giant.

Victoria was too small to be of much help when her mother made her climb a stack of folded mattresses and peek into the Nunus' courtyard, nor did Najia's explanations, which were illustrated by loud kissing sounds, mean anything to her. She had just begun to grasp nonetheless that something horrendous was happening when she and her mother were forced to beat a retreat by Abdallah's sister Hannah, who loudly told them to stick their faces in excrement.

The rumours became daily grist for the women of the household. It did no good for Michal to scoldingly point out that they might be libelling innocents. Najia's imagination was inflamed by the house next door. The slightest peep from there was enough to make her gallop up the stairs, dragging Victoria behind her to the tin balustrade. Victoria strained to see but felt a weight in her heart, as if the most despicable sinner were herself. Gradually, she came to understand the truth: her three neighbours, father, son-in-law, and daughter, were trapped in a vortex that sucked them into it each day. Although her mother kept dragging her up to the roof, she was sickened by what she saw there, as if it were a special treat that she had been forced to eat until it tasted like medicine. She began to fear for her sanity. Her three neighbours invaded her dreams with horrid masks on their faces, but instead of Nuna's lewd giggle behind locked doors, the laugh she heard was her own, and the place of Nuna's squat husband knocking in vain was taken by Ma'atuk, a stooped figure with a hump like a clay barrel on his back who drooled the babbled phrases of a baby. She longed to trample his hideous form and hear it splatter like a cockroach. Abdallah tried to hide his laughter, which only made it sound more venomous, and each time she woke she was struck dumb by the same delicious terror. It was her father who had laughed in her dream, not Abdallah Nunu, and as he approached, a conquering giant, the mockingly closed door dissolved.

Eventually, she refused to obey her mother's orders to follow her up to the roof. Yet Najia's tongue not only kept wagging, it cast aside all restraint and made the child's guilt even worse. Victoria stopped playing Miriam's favourite game of making themselves up like women and subtly rebuffed her father's affectionate overtures. When he asked her to soap his back while he bathed in the basin, she did it with closed eyes. The exciting gifts that she received from him, such as a red Persian apple or a gold earring, were passed on to her mother as a bribe and sop to her conscience. She loved her father deeply. It was hard not to love him. He was the sultan of the household, an unfailing source of bounty, not at all like the sickly, spartan Yehuda or the perennially bankrupt Eliyahu. None of the women in the courtyard, not even the young brides, were indifferent to his captivating presence.

Now, warding off the roving fingers on the bridge above the cresting river, she wondered how her mother had been so quick to notice her young love for Rafael.

By the age of eight, the boys had stopped playing and wrestling with the girls. Only a few couples continued in secret, and Rafael, who took to ignoring girls even earlier than the other boys, was not in their ranks. To Ezra's dismay, he stopped playing with boys his age too and became a stranger in the building he was born in. Already too old at heart to join in their pranks, he was not a grown man either, and he remained aloof. Both at home and away from it, adulthood meant imposing a centuries-old reign of terror; the fear of men—especially of strange or new ones—was considered basic hygiene for a woman; and in declining to play his preordained role, Rafael ruled out a friendship with his peers. Yehuda and Izuri let him go his own way and sighed with relief when they saw that he was able to support his family and forestall his father's business failures, which Eliyahu no longer needed to be bailed out of. Gradually, Rafael forced his two uncles to treat him as an equal, and while Izuri kept a chilly distance, Yehuda was taken by the young man's charms.

On Najia these had no effect. She was immune to them. Her opinion of Rafael never changed: he was more dangerous than the most violent of men, more deceitful than the most obsequious, dissipated through and through despite his polished manners. She did not say this to his face, of course. Her poison-tipped thoughts were kept for Victoria, into whose ear she launched them at every opportunity, while cooking, washing, and nursing. Victoria refused to listen. She was happy to be in love with Rafael, not least because it made her feel sane. Her father no longer lurked in her dreams, and she felt that she had bested her mother too. She nursed her love and basked in it without confessing it even to Miriam, let alone to Rafael. On the contrary: the stronger her feelings for him, the more she kept away from him.

But Najia guessed anyhow—hence her prophetic smile at the sight of Rafael's unslept-on mattress. For four anxious days no one knew where he was. Someone at the far end of the neighbourhood reported having been awakened at night by the crack of a pistol shot. Someone else spoke of hearing a man's death rattle from an altogether different direction. But no body turned up and Jews did not go to the police in such matters.

The more everyone worried, the more Najia smiled. Curious and covetous, the neighbours advised Rafael's father to break the lock on the big trunk in which he kept his clothes and belongings. Victoria went upstairs and found Michạl on her rug, grumbling "the dogs!" with each blow of the hammer. Eliyahu and his brothers were vexed to find no treasure, which only increased their grief. Rafael's loafers, suits, and silk shirts were laid out in the basement on stools like worthless plunder.

It was at this juncture that Rafael returned in one piece, bursting furiously into the basement to the sound of frightened screams. Shoving away his father and lashing out at his lamenting mother, he turned on the despoilers with merciless kicks. A porter with a donkey was waiting outside.

"Where are you going?" wailed his mother.

"Away." His hair was unkempt, his eyes were bloodshot, and his face was drawn.

Victoria, who had been leaning against the second-floor railing, felt faint, even though Rafael was as repulsive to her at that moment as if he had stepped out of a cesspool.

"And the bindery?" asked his elder sister in despair.

"Sold."

The porter's body vanished beneath the big trunk, which seemed from Victoria's vantage point to bob unassisted in air while Rafael walked behind it like a sorcerer.

"A little more to the left! Lower, or you'll hit the lintel. Now right!"

The trunk obeyed him, passing through the doorway while the household watched with expressionless faces.

That same day Rafael, who was fifteen years old and already the lover of a chanteuse, headed across the desert for Damascus in a covered wagon.

Hunger descended on the basement once more.

3

The flags changed again on the towers at the ends of the bridge, and the crowd spilled into the vehicle lane. This time the honking cars approached from the other direction, so that for a moment it seemed that they were the same ones that had passed before, jokingly returning to force the pedestrians back onto the packed sidewalk. Victoria spied two women, veiled like herself and dressed in the coarse woollen cloaks of the poor, signalling that they saw her distress. In a jiffy they had joined her, flanking her on both sides and slightly to the rear to shield her from the male hands that assailed her. Their cloaks had a harsh smell and they spoke in low murmurs and stifled bursts of laughter. The way they clung to her suggested more than the innocent desire to protect her.

Behind her double veil, Victoria felt her eyes bulge. What if the two were men pretending to be women in order to rob or molest her? But their muffled laughs could only have come from women's throats, young ones at that, and her last doubts were removed by the pressure of their firm breasts. Although she could not make out their faces, the warmth of their eager thighs was pleasurable against her own in the chill wind coming off the river. A sweet shiver ran down her and she felt herself blush. The two cooed to her in soft voices. They were no longer frightening or distasteful. Her sweat-smell mingled with the fragrance of the scents absorbed by her cloak in better days. With an irrational pride she thought that she smelled better to her accosters than the horses or the wild river.

The realization struck her that she was still alive and breathing. Why, she had left the house as good as dead!

When had she last heard such tender voices? Though a lump

still smarted in her throat from the indignity, something stronger than herself drove her to submit to the strange touch and to feed on its animal, even though female, warmth.

"O my beauty. O my darling. O light of my eyes," sweetly murmured the voice on her right, drowning out the din of the bridge.

"You smell like the jasmine in Paradise," said the murmur on her right above the roaring water.

The thrill awakened by the unfamiliar contact turned to a feeling of vertigo. Though she was desperate for air beneath her veils, she was afraid to remove them, and when she shakily fanned her face with them the women only sidled closer, thinking she was whispering back. Victoria bit her lips against the dark mist descending on her. Leave me alone, she wanted to cry out loud. It chagrined her that her faintness came more from plain hunger than from the assaults on her body, and she tried telling herself that someone about to die should not be afraid of such things. And yet here, on this bridge, death had gone off and left her with them. She had not eaten before leaving home, although she had remembered to feed little Suzanne and Kilmanteen and to make sure that her sister would look after them until her long absence was noticed by the household. And nothing, she thought, feeling yet another twinge, this time in her heart, was longer than death.

But her hunger pangs were insistent. They made her think of the famine in the basement that winter long ago.

Shortly before Purim word reached them from Damascus that Rafael was living there with his chanteuse. Who was supporting who was the subject of much spiteful speculation. Aziza alone refused to cast a stone. "He would never live off another man," she said, "so he certainly isn't living off her. He's got balls, that boy."

"Woman," said a shocked Yehuda, "watch your tongue!"

Aziza laughed as if she had mentioned an amusing toy. "Miriam," she said, "don't believe all their crap." And looking straight at her brother-in-law Izuri, she added: "Rafael has the balls *and* the brains of a grown man."

Izuri turned away. Victoria winced to hear her uncle's wife speak like that to her father and waited for him to say something. But although a piercing glance from him was usually enough to silence any backtalk, he now paled and shifted in his seat like a man whose clothes were too tight. He ground out his cigarette with the tip of his shoe and lit another uneasily, as if embarrassed by the smoke drifting up from his bushy moustache.

Once again, in one last righteous outbreak of charity, Izuri and Yehuda put their debauched brother back on his feet. Together with Michal they paid off his debts and rented and equipped a new bindery. Eliyahu lasted in it almost until Tisha b'Av. For months he put up with having to earn a living while stalking the house like a prisoner whose cellmates aroused his abhorrence. He seemed to be listening to the unfamiliar strains of something far away, and in the end, like so often in the past—like Rafael—he disappeared. Once more his sons and daughters crept back into the dim basement, excommunicated by the courtyard. The crimes of the deserters were always paid for by those who stayed behind.

Victoria's tears confirmed her mother's predictions, and Najia enjoyed catching her with them. If she went on ignoring every normal young man for one as flighty as the steam from a basin of hot wash, Najia told her unceremoniously, she would indeed end up crawling into Rafael's bed, no better than Nuna Nunu.

Najia could not control her tongue. She had stopped going up to the roof, she told Victoria, because she had learned all the Nunus' tricks. "To think what an idiot I was, what an imbecile!" she exclaimed, scolding her slowness in discovering the truth. Transformed into an inspired chef, she moved her cooking board out of the kitchen and prepared her family's meals under the noses of the basement's famished inhabitants. Every day a delivery boy arrived from the market, bringing fresh vegetables, grapes and dates. She seemed reborn as she stood quartering chickens, slicing fish, and marinating lambchops while crooning to herself with dancing shoulders until Grandmother Michal exclaimed sharply from her carpet on the second floor:

"Have some fear of God, woman!"

As though flushed by this cry from Najia's siege of plenty, a silent column of starved creatures appeared from the basement. Led by their mother Hanina, a pot in her hands, they seemed to belong to two different species, half stout and swarthy like her and half tall and fair like their father. Fearful of the Evil Eye, Najia hurriedly covered her meat and fruit with a thin cloth, but the procession swung around her, oblivious to her laden cooking board, and marched to the kitchen doorway. There it huddled while Hanina knelt by the third stove and lit a fire of twigs beneath the pot.

Meanwhile, the bickering between Miriam's parents erupted into a loud quarrel. A large crowd had gone to the Great Synagogue that day to hear a sermon by Rabbi Shimon Agasi, in which—albeit tardily—he had addressed the revolution of the Young Turks; the drought that was already in its second year; the conscription of young Jews into the hated Turkish army; and the recent rise in prices. Yehuda felt suffocated by the congestion and exhausted by the endless sermon, and when the rabbi assailed the spread of loose morals among the city's Jews, which had invoked the wrath of the Almighty, his shoulders felt the full brunt of their sinfulness. He returned home crushed, headed straight for the couch, and lay there ashen-faced and dull-eyed beneath the compress of vinegar that Aziza put on his forehead. Pointing with his beard to Miriam, who was busy braiding her hair in front of a mirror held by Victoria, he said in a whisper:

"That's just what the rabbi was talking about."

"Why don't you and your rabbi stick to the Torah and leave the child alone," said Aziza. "What has she done to you?"

"Look at her dress. Her legs are bare almost to the knees."

"And that's why we've had no rain for two years? Don't make me laugh. I'd like to know what sin your bad heart is a punishment for. Or your other illness, which I don't even want to talk about, the one that left you such a wreck. You have a lovely daughter, and if the Turks are crazy enough to start taking our sons to the army, don't blame it on Miriam's dress."

"And Ezra," said Yehuda miserably.

"God help us. Did your rabbi talk about him too?"

"Every word."

"Over my dead body he will! Ezra goes to a Jewish high school," Aziza boasted. "He's the only high-school student on the street."

"The rabbi could have had him before his eyes. He's cut his side locks off. He studies foreign languages instead of the Torah."

"That's just envy talking."

"Woman!" chided Yehuda. "The rabbi is a saint."

"God save us from your saints. It was a drought that made Jacob send his sons to Egypt. There was hunger in the world before there were French-speaking high schools. People starved to death even though their wives dressed in black from head to toe like Bedouins. Tell your rabbi to stick to his prayers and let us be."

"Go talk to a woman," sighed Yehuda.

Aziza lost her temper. It was all she could do to keep herself from hitting him. "Look who's the big expert on women!"

A cold sweat covered Yehuda and he felt a growing pressure in his chest. He tried to calm himself. Although it was only fair to remember Aziza's love and devotion, all he could think of was her barren laughter and his own impotence. His anger mounted. "Get away from me!" he wheezed. Aziza shrugged and smiled to herself, pushing her heavy body off the mat with her arms. She was a large woman with a big appetite, and she knew that men still found her attractive. "There are some sugar rolls left," she said. "I'll warm one up for you."

"I don't want your roll."

"Oh, lordy," she pouted. "Ezra, do you?"

When Ezra came downstairs, he was absent-mindedly munching a roll soaked with butter on which grains of sugar sparkled like tiny diamonds. Since Rafael's departure, the courtyard had been for him like a desert island. Now, noticing the stony mass of his cousins in the kitchen doorway, he changed his plans to go out, sat down beside them, and smiled. "Who wants a bite?"

Eyes glittered but there was no response. Young as they were, they knew that nothing came free. For a piece of the butter-drenched sugar roll, Hanina's two youngest sons would gladly have let Ezra pull their ears or ride them like horses ten times across the courtyard. A few weeks ago, with a strong tail wind at his back, Asher had leaped the narrow lane outside—from Sha'ul the peddler's roof to one-eyed Kaduri's—for a plate of kubbeh. Far from being a sadist in their eyes, Ezra seemed to them a privileged being who could be forgiven everything except the failure to state his price.

He reached out for the two nearest heads and pulled them closer to him. "Who'll sneak into Nuna Nunu's bedroom and hide beneath her bed to see who gets on top of her?" He held the sweet-smelling roll close to the two boys' black forelocks. They swallowed. Asher, who was one of the short, swarthy ones, went for the bait. "And the sugar roll?"

"You can have all of it."

"Now?"

"I'm not that dumb."

The deal fell through to the disappointment of all, including Ezra, who looked hollow-eyed at the deserted courtyard. Glumly, he finished his sugar roll, which did not even taste good any more. Hanina's youngest son fell on his hand and avidly licked the sweet goo from his fingers, working his tongue into the spaces between them and even beneath the nails. Ezra cringed with an embarrassed grin, as if masturbated on by a dog.

"What is your mother making?" he asked apathetically.

As if sworn to silence, his cousins exchanged determined looks.

"I don't smell anything cooking."

"There's lentils, and rice, and even sesame oil," boasted the tallest and most light-skinned of them. The others imperceptibly closed ranks to hide their mother and the pot. Ezra could have easily broken through the cordon—anyone could do what he wished with them—but their do-or-die look warned him off.

Out in the passageway Miriam said:

"I'll bet they're just boiling water with a bit of wormy old rice. Turn around and I'll comb you and do your braids. He should never have run off with her."

Victoria nodded. Shutting her eyes, she entrusted herself to Miriam's hands and allowed blasphemously:

"No. He shouldn't have."

"They get into the Nunus' from our roof and rob their pantry. Mama says that the minute she turns her back they steal from our pots."

Victoria harboured other doubts too. About Grandmother Michal, for instance, though everyone stood in awe of her and knew that she was a saint. The grown-ups swore by her, whole packs of lies collapsing when they did, and she had once even come to the rescue of a dying rat. For years the rats and the household had got along, the former stealing precious food and the latter obtaining its revenge by seeing the corpses of the culprits dangling from the cat's jaws, until one day one of them bit a baby's nose and the courtyard was thrown into a turmoil. Rafael rushed out to buy a trap, and when it banged shut in the middle of the night the men jumped out of bed in their underwear and stood staring with the women and children at the terrified little grey ball in the corner of its cage. Rafael boiled water and poured it over the rat, and the children cheered until, gripping the second-floor railing, Grandmother Michal rose from her rug and called down:

"I won't have it! If we start with rats, who knows where we'll end up? God created snakes and cats, and it's their job to catch pests, not ours. An animal's screams are nothing to laugh at."

Her sermon came too late to save the rat. Its corpse was thrown out and the trap put away on a grimy shelf and forgotten until Jamila the fortune teller, who was also a matchmaker, keener, spell remover, and midwife, was urgently summoned to the Nunus'. For two whole days Abdallah had been unable to pass water, and now he pleaded: "Please, God, You created rivers and oceans—what, begging Your pardon, is a drop of urine to you?" "Try, Father," coaxed his son-in-law, whose name no one on the street remembered, loyally holding the chamberpot between Abdallah's outspread legs while cajoling him in quiet tones. "You're afraid of the pain, but you'll see, it's only the first few drops that hurt." Abdallah's sister Hannah was sure he had been bewitched by his banished wife, and Nuna's attempt to thaw out his system by pouring hot oil on his stomach did no good at all: Abdallah bellowed and Nuna sobbed while her husband stood helplessly by with the dry potty. In the end, she decided to milk him like a goat. Abdallah let out a scream and a suspicious liquid oozed into the potty. "Blood!" he shrieked. "It's the plagues of Egypt!"

Hannah and the Kurdish housemaids ransacked the house and found a mouse trap smelling of death beneath the sick man's bed. "I told you so!" Hannah said, "I told you!" Jamila was called to remove the spell, and she ordered the trap to be burned by the trunk of the date palm, threw the ashes from its wood in the drain, and took its twisted metal frame home with the promise to leave it on the doorstep of Nuna's mother. Abdallah recovered. Within a few days he was well enough to give a party at which he regaled the guests with a description of his son-in-law's expression as he held the potty between his legs. "I swear," he said, "a man like that is a godsend. What a soul!"

Although Ezra's motives were unclear, the courtyard did not scold him for his prank. Not everything called for an explanation. Ghosts, jinns, Evil Eyes, magic spells, miracles, and dreams that told the future were daily occurrences.

When the pot in the kitchen came to life and its lid began to clatter like possessed cymbals, Hanina rose, grasped its handle with the aid of a rag, and marched her children in silence from the sooty kitchen to the basement, into the dark maw of which they vanished. Najia, who was busy slaughtering tomatoes and draining their blood on her cooking board, remained in the kitchen with Ezra, who wiped his sticky fingers on his pants. Both were as blank-faced as a pair of actors that has been walked out on by its audience.

Her hair transformed by Miriam's fingers into two black snakes, Victoria wondered why Grandmother Michal did not speak up.

4

Her black veils hid Victoria's flushed face from the eyes of her two accosters and kept them from guessing her state. When her cloaked form did not respond to their increasingly insistent advances, they jabbed her with their knees and pinched her breasts and buttocks, until their vengefulness abated and they broke away from the impenetrable, splendidly curved cloak that moved along, frigid as death, like a windowless, black jail cell. As they sought to veer off, however, a solid human wave drove them back, and they struggled to break free as though trapped in a whirlpool with a corpse, the fear of which was greater than that of being dragged down to the depths. They did not know that Victoria's initial resistance had faded with the passing of her dizziness, and that she was now ready to yield to—indeed even craved—the delicious warmth she had at first felt ashamed of.

And yet fearful of where such novelty might lead, Victoria felt relieved to be abandoned by the two even as the cessation of contact left her with a painful sense of loss. Suppose that, put off or even repelled by her, they had chosen to stick her with pins or rip off her cloak, exposing her, an unchaperoned woman, in a house dress flecked with kitchen stains and baby drool amid a crowd of predatory men! She bit her lips and seized the railing of the bridge, clinging to it even though her arms were nearly torn from their sockets. A few seconds were all it took for the two women to be carried away by the flow. She felt the railing dig into her; someone rammed her with his knee, a faceless hand pawed at her cloak; she choked back a scream as a man's fingers squeezed her breast; but the two were soon gone, and she let go of her grip and let herself be swept along again.

She felt shattered, exhausted. A sense of numbness enveloped her once more, though her hunger, humiliation and fatigue were pierced by the gnawing question of what to do at the end of the bridge. She could not afford to appear indecisive. From childhood on she had been taught to do nothing in public that lacked an obvious purpose or suggested an availability for illicit pleasure. A lone figure in a cloak should proceed mechanically, unthinkingly, to the nearest destination. Turning around and heading back in the middle of the bridge would only cause more than one bristlingly whiskered male to volunteer to be what she was looking for.

The muddy waters of the Tigris roared like the sandstorms that sometimes shook the roofs of the city. The wild torrent scared her. For a moment the water seemed to stand in place while she and the crowd flowed on; then, all thought deserted her as she saw, halfway across the bridge, a man thrust into the traffic lane. Each time he tried amid howls of laughter to regain the pavement, a welter of arms and legs drove him back into the path of the snarling motors and charging horses, until gasping for breath he gave up all hope of rejoining the human ranks that had ejected him. In front of him rattled a wagon piled with crates, its barefoot driver racing before it with the bridle; behind him sped a cabriolet, its shiny leather top rolled down and its passengers smiling grimly from their high, springy perch while the coachman ran with the horses and sought to calm them.

And so Ma'atuk Nunu was forced to sprint at a frightening pace, sweat pouring from the roots of his hair despite the chill wind. He had continued to dress in traditional garb even after unexpectedly coming into money, and now he stripped off his elegant camel's-hair cloak and threw it over his shoulder like a bath towel, baring the shameful, inciting hump on his back. Not even as a child had he ever run like this in the street.

Watching him comically flap his arms like a fat rooster trying to fly, Victoria forgot her own distress. There was a dark side to this City of the Rooftops that many preferred to turn a blind eye to. Others blamed it on the jinns. Perhaps it came, this callous treatment of the misfit, the freak, the living thing that did not perform its function, from the harsh and distant, desert-dwelling past of the city's inhabitants. Horses that stumbled while pulling a carriage were whipped till they bled. Children tortured cats and tormented helpless old men. Boys hunted madmen, who fled volleys of garbage and stones shrieking with pain or laughing dementedly. If you fell flat on your face in a puddle, you would look up to see more grinning faces than helping hands. Victoria knew that the jiggling figure of the hunchback was a perfect outlet for such dark passions. Ma'atuk's terrified look told her that he too was aware of how easily the hidden devil could be aroused. "Run, you son-of-a-bitch, run!" guffawing shouts could already be heard. The driver behind him cracked his green-beaded whip over Ma'atuk's head and the crowd broke into a cheer.

In the land of tyrants, no tyranny is worse than the mob's. Not a kind word was spoken, not one person had the courage to reach out and gather Ma'atuk in. His red slippers pattered like tongues. The crowd resented his struggle to retain his dignity, which was something he did not deserve to have, a performance-spoiling ruse. He tripped, and for a moment it seemed that he was about to go down beneath his hump and scamper on all fours. The mob's roars drowned out the river. The whip cracked again, catching the cloak on Ma'atuk's bobbing shoulder and coiling around it. Like a hunted lizard shedding its tail, he flung it away and grabbed hold of the back of the wagon with a desperate lunge. Victoria caught a last glimpse of him, dragged along like an old sack until he vanished to the jeers of the crowd.

And this was the man that years ago her mother had wanted her to marry! Perhaps it was the prompting of his own mother that had made Jamila come one day to the courtyard, dressed in her finery and smiling her matchmaker's smile. At first everyone thought she had knocked on the wrong door. She looked absurd in a flowery dress that was too big on her and that must have been given her by a fat woman in payment for one of her services. In those days she was already gaunt and juiceless, and her henna-dyed toenails and rust-painted lips were as ludicrous as the cheeks that had sunk into her toothless mouth, bringing out the blue tattoo marks on her chin. Fully conscious of her blowsiness, she sat with her legs spread, lit a cheap cigarette, and hoarsely asked for some tea. Yehuda, who was home sick that day, retreated to the rear of the passageway, repelled by the batting of her eyes that were made up with coal dust. "Give her something to eat and drink and get her out of here," he snapped, fanning his pale face with a big fan.

Jamila did not take offence. Being insulted was the privilege of women more pampered than she was. Her bony knees moved like the handles of a bellows, pumping red flowers from her dress into the summer air. "I can't tell you how good it is to see you," she said fawningly to Yehuda.

"You must be blind then!" Aziza welcomed her heartily. Her blunt language was nothing new to the group of young women and girls around her, who were used to hearing it echo over the rooftops. "What are you doing here?"

"Do I need a special invitation to visit the House of Michal?" asked Jamila. "Touch wood, I can't believe how the girls have grown up. Backsides ready for a man's hands and breasts for a baby's lips! Each cheek a Persian apple! And look at those bellies, just waiting for a tumble!"

"Shut your mouth," scolded Aziza. It was hard to tell if she was indignant or amused. "Our girls don't need your brand of goods."

"There's many a pearl been found in the dirt. Why not? It's all up to God. And meanwhile my mouth is dry and I'm still waiting for my tea."

"Victoria, make our guest tea."

The women turned to look with amazement at Najia, who was nursing her latest baby. Victoria blushed. Her mother's request, she realized, was no accident. Jamila, whom she never had liked, now revolted her.

"You heard what your mother said, sweetheart," Jamila

shrilled, running a practised eye over Victoria's shoulders, breasts, and thighs. "The kettle's on the table and the fire's in the kitchen. Wait till you hear the good news I've brought you, my beauty."

Victoria fled to her family's quarters and sat listening behind closed doors to the whoops that broke out in the courtyard when Jamila revealed that the news she had brought concerned the hunchbacked Ma'atuk. She sat there perspiring for hours and only opened the door when Michal scoldingly ordered her to come out. The whole thing, her grandmother assured her, was but a feeble-minded joke.

Ma'atuk Nunu did not remain a bachelor. He was long married and the father of many children by the time Victoria married herself. Dressed in his one good Sabbath cloak, he hobbled down the street on her wedding night and sat with the other male guests. It was a very small wedding. Indeed, it resembled a pauper's, because her father's business had fallen on hard times, but Victoria was too dazed and excited to pay attention to such things. She was hardly even aware of who was there.

Ma'atuk Nunu did not have to walk far that night, since he now lived in a rented room at the top of the street with his mother, wife, and children and owned a small grocery store on the ground floor of their building, from the door of which he could see his father's house. The grocery smelled of halvah, laundry soap, sticky sucking sweets, kerosene, mouse droppings, and henna and served the street's poor inhabitants. Sometimes his father's Kurdish housemaids, who had raised him as a child, came to make a purchase. They spoke in low voices and stared at the ground while he waited on them unblinkingly, never tilting the scales or overcharging them. When the crushing noonday heat drugged the street and sent all fleeing to the shade of their homes, Ma'atuk went on sitting in the entrance of his store, staring at his father's grandly studded door, from whose horn of plenty he and his mother were exiled in his youth. No one knew what he was thinking, and his mother too remained a closed book until her death. Any shopper who tried drawing him out received a blank stare and no answer. Such customers spread rumours that he was nursing dark, hateful plots and that it was not by chance that he had rented the store opposite his father.

The only mourners at his mother's funeral were himself, his wife and their children. Abdallah Nunu went about his business, riding his white mule with its colourful tassels even though the deceased had been his wife. And yet no one heard Ma'atuk utter a word of complaint about either his father or his sister, who spent the week of mourning in her usual fashion behind the studded door that he resumed staring at when he re-opened his store. He was like a man waiting with the patience of Fate for something to happen.

There was Rafael and there was Ma'atuk Nunu.

Would she have shut herself up in the sunlit room today too and threatened to starve herself to death as she did then? The hunchback, who had never shown her anything but kindness, was now a thriving businessman, while Rafael must already be dead. And yet, yes—she would do it all over again. You're a fool, she chided herself, not knowing whether to be happy or sad at the thought that, even dying or dead, she still loved Rafael. What had Ma'atuk Nunu been doing on the shaky bridge? Not since the great flood before the war that had inundated whole sections of the city and swept away many houses could anyone recall such high water, which was the first serious test of the new bridge built by the English after taking the city from the Turks. Ma'atuk had his own offices now, with a private bookkeeper and a footman, but no one could forget he was a hunchback. There were things that not even money could paper over. Victoria wished she had not seen him humiliated on the bridge. Throughout all the hard years she had admired his reserve—and now here he was, dangling like a rag while everyone howled with laughter! What's the point, she asked herself, biting her lips behind her veils.

5

Miriam winked at Victoria and pointed at the childish rear of Toya, who was intently walking backwards in their direction while using the burned end of a stick to draw black squares for hopscotch on the roof. Though she was only a year younger than they were, she was so short that she looked no more than eight. Her voice too had a dewy, dainty tone that matched her petiteness. She had made the hopscotch squares too big, and Victoria and Miriam had to back off to the tin balustrade that separated their roof from the Nunus'. Unable to resist, Miriam gave the little rear end showing through its dress a pinch. Toya jumped and threatened Miriam with the sooty stick. The three of them started to yell.

"All right, the party's over," Abdallah Nunu good-naturedly rebuked them from next door. "Get off the roof."

"We were just playing, Uncle Abdallah," said Miriam.

"Then play quietly," Abdallah said with a fond look at the green fronds of his date palm. He ran sensual fingers over its rough trunk.

Nearby his son-in-law was fertilizing it with male pollen from a yellow pod. "Look at all the clusters we'll have this year," he said, eager to find favour. "Just look."

"I am looking," Abdallah Nunu replied coldly, not wishing to arouse the Evil Eye.

It was a cleansing spring morning, the kind that sometimes followed a night's sandstorm. The sky was deep and blue, and Victoria gulped the clear air, thrilled by the sparkles of sunlight. Excited by her happiness and the beauty of the birds winging through the pure expanse above her, she was impatient for Toya to be done so that the gale of energy inside her could be released.

She stood waiting to go first on the black-squared roof that the three of them had wiped the sand from, in her fist a dry peach pit instead of the usual stone.

Najia's voice rasped from the courtyard:

"Victoria, it won't do you any good! You can't hide from me. I'm not working like a donkey for your father's worthless guests. All they do is eat themselves sick. It's too much for me."

Miriam regarded Toya's backside. Although the guests were hers even more than Izuri's, Toya was either pretending not to have heard or really hadn't. Miriam glanced down at the courtyard. "She's nursing Salman," she told Victoria. "I'd like to bean her with a jug. If I were you, I'd pray to be an orphan."

"You're a very naughty girl," said Abdallah from beyond the balustrade.

"It beats me how she has such good-looking children," Miriam mused out loud.

"That's because she was once good-looking herself," explained the invisible Abdallah. "Take a good look at her. She was once very pretty."

Miriam moved out of earshot to the far end of the roof. "Toya," she whispered, hoarse with excitement, "come over here."

Toya straightened up and went over like an obedient poor cousin. The sooty stick still in her hand, she stood drawing perfect circles in the red sand.

"When are you going to have a baby?" Miriam wanted to know.

Their three heads touched like the petals of a black flower.

Toya smirked forbearingly. "How can I have a baby when I haven't got my period yet?"

Annoyed by her own lesser knowledge, Miriam scanned the little face suspiciously. "What's that got to do with it?"

"That's what my mother told me," Toya said. "And that's what the woman who prepared my body for Dahood swore too."

"There's never any telling with you people," Miriam grumbled, no longer so sure of herself.

Toya bowed her head, ready to reveal all if asked nicely. "I don't know how much you know."

"They say that your mother and Dahood came to an agreement. It's because you don't have a father and are poor. She'll let him marry you and take you to live with him, but he can't stick it into you until you get your period."

"That's right," said Toya matter-of-factly. "That's what they agreed."

To Victoria, their curiosity did not seem a sufficient reason for subjecting Toya to all this.

"He's not keeping his promise, though, is he?" Miriam asked. "Come on, you can tell us."

Toya smiled. She did not mind being interrogated. Though Miriam was older, Toya could see how intrigued she was and wanted to please her. "You're right," she whispered. "He isn't."

Miriam shut her eyes. "So he's been sticking it into you all along down there."

"Yes," said Toya with a glint in her eyes.

Victoria felt faint. Miriam's voice burned like hot coals in her ears and Toya's blitheness baffled her.

"I swear, I can't figure it out," said Miriam. "So how come he promised that he wouldn't?"

"It wasn't because of having babies and all that. It was because in a girl my age, everything is still small. I'll bet it is in you and Victoria too. When a man does it to you, he can tear things. It's dangerous."

Miriam looked at her questioningly. "And Dahood doesn't tear things in you?"

"It hurt a lot at first," said little Toya triumphantly, as though enjoying a private joke. "But now . . ."

"Come on," whispered Miriam, putting an arm around Toya's shoulder. "I want you to tell me everything."

Abdallah's head appeared above the balustrade in a red fez. "Girls," he called, causing the black flower to open and three faces to turn his way at once. "You have a clear view from your roof. Try to see if the river has really burst its dykes and is carrying away houses. Nuna is shaking with fear, and my sister is driving us crazy too." He sounded his usual, unruffled self. "Climb up on that stool and have a look," he gently urged Miriam, who stood there as though transfixed.

Miriam did as she was told, shading her eyes with one hand as she surveyed the horizon. "No, everything seems all right. There's a lot of water shining in the sun but the houses are all still there."

"What did I tell you, my darling," chuckled Abdallah over his shoulder. The fez disappeared behind the balustrade while his voice went on sounding over the rooftops, invoking stately merriment. "When your father tells you something, you can believe him. *You*, where's that hookah you were bringing me? The man hears 'flood' and passes out from sheer fear."

Encouraged by his tone, the three girls made bold to approach the balustrade. Nuna Nunu was sitting in a velvet chair carried up into the warm sunshine by one of the Kurdish housemaids. On a tray beside her were some fresh leaves of lettuce and dried dates. Though she smiled winningly at the girls when she saw them, her anxiety was apparent. And yet even then, her beauty was beyond all imagining, like none they had ever seen; it was like that of the stars and the birds, impervious to illness or want. They stared at her reverently, taking in her jewel-studded slippers, the dress that caressed her shapely body, the curls gracing her delicate shoulders. They waited with baited breath to hear the languid timbre of her voice.

Abdallah Nunu swelled with pride at their worshipful glances. "Damn your soul!" his masculine voice rang out. "What's taking you so long down there?" With the tip of his shoe he nudged a yellow pod of pollen along the roof as his son-in-law came up the steps, a scrawnily assiduous young man who hugged the hookah like a Torah scroll. Instead of placing it like a well-trained servant at Abdallah's feet and stepping back, he handed his father-in-law the mouthpiece and followed him in wide circles around the date tree with the vase of bubbling water in his arms. Victoria bit her lips and turned away as puffs of clear smoke rose from Abdallah's moustache. Why, it was worse than degrading, it was treating a man like a tame bear! There was an amused smile on Nuna's lips. The swarthy face of her little husband, who was busy making sure that the tube was not too taut or slack, darkened even more at the sight of it.

"Victoria!" came Najia's voice again from the courtyard, which was now receding into shadow. "The meat will rot and the cats will get the fish. What will your father serve that wolf pack he's invited for dinner?"

"Don't listen to her," said Miriam, trying to stir up rebellion.

Victoria headed for the stairs.

"What about the hopscotch?" Miriam asked.

"I have to help with the cooking," said Victoria. "Do you want to give me a hand, Toya?"

Toya was afraid to descend to the courtyard before Dahood, her protector from his sister Najia, had got out of bed. "I'll stay up here," she said with a shrug and a squirm.

"What are you wriggling like that for?" asked Victoria.

"I'm dying to pee, but I'm too scared of your mother to use the bathroom. Peeing hurts me a little. Since Uncle Dahood started playing with me, I have to go all the time."

"You can go right here on the roof," suggested Miriam.

"But suppose Abdallah sees me?" asked Toya.

"He's smoking his hookah. Go on, dear, pee," Miriam advised in a motherly tone.

Toya pulled down her pants and squatted. Victoria froze. She and Miriam stared hard, as though expecting to see some special sign of Toya's deflowering.

Before going downstairs, Victoria took one last look at the neighbours' roof. Nuna was still in her chair and Abdallah was serenely circling the date palm with his son-in-law on his heels. In a voice soft as a lullaby he said:

"Let's have a smile, my darling. You heard Michal's granddaughters. The flood is far away and your father has built a strong house. And if anything, God forbid, should happen, we will carry you from here on our shoulders."

And scratching his chin with the mouthpiece of the hookah, he added:

"If you're still worried, we can always go to Hannah's house."

Victoria did not understand how a heavenly being like Nuna, protected by such a father, could be worried by a flood. She went downstairs, tiptoeing past the napping Michal's carpet so as not to wake her. Her uncle the zither player stepped through the jute curtain of the alcove with a yawn, running a hand through his hair. He mugged a clownish grimace when he spied Najia with her baby at her breast and was cursed by her under her breath. Victoria sat by the cooking board, thinking how rude it was of Aziza to laugh openly, her great belly making her huge breasts quiver. Dahood, though he was entranced by the rolls of her flesh, or at least made believe that he was, and the buttery laugh with which she yielded to his masculine wiles, upset Victoria even more than the way Abdallah looked at Nuna.

"You better watch out," said Aziza, shaking like jelly. "More than one little devil Toya's age has buried her husband before she even grew breasts."

Dahood, who felt the spring weather in his veins, did not try to hide his high spirits. "Believe me, mother of Ezra, I can't think of a more blessed way to die." He had an inveterately dirty mouth and would have liked to send Aziza into a new spasm by telling her what little Toya did to him, but he thought better of it and kept his bliss to himself. Although during his wild life he had known many women who could have taught Aziza a thing or two, none had ever sat naked on his knees or bit his private parts with such childish shamelessness.

"You can invite me to the funeral."

"Mine or hers?"

Dahood scooped water from a bucket and rinsed his face with it. A mouse scurried out from behind the drinking-water barrel and stood surveying its surroundings with a tiny head as if trying to decide whether to venture further. Aziza, Najia, and Victoria followed Dahood's glance intently as he wondered if the mouse could make it safely across the courtyard. In the end it crossed unharmed, boldly evading two cocky roosters and the frisky cat, and stepped out into the street.

Victoria could feel Aziza's irritation grow until her forced smile vanished and she said carelessly:

"Toya is made of steel like Nuna Nunu. Don't be fooled by how fragile she looks, Dahood. Little tarts like her can live forever just like some saints that I know of."

Victoria caught her breath. No one in the household had ever dared talk that way about Michal. How could her good-natured, easy-going aunt be so wicked in front of everyone?

Dahood wisely brought the conversation to an end before it got out of hand. "Children and zithers bring happiness to the world, and I thank God every day for his gift of them."

"At least a zither can't get pregnant. It won't turn your old age into a nightmare of screams and baby shit."

"God is great," said Dahood with a flourish of piety that was meant to draw a last laugh. When it didn't, he asked with genuine concern:

"Aziza, what's going on with you?"

She looked away and said nothing. Dahood was a connoisseur of women and she had no wish for him to notice the hot flash that had passed over her. Although she was almost the same age as Najia, her sister-in-law went on having children while all she had were these confounded flashes that heralded her change of life. She was glad Izuri wasn't home. She was afraid of his finding out, as if it were something she had done wrong. She had always believed herself a desirable woman—and now, apart from this, she was growing hard of hearing and had secretly had two rotten molars pulled. It vexed her that Najia's body was bearing fruitfully up beneath the years while hers was falling apart. Could she have caught some disease from Yehuda? Though Dahood was in thrall to his little bird of a bride, he still had not learned to keep his caressing eyes to himself. She felt another flash, and her face and neck burned hotly. "Well, be careful," she advised him. "Getting pregnant is something that women have a knack for."

"Allah is merciful," he replied with the same mock piety as before.

He had never in his life counted on Allah for anything. Not that he doubted that the Creator, like an anxious mother, tried to keep a clean house; but he, Dahood, always left messes behind him. At first he had gone with his request to Rabbi Juri Chittaiyat, who ignominiously shooed him away. Next he tried Jamila, but it was soon obvious to him that a fraud like her was not to be trusted in such matters. Finally, he threw caution to the wind and went to the Shi'ite quarter of el-Kazamiya, where he pleaded his case with a blind healer he had met years ago. The powder given him was now in his purse, and he hoped it would have the desired effect and no worse, so that the child might go on budding like a jasmine bush until the day he died, all aromatic beauty and no fruit. Every day an exact dose of it went into her food, which so far she had downed unsuspectingly.

And indeed, Toya suffered no unintended damage. She lived to an old age, kept the gleam in her eyes even after two world wars, and was eternally grateful to Dahood for never complaining about her childlessness or blaming her for it.

The fact was that Toya had changed his life. Though he continued to earn a living by playing his zither at parties and gatherings, he now gave up his dissolute and once enigmatic existence. He had always, even while having his bucolic orgies with Eliyahu, provided faithfully for his two sons and his daughter, and when their mother went insane after her last baby fell from the roof as she was holding him, Dahood beat his fists against her head in furious anguish. Her legs folded beneath her, she sat endlessly in the dirt of the unpaved street counting from 16 to 112, the number of weeks and days that the infant had lived.

Even during the five mysterious years in which he vanished completely, Dahood saw to it that an anonymous source transmitted money to his mother for his wife and children. Many people had tried getting him to talk about those years, especially when he was drunk, but their secret was never revealed. Though

Najia claimed that he had spent them with their brother, a Turkish officer in Constantinople, no one took her ravings seriously. Another story had it that he had fallen in love with a Shi'ite girl from el-Kazamiya and become a Moslem in order to marry her; when she died, young and childless, from cholera, he returned home and to the Jewish faith despite the death penalty decreed for lapsed Moslems. This romantic tale had several corroborations, among them the fact that ever since reappearing Dahood had a deeply melancholy expression even when clowning in his usual fashion. He also plucked his eyebrows religiously, dyed his beard a flaming red, and padded his clothes when he went out until he seemed twice his size. When invited to play at Moslem gatherings he never sang with the ensemble, and he adamantly refused all invitations to appear in the vicinity of el-Kazamiya.

Dahood's marriage to Toya, which took place about a year after his first wife's death, was a sore point with Najia. She had disliked Toya from the start. She was sure that she was not a real little girl but a dwarf in disguise who was best avoided, and that she practised black magic. How else explain something as unnatural as her brother's falling in love with her? "It's been known to happen," she said when asked by Aziza to be more specific. "There's a male organ under the female one. Some people are born that way. You remember the time Abu Nifata invited the whole street to his son's circumcision? The boy came after nine daughters, and there were drinks and sweets and cakes and a big celebration until the circumciser discovered that there was nothing there for him to cut. Abu Nifata and his family left the street in a hurry, and the baby got to wear his sisters' hand-me-downs. I know my brother. He's as weird as they come. That's just the sort of thing he would go for."

Aziza scooped the little bride up with one hefty arm, sat her on her knees, and ran her hand as carefully over her as if she were a chicken being bought for the Sabbath in the el-Hanuni Market. The frightened girl, who had no idea what it was all about, stared panic-stricken at her laughing aunt until convinced that she was not being searched for stolen property. The affectionate slap given her pudendum at the end of the examination hurt so much that she had to run straight to the bathroom to pee.

Still, Najia did not protest when Izuri gave his blessing to the couple and offered them the former storeroom that Eliyahu and his family had been banished from. The great man was not unfeeling, and believing the story of Dahood's double apostasy, he knew the danger his brother-in-law was in and took his pledge to reform at face value. Izuri presented the newlyweds with a handsome sum and promised Dahood a seven-day wedding feast, the idea of which captivated even Najia. During it she ate great amounts and almost smiled once or twice, but on the fourth day she ceased to cook. It was simply too much for her to cope with, and had it not been for Aziza and Miriam, who in turn pressed Victoria into service, she would have been buried beneath the piles of fresh produce that Izuri sent every day from the market with one-eyed Kaduri.

Within two hours of Victoria's coming down from the roof there was a growing sense of disaster. A steady stream of out-of-breath arrivals reported that whole streets were under water and the Tigris was on the rampage, which made Victoria ask her mother what point there was in cooking so much meat and fish, since none of the guests would show up anyway. Najia, however, merely grunted. She was a woman of strange whims, and now she had laid her baby down on the shaded sofa and was cracking walnuts from a bowl, giving each an angry blow with a stone. Bits of them flew from under her hand and were snatched by her sons and daughters before she could gather them up. Her eyes glinted ravenously. "You little beasts!" she scolded, licking her lips. "Save some for me. Don't be such pigs."

Victoria turned to Dahood, who was sitting near the drain, absorbed in clipping his toenails.

"Is that all that's worrying you?" he said. "Go ahead and cook it all. Nothing goes uneaten in this house. Tell me, what is Miriam tailing Toya for? She even follows her to the bathroom. They've gone out together now."

She did not want to ask Aziza, whom she had seen going off poker-faced to her room, and so she sat by herself in the sooty kitchen and built up the fire beneath the pots. Before long the cooking meat gave off a good smell and slices of fish sizzled in the frying pan. Mollified, she forgave everyone. She liked to sit staring at the flames, and after thinking of the anxious glow of Nuna Nunu's beauty, she smiled as she pictured Toya swiftly pulling down her panties on the roof. A spring breeze blew through the smoke-filled kitchen. Her hair whispered sultrily to her shoulders and neck, and a sweet shiver ran down her when, bending to stir the pots, her knees brushed her breasts and her buttocks skimmed the low stool she had placed in front of the stove. She gazed at the dark canopy of spiderwebs above her and wondered if she would see Rafael again.

It felt good even to sit brooding, and her thoughts did not keep her from expertly tending the six pots and the frying pan. The fish was done right, the rice came out puffy, and the lamb grew tender without burning—seven flames feeding the irrepressible flame within her, so that, carried off on a swell of emotion, she at first failed to hear the din of shouting boys and women outside. And when she did, she merely smiled to herself. What did she care if the Tigris unleashed itself on the city? Not even the distant keening that now reached her, like a lament for the victims of a plague, could shake her from the grip of her reveries. She stirred the rice and turned the chicken in its pot. She would move away from here one day. She and her husband would rent a small room nearby, and on their wedding night, when all the guests had departed . . . She blushed and pressed her breasts so hard against her knees that they hurt.

A new commotion from the courtyard, no doubt on account of the river, woke her from her trance. Since she could not easily put out the cooking fires, which were stoked with dry twigs, in order to go see what the matter was, she made do with a quick peek from the kitchen doorway and returned to her pots. And so it was that she missed seeing Rafael's brothers and sisters come flying out of the basement, Najia put down her bowl of nuts and flee with her baby to her room, Grandmother Michal wake from her nap and sit staring on her carpet at the hallway leading to the front door, and Miriam and Toya run hand-in-hand through the courtyard to Ezra, who had raced down from the second floor. The lids of the pots rattled and the frying fish sneezed in its pan, spraying hot oil and forcing Victoria to concentrate despite the pandemonium outside. Carefully she took the pots off the flames, wiped her hands on the thighs of her dress that was too small on her, and stepped red-faced out of the kitchen into the cool courtyard.

The crowd in the hallway flew apart and out of it stepped Rafael and his father, Eliyahu. Not a generation, but an entire era, seemed to separate them. Eliyahu wore a striped woollen cloak belted with a broad sash at the waist and seemed to tower in his red fez, on his face the haughty look of a passenger in a grand carriage impeded by a crowd of shiftless pedestrians. Rafael had on a suit and blue tie, spiffy shoes, and an elegant overcoat folded over one arm, and in his free hand he carried a suitcase. Having arrived together by sheer accident, the two now ignored each other, springing away when their shoulders touched in the crush. Though they were coming from different places, Eliyahu rousted from his pleasure dome by the flood and Rafael back from the arms of his chanteuse, both acted like tourists who owed no one any explanations.

At that exact moment, Victoria could think of only one thing. Miriam was standing next to Toya, washed and clean in a pretty dress, while she herself was still teary-eyed from the kitchen, her raw hands greasy with fish oil, her uncombed hair falling in thick clumps, and a stained, ill-fitting dress on her body.

Miriam went wild. Pushing aside her brothers, she threw herself impetuously on her cousin, daring even to grip the hand beneath the overcoat, and exclaimed:

"Rafael!"

Toya, who hardly remembered Rafael, threw back her shoulders childishly and stuck a thumb in her mouth.

As in a lush forest, the household's wounds and grievances

were quickly overgrown, its anger at father and son for having abandoned a nest of hungry mouths now silenced by its cries of joy at seeing them alive and well. As usual, Najia was the one exception. Stepping out of her room long enough to order her small children into it, she thrust out her pointed chin, puckered loathing lips, and spat three times. Rafael stared at her with contempt, while Eliyahu smiled tolerantly as at a madman and Victoria fled back to the heat of the kitchen.

The procession disappeared into the basement, soon after which Eliyahu chased everyone outside, his wife and children too, and stretched out wearily on the bed. Meanwhile, Ezra invited Rafael up to his room to rest, and Rafael gladly accepted.

Miriam scooted up the steps after them. Toya remained standing in the kitchen doorway, tapping her teeth with a thumbnail like an old man. "He must be a fucking wonder in bed, that Rafael," she remarked, "just like everyone said."

Coming from her, the words were so shockingly obscene that Victoria wanted to stop her ears. Miriam entered the kitchen excitedly, carrying two Sabbath dishes. "He's all skin and bones! He ate nothing for ten days while crossing the desert but bread and dried dates."

Without a word Victoria lifted the lids of the pots.

"I can't decide," beamed Miriam. "You choose."

Victoria filled a plate with saffroned rice garnished with raisins and extravagantly added two drumsticks still attached to their thighs. In the second plate she laid some slices of browned fish. It upset her not to be bringing Rafael the food herself and to have to listen to Miriam thank her for him.

Najia's shadow loomed over the pots. "You filthy bitch," she yelled at Victoria, "what do you think you're doing?" And turning to Miriam, she shouted:

"Put it all back! You're a thief just like your mother!"

Miriam clutched both plates, one above the other, tightly between her breasts, which were more developed than Victoria's, and held out her other hand defensively. Left out in the cold on the second floor, Najia's baby began to cry piercingly. "Let's have it," said Najia, stepping up to Miriam's steaming bosom. Miriam bared her healthy teeth, which would chew such mountains of food in years to come that she would swell into a good-hearted zeppelin, as if threatening to bite off her aunt's grimy fingers. Through her own clenched teeth, Najia spat out words as disgusting as maggots:

"A stinking tart sucked his blood, and now he's run away from his alley bitch like a mangy dog, reeking of shit and piss. He eats every woman alive with his eyes, and the two of you run to him like servant girls creaming in their pants!"

She was so mad that she kicked over a pot of kubbeh, sending bright cinders flying over the kitchen.

There was a cluck of admiration from Toya at her sister-in-law's powers of rhetoric. For a moment, Najia squinted at the little creature; then she dug her nails into the child's ear. Toya screamed, and Miriam, whose free hand was still guarding the two plates, lowered her head as if to butt Najia out of the kitchen doorway. Victoria stood with her back to the pots, ready to protect them against her berserk mother. It had already happened once before that a meal meant for her father's guests had ended up in the dirt, leaving them to dine on bread and stale cheese. Had he been here, he would have dragged her mother off to a corner and stopped her mouth with one hand while beating her about the head with the other. She and Miriam were still facing each other with flashing eyes when Dahood appeared on the scene. Toya felt her ear gingerly and looked at her finger.

"There's no blood," her husband reassured her, his heart stirring at the sight of the scratched ear. "Animal!" he snarled at Najia. "You could have torn the child's ear!"

"The child!" breathed Najia. "I suppose you'll tell me that you change her nappy at night and give her a bottle every morning. The poor dear!"

"You're insane," said Dahood, only making things worse. "I would have thought you would want there to be at least one person in this house who won't be thrilled when you break your neck."

"You'd like me to die yourself because of that little slut of yours. Don't think I don't know what she whispers to you at night! I knew it all along. You've got a witch on your back and it will be the ruin of us all. Since the day the two of you moved in, all I have is bad dreams. I wake up sweating at night and with a dry mouth. And the children keep tripping and having accidents."

For years before her marriage, Dahood had beat her regularly. Her stupidity enraged him. Now too he was angry enough to teach her a good lesson, but remembering that he was only a tenant in a house maintained by his brother-in-law, he gritted his teeth and controlled himself. In fact, he was not even a tenant, since he could not afford to pay any rent and subsisted on Izuri's good graces. The long drought and the rumours of war had caused people to scrimp on celebrations, so that his zither had not been in great demand. And now this damned flood would make them spend whatever money they had left on repairs! He gave his sister an outraged look and said:

"We'll buy you a cane to keep you from tripping, and God will look after the children."

Victoria did not particularly like her uncle. Like many entertainers, he was too concerned with his looks and only nice to those he considered useful. There was a hidden hardness in him that made children and adolescents feel like pests. He had just put his hand on Toya's shoulder and was about to lead her off to their jute-curtained alcove when Izuri's voice thundered in the courtyard:

"Mother! Najia! Aziza! Women! Get dressed and round up the children! The city is going under! The river is rising and taking houses with it!"

6

Miriam, with the chicken and rice still steaming between her breasts, turned pale with fear. But Najia appeared not to have heard. Deliberately she shoved her brother aside, pushed Victoria out of her way, and bent over to spit into the pots and the frying pan, after which she turned on her heel and left the kitchen.

Izuri stood in the middle of the courtyard, the silver-bearded Yehuda on his right, and on his left Victoria's oldest brother, Murad, wagging his head at his father's every word. He was the same age as Rafael, a decent, upright young man, purer and more innocent than anything that courtyard had ever seen. The sharp-tongued Ezra had long ago delivered his verdict on Murad: He was pure because he was a coward, and the truth was that he was an out-and-out hypocrite.

The three men, who had hurried home early from work, were dressed in traditional garb: gowns, *abbayas* and fezes, and at that moment they looked like awe-inspiring representatives of authority. "Where to?" asked Grandmother Michal from her rug.

"We'll spend the night in the warehouse, Mother." It was only to his mother that Izuri spoke so respectfully.

"We're more than sixty souls, God save us."

"We'll manage, Mother."

Murad kept nodding his head, basking in the borrowed glory of his father's authority. The black tassel of his fez bobbed towards his own mother, showing her the same reverence as his father showed Michal. Najia, suspicious and persecuted in her own home, did not know how to react to these respectful gestures. Her relations with her son Murad embarrassed her.

Michal banged on the second-storey railing with the wooden spoon she always kept about her. "Your brother Eliyahu and his son came home an hour ago."

Izuri glowered in silence, and Murad's face fell. Yehuda's eyes lit up as he looked around for a stool to sit on. The rapid walk from the shop and then standing in the middle of the courtyard had strained his heart and exhausted him.

"The warehouse is far from here," said Michal. "I'm staying here. I haven't got the strength to walk such distances any more."

"I'll carry you on my back, Grandmother," said Murad.

"Nobody's going to carry me on his back like a sack. I'll sit on a chair. Go and call Shaul the peddler and his friend Kaduri."

"And the clothes?" demanded Aziza. "I've been sewing Miriam's trousseau for years."

Yehuda cupped his beard in his hand as a sign that he was not an authority on such matters. He turned to his brother for advice. Izuri's reply was as firm and clear as if he had been practising emergency evacuations in the face of floods every day of his life. "One small bundle for each family. Including jewellery and gold rings, of course, if there are any. We're leaving immediately. It'll be dark soon and we won't know how far the water's risen."

A frenzy gripped the house, on both its floors. Hiding-places were exposed and treasures were collected. Babies cried and women bared their bosoms as they scrambled. A door slammed on Ezra's finger and he avenged himself by aiming a vicious kick at a passing cat. The boy wailed and the cat screeched. In all the commotion Victoria noticed that her mother was losing her wits. First she snatched up the baby and laid him on the wet, sticky cooking board, then she sat Nissan, a three-year-old menace, beside him. And with the baby already shrieking in pain she carried him to the arcade, dragging the sharp-toothed culprit behind her, and stood in the open courtyard wringing her hands in despair. "What did I break my back cooking for?

Everything's lying there in the kitchen. And what about the guests we're expecting tonight?"

"Never mind the guests!" snapped Izuri. "Is that all you've got to worry about? The river's sweeping the houses away!"

And as if she hadn't heard him she said: "Victoria's in a fever because of those two bastards who've come back from their whoring." And as if to confirm the news of his return Eliyahu emerged from the basement with an angry expression on his face. "What is this—a madhouse? I told you I wanted to rest." His eyes encountered Izuri's stern look of rebuke, and he fell silent, turned around and threw the basement key over his shoulder muttering: "I'm tired, I have to sleep."

"The river might flood the house," said Yehuda.

"Let it," growled Eliyahu.

"Not everybody gets the death he desires," said Izuri in disgust.

"Izuri!" Yehuda rebuked his brother in a tone of mild reproach, and he shuffled over to the basement entrance and called: "Eliyahu, the basement's dangerous, the water might reach the house. At least go up to the roof."

"In this cold? I'm already asleep, leave me alone."

Yehuda said no more and unnecessarily kissed the *mezzuza* on the basement doorpost. Like a knife the pain stabbed his chest, and he gasped for breath in a terrifying fog of suffocation and began the ascent to the second storey, his feet stumbling on the steps and his forehead shining with sweat.

Victoria got her brothers and sisters ready for the hurried departure and Murad helped her in silence, ignoring Ezra's sneers at him for doing a woman's work. Their father too joined them upstairs, after despairing of their mother, who remained rooted to the spot in the courtyard as if she had forgotten who she was. In the scurrying anthill of the house there was a sudden piercing shriek from Najia. "Look and see if someone's sawing her legs off," Victoria's father said to her. The sight that met her eyes was no less shocking.

Eliyahu's children, emaciated from their long hunger, had

invaded the kitchen and they were snatching the food straight from the boiling pots and devouring it in blind greed. One of them choked on a bone and vomited. They chewed with their mouths full, they burned their snatching fingers. The girls lifted their skirts shamelessly and shovelled pieces of lamb and joints of chicken and scalding rice into their dresses. Their hands dripped with oil, gravy ran down their chins. And Najia was beating their backs and slapping their faces, ready to rip off their sleeves in her fury as she struggled to rescue the pieces of meat into which their nails were digging, while the children, frantic with greed, ignored her. Pots overturned. Bare feet were scalded by the steam. In the end the children fled, their mouths and pockets crammed with meat and rice.

Najia flew after them, intent on reaching the stairs before them and barring their way to the roof, as if she were trying to force a cat to give up the Sabbath chicken it had stolen from the cooking board. But Izuri's mighty arms plucked her from the third step and lifted her into the air. For a moment Victoria was afraid that he would throw her onto the tiles of the courtyard and smash her head in. Her mother's feet were close together in the air, her little eyes looked straight into her husband's big ones. "Woman," he groaned, "woman, woman . . . they're children. My brother's hungry children, damn him, damn him, damn . . ." Victoria didn't like the sound of her father's voice. She hung onto her mother's legs and pulled her down, wailing: "Father, it's not her fault, she's confused because of the flood . . ."

Izuri shook himself, dropped his wife into his daughter's arms and clapped his hands as if to rid them of dust loathsomely drenched in dog pee. As soon as Najia's feet touched the ground she turned on Victoria and punched her on the shoulder. "It's not the flood, you imbecile! It's him! He knew when to come back. He's scheming to rob me of everything."

"What's she jabbering about?" asked Izuri in disgust.

"Even if the house is flooded he'll swim and poke and pry and steal everything."

"Victoria, a devil's taken possession of your mother."

"I'm not crazy," she shrieked at him. "For years he's been waiting for the chance to rob us. A family of thieves."

A look of horror came into Izuri's eyes. Death was dealt by God; madness came from Satan. His wife was foaming at the mouth. Who knew how far the curse would reach. Perhaps his seed was infected too? How to explain the bawling of the latest baby, Nissan's sharp teeth that dug into every living flesh?

"If we leave the house," demanded Najia vehemently, "I want him to leave with us."

"Has she taken leave of her senses?" asked Izuri.

"It's Rafael," whispered Victoria shyly.

"What can he steal from her already, a filthy slut dressed in rags . . ."

"For years Mother's . . ."

"Shut your mouth!" Her mother stamped her foot.

Satan or no Satan, Izuri's patience snapped. "Let her speak," he said sternly.

"She's lying."

"Quiet."

The house, which had been built decades before, was home to countless hidden occupants: ants, fleas, worms, ticks, scorpions, beetles, mice and snakes. What with the want, the deadly seasonal diseases and the cyclical epidemics, the human occupants humbly recognized their transience. Consequently they invested a minimum of effort in the upkeep of the building. Months went by before a broken window pane was replaced. Sometimes it was replaced by wooden boards or cardboard. The cesspits were emptied only when they overflowed. Broken floor tiles were left to disintegrate. The present occupants were in no hurry to wield hammers and picks. The line between the natural and the supernatural was thin and fragile, and few dared to touch it or cross it. Young and old, the members of the household believed that under the floor the earth was alive and kicking with demons and harmful spirits. It was better to ignore a cracked tile than risk startling the vengeful forces of the underworld from their slumbers.

In contrast to the human beings, the lords of creation, the hidden occupants worked diligently generation after generation to improve their dwellings: little holes grew into miniature caves, ant-sized cracks were transformed with time into mouse-holes. And like these hidden occupants, Najia too hoarded in the days of plenty for the lean days to come. From the weekly allowance she received from Izuri she secretly set aside a few pennies, and from time to time she would covertly meet Salman, who even in the blazing heat of summer wore his heavy patchwork coat. From a hole in the lining he would extract a gold coin and sell it to her at an exorbitant exchange rate. Najia would go home thrilled with her little treasure and hide it in the cracks and holes of the walls. Jewels purchased with the hoarded coins too found their way into the walls. But the suspicious woman guarded her secret so jealously that there was nobody to help her remember, and she herself had forgotten the extent of her treasure-trove, and where exactly it was hidden. Once a rooster was found pecking at a diamond studded brooch it had dragged from some hole, and another time a crow swooped and soared with a gold bracelet in its beak. None of the women complained of her loss, and Najia too did not lament, for she had completely forgotten that the bracelet had ever been in her possession. Michal claimed the diamond brooch which was rescued from the inquisitive rooster, and with the proceeds she bought a few trinkets for Victoria from the goldsmith.

When Izuri understood, from Victoria's hasty explanation, why his wife was afraid to leave Rafael in the house, he looked at her sternly and urged the occupants to hurry up. He had no time to worry about his wife. The people at the observation posts on the roof announced that the river was still rising and inundating the houses.

Victoria did not remember much about that day. The main events were blurred, and only insignificant images survived the filter of her memory. The sight of her cousins snatching food from the pots was too dim to shock her when it rose vaguely before her eyes, and even the spectacle of her mother hoisted high and hanging from her father's arms she almost succeeded in suppressing. On the other hand she remembered vividly how Grandmother Michal was carried in regal splendour on a blue velvet armchair by the two stalwarts, Shaul the peddler and the one-eyed Kaduri, seller of candied turnips. The three of them advanced in the middle of the procession. The old woman sailed through the air, above the babbling of the household trudging through the puddles left by the last rain, greeting the men and women clustering in their doorways, who had no refuge to flee to, and they responded fervently to the greetings of the crone who was reputed to be a saint, hoping that she would bring salvation to her well-wishers. At the head of the procession walked Yehuda, who had somewhat recovered from the pressure on his chest and was holding a burning storm-lantern in his hand. It wasn't completely dark yet, and the sight of the shocking waste of the lamp burning in the twilight deepened the premonition of disaster in the hearts of those remaining behind. The adults in the procession walked in grim silence, the whispering children clustered round the blue velvet armchair with its carved ivory arm-rests. Eliyahu had ignored all their pleas and gone back to sleep. Rafael had joined the procession last, after locking the house with the enormous, foot-long key. Najia kept turning her head to scrutinize his face and examine his suit pockets for suspicious bulges.

The Nunu family too emerged from their house at the same twilight hour. In the gentle breeze the palm fronds swayed forlornly on the roof, like abandoned souls. Nuna's fair face, so touching in the pure delicacy which was now exposed to all eyes, betrayed no fear of the flood. The silk *abbaya* lay draped on her shoulders. She was the only woman in the alley who painted her face on weekdays, and she looked to them like an expensive china doll, the kind imported from overseas. She was already a mother of two, but the purity in her wondering eyes made her look like a child herself. Never before had Victoria encountered a gaze so frank, innocent and full of goodwill. Nuna smiled at the procession from the House of Michal, and at the walls of the houses eroded by time, and at the narrow, winding strip of sky between the roofs, and at the people with no shelter to go to standing in the doorways of their houses, and they all smiled back at her as if they were grateful for the smile of affluence as well, as if it too could bestow the blessings of the saints. Apart from Najia, no one dreamed of condemning the little beauty, and she was even welcomed gladly when she and her father and their servants joined the procession. Abdallah did not trust his son-in-law and carried his grandchildren himself, the little one in his arms, and the red-headed firstborn on his shoulders. The child's little arms encircled the man's forehead and pressed the grey head to his stomach. The dark-faced husband brought up the rear with the servants carrying neatly wrapped and well-tied bundles. Little Toya broke away from Dahood with his dyed beard, who was carrying his zither on his back, and hurried to catch up with Nuna Nunu. She gazed at her like a timid animal, touched her *abbaya* and the lace on her elegant dress as if spell-bound, and then plucked up the courage of the diminutive to fondle Nuna's hand and stroke her beautiful face with her finger. Nuna filled the narrow space of the alley with peals of laughter.

In those days, the days of Victoria's youth, the poor admired God's chosen unstintingly. They all lived together in the crowded quarter and they all respected the eternal gulf yawning between opposites. Thus Rabbi Juri Chittaiyat, who knew how to heal broken bones and was conversant with the *Zohar*, the Kabbalistic Book of Splendour, and Rahma Afsa, who was spending her weekly day off with her sister, were to be found standing opposite each other, door opposite door, and watching the procession. Apart from the tattoo dots decorating her chin and brows, Rahma the prostitute's face was free of make-up. Her clothes were new and relatively expensive, but perfectly modest. She was widely respected for the generosity with which she fed her sister's large family. Men worn out by hard work, who could ill afford it, coveted Rahma's ripe body, but none dared approach her on her day off in the alley, because on that day she was to all intents and purposes a pious, respectable woman. And if anyone dared to approach her nevertheless, the mischievous Ezra would open his mouth and howl like a cat, yap like a puppy-dog, and even go so far as to wink at her brazenly. Rahma and her sister and brother-in-law indulged him. For he was a student at the *Alliance Israélite* high school and the son of the silver-bearded Yehuda.

How far those days were now. All this was before Ma'atuk Nunu rented the shop and set up house within eye distance of his father's home, about six years before the new raft bridge was built and called after the British General who conquered the town from the Turkish army, the very bridge upon which Victoria was to step in an *abbaya* and two veils in order to drown herself in the raging river.

But on the day when they fled from the rising river her eyes were sparkling, and her breasts were firm, and her soul was like a flower blooming in spite of the harshness of its surroundings. Her baby brother was in her arms, and Miriam begged to be allowed to carry him for a while, because he smelled so good, and when the infant was placed in her arms she kissed him on the forehead with a smacking sound which threw Victoria's senses into a turmoil, because it was clear to her that the kiss was in some way connected to Rafael, who had returned from the desert in the silence of a man.

They left the al-Shorja market and entered the heavy gloom of the fabric bazaar. For reasons of economy this place was omitted by the lamp-lighters. Only the alleys of the residential quarters were illuminated at night. Victoria remembered that her father had walked at the head of the procession, taking the lamp from Yehuda who fell behind again until Aziza caught up with him and gave him her arm. Ezra and Murad too carried lamps and walked on either side of the procession. Rafael with his lamp brought up the rear. Through the fog of the years Victoria could not remember if they had been hurrying, panic-stricken by the flood. If they had, perhaps she would not have noticed a little detail like Abdallah Nunu's hand waving goodbye as he and the members of his household parted from them at one of the turns in the road.

Vividly she remembered how she and Miriam had stopped several times to peek at Rafael's face lit up from below by the lamp in his hand. They heard him reassuring a pregnant woman in his clear voice, telling her that the figure which had suddenly loomed up in front of them and disappeared into a side alley was not a ghost but a man frightened by the dark. The young woman nodded politely, but her teeth went on chattering hysterically. Najia slapped her face and dismissed Rafael's words in contempt: "Don't talk rubbish, that was a murderer and a robber!" In her excitement Toya forgot herself and announced loudly: "A devil hit Aunty Najia!" Her aunt retaliated immediately: "May the devils out of hell burn your hair, you little bitch, may you never grow any taller, may you always take tiny steps like a blind backward midget." Aziza, who had Yehuda's arm resting on her shoulder, burst out laughing. The pregnant woman, who thought that the demon was mocking them and mimicking Aziza's voice, screamed again, and Rafael ordered her husband to calm her down. "Look how he's not even tired after travelling through the desert," Miriam said proudly. As they walked Ezra collected the boys in a group around him and Toya joined them. Dahood grabbed hold of her shoulder and whispered that she should behave in a way befitting a married woman and walk next to him. But she took no notice, and he was obliged to walk with the youngsters too, until he felt that he was making a fool of himself and resumed his place in the rear, next to Rafael.

And Victoria remembered, too, a big square and two strange men feeding fires under kettles which gave off a refreshing smell of strong tea. And there was a smell of fresh pitta bread too, and salty cheese, and clusters of dates shining in the flames. Her father stood next to the strange men and dished out snacks to the hungry and urged the women into the warehouse, because it was growing chilly. Shaul and Kaduri put the armchair down and bent over to kiss Grandmother Michal's hand, and they asked Victoria's father for permission to spend the night with them. They were afraid of making their way back home in the dark alleys, perhaps the pregnant woman, God save her soul, was right, perhaps she really had seen something. They promised not to touch the food intended for the children. In the end they all sat down next to a pitted wall and devoured the food which had been prepared in advance, and Victoria smiled at Rafael's brothers and sisters, whose stomachs were still full of the food they had looted in the kitchen, but who could not withstand the temptation to eat another meal. In the light of the lamps standing on the floor her father's shadow looked like a big cloud, and babies' mouths closed round the pink nipples of full breasts. In the darkness shrouding everything children went on growing and adults went on aging. Victoria's mother disappeared into a corner and her little brothers clung to her skirts until they fell asleep amid tears and laughter and whispers. Before entering the warehouse she had looked up into the sky and not seen a single star. The square was covered with a vaulted tin roof, as was the custom in the commercial section of the town. Ezra's lamp flickered next to Rafael's, and her brother Murad's lamp delineated an area of darkness between himself and them.

She remembered that she sat with her back against a pile of bolts of cloth. After a while she woke up for a few minutes and smiled to herself in the dim light of the lowered flames of the lamps. How fortunate I am, she said to herself, how fortunate I am to be fed and clothed and protected and wanted in a cold, hungry world in danger of being drowned like a litter of mice. Just before she fell asleep again it occurred to her that the mice in the basement would drown together with Uncle Eliyahu if the river flooded the house. And where would they live then? And the water in her dream was white as milk, radiant in the noon light.

7

Baghdad has existed for over a thousand years. The great city, which developed from a remote village on the outskirts of the Sassanid kingdom, owed a lot to Victoria's ancestors. Jewish doctors, scientists, philosophers, statesmen and men of letters made a considerable contribution to the Arab culture which flourished there. But generations of conquests, floods, plagues, persecutions and massacres not only dwindled the spiritual resources of the Jewish community, they also caused it to lose its memory. The Jews huddled together in a cramped quarter, and most of them were born and grew up and grew old and died without ever leaving its confines. A community whose forbears had composed the Babylonian Talmud and whose aspirations had encompassed the world and the fullness thereof, narrowed their horizons drastically.

On the day that Victoria crossed the bridge over the river these thousand years had already been effaced from her consciousness as thoroughly as the ancient graves of her ancestors, which were made of clods of dirt, had been wiped off the face of the earth. The Arabic she spoke too was an old, refined, urban Arabic as opposed to the Moslem Arabic which had recently invaded the city together with the encroaching desert eroding its environs and making them barren. A barrier of suspicion, ignorance and forgetfulness thus separated Victoria from the rabble of Shi'ites and Sunnites, Kurds and Syrians and Turkmans and Persians crossing the Tigris with her. With a pounding heart she realized that the entire length of the bridge was already behind her, and she found herself standing in a spacious square in front of a line of cars and wagons waiting for the flag to change on the tower. The crowd which had spilled off the bridge with her spread out like a huge fan and scattered over the square. A few of them turned towards the dirt alleys whose buildings were covered with a film of dust. The Jewish strollers didn't dare explore these alleys, especially in view of the rumours that the bridge would not last till evening, the swelling tide would tear it from the river which was raging out of control. Their curiosity waned, and they began turning back to recross the bridge, afraid of being cut off from their homes on the east bank of the river. Inside her *abbaya* Victoria froze in despair. A married woman, the mother of two children, she stood there like a helpless child crying out for some familiar man, or even boy, to take her hand and lead her in a world ruled by men. The very thought that she was standing there alone on the exclusively Moslem west bank filled her with terror. She was sure that even her brother Murad, long a man among men, had never set foot here. How had she dared?

She tried to overcome her panic and not to stand apart from the crowd. Men lay in wait everywhere. She turned quickly on her heel and joined the crush of people crowding onto the narrow bridge, her body once more the object of pinches, her buttocks of hooked, prying fingers. She was soon swallowed up in the solid mass which she was afraid to be part of, but even more afraid to be left out of. The thought of suicide had already been forgotten. Kilmanteen and Suzanne must be hungry by now, with nobody to take care of their needs. She had sold her wrist-watch with the rest of the jewellery to pay for Rafael's trip to Mount Lebanon, but it seemed to her that several hours had passed since she left the house. Now she reproached herself bitterly for having contemplated abandoning the little girls to her mother's caprices, and she saw them in her mind's eye huddled in a corner and crying their hearts out, and at the same time she remembered the keening noise which had escaped her mother's throat at about midnight on the night of the flood.

She had awakened from her sweet dream to see her father passing between the people lying next to the bolts of silk and velvet. Between his thumb and forefinger he gripped the slender neck and shook her mother's head until the kerchief slipped off. "Keep quiet, you idiot. These poor people are worn out."

Aziza turned over like an enormous buffalo. "Try to understand, Izuri. She's upset about her loss."

Najia's temper flared. "I can do without pity from snakes."

Aziza closed her eyes. "You're right. Even the pity of snakes is too good for you."

"Listen to her."

"Keep quiet, I told you."

"Where's Rafael?"

"Lying outside."

"Then his father's busy robbing us of house and home. He didn't insist on staying behind and endangering himself for nothing."

Michal, who had elected to remain on the armchair rather than joining the others on the floor, coaxed her son:

"Be nice to her. The fear and the flight . . ."

"To hell with the fear and the flight," Najia interrupted her. "It's your fucking son who's sucking my blood right now."

The shocked Yehuda clucked his tongue. A heavy silence fell, as if the very walls were exhorting Izuri to clobber the rebellious shrew on the head. Victoria held her breath—Dahood's first wife had gone insane from a blow to her head. Her gigantic father's hand was capable of killing. But this time too he hit her with moderation, and stalked out of the warehouse, leaving her whimpering mother to cry herself to sleep like a child.

The river did not wreck the house in the flood.

When the sun rose they returned to the alley. Najia rushed ahead, striding out until she lost one of her shoes, and then she ran at a limp until she took off the other shoe too and went barefoot. She arrived before Rafael, who had the key, and banged on the door with her shoe. The clan lowered their eyes at the sight of their neighbours who had been abandoned to their fate during the night, and now stood watching the deserters who had fled for nothing. When Rahma Afsa departed that morning for her forbidden haunts she was astonished to see Najia pounding savagely on the door with her shoe. Rafael hung back maliciously at the end of the procession until Izuri growled: "Go and open the door, man."

In the meantime they all moved aside, for the Nunu family had entered the narrow alley. This time Nuna and her father were mounted on impressive white mules. Abdallah thought that the House of Michal had lost their key, and with something of a swagger he kindly offered to break the door down with his shoulder. Offended by this slight to his own shoulder, Izuri repeated angrily to Rafael: "Get a move on, man, open the door!"

Rafael turned the key in the lock and moved aside. Najia flung the door open and stood frozen to the spot, looking as if she had seen a ghost. From lintel to doorstep Eliyahu filled the doorway with his rumpled hair, his glaring drunken eyes, his smooth narrow chest, his dark nakedness and his heavy testicles. The woman covered her eyes with her hand and shrieked, "*Wai*!" and without bothering to drop his robe and pull up his long underpants he said in disgust: "Madwoman, can't you even let a man shit in peace?" And with regal disdain he turned his muscular bum on her and returned to the lavatory.

Najia swooped on the cracks in the walls and scratched in the holes with her nails until the eroded bricks were stained with blood. Perhaps in her frenzy she did not search properly, and perhaps she did not believe from the outset that there was anything left of her treasure, and her frantic scrabblings were only intended to prove the rightness of her suspicions. Or perhaps an anonymous hand had indeed emptied all her hiding-places of their loot. In any case, she found nothing. Sometimes she stopped searching and hit herself in the face like a mourner until her forehead and eyelids and cheeks were smeared with blood, and when she screamed it looked as if her face had been cut to pieces and she was screaming in pain. A note of pity crept into Izuri's voice: "Woman, calm down. If you keep this up you'll scrape the walls bare. What have you lost, ten bracelets?

Twenty earrings? I'll replace whatever's missing. Just calm down." But she was afraid to reveal the full extent of her treasure to him, partly because she could not rid herself of the guilty feeling that she had taken the money from the mouths of his children, and partly because she feared he might demand the lost treasure for himself. "Your cruel brother and his gangster son, they're the ones to blame."

Eliyahu went up to the drinking-water jar, and in the cold of the morning he splashed icy water onto his head and neck and smoothed his wet hands over his bare chest.

"Eliyahu," called Izuri.

Eliyahu looked his sister-in-law up and down with loathing.

"And don't forget his son," shrieked Najia. "They don't talk to each other but they joined forces to rob me blind!"

"Rafael!" thundered Yehuda.

"Leave them both alone," said Michal. Shaul the peddler and his one-eyed friend Kaduri carried her up to her rug on the second-storey gallery. She pointed to the courtyard with an obscure gesture and left it at that, not wishing to add fuel to the flames by her interference. And Izuri shrugged, turned his back on his wife, and left for the shop without waiting for breakfast. It seemed to Victoria that her grandmother was silently accusing her Aunt Aziza, and she felt uncomfortable. She had not forgotten that her aunt had suckled her at her breast, and she knew that the laughing, good-natured woman really loved her sincerely. It can't be true, she said to herself, it can't be true. It must be somebody else. Her mother went on circling the courtyard and feeling the walls and leaving bloody trails on them. A merry, metallic sound rang on the tiles and silenced Najia's lamentations for a moment. The gold coin which Michal had flung into the courtyard caught a ray of sunlight and twinkled mischievously. Najia kicked it. "I don't need charity," she said and she picked it up and ran to the gutter and threw the coin into the hole. The women groaned at the sight of the lost gold. Najia clapped her hands and cried bitterly: "There!"

In the afternoon the house settled down. Rafael's eldest sister sat on the middle roof with her little brother trapped between her knees, picking the lice from the tangled mop of his hair. Victoria, Miriam and Toya went into a huddle at the end of the roof. "A bit higher," Toya instructed Victoria, who was holding the little mirror as Toya plucked her eyebrows.

Victoria smiled at the sight of the little girl's serious face as she pursued this grown-up occupation.

"Your brother Ezra," said the tiny flatterer to Miriam, "is a good looking boy, he's got fire in his eyes."

Miriam's voice was hoarse, as it always was when she was aroused. "Never mind Ezra. We're talking about Dahood. The stories he tells about you are the biggest lies in the world. My mother says that men like him aren't men at all."

Toya smothered a giggle, for she of course knew the truth, but at the same time she was eager to please Miriam. "He's got all the equipment a man needs," she said with an apologetic smile.

"That makes no difference," Miriam insisted.

Toya stopped plucking her eyebrows and looked anxiously into Miriam's face. She would have been ready to agree that Dahood was an elephant or a wasp, as long as Miriam wasn't cross with her. "He's good to me," she said.

"Is my mother lying?" Miriam sprang to her parent's defence.

"God forbid." There were tears in Toya's eyes.

"Dahood paints his face and dyes his hair like a woman. And my mother says that everyone who plays the zither at parties is that way."

"You mean crazy?" Toya sacrificed her husband's sanity on the altar of friendship with alacrity.

"I mean that men fuck him the way you say he fucks you."

"Oh, that." Toya let out a sigh of relief, straightened the mirror in Victoria's hand, and resumed her eyebrow plucking. "Let them fuck him, what do I care. Is it so terrible?" she inquired innocently.

"It's impossible to talk to you," said Miriam sulkily.

The little girl was filled with anxiety. "I love you, Miriam. If you like I'll fix it so you can peek at us tonight. Just don't be cross with me. You can see everything. Really."

Miriam was overcome with terror. "No! No! Your Dahood is a bastard and the son of a bastard. If he finds out he'll tell my father."

"You're not cross with me any more?"

"No."

"Then let me kiss your fingers."

"Take them," Miriam consented with the haughty gesture of a princess.

Toya's face fell. She had hoped that Miriam would give her, or at least lend her for a day or two, her hair-clip that was decorated with white beads. And now that she had disappointed Miriam she probably wouldn't be invited to eat at Yehuda's table either. She really didn't understand how men could fuck Dahood, who was a man himself, and perhaps Miriam was asking her to admit to something that couldn't possibly be true. But still she reproached herself for not responding immediately to Miriam's probing. And she sighed in resignation, and saw Victoria looking into the crystal blue sky and saying to herself: "That's not a bird."

The tiny white object sailed through the sky, trembling delicately like a bird abandoning itself to invisible currents of air. "It isn't falling," said Miriam. "So it has to be a bird."

Toya made haste to agree with her. "Yes, it's turning round and round in the sky. Maybe it's looking for food." And unthinkingly she stroked her empty stomach.

"It's paper," said Victoria. "It's a piece of paper. I'm telling you."

Toya smiled humbly at Miriam. "Maybe it's a love letter."

"It can't be," said Miriam with crushing certainty. "You don't just cast a love letter into the wind. You tie it to a stone and throw it exactly where you want it to go."

"You're a hundred per cent right," Toya quickly agreed.

"It's a piece of paper," insisted Victoria.

Grandmother Michal too watched the piece of paper trapped

in a kind of compulsive dance in the sky over the courtyard. The paper caught the gold of the sun and for some reason she imagined she could hear a whispering laugh. "*Shma Israel*," she mumbled and dropped her eyes. Perhaps it was a soul from her girlhood, homesick for its earthly abode.

The three girls climbed on tiptoe to the upper roof. Aziza saw them stealing past, even though her hardness of hearing prevented her from hearing their footsteps, and a flicker of fear and sadness flared up in her heart. An unwonted resentment crept into her voice. "You're going to spy on the Nunus again. Why don't you just move in with them?"

The piece of paper, exhausted by its celestial dance, landed on the outer edge of the gutter. The three girls held their breath. The flutter of a butterfly's wings, it seemed, would suffice to dislodge it from its perch. "As true as God, it's a letter!" breathed Miriam, recovering her usual good nature and high spirits. And the letter was going to fall off the ramshackle gutter at any moment into the abyss of the alley below. "Who knows what's written in it!"

"Hang onto my legs and I'll get it."

Miriam studied the little girl who was prepared to risk life and limb in order to please her, and refused to take part in the adventure. "No, you might fall."

Toya was already lying flat on her stomach. "Hold my feet," she cried to the other two, and they quickly grabbed her little feet and held on with shaking hands as she inched forward and snatched the paper. Then all three of them stood on the roof and stared blankly at the curly, elegant script. None of them knew how to read. The square letters looked like the print in the holy books, so perhaps they were Hebrew letters. They passed the paper from hand to hand and smelled the old ink. Miriam ground her teeth. "The stupidest donkey with the crookedest prick goes to *cheder* and learns to read and write— and us?"

"It could still be a love letter."

"You keep telling us that Dahood rides you every night like a man, so why are you wetting your pants because of some old love letter?"

"He's good to me," the little girl defended herself. "But I love you more."

Miriam was speechless, and then she smiled. "It's impossible to be cross with this crazy creature."

The overjoyed Toya wagged her head as hard as she could.

"Let's go and ask Rabbi Juri Chittaiyat to read it to us," Miriam suggested. "Maybe it's just an amulet."

"The Rabbi doesn't do anything for nothing," Victoria reminded her.

Toya tapped a tiny purse tied round her waist with a string and hidden in her panties. "I've got a few pennies."

The Rabbi glared at them and questioned them sternly, suspecting that some ruffian might be playing a trick on him. Victoria and Toya trembled at the sight of his wrinkled face and his eyes terrifyingly magnified by his thick glasses. But Miriam seemed to be making an effort not to laugh. The learned Rabbi fixed his eyes on her. "The handwriting is familiar to me. Aren't you Master Yehuda's daughter?"

Miriam was afraid to open her mouth, lest the laughter penned up inside her burst out, and she nodded her head.

The pious neighbourhood healer waved the paper at her accusingly. "Perhaps you stole it from your father?"

"It came on the wind," Victoria replied instead of Miriam, who was choking with silent laughter.

"And you're Master Izuri's daughter?" the Rabbi asked in a kind of wrathful whisper, and proceeded to read the note to himself.

"*Jamiya al Allam yitlebun rizzek min Ha-Shem Yitbarech v'hu yati-hum . . .*"

"What's written there?" piped Toya. "I can pay."

The Rabbi's left hand reached out and tightened round the coins, while his right hand steadied the note in front of his spectacles. Miriam could no longer restrain herself and ran outside to release her laughter. The Rabbi began to read and interpret the note, which was written in Judeo-Arabic. "Everyone asks the Lord, blessed be He, for a living, and He gives it to them. But there are three trades, which when their practitioners pray for a living, the Blessed Lord does not accede to their request. One is the healer who desires a living, and his living means that people should fall ill so that he can cure them. The second is the coffin seller, whose living depends on people dying. And the third, begging your pardon, is the whore. These three, when they pray to Him for a living, the Blessed Lord turns a deaf ear to their prayers."

The Rabbi-healer cleared his throat and Victoria did not know if he was angry or suppressing his laughter. On the threshold she heard him muttering: "Wonderful, so now Rahma Afsa and I are in the same boat!"

It didn't enter Victoria's head to ask him for the note. Outside Miriam was still writhing with laughter. "What's got into you?" smiled Victoria.

"That holy man who takes care all year long not to touch a woman's hand—I couldn't stop thinking what he would do if he knew where the money had been before he laid hands on it."

8

Three months after the flood the residents of the courtyard were listening to Najia's dream. Dreams were always taken seriously. People remembered their own and others' dreams for years. In their eyes a dream was a prophecy with the power to determine the future. Najia's dream gave her a surprising vitality and attraction that seemed incompatible with her hostile aloofness. Her wish to confide her dream in them was in itself surprising, and since she was a downtrodden, persecuted woman they expected it to come out stammering and awkward. But instead her language rose to such heights of creativity and eloquence that her audience listened with bated breath. She sat in the courtyard, near the basement doorstep, her legs crossed, her back straight, her eyes like the eyes of a dervish greeting the rising sun.

Yehuda had stayed home due to the pains in his heart which had kept him up all night, and he sat leaning against the second storey railing with the space of the courtyard between him and Michal's rug. There was a sheet of paper propped on his upright knee and he was writing intently. The women thought that he was doing the business accounts, and they soon forgot the presence of the scholar in their midst. Even Michal, concerned as she was at the sight of her son's suffering face, pricked up her ears so as not to miss a single word of Najia's dream. Aziza hushed Toya and Miriam who were talking loudly in the arcade, and went to sit opposite Najia, where she cupped her chin in her hand and turned her less deaf ear towards the woman unfolding her dream.

Najia pinched the corners of her mouth between her thumb and forefinger, stretched her pursed lips, and said: "Not in her winding-sheet but in her pure-white bridal gown she came. On the wings of a dove she glided into the courtyard and sat opposite me as clear as you see me now."

And Yehuda wrote: "What is the point of waking up in the morning like a plough-shaft dug up from underneath the ruins?"

"So fair was my grandmother," said Najia, "that the moment my grandfather set eyes on her he forgot himself. In those days the Jews were still paying a poll-tax to the Sultan to gain exemption from military service. But he was a wealthy man and did not demand a dowry from my grandmother's parents. She never had to lift a finger. She was his pride and joy, the crown on his head. That was my grandmother, may she rest in peace."

"And what does it benefit a man," wrote Yehuda, "to leave his house and go out into a street which is all crooked nails, and coax customers who are also crooked nails, and sit in a shop full of nails which are also useless junk?"

"Stand up, granddaughter. Her voice was like cool water on a blazing day. They kick you and you fall to the ground and think yourself no better than a pile of rubbish. Stand up, my daughter," said Najia.

"And the pain splits you in half and freezes your fingers," wrote Yehuda, "and Aziza is a garden in bloom and I stumble at the gate."

"Stand up, granddaughter, the colour of the grave is yellow and green and black, and it lies at the foot of the wall. You'll know it at once."

Michal's eyes were fixed on her daughter-in-law sitting below. She left off drinking the sweet tea so that Najia's words would not be lost in the noise of her slurping. The women hushed each other, and Michal was swept along with them in one of those magical moments which united the courtyard into a real family with its own code of behaviour.

"The grave described by Grandmother, may she rest in peace, was the strangest grave I ever heard tell of. Whoever heard of a grave painted like a flag?"

"Even the dream of this silly goose," Yehuda went on writing, "makes more sense than mine. I am ashamed to tell it even to my wife. A strange corpse, God forbid. The upper half of a man and the lower half of a woman. And the corpse is naked and smiling lasciviously as if inviting someone to come and have his way with it. God, have mercy on your servant, to dream such a dream is a disgrace."

"And I beg her," said Najia and blew her nose loudly on her head-kerchief. Suddenly she looked beautiful to Victoria, the way Abdallah Nunu had described her. "Grandmother, where will I find such a grave? And she replies: It moves hither and thither. So said my grandmother, may she rest in peace. It lies at the foot of the wall, but in every alley you may meet it."

"How Aziza devours Najia's dream," wrote Yehuda. "A handsome, hard-working woman God gave me, but he gave her to me as punishment. To place a ladder before a cripple and say, ascend to the glory of heaven. It is not for nothing that she spreads her smiles before Izuri, and only the loyalty and honesty of my brother keep us from disgrace."

Najia fell silent. "Is that all?" exclaimed Aziza in disappointment.

"So said my grandmother and went away," said Najia on a concluding note.

Michal raised the little cup of cooling tea to her lips. It was the war, the war that was advancing like a storm of fire. The alleys would be turned into graves, God save us.

Victoria felt gratified. She was proud of her mother, who had produced such fine sentences and made the whole courtyard listen to her. And she was proud of her mother's grandmother too, as if she had really visited the courtyard. She stood up and gave the baby she was holding to Toya, and went to make strong tea for her mother and Aziza.

On the second story Yehuda's face turned grey, but he went on writing: "And these are the words of Rabbi Shimon Agasi in the synagogue: 'Woe to the woman who provokes the lust of young men. And modesty demands that even when she lies with her husband there should be no laughter and heedlessness and boldness, God forbid, but everything should be done in modest seclusion and the fear and dread of God. As it says in the verse, and she ate and wiped her mouth, which teaches us that even in the act of intercourse, referred to here as eating, there must be modesty and shame before God, to whom all mysteries are revealed.'" He stared into the space between himself and his mother sitting on the other side of the courtyard, and added in Arabic in Hebrew script: "And perhaps I deprived her body of joy precisely because of that accursed fear and dread. It paralysed me on that first night, when I was in my prime, and now I am paralysed by illness and old age. What wonder she laughs like that for Izuri, and even for that child Rafael."

And he went on writing, but after a while Miriam saw that her father's head had fallen onto the railing, and she hurried up to him and called her mother. Rabbi Juri Chittaiyat was immediately summoned, and the ancient healer agreed to leave his house only out of respect for the learning and family of the patient. Bent as a bow, leaning on a stick and supported by his two grandsons, he traversed the short distance between the two houses. He diagnosed what was already common knowledge: a mysterious power of corruption had affected Yehuda's heart, and his spleen too was damaged. And he prepared an amulet for him, and to strengthen his body he prescribed well-fried mutton liver, and for breakfast *zibda* made from buffalo milk and sweetened by date honey. Nobody noticed when he swept the notes strewn over the patient's mat into his cloak.

Najia's star, on the other hand, waned, and nobody paid any more attention to her fears. And so she turned to Jamila the fortune-teller, and occasional midwife and professional wailer. For a penny the fortune-teller told her that the dream had come from a sudden fright which had clouded her blood. Najia dismissed her explanation—she was always frightened, she said. Jamila couldn't know what it felt like to hang in the air in the hands of a giant, not knowing if she was about to be hurled to the ground or smashed against the opposite wall. No, she said, with a touch of pride, nobody could call her a spoilt mare. She was already immune to all kinds of frights. And in lofty language she repeated the description of the colourful grave, until Jamila understood and she smiled and said: "It's not a grave, it's a person."

"A person?"

"A person," emphasized Jamila, well-versed in the convolutions of the human heart.

Najia regretted the penny she had spent in vain—she had already guessed this interpretation for herself. She went home and collected the coins she had accumulated in the meantime, and before setting out to search for the mobile grave she instructed Victoria: "You'll do the cooking today by yourself, and Toya, instead of standing and sucking her thumb like an imbecile, will help you to look after the little rascals. What's the matter with you?" She looked at Victoria's face, where laughter and tears seemed to be pursuing each other. In her own way she loved the girl. Although Victoria's presence made her bitterly aware of her own insignificance, without her she would have lost her only support in the hurly-burly of the hostile courtyard. "Are you ill?"

"No," said Victoria, marvelling at the warmth in her mother's voice.

It was almost noon when Najia set off to look for the yellow, green and black grave. It wasn't easy to find Salman, whose patched coat was heavy with gold coins. Nobody knew where he lived. Many people had followed him, guessing at the fortune he carried on his body, but none had succeeded in discovering where he laid his head at night. He drifted about like a ghost, on holidays and weekdays. The air imprisoned in the narrow alleys shimmered in the blazing heat, and after crossing flaming lakes of sun Najia was streaming with sweat inside her black *abbaya*. She dragged herself tirelessly from market to market and synagogue to synagogue, until she finally found him sitting on an ancient mound of earth which had been absorbing human and animal urine for centuries. The sun beat down on his head, and his colourful coat, shiny with the grease of congealed filth, enclosed him like armour. His fingers picked at the rotting flesh of a watermelon, and from time to time he broke off a piece of the dry pitta in his lap, which he had received as alms, and pushed it between his disintegrating teeth.

"Wait till I've finished," he belched.

"You don't have to unpick the lining of your coat. I've finished with gold coins."

Salman had never given anyone advice in his life, certainly not for nothing. For advice was rewarded by curses and abuse, and sometimes worse than that. Nor had he ever uttered a superfluous word liable to betray the secrets of the city thirsty for secrets. Therefore he did not disclose the name of the woman who had been bringing him gold coins to change, even though it was clear to him that the gold was Najia's. He made a pretty profit from the two women and saw no reason to upset the arrangement. At the end of his meal he wiped his mouth on the coarse sleeve of his coat until the sores on his lips bled, and asked in a gloomy voice: "What do you want then?"

"To deposit the money with you for interest. The house is no longer safe."

"I'm not interested in your house. And what will you do with the interest?"

"Let it give interest too."

"As you wish."

When she returned she saw that the smiles and the sadness were still chasing each other on Victoria's face. She asked no more questions, for it was not their way to open their hearts to one another. Victoria avoided her mother as she avoided all the adults in the courtyard then. That morning, immediately after it happened, she called Miriam into the glass-walled room, which was kept closed in the summer, and told her. Miriam went down to the courtyard and she was left alone in the stifling heat of the empty room. At long last she was a woman. Miriam had preceded her by almost a year and a half, and all that time she had tried to console her by repeating her mother's words, that a girl who was late in getting her period would be tall and shapely, and not short and fat. Victoria was not comforted. Men preferred fat women. Ever since morning she had been daydreaming and thinking of the foreign word "theeayter" and fighting the irresistible craving for sweets. In her mind's eye she saw herself leaning against the Nunus' palm tree, while a pure white dove caressed the chapped skin of her hand with its beak. As soon as her mother left to look for Salman, she went to Ma'atuk Nunu's grocery store on the corner of the alley. He was already married. She put the money on the counter, and Ma'atuk rummaged in the rusty tin next to him with his six fingers and filled a paper cone for her with embarrassing generosity. "That's too much," she smiled at him. "You deserve more," he stammered, blushing, his hump looking as if it was about to crush him to the ground. She walked home with a dancing step. Her period and the theeayter, the theeayter and her period.

Every day she and Miriam did their utmost not to miss Rafael when he set forth. At that time he was growing a cheeky little moustache. He shaved sitting down in front of a mirror with a folding stand. Towards evening he would set out, his hair parted in the centre, a bowtie adorning his dazzling shirt, his hand twirling a silver-knobbed cane. Apart from the Nunus' palm there was not a single tree in the whole alley, nor a potted plant or flower. Between the old walls the eye was accustomed to the shabby clothes handed down from father to son. And so Rafael's every appearance was like the vivid renewal of the seasons. His voice was restrained in the screeching of the courtyard, and the alert look in his eye gave you the feeling that something thrilling was about to happen in this grey, humdrum world. He came home late at night, and many of the residents of the courtyard predicted that he would meet his death at the hands of a deserter from the Turkish army.

Once Victoria tried to get details about the theeayter out of Murad. Her naive brother repeated his father's unequivocal statement: "A den of vice." More than this he did not know. And she and Miriam and Toya went to ask Ezra. His description was more lively. "Lux lamps burning in every corner of the hall with a light like the sun in summer. Women younger than Rahma Afsa in tiny little panties dancing and singing. Sometimes there's a band and sometimes there isn't, and they drink all the time."

"And what do the men do?" asked Miriam.

"I told you, they drink all the time. And they look. Some of them sing along with the dancers."

"You sound as if you've been there."

"And how I have," he lied without blinking an eye.

They didn't believe him, although it seemed to Victoria that his description was accurate enough, especially in the matter of the tiny little panties. In her imagination she saw herself wearing them and capering about in front of Rafael. And she shivered at the thought: what kind of a woman will I be? A punching bag like her mother for someone like her father to satisfy his lust on? Or a tigress like the women who made the roof shake on summer nights? Or perhaps a delicate creature with a shining angel face like Nuna Nunu? And if Miriam took Rafael, would she be a tigress? And what would happen if she, Victoria, was saddled with a husband like Uncle Yehuda, suffering and sickly and pious and God-fearing? Or someone like her brother Murad, hard-working and obedient and boring? And what good would it do her to fill her head with thoughts of a burning brand? You couldn't trust types like Rafael any more than you could trust the Devil. But Rafael wasn't the Devil. He was the one who had saved Eliyahu's family from starvation, it was thanks to him they had food on their table. And now he was keeping his promise to his sisters, that they wouldn't die old maids. He had taken a loan and returned it after a few months, his shop was prospering, and he had found husbands for his sisters and paid the dowry out of his own pocket. Even his father came to him for pocket-money. Rafael was generous to a fault. He had given a gold tiara studded with jewels to his mother, the quietest and most modest creature in the bustling courtyard.

Both she and Miriam lived in suspense. A young man who did his duty and married his sisters, himself an eligible bachelor.

But Rafael was silent. He didn't drop a hint, and he gave no encouragement to Miriam's parents either. Was there some other girl? And perhaps a new demon would take possession of him and he would set out on his travels again?

9

The men digging into the dust of the ancient courtyard breathed heavily. Unaccustomed as they were to the job, they were already in a stupor of exhaustion, but they went on wielding their picks and spades and packing their baskets with the damp, decomposing, yielding earth, full of the memories of previous generations. They were already working in their long underpants and loose shirts, and their skin was gleaming with sweat. From outside their heads looked like black balls floating on the darkness of the pit, which was growing deeper and wider every day, for the third day running. From time to time they changed shifts, and the work continued day and night without a pause. The women, girls and children lifted the full baskets and carried them upstairs where they scattered the earth on the upper roof. The men worked in oppressive silence and in dread, all except for Kaduri the candied-turnip seller, whose blind eye exempted him from death. The lame and the blind swaggered around the markets and the alleys as confidently as if they were immortal. The whole and healthy envied them. Some pretended to be cripples and limped with bent backs or shuffled with canes and groped with their free hands like blind men. People hardened their hearts to the handicapped, unable to distinguish between the true misfortunates and the imposters. Beggars whose lameness had been their meal ticket up to now died of hunger.

The men in the courtyard grew beards to make themselves look old. A grey beard was worth its weight in gold. Dahood stopped plucking his eyebrows and dyeing his hair. Within a month he was transformed from a man bursting with vitality to a wilted greybeard. Toya was astounded. The dissolute Eliyahu, who had always been so proud of his youthful appearance, now cursed his beard which refused to go grey. He worked like a demon at the bottom of the pit and urged the others to dig deeper and deeper, like a prisoner digging a tunnel to save his life.

He was already considered a deserter, and if they caught him he would no doubt be sentenced to death.

The residents of the courtyard had no idea where the war had broken out or why. It was as remote as the snow which capped the Turkish mountains in winter and flooded the Tigris in the spring, as if trying to drown Baghdad. The invisible monster terrified them. It had already devoured many men. Among the first to go was Nuna Nunu's husband, whose name nobody remembered. Ma'atuk's crooked back and six-fingered hands were a guarantee of life. Now he set a stool before the shop and in his free time he would sit and stare at his father's door, with its huge, fortress-like nails. The certainty that he would go on living made him bold, and when his second child was born he bought two houses. His father was not impoverished by the war either. The Turkish army confiscated half his mules, but the remaining half brought in a handsome profit.

The terrors of the war were exemplified by Eliyahu. He disappeared for a few weeks, and it was generally supposed that he was carousing in one of the pleasure groves on the outskirts of the town. For otherwise he would surely have heard the beating of the drum and cries of the herald proclaiming that the Turkish Empire, bearer of the sword of Islam, had embarked on a great war. For many generations the Jews of Iraq had not known war. Many were under the impression that wars were still fought with bows and arrows, swords and horses. That cruel armies besieged cities and slaughtered their inhabitants. The more sophisticated reassured them that this war was being waged at distances too far to imagine, there was no danger of some Nebuchadnezzar breaching the walls of Baghdad and leading the Jews into slavery and banishment. In previous generations the Jews had paid a special tax exempting them from serving in the Moslem army, all of whose wars were holy Jihads. And so the belief had taken root that battles were fought exclusively by mighty warriors. With the revolution of the Young Turks the old order was overturned. The tax was abolished, and Jewish men faced conscription in wartime like all the others. The Jews were thunderstruck when they realized that as soon as they reached manhood their young boys would be sent to the slaying fields. They failed to understand what good a man like Nuna Nunu's husband, for example, could do the mighty Sultan. When he couldn't even break down the door to his own wife's bedroom. And what use would even Dahood or Murad be to him? They were sure that the conscripts, who had never set foot outside the city or spent a day outdoors, would soon be sent home. They must have been taken for some kind of forced labour in a time of emergency, as in the floods. The Jews would only get in the way of the mighty warriors of the illustrious empire. In spite of the determined hunt for the young men, the Jews went on cherishing false hopes and smiling, until Eliyahu returned.

They almost chased him away when they saw him standing on the doorstep. They thought he was a Shi'ite pilgrim, lost on his way from Persia. He gave off a terrible stench. His feet were bound in stinking rags instead of shoes. The tattered rags on his body looked like the filthy spiderwebs in the kitchen. His body was full of sores and lice. And he fell on his knees and kissed the floor of the courtyard, and wept in a voice made hoarse by the sun and the wind of distant fields.

Toya held her nose and pulled a face. Najia panicked and cried "*Kush! Kush!*" as if to chase away a cat. Izuri shouted "What's this?" confident that the sound of his roar would send the pilgrim scuttling to find shelter elsewhere. Only Hanina cried: "It's my husband Eliyahu!"

Like Najia, Hanina was a little woman, but her voice was never heard in the courtyard. She bore her suffering in silence, avoided arguments, and did not react to her husband's exploits, with the result that nobody knew what she really felt. Now too, she refrained from asking Eliyahu where he had been and why he had come home in such a state.

Having knelt down to kiss the floor, Eliyahu couldn't get up again. On all fours he crawled to the shaded arcade, and Hanina hurried over to him, thrust her thin arm under his armpit, and implored him to stand up. Convinced that he was drunk, she was surprised that he did not abuse her, and alarmed when he asked for her sympathy. "Woman, I've seen death face to face."

She helped him to lie on the bench. Dahood, his companion in the wenching of the pleasure groves, began to fear for his sanity. "Where were you?"

"In the war . . . or near it," he stammered from the depths of his hollow chest. "I was on the way to the war. The men died of exhaustion, they were mowed down by Turkish bullets. They went mad with hunger and hunted field mice until they gave up the ghost in the wilderness."

The residents of the courtyard crowded round the arcade and surrounded the bench. Michal gave the command to be taken down from her rug, and Izuri carried her down the stairs on his back and seated her on a stool at the feet of her son. The news spread through the alley, and many whose relatives had been torn away from them hurried to the courtyard. Hanina sat on the floor with a basin of vinegar, soaking strips of cloth and putting them on Eliyahu's forehead.

"Did you meet Nuna's husband?"

Eliyahu glared at the prosperous cattle dealer, scowled and retorted with his usual rudeness: "The question of a fool. Where do you think I was? Carrying the Torah round the synagogue on *Simhat Torah*? I wouldn't have recognized my own mother there!"

Abdallah Nunu smiled and chivalrously ignored the affront to his honour. "The man has vanished like a drop of piss in the river, and left my daughter an abandoned wife."

Eliyahu took no notice of him. "God knows how I landed up in that hellhole. I saw pale-faced men lined up in the square, with soldiers guarding them with guns, and a Turkish officer counting them. It seemed a little strange to me that there wasn't a single man among the onlookers. Only women and children were standing there and staring at the unfortunate wretches."

"You hadn't heard that war had broken out," said Dahood.

Eliyahu's body was convulsed with sobs again. "No, I didn't know."

Hanina waved her hand to make the people crowding around him move back. She knew about the man hunt, and when he failed to return home she suspected that he had been caught, and she had mourned him in secret, far from the gloating eyes of the residents of the courtyard. And here he was, alive and breathing before her, the lecher who had turned her nights into a desert of loneliness, the wastrel who had never put bread on the table. But even a man like him was better than a dead man. Carefully she unwound the stinking rags wrapped round his feet, and thankfully she washed the toes which had come back from the fields of death, as if he had done her a favour and endured great hardship in order to save her from the humiliation of being a widow, with people hiding their happiness from her for fear of the Evil Eye.

Eliyahu stared at the little girl who pushed her way to the front row and listened wide-eyed with her thumb in her mouth. He didn't remember Toya, and he made no effort to remember who she was. The courtyard was always swarming with children, and he couldn't be bothered to find out who they belonged to. All he wanted to do now was pour out his heart. "The officer called out the names of the men. There were Jews there too. Some of them wet their pants from fear."

"So maybe you did see Nuna's husband," Abdallah broke in. "That sounds like him."

From the exalted heights of his martyrdom the penniless ne'er-do-well snapped at the wealthy merchant, "Shut up!", and resumed his tale of woe. "The Jew-hating Amalek must have been short of a conscript. Suddenly he yelled at me: 'You're Muhammad ben Ali Nazim from the town of Diwaniya. Get in line.' I felt my legs collapsing underneath me. One of the officer's fiendish henchmen slapped my face."

"May his hand wither," said Hanina, suddenly in sole possession of her man. His brow responded gratefully to her touch.

"I wept. I told him I was Eliyahu, son of Michal, and long

past forty." His body jerked upright, as if reliving the terrible experience. "The officer didn't say a word. He drew a pistol and fired a shot between my legs. Izuri, is that girl yours?" Somehow the finger in Toya's mouth seemed incompatible with the knowing look in her eyes.

"You've forgotten, brother. That's Toya, Dahood's wife. Don't you remember how drunk you got on her wedding night?"

Hanina brought a clay mug and poured water on the ground, kneaded the mud in her hands and smeared it timidly on his brow, as a remedy for fright and shock, as if the terrifying shot had only just gone off between her husband's legs.

"A sergeant kicked me in the arse. They told us to move and we were afraid to ask where to. They led us through the streets until we left the city. I felt as if I was being torn out of my life. They whipped us on like cattle. Further and further north. At night we fell down where we stood. We dragged ourselves forward, thirsty and hungry. After a week my shoes fell to pieces."

And he broke into embarrassing sobs again. "People, we have to hide. So those sons of Satan won't see us. You don't know what they're like. They dragged the sick to the side of the road, and that Amalekite officer shot them dead without even getting off his horse. They left their corpses for the birds. Go tell Rifka Muslawi and Naima Halali that they're widows. I saw it with my own eyes."

The women listening slapped themselves in the face. Hanina, saved from this fate, was ashamed of the joyful smile spreading inside her.

"Go," he went on in the same keening, hair-raising tone, "and tell the parents of Karim Gabbai and Benjamin Fattal and Yehoshua Ghali to sit *shiva* for their sons."

Like a tempest the keening lamentation swept through the women crowding round the bench.

"Rafael," whispered the beaming Hanina. "Come to your father and praise Allah for bringing him back to us safely."

"He's here?" asked his father.

"I'm here," announced Rafael in a tone of qualified sympathy.

Suddenly Eliyahu's voice filled with touching paternal concern. "Run, my son. Run away before they catch you."

Rafael's face hardened and he said nothing. It seemed to him that his father was deriving a peculiar enjoyment from his status as the prodigal son safely returned to the bosom of his family.

"We left the city in a column of one hundred and eighty men," said Eliyahu, "and within two weeks that crazy bastard had reduced us to less than a hundred. People in the know said we had a march of many weeks before us, we would have to wade through rivers and trudge through snow in the miserable clothes on our backs. Then they would give us guns and line us up facing the Muscobites, so they could mow us down with their cannons. And if anyone was left alive the Cossacks would fall on them and slice off their heads with their swords."

"God save us," said Michal.

"Which of us knew anything about living under the open sky? Many died in the heat of the day and the cold of the night. They would have been better off dying from the officer's bullets. The rations ran out. And we went on crawling forward with no food in our stomachs. Every day the officer sent another squad to invade the villages and commandeer food. The peasants ran away, but some of them ambushed us and killed us. When we reached the mountains of Kurdistan, the head of our squad made a big mistake, and laid hands on the daughter of a Kurdish *mukhtar* as well as his food. They killed him on the spot, together with the other members of the squad so there wouldn't be any witnesses. I saw the barrel of a gun opposite me with a face of stone behind it. I shouted '*Shma Israel*' and the barrel pointed downwards, and stayed there for a long time aimed right here, at the groin, while someone roared inside me: Don't castrate me, kill me and be finished! *Shma Israel*! It turned out that there was a Jew in the village, and it was this same Jew who held the hand of that Kurd and persuaded him not to shoot me. I fell to my knees and wept, and shat in my pants too, begging your pardon. They hid me in a cave, and a few days later the

Jew took me to a spring and told me to follow the water course until I reached a river, and to beg for food in the villages on the river banks until I came to the Tigris."

"And you came by foot, alone among the gentiles, from Kurdistan to Baghdad?" asked the astounded Dahood.

"Alone, by foot."

In the afternoon the heads of the diggers disappeared from view. "Enough," said Eliyahu, again in the grip of a panic which seemed to have been in abeyance for a while. "Enough, let's put up the frame and cover the pit already. We don't need a palace to hide in." But the other diggers paid no attention to him. A trail of earth lay scattered over the path to the roof and covered the courtyard and the stairs. That morning Yehuda had taken a hoe and descended into the pit to try his hand at digging. After a few minutes he turned pale and the hoe slipped from his hands. Arms resembling hairy branches pulled him up and dropped him at the edge of the pit. Najia was the first to hurry up and give him water to drink.

Michal sat up on her rug and banged on the second-storey railing. "Izuri, the Sabbath is beginning."

"We'll go on working until we finish," her son's voice answered her from the pit.

"I'll go and light the *kuraya*," said Michal and called Miriam to help her.

Kaduri sat on the edge of the pit, his good eye surveying the courtyard and his white eye frozen as a hailstone. "Sabbath," he announced. "I have to stop now."

"So we won't work for pay," Shaul the peddler's voice rose from about two metres below him. "We'll work for nothing." He himself was eligible for conscription and he knew that there would be no shelter for him. He was too poor to hide. He had to feed his family.

"My stomach's rumbling," protested Kaduri. "Let's have a bite to eat at least."

The peddler climbed up and sat down beside him. He whispered shyly, as usual: "I think you're right."

Tongues of fire painted crimson patterns on the faces of Miriam and her mother, who were in charge of the pots in the kitchen. The men and the boys came up from the pit and washed and prepared themselves for the hasty Friday night meal. "Where's Najia?" asked Izuri. Victoria spread her hands as if to say, don't ask me. Her brothers sat silently at her back. Their father clucked his tongue. "It's nearly dark, what the hell is she up to outside?" Nobody stood up for the absent woman. In the condemning silence Victoria said: "Then I'll light the *kuraya.*"

The *kuraya* was a glass dish full of water and a layer of oil. Victoria went up to the wooden sticks wrapped in cottonwool which were standing in it, covered her head with a shawl, and the flames shone inside the *kuraya.* In the silent, empty room she felt as if she were bathed in a pure light. In the busy, crowded house it was only rarely that a person found himself alone. It seemed to her that she was floating with the little flames on the pure oil, and two words broke out of the depths of her being: God and Rafael, Rafael and God. She saw Rafael sitting at the festive Sabbath table radiant in a white robe, while God hovered overhead. And Rafael winked at her with a mischievous smile, which said as plainly as words "Be fruitful and multiply", and raised the delicately engraved silver Kiddush cup. The whole room was at their disposal. A smell of wood and fresh paint rose from the chest and the two-mirrored wardrobe. The polished brass knobs on the bed reflected the tiny flames. And as if with God's blessing and permission Rafael approached her with the Kiddush cup in his hands and lifted the skirt of her dress as his voice rose clearly in a smiling blessing. The tips of his fingers caressed her and she laughed in her heart. The upper half of her body received the Sabbath, and the lower half was in a delightful turmoil. Her hands holding the shawl were still, only her hips wriggled, her lips murmured the blessing and her skin prickled with goose bumps.

"Are you lighting the *kuraya* for the Sabbath or chasing ants out of your pants?"

Shame and anger flooded her. All this time she had been

afraid of hearing the thunder of God's own voice, but not this hoarse, smoky voice.

"Father was looking for you," she said coldly.

"And you couldn't wait to usurp me, to take over the *kuraya*, you bitch."

And already she was on the defensive. "It's late, nobody knew where you were."

"Salman," said her mother and spat into the air, so recently full of sweetness and grace. "Vanished, as if he's drowned in the shithouse."

Victoria tried to reassure her mother. Whenever she was so agitated she ended up doing something rash, and her father beat her. "You never see him in the streets on the Sabbath," she explained.

"Nobody's seen him for over a week."

"A lot of people know about the fortune in his coat. Robbers, murderers, who knows."

"Shut up! He's alive. Alive, I tell you." She didn't tell her daughter that she had invested all her savings with the weird tramp. As always, she was alone in her troubles.

"Has Father seen you? He must be hungry."

"Why should he see me?" pounced Najia. "His eyes gleam when Aziza serves his food. And the way she shakes her whorish tits at him!"

The next day, when the Sabbath was over, the work on the hiding place was completed. On a sturdy wooden frame rush mats were spread, over them a thick layer of dirt was scattered, and the tiles were returned to their places. The narrow entrance was hidden with the clay drinking-water jar, which was removed from its usual alcove in the wall. Eliyahu went down first, terrified out of his wits. Hidden underground he would grow a beard, stop washing and cutting his nails, and even abstain from alcohol.

After him went his son Rafael, Victoria's brother Murad, Rafael's sisters' two new husbands, and another five young men. Ezra refused to hide in spite of the pleas of his mother and father. Dahood announced that he was going down to the pit with the zither, in order to entertain the others, and it was clear that he wasn't joking. His beard was showing a promising growth of grey, and hairs sprouted from his ears and nostrils. His suspicions grew. Why did Ezra refuse to go down the pit? He didn't like the way the boy looked at Toya, and she seemed far from indifferent to his attentions.

At first the women stepped on the tiles in fear and trembling. The very idea of the men hiding under their feet made them shudder. Up to now the bowels of the earth had been populated exclusively by demons. In the evening the married women parted damp-eyed from the courtyard and lay down on their beds feeling like sinners. The men who were still above ground, too, slipped like shadows, full of uneasiness, past the women whose dear ones were huddled together in the damp and the dark. After a week of gloom, Michal banged on the railing with her spoon and pronounced: "The children are entitled to play and laugh, and the adults should enjoy the food they bless. We should thank God that they're safe down there, instead of dying in the desert."

Two days later Ma'atuk Nunu came into the courtyard and looked up at Michal and wrung his hands and said with sincere pain: "I've heard terrible news, Umm Yehuda, and I don't know what to do. Nuna's husband has been killed."

"Then go and tell your father and sister, my son," said Michal in a tone of mild rebuke. "She must sit *shiva* for him."

Toya stopped braiding Victoria's hair in the corner of the courtyard. Ma'atuk's eyes slid over Victoria's face and her straight shoulders leaning against Toya's childish stomach, and he blushed and kept quiet.

"It's inconceivable," continued Michal, "that out of hatred for your father you should fail to perform this duty. It's your duty, my son."

"May God lengthen your life, Umm Yehuda. You're a good woman."

"Then forget your grievances against them and knock on their door."

"It's not hatred, Umm Yehuda. I'm afraid of my father's laughter. You know him, Umm Yehuda, not even Satan could stand such laughter, and I'm not Satan."

Michal was silent. Her heart was touched. That Nuna Nunu's husband, whose name nobody remembered, should arouse such sympathy in a man whose heart might understandably be poisoned with hatred . . . And she shuddered when she tried to understand the deeper meaning of the fact that this cripple was standing on the heads of men in hiding, and of the news he had brought, that another man had been killed. Like the sacrificial chicken on Yom Kippur, she thought and shivered, like the chicken sacrificed to expiate our sins.

"Go back to your shop, my son. I'll tell Azuri when he comes home from work. He can take the news."

"Thank you, Umm Yehuda, thank you," he said and took a step backwards, glancing again at Victoria's face in the frame of Toya's arms, and he mumbled something and left the courtyard.

Toya pulled Victoria's hair. "The cripple's crazy about you."

Victoria smiled, and then they remembered that the hunchback had brought news of death, and they fell silent.

The nights were astir with movement and loud with whispers. When the sun went down the motions were repeated like some ancient rite. After the removal of the cooking boards Victoria, together with the rest of the residents of the courtyard, would watch her father bend his knees and embrace the big water jar, whose shape and weight made her think of Aziza's big body, except that the smooth and slippery jar wasn't easy to hold like a woman's body. Straining his massive muscles her father would straighten up with the jar in his arms, and Ezra would quickly move the stand a couple of paces away, and her father would cross the fearful distance and deposit the jar in its new place. Only then would Victoria relax her pursed lips and release the air in her lungs in a long whistle of relief. Then she would run to the kitchen and hand Miriam and Aziza the trays and dishes, and they would hand them to the arms growing out of the darkness of the pit. Occasionally she caught a glimpse of Rafael's arms among them, but everything happened so quickly, amid urgent whispers to hurry up, that before she knew it she found herself surrounded by empty dishes and men's dirty clothes, and sometimes she was handed a stinking pail of pee and excrement as well, and in the meantime she heard Rafael address Miriam in a voice which despite the darkness and the stale air and the heavy smoking was still as clear as ever. Pierced by the pain of lost opportunity she would go to the lavatory to empty the pail, and her father would block the entrance to the pit with the clay jar again.

Night would descend on the courtyard all at once. The shouts of drunken soldiers terrified her. Her father suspected that the watchman was taking advantage of the chaos to steal bolts of cloth from the warehouse, and Yehuda didn't want to listen. Bad news made the pressure on his chest worse. Even on those nightmarish nights Victoria's father found solace in her mother's body, worn out by the search for Salman's coat. Her stomach was swelling again. She could hear Toya squealing again underneath the bulldozer of Dahood's body, the war having left no customers for his zither. At the same time Miriam began creeping into Victoria's bed. Nobody saw anything wrong in this intimacy between the cousins. Miriam would put her lips to Victoria's ear and set her on fire: "The way that Toya loves to swallow. She's only a few fingers high and an oar like that can get inside her." And she would raise herself slightly and look over to the corner of the roof, where the couple were lying. "Listen to her, just listen." And Victoria listened, and her face burned. "She wants more. Dahood's too old and tired for her. Oof! Oof!" groaned Miriam. "Touch me here, go on, touch," she said and pulled Victoria's fingers to her breasts and below. "I think about Rafael and it sets me on fire. Damn him, how I think about him. Today he touched my hand when he took the dish." She gurgled with laughter. "He hasn't got any whores in the pit. I'm telling you, he fucked me through his hands. Touch, touch me some more. Look how wet I . . ." But this time Victoria's shy hand refused to respond. "Damn the war. He could have chosen one of us now that he's married his sisters."

Like a big cloud Izuri's body passed over Najia's little body. He turned on his side, ready for sleep. "Quiet, chatterbox," he grumbled.

Miriam went on whispering. "Do you believe that your father fucked my mother? I would have given anything to see them doing it."

And Victoria stopped her ears and tried to think only of Rafael.

10

Shortly after stepping off the bridge she sensed him, without turning her head. A man was following her. A predator stalking its prey. Here too she found herself in the same quandary: how to avoid pressing up too closely to some group, so that he would not force himself on her under cover of the crush, while at the same time not isolating herself from the crowd, so that he would not see it as a sign that she was giving him an opportunity to approach her. In spite of her tension, she did not give way to a paralysing panic. From her own experience and the stories of other women, she knew that she was in no real danger. Within the shelter of the *abbaya* and behind the anonymity of the veil, many women even derived a certain pleasure from such adventures. Weeks after the incident had taken place they would still avidly describe the details of the stubborn pursuit. Once Aziza told them, with a hint of pride which was not at all to the liking of Yehuda and Izuri: "He wouldn't leave me alone, the cur, he followed me all the way to the front door. It gives me gooseflesh. Now he knows where I live. What if he's waiting for me round the corner?"

It was a game, an exciting game and no more, Victoria reassured herself. In view of the barrier of strict prohibitions segregating men from women, the fascination of the anonymous pursuer stirred the souls of women with lively imaginations. The pursuit almost always came to nothing. If the pursuer received no signs of encouragement, he would not dare to come too close, he hardly ever opened his mouth, and when he did so it was only to mumble broken words in a voice faint with excitement. In many respects the predator was no less panic-stricken than his prey. The violent perverts went to el-Kazamiya.

Ordinary men and boys who harassed women in this way in broad daylight were intimidated by the very knowledge that they were violating a sacred moral code. And that wasn't all: one scream from a pursued woman was enough to bring a few self-righteous stalwarts running, and they would set upon the pursuer even if he was a Moslem and the woman was a Jewess. Consequently his mouth was as dry as hers, his knees as weak as hers, his heart beat as wildly as hers.

At the entry to a wide alley she quickly turned her head and caught a glimpse of him. A boy, just a boy. Innocent as a boy, dangerous as a boy. An arrogant moustache and a delicate face. Definitely an Arab, in a European suit, and obviously terrified by his own boldness. But Victoria, whose dress underneath the *abbaya* was stained by her babies, and whose face bore the marks of her tears, a woman who had set out to drown herself together with the unwanted foetus in her womb only a few hours before, was in no mood to concern herself with the panting of a randy boy behind her back; she was not really worried by his presence, but the knowledge that he was watching her every movement confused her. Despite the cold she broke into a sweat, her feet stumbled, and her self-conscious indecisiveness about how to hold her head made her neck stiff and sore. He whispered something, she couldn't understand a word, but from the hoarseness of his voice it seemed to her that he was about to pounce, and she forced herself not to pick up her heels and run. All she wanted now was to reach the alley from which she had parted, cursing it for ever, only a few hours before, and she suppressed the urge to shout that she was no longer a girl, to open the *abbaya* and display her swollen stomach, to tear off the veils and show him her face, stamped with the signs of defeat.

Or perhaps they were the signs of victory? For she was safe and sound, she had come back alive from her journey to death.

A noisy group of men, out to enjoy themselves for the night, advanced towards her. Instead of stepping aside, as befitted a modest woman, she threw back her head and stood firm as an island, obliging them to part and flow around her. Whistles of admiration for the tall, black-robed column rose into the air, and she knew that they were turning their heads to look back at her. Her impressive height was an inheritance from her father. The pursuer was apparently swept backwards with the little group of men, borne away on the tide like the terrors of the Great War itself. Under her veils she smiled as she remembered how the little Jewish courtyard had defied the mighty Turkish Empire, and beaten it.

The residents of the courtyard were like insects in their own eyes, as opposed to the omnipotent Ottoman giant. Nobody knew if the Turks were winning or losing the distant battles of their war. And even as the men were being taken north and falling like flies on their way to the battlefields on the Russian border, news came that the English had landed in Basra, and its Jews were saved. In the meantime the giant devoured more and more men in its war. And in the middle of all this, the wretched Jewish courtyard rose up and revolted against the powers that be. They were all aware of the direness of their deed, and a feeling of fraternity in the face of the common enemy united old and young, male and female, daughter-in-law and mother-in-law. Najia pursed her lips, shrewd and clear-sighted, without any illusions. She did not believe in fraternity: it only served the interests of the strong and powerful in the hour of their weakness. In the end, when the emergency was over, the bullies would assert their authority over the courtyard again.

Nobody listened to her. The elderly girded their loins and provided for the families of the men in hiding as well as their own. The children were on the alert for any suspicious noise outside the courtyard, even at the height of their games, so as to give warning of search parties. Aziza and Miriam took charge of the cooking for everyone and worked Victoria and Rafael's two sisters to the bone. Even Toya put her shoulder to the wheel.

One day Michal looked at the fallen faces of the young married women and banged her spoon on the railing. "Izuri, we're guilty of a grave sin, may God forgive us."

Izuri bowed his head.

"Under the ground men are sitting in the dark and eating their hearts out with fear. Above the ground the women are suffering. We must take pity on them, Izuri, it's a *mitzvah* . . ."

Izuri blushed to the roots of his wartime beard. He hadn't expected this. "It's dangerous. The Turks make surprise raids."

"One night a month. Everyone will keep guard."

Murad, Victoria's brother, also emerged from the pit, and after bathing and eating a dinner fit for a king, he took up his post together with the other bachelors, the only one among them who couldn't understand why it was that he had to stand guard over the married men. At that time Ezra had begun to smoke, but in secret because he was ashamed of his father finding out. He sat down next to Murad and sucked at his cigarette, coughed, stuck it between his teeth, clapped his hands and said to his cousin: "Can you smell?"

Murad sniffed the air cautiously. He was already familiar with the boy and his tricks. "I can't smell anything and you leave me alone."

"How come?" said Ezra in surprise. "The whole house is swimming in it, like sticky date-juice. Didn't you see the men's eyes and the women's bums?"

The naive young man couldn't see what eyes and bums had to do with anything, and he lit a cigarette of his own and wished that this nuisance would go away. His face closed up.

Ezra explained in Moslem Arabic: "Tonight's *le'el haneitch*."

"Ah," said Murad knowingly, and sighed with relief when the joker went away. Later he accosted his Uncle Dahood: "Ezra's nattering about some *le'el haneitch*. What is it?"

"The fucking night, my son," said Dahood bluntly, but thoughts of Toya kept him from bursting into his crude laughter: the cheeky Ezra's maturity filled him with foreboding.

"But what exactly is this fucking?"

Dahood's mouth fell open and he looked pityingly at the overgrown boy. "It's a stupid game, my son. The man gives something to a woman and persuades her that she needs it, but he always takes it back again."

"I didn't understand a single word."

The zither player showed more patience than was his wont. "It's just a silly game, like the game of hiding the *afikoman* at the Passover Seder."

The devout lad was shocked. "The *afikoman* isn't a silly game."

"You're right," sighed Dahood. "Most men think that fucking is a matter of life and death too. And now please leave me alone."

The young women returned from the baths flushed and fragrant. Some spoke openly and others giggled in elated anticipation. The children's spirits soared in the general atmosphere of festivity and goodwill. Nobody scolded them. The men washed themselves until they shone with cleanliness and stepped leisurely and spoke gently, as if something had slowed down in the bodies tensed to scale the long-awaited peak ahead. Even Najia almost smiled. That morning she had finally tracked Salman down. He had escaped the hardships of the war unscathed. She found him sitting at his ease after a sound sleep in the synagogue next to Abu Sifein, nibbling wormy almonds and raisins left over from last season's stock. He reassured her and informed her that her capital had grown by a quarter of a gold coin from the accumulated interest, and slipped the coin she had brought with her into the hole in his coat-lining. As evening fell she was sure that she would give Azuri the most beautiful son the courtyard had ever seen.

Rafael sat in a tub next to the basement door. The face uncovered by his shave was pale, his flesh was emaciated by long confinement in the dark of the pit. His eyes had grown bigger. Victoria could not ignore his presence. When he poured water over his skin from the pail standing next to the tub, she was riveted by the sparks flashing from his gleaming body. In the courtyard eyes were always open, watchful for the slightest move or look. The courtyard had very little faith in innocence, and none whatever in coincidence. There was a reason for everything that happened, an intention behind every act. Victoria realized that her stolen looks were being noted in somebody's mind, and she blushed, but she couldn't keep her eyes off those sparks. Before he got into the tub he had set a stool next to it, and while the other men were putting on their loose nightgowns, Victoria was astonished to see his mother laying his narrow trousers and his jacket, his silk shirt and bowtie on this stool, and placing his light shoes on the floor. He was supposed to be guarding the married men, so why was he getting dressed up to go out? Only a lunatic would go out at night in times like these. His mother pleaded without any conviction in her voice: "Perhaps you should think twice."

His open mouth was a red stain in the foam covering his head. "I can't hear you. My ears are blocked."

His mother bowed her head in submission and turned towards Eliyahu, who ordered her to scrub his back.

Michal was outraged. Rafael's scheme to go out at night was tantamount to open rebellion, unlike the classically Jewish rebellion of the courtyard. "When you tempt fate you provoke God," she scolded.

The tender smile Rafael sent his grandmother touched Victoria's heart. His wet skin caught the coppery sunset, and he put his foot on the rim of the tub and cut his toenails with supreme concentration, as if he were purifying himself for something. The sight of his muscular legs stirred Victoria's soul. Then he stood up in the tub with a towel wrapped round his waist, covering his childish buttocks. His body looked so smooth, so vulnerable. People who turned their backs on God were called idol worshippers—and now Rafael stood before her like one of those very idols and she was spellbound. Najia spat three times to express her contempt for all forms of idolatry and said in a whisper: "May you leave the house and never return to it alive."

"Look, look," said Yehuda in his hollow voice, pointing his white beard at the shapely body, and nobody knew if it was admiration he was expressing or indignation.

Victoria noticed a rare agitation in Aziza's perpetually smiling eyes. Aziza's eyes darted from Rafael's tub to Izuri, as if she wanted to remind him of forgotten, enchanted realms which this breath-taking living statue called to mind. Her feelings were so complicated and contradictory that in the end she retreated to the arcade, where she sat down on the floor and scratched her thigh fiercely, an obscure bitterness swelling in her soul.

Izuri himself seethed with rage. Without addressing Rafael himself, he said as if to a third person: "Tonight we'll lock the door and bolt it from inside, like we do every night, and we won't open it for Satan or for an angel. Tell him. Let him listen. I won't allow anyone to touch the bolt, not even if it's a question of life and death. Even professional murderers hide at night for fear of the deserters from the army."

The silk shirt slid over the towel round his loins. Rafael stepped out of the tub and seated himself on the stool and slipped his leg into his trousers. His movements were deliberate, even insolent, until Dahood felt impelled to intervene: "And all for what? To die for some woman you'll have forgotten an hour later."

"Woman? What woman?" said the bewildered Murad, who was the same age as Rafael. "He's not married. Right, Father?"

Michal suppressed a smile, her anger somewhat subsided, and Ezra found the courage to pipe up gleefully: "Rahma Afsa!"

"Don't dirty your mouth with such names," his father rebuked him mildly.

"He's going to her! She's crazy about him."

Aziza stopped scratching her thigh. She was dying to ask her son how he knew all this, but she was afraid that Izuri would take his anger out on her, and she kept quiet.

Thoughts scurried round Victoria's mind. Surely Rafael didn't intend meeting the whore in her sister's house in the alley? No, he intended going to the sinister al-Kilachia district. She didn't even know where it was, but people pointed to it with a gesture that made it seem as remote as the mountains of darkness.

That night her father sat isolated on a corner of the roof and smoked, taking deep drags on his cigarettes. He and the young boys and bachelors kept their eyes open and their ears pricked when the men rose from the pit as if borne on the storm of their senses. The old women too kept watch over the dark alley below. Victoria was sure that her father was so tense because he was waiting for Rafael. And when he appeared below, Izuri would rise to his full height and his voice would thunder from rooftop to rooftop: "I told you. The door stays shut."

But Rafael didn't come back that night.

In the morning too, when the men of military age went down to the pit, he didn't appear. Izuri lifted the heavy jar and lowered it onto the entrance to the pit. "Nobody will move anything if that idiot comes back during the day," he said angrily, and refusing to eat his breakfast he left for the shop without so much as a cup of tea.

A mournful silence descended on the courtyard as the hours passed with no sign of Rafael. Najia clucked her tongue whenever Victoria walked past, and Victoria averted her face so that her mother would not see her anxiety. Before the men came back from work the women surrounded Ezra and urged him to tell them everything he knew about the relations between Rafael and Rahma Afsa. He complied with a will, but they soon realized that he was making it all up. Miriam begged him: "Go and ask Rahma's sister."

"What else?" shrieked Aziza.

"Maybe at this very minute he's being led to war, hungry and thirsty."

"Supposing he has fallen, God forbid, into the hands of the Turks," said Michal sensibly. "How would that woman's sister know?"

Victoria did not dare speak up before such a big audience.

But Miriam stood her ground. "Maybe he's hiding at Rahma's and waiting for dark. We should try to find out."

"Okay, I'll go and find out," Ezra volunteered.

Aziza opened her eyes wide. "How do you know the way?"

"When Rafael was my age . . ."

"Tie the rascal up with a rope," Michal interrupted her grandson.

As if this was all the young virgins were waiting for, they threw themselves on the lad with gusto. They tied his legs together and strapped his arms to his sides and laid him in the shade like a long parcel, taking no notice of his waving fists and tears of rage. When he complained that he was thirsty, they raised his head and gave him water lying down. Then he said that he needed to urinate, or else he would burst. After a short discussion, his request was denied. "We permit you to pee in your pants," Miriam laughed in his face.

At this he seemed to go berserk. He rolled rapidly over the courtyard, overturning and scattering everything in his path, and tried to bite the legs of his tormentors. Cries of fright and glee rang out in the gloomy house, and the men hiding in the pit held their breath, not knowing what was happening above them.

"If we put you on your feet," Toya suggested gravely, "and you behave yourself, I'm prepared to take it out for you and you can pee to your heart's content."

"Najia," cried Aziza, fit to burst her girth, "Najia, you don't know what a minx your brother found himself! She's hardly out of diapers and just listen to her!"

"Mother," yelled the boy, "I'm going crazy!"

When his mother went up to untie him, all the girls except Victoria fled to the basement and barred the door from inside with their bodies. Ezra pulled out his member, and as a sign of protest he encircled the courtyard twice, pissing as he went. His mother melted with pride. With a prick like that, she said to the crones, so big and thick and cheeky, he'll go far. After his second circuit Ezra emptied what was left on the basement door, behind which the girls were hiding.

At this moment Rafael entered the courtyard.

Nobody thought of asking him where he had been. He waited patiently until evening, ate his supper outside, and then descended into the pit. He and Izuri ignored each other.

The days passed, and the growls rising from the bowels of the earth grew into an ominous roar. There were already nine men packed into the dark, narrow pit. Their nerves were fraying in the stale air reeking of excrement and sweat, mouldy earth and rotten teeth. There was no space to stretch their limbs or lie down comfortably on their mats. They took it in turns to curl up in the foetus position to allow the others to stretch out and sleep. The talkative ones infuriated the more taciturn with their chatter.

The younger of Eliyahu's sons-in-law liked telling jokes, while Murad quoted the Torah with the self-importance of a teacher in the *Beth Midrash*. The older son-in-law sobbed shamelessly in the wee hours of the night, when the silence deepened outside and flowed into the pit like a dense liquid intent on drowning its dwellers. He was convinced that he was doomed to die in a strange land from the bullet of a stranger's gun. Murad ground his food with a noise like footsteps on gravel, while Rafael ate as soundlessly as a bird. After a while Rafael demanded a supply of candles and the books from the chest where he kept his belongings. The flame of the candle burning at his head bowed over his books had a strange effect on the group of men. The fire burning without a flicker looked like an unblinking eye staring at them severely. Some of the men surrendered to it as if hypnotized, and in a kind of trance, laughing and crying, they would regurgitate secrets buried for years. Murad dissolved in tears, as if Rafael had just this moment pinched him in the *cheder* where they had studied together as children.

In the dim light human flaws and shortcomings were thrown into loathsome relief.

"Shit into the pail for once, like a human being," Rafael castigated his father. "And hold your crow down. You're flooding the mats with pee."

"Show some respect to your father," groaned Eliyahu, in agonies of constipation and piles.

Rafael ground his teeth. "To find myself buried alive with you . . ."

Like the other residents of the courtyard, his father treated him with a certain degree of caution and respect, perhaps because he realized that he would be dependent on him for the rest of his life. "Death is stalking the world outside," he attempted to appease his son. "All we have to do is sit still and let the storm pass over our heads."

"So stop hogging a mat and a half to yourself all day and night," Rafael upbraided him. "Give somebody else a chance to stretch his limbs."

Eliyahu's eyes flashed above the pail. "Damn you to hell. It's your fault I can't shit. And the harder I try the more I bleed. Show a little consideration after what I've been through."

Rafael yelled and his father yelled back, they slapped the floor and pounded the crumbling walls of the pit with their fists, Eliyahu kicked the pail, while the others implored them to control themselves and think of the situation.

Outside the shouts sounded as if the men were tearing each other's throats to pieces. The women banged on the tiles and the water jar and begged the squabblers to keep quiet and not to attract the attention of the Turkish search parties. But the uproar grew louder. From the day they had descended into the pit Victoria had anticipated a clash between the father who behaved as if he was alone in the world and never lifted a finger for anyone else, and his son Rafael, who although he sometimes kicked over the traces and took off on his own, usually showed a highly developed sense of responsibility and acted for the general good. And since the father knew that he and the rest of his children were dependent on Rafael's good graces, he landed up behaving like a rebellious child himself, while Rafael acted the part of a father who had failed in the education of his son. A single spark was enough to ignite the hatred smouldering between the stubborn pair in the enforced proximity of the shelter. And perhaps, thought Victoria, it was their respective attitudes towards their imprisonment which caused the explosion. Nobody could expect a man like Rafael to accept confinement for long. His father, on the other hand, was prepared to stay underground until the final collapse of the Ottoman Empire, and he spent most of his time dozing, as if he were a hibernating beetle.

The day after the quarrel, when they served the men their food, Rafael climbed out of the pit and announced that he had decided to remain above ground. This time too he bathed, but he did not deck himself out in his finery. Again Victoria's father warned him that the door would be bolted from the inside, and that nobody would open it to him after sunset. About four hours after the sun went down Rafael returned and stood in the alley and shouted: "Uncle Izuri, I'm back." His clear voice expressed neither resentment nor supplication. Victoria listened with the rest of the household. Her father and Rafael always spoke to each other in a calm, matter-of-fact way, covering up their feelings. Her father delayed his reply, since a prompt response might be interpreted as weakness. "I warned you," he said.

"I had to go out, Uncle Izuri."

Victoria shivered, but not from cold. Since the beginning of the war the lamp-lighter had stopped coming with his ladder to light the lamp at the beginning of the alley. The darkness was as dense as soot. It took a lot of courage to stand between the silent walls and call up the powers of hell with loud cries.

"Nobody's going down to open the door for you," her father stated. "A catastrophe has overtaken the Jews, and you amuse yourself and endanger the others," he went on, openly defying Michal's pleas for lenience.

"Rafael, come to us. I'm coming down to let you in," called one-eyed Kaduri from the roof of his house.

A sigh of relief passed over the roofs. "Good for you, God bless you!" someone congratulated the pauper who had dared to oppose the high-and-mighty Izuri, especially in view of the shots and shouts audible in the distance.

"No thanks," replied Rafael to the turnip seller. "I have a home."

Izuri lit a cigarette, torn between rage at the stinging insult of the invitation and satisfaction at Rafael's declining it. Someone let a storm-lantern down from his roof on a rope, and in the bewitched darkness in which Rafael was drowning it shone like a brilliant floodlight. Heads appeared against the background of the stars along the balustrades of the roofs. Miriam threw herself onto Victoria's bedding and burst into tears. "They might kill him," she cried.

"We've turned into heathens," said Michal.

Izuri lay on his back and looked at the sky and gritted his teeth, ready to argue his case with the Almighty himself.

"He's disappeared," whispered Aziza.

Shortly afterwards footsteps were heard and a tremor passed through the roof. It was Rafael. He made straight for Izuri's mattress. "I'm here," he announced.

Izuri sat up and then rose to his feet, so as not to give Rafael the advantage of height. "Who let you in?"

At that moment Victoria could have kissed Ezra's hand. Rafael fell to his knees on Izuri's mattress, whether from exhaustion or as a sign that he was at his uncle's mercy. He lit a cigarette and his face looked sombre in the light of the match. Izuri folded his arms on his chest and waited for the trangressor to beg for forgiveness. Najia tried to put as much distance as possible between Rafael and herself, hitting the blanket and panting ostentatiously in her pregnancy, to demonstrate her indignation at this invasion of her privacy. All the residents of the courtyard came rushing to the upper roof. There was no doubt in their minds that Izuri and Rafael were putting on an act to save each other's honour.

"Just a minute," cried Michal from the middle roof. "Either the two of you come down here, or someone take me up there."

Without a word Rafael flicked his hand and his cigarette stub went flying into the darkness of the alley. A few minutes later he reappeared on the roof carrying his grandmother like a hump on his back, her knees digging with an old woman's shamelessness into his loins, while Ezra brought up the rear with her withered bum cupped in his hands.

"Get up," Izuri ordered his pregnant wife, who was pretending to be asleep, forcing her to give up her place to her mother-in-law, with whom she had not exchanged a word for the past three years.

"Roll me a cigarette," the matriarch of the clan instructed Rafael, and after inhaling and blowing out the first drag, she said: "Now you can carry on."

"I'm taking the whole family to Basra," said Rafael.

Michal took three puffs running and sent the smoke up to the stars. "It takes weeks to get there by cart, and that's in peace time," she said.

"Correct," said Rafael.

"Lunatic, madman," Izuri burst out.

"Quiet, Izuri. And how do you intend getting there? The English captured Basra, and in the meantime we've heard that the Turks socked them between the eyes next to Amara. There's talk of columns of prisoners of war, blond-haired boys and black-skinned Indians. They marched them through the streets of Baghdad. How do you think you're going to get through the warring armies with women and babies and men who're supposed to be fighting themselves?"

"Some people have made the attempt and succeeded."

Izuri sneered. "Only an idiot would be willing to drive you through the cannons in his cart."

"Shaul's ready to do it. He's a peddler, he's travelled around the villages, he knows all the roads."

"With that decrepit old mule of his," Izuri scoffed. "As soon as you've left Baghdad you'll have to carry it on your backs."

"That's why I was late. I bought what we need this evening."

Izuri made an effort to hide his admiration. He cleared his throat.

"And your father?" he asked.

Rafael always answered his uncle politely. "My father had a bad time outside. He'll stay in the pit."

"And what about Shaul's family? How will he abandon them to escape to Basra? He'll be stuck there for years, until the end of the war. He's not the man to desert his children."

"On the contrary. He's enthusiastic about the whole idea. In any case he endangers himself every day. He helped me choose the horses himself. He made only one condition. By the way, I forgot. Dahood, Najia, listen. We bought the horses from a stable near your mother's house. You must go there tomorrow to sit *shiva*. There's bad news of your brother."

Najia tore her hair, ripped her dress and beat her swollen breasts. "Moshe, my soul, poor Moshe!"

Unusually for her, she gained the sympathy of the residents of the courtyard. Izuri wiped his eyes on his sleeve, and in order to disguise his emotion he turned to Rafael: "What's Shaul's condition?"

"As Grandmother said, he'll be stuck in Basra for a long time, and he wants someone to provide for his children in his absence."

"We're Jews," declared Michal. "We won't close our eyes."

Rafael smiled sadly. The old made promises, but they were powerless to keep them, especially in wartime.

It hurt Najia to see how quickly they had resigned themselves to the loss of her brother. She scratched her face with her nails, and her wails churned up abysses of grief in the alley. Widows' lamentations swept from roof to roof.

Izuri pulled Rafael to the stairs. "Can't you see that you're committing suicide together with your whole family?" Izuri and Rafael had never seemed so close to each other in Victoria's eyes.

"If I stay here the Turks will catch me," said Rafael.

The next morning Rafael's family packed their bundles and waited. His sisters' husbands were taken up from the pit, barely able to stand on their feet after their long incarceration and immobility. It was evident that it would be impossible to get the cart and the two horses into the narrow alley, and Rafael and his family set out to meet them in a long column, their bundles on their backs, disguised as Moslem peasants.

With a quick glance Rafael parted from Victoria, while Miriam and Ezra accompanied them to the beginning of the alley. After that a crushing loneliness descended on the courtyard, as if it had been emptied of all its inhabitants. Najia's wails beat against the ancient walls, until Izuri turned to Dahood: "Take your sister and go to your mother. I'll send you all you need from the market."

"Toya will stay here. Where is she?" He was afraid of what might happen between his wife and his sister during the enforced intimacy of the seven days of mourning, just as he was worried about what might happen between Toya and Ezra if she stayed behind.

11

The oil lamp spread a ruddy glow, and the grains of sand borne by the gale whirled round in the covered arcade and settled on the floor, the rush mats and their faces. The sand gritted their teeth and whitened their bare heads. Because of the dust on his face Eliyahu huddling in the corner looked like a sullen ghost. The wind shrieked between the alley walls with the roar of a wounded animal, carrying scraps of torn washing, the cries of distant women, and the smell of the desert. Yehuda shook the dust from his beard and went on fervently reading from the Book of Psalms. The tin partition on the upper roof was torn from its place and flew across the floor with a rasping clatter. With every fresh gust Aziza would jump to her feet and beat her heavy breast. "God save us!" Toya squealed after her, burying her little fist in her mouth, evidently as overcome by anxiety as Aziza herself. Her fragile bones wrapped in a woollen blanket, Grandmother Michal, who had been carried down from her rug, peeped over its edges and fixed her eyes on the embers smouldering in the brazier. "God save us!" Aziza leapt up again. "Izuri, the water jar over the pit's shattered, something must have fallen on it."

Toya rushed out of the shelter of the arcade into the courtyard, and returned with a reassuring look. "It's not the jar. A piece of iron broke the table."

Victoria saw her mother's arms clasping her stomach. The people sitting in the arcade tried to ignore the fear on Najia's face. She bit her lower lip, and Victoria understood that her mother was craving for a little cup of sweet tea from the kettle on the brazier, but she was afraid to pour one for herself or ask someone else to pour one for her in the middle of this catastrophe, and Victoria herself was ashamed to get up and fetch her mother tea when others were in such real danger. The floor of the arcade trembled, and Aziza hurried to the front. "God save us! If the top floor collapses into the courtyard they'll all be buried in the pit!" Yehuda's eyes were wide with fear and Izuri was afraid for him and whispered gently: "Aziza, enough. You're going to give him a heart attack. Nothing's going to collapse. The house has withstood worse sandstorms than this. Go back to your blanket. Perhaps we should wet our throats with a little tea." Najia's eyes lit up avidly.

In the terrible roar which shook the house Aziza clutched Izuri's arm and hung onto it. "What's this?" Victoria was shocked. In spite of the dreadful din she couldn't take her eyes off the sight. Aziza's body engulfed her father's arm. She had never seen a woman touching him like that before. One of the boys went into the courtyard and came back stunned.

"What did you see?" demanded Izuri and extricated his arm from Aziza's clutches. "What's happened?"

The boy waved his arm. Michal realized at once that he was paralysed with fear. "Speak, child!" she said severely.

Izuri was already in the courtyard. In the dim light of the lamp, through the haze of sand, they could see him standing still and staring up in astonishment. A moment later Dahood was standing bravely next to him, clapping his hands in horror, and exclaiming: "The Nunus' palm tree has fallen onto our roof!"

"Then the roof's going to fall in too," said Aziza. "Izuri, the pit. The men under the ground." Her son Ezra, who had begun to sprout a beard, had joined the men hiding in the pit.

"It's an evil omen," said Najia in a measured tone, detached from the roaring of the storm. "A tree breaking in a house means someone will die before the year is out . . . That's it," she added, "the contractions have begun . . ."

"A fine time you chose," protested Aziza.

"She can't help it, nobody lies about things like that," said Victoria.

Aziza stared at her. It was rare for Victoria to open her mouth in public. Izuri too looked at his daughter, and Aziza grabbed his arm again and begged: "Save them first, Izuri."

He went out into the sandstorm and lifted the mighty jar in his arms and cried into the pit: "Come up, all of you. The Turks won't come in this weather."

As soon as the men emerged from the pit, bending their bodies to face the wind, and entered the arcade, the terror of the storm subsided. The fronds of the broken palm were still flapping over the courtyard, the wind wailed as strongly as ever, but under the roof of the arcade the unexpected meeting was greeted with cries of joy. Toya hid behind Dahood's back and stared at Ezra, seemingly oblivious to the voices around her. Miriam helped Victoria to serve the tea in little narrow-waisted glass cups. In the storm raging around them, the residents of the courtyard came together in a spirit of reconciliation and loving kindness. Now they looked encouragingly at Najia, as if they expected her to perform a miracle. Yehuda's voice rang out joyfully as he read the psalms, and it was clear to him that it was these words which were rescuing them from disaster.

Eliyahu was withdrawn and detached from the festivities. His face was lined with the suffering of a drinker sentenced to abstinence. Some were tempted to believe that he was grieving for his family, who had gone off and left him all alone. A few days after they had left Baghdad he climbed out of the pit and shut himself up in the basement for a week, and when he emerged from it the residents of the courtyard were shocked by his appearance. He seemed to have aged by twenty years. His face was furrowed by deep lines, his shoulders were stooped, his back was so bowed that he was forced to look upwards, and it was evident that he was unable to straighten it. Whenever anyone addressed him he inclined his head, cupped his hand round his ear as if he were deaf, and shouted rudely, like an irascible old invalid: "What? Ha?" and the speaker mumbled apologetically that he hadn't said anything. Even the tolerant, smiling Aziza gave him hostile looks, suspecting him of mimicking her. He would shuffle around heavily in unlaced shoes, treading their backs down with his heels, and talk to himself in a worried, quarrelsome or indignant tone. Outside the house he would suddenly lift up his gown—revealing that he had no underpants on—and piss on any convenient wall. Once he relieved himself on a high-bred horse whose mane was decorated with green beads and whose muzzle was buried in a bag of oats, and he couldn't understand why the Turkish officer pounced on him and cracked his whip in his face, and in the stupor which overcame him he pissed on this Jew-hater too. There were almost no teeth left in his mouth, and his beard was grey and wispy. Michal and Izuri tried to send him to Rabbi Juri Chittaiyat, but he refused as if he had resigned himself to his fate long ago, and all he wanted was for his allotted time in this vale of tears to be over.

Najia gobbled sharp green chilli-peppers, as was her wont when her time drew near. "He's putting on an act," she said with the old smile on her face.

Aziza was jealous of the woman who was blessed every spring in spite of her advancing years, whose health was good, whose hearing was unimpaired and whose feet were light, and who had never had a hot flush in her life. "Look at his toothless gums," she rebuked this sister-in-law who was like a rival second wife to her.

"His teeth were like rocks, he pulled them out himself with cobbler's thread, and he tears the hair off his head and his chin with his own hands. The miserable cur burns the skin on his face every few days and rubs it with dry pomegranate peels. He's a fraud, the bastard. You'll see how he'll still rob his two brothers blind."

The other women agreed with Aziza and clung to the touching story of the decline of the interesting man. The man was truly grief-stricken, they said. True, he was a lecher, but he always returned to the bosom of his family. And now they were all gone—his sweet wife, Rafael the glory of the courtyard, his modest daughters. The war had swallowed them up. Some people had reached Basra safely and sent messages home. Who knows, perhaps Eliyahu's family had perished at the front, or perhaps they had been murdered by robbers. And now Eliyahu stood alone like a naked tree in a burned-down forest. He didn't talk to himself like that for nothing. And look how he'd stopped drinking.

"Have any of you smelled his breath?"

"Look how thin he is. With tears in his eyes he rejects the dishes pressed on him by kind-hearted women."

"His body has always been dry, just like his accursed son. At night he steals into the kitchen and eats from the pots like a cat."

"You're wicked, what a wicked woman you are. Look at the way he takes orders from your husband, slaving for a pittance in the business. He's almost as God-fearing now as Yehuda. What else does he have to do for you to admit it?"

"I've seen his eyes sticking to Toya's arse. I've heard him pant whenever he gets an eyeful of your daughter Miriam's tits sitting on her fat belly. Once his eyes strayed and I caught them squinting at me too."

"At you!"

"Yes, at me." She raised her head proudly above her burgeoning body.

Victoria preferred to believe her mother's version. She didn't think that Eliyahu was in mourning for his family. It hurt her to see the courtyard in such a hurry to write off Rafael and his family. When Eliyahu recovered from his first fears and sat staring into space at the basement door, her father offered him work as an employee in the family business. Yehuda's health had declined even further, and all Rabbi Chittaiyat's charms didn't help him. Walking to the shop tired him out, and on the days when the pressure on his chest was bad, he had to stay at home. So he was pleased when Eliyahu accepted Izuri's offer and followed him meekly to the shop.

The day after the sandstorm the residents of the courtyard's eyes were red with sand and sleeplessness. Yehuda alone greeted the crystal clear sky with fervent thanksgiving. He felt as if his illness had dropped away from him, he rejoiced in the waves of vigour surging through his blood. From the depths of his being the exultant cry broke out: "May the name of the Lord be blessed and extolled!" The crest of the palm still hung over the courtyard sky. The birds seemed unaware of the death of the tree, and they went on warbling from the still fronds in the clear air.

The men descended into the pit again and Izuri closed the entrance with the heavy jar. "We'll have to tell Nunu to bring workmen to remove the tree," he said. "It's shutting out the light."

"It's pretty like this," said Aziza in a romantic tone.

Izuri smiled and put on his red fez, and he saw Toya standing next to the big jar with her little foot stroking the tiles. He didn't understand why there were tears glittering in her childish eyes, and he didn't ask. He looked appraisingly at Najia's stomach, and his concern touched the woman's bitter, disillusioned heart, and she murmured with rare tenderness in her voice: "Go, father of our children, to earn our bread. Someone will call the midwife if I need her."

He went, and Eliyahu walked behind him as if attached to him by an invisible cord, shuffling his feet and looking at the ground.

Aziza stood next to Yehuda and forced him to finish a saucer of apple jam and a hunk of goats' cheese. He held his fez on with his hand and threw his head back and addressed Michal on her rug. "May God give you health, Mother. I'm going out."

"Don't go out."

"I feel well, I feel very well."

"Don't go out, my son." The fronds of the fallen palm tree almost touched her head and they swayed in the gentle breeze like a huge fan for chasing away flies.

"I feel so well this morning, Mother, frisky as a young bridegroom."

Najia did not bother to hide her sneer when her eyes met Aziza's. When Izuri was a young bridegroom, she said to herself.

Today Aziza had to go up the stairs sideways, and she would probably get even fatter and more bloated until they would have to hoist her up to the roof in summer on ropes. Let her saunter round the courtyard like a fattened cow. There was one thing she would never be able to change: Izuri was Izuri and Yehuda was Yehuda.

But at that moment Aziza was thinking of Toya. With a troubled spirit she saw the child-woman standing at the entrance to the pit with tears in her eyes, and her heart was wrung within her at the sight of the sadness on her face. And for fear of where this sadness might lead, she decided to open Dahood's eyes and tell him to restrain his wife.

Michal's voice went on pleading from the second storey: "Stay at home today, Yehuda."

"For God's sake, Mother," the man protested.

"Come up here, my son. Come up to me."

He went up and on the eighth step he felt the cruel invisible hand gripping his heart. Sweat poured down his neck, and he bent over his mother glassy-eyed with fear. From below it seemed that the mother wishing to reassure her son laid her cheek on his shoulder in a rare gesture of intimacy, and the women watched, and when the terrible scream rang out it seemed to be escaping from the very walls themselves rather than the throat of the mother lamenting her first-born son. But there was something strange on the rug. It was Michal's face, held fast on Yehuda's shoulder, which was lifeless. A long moment went by before they understood that the despairing cry had broken from the mouth of the son proclaiming his mother's death, followed like an echo by Najia's scream in the enclosed space of the arcade.

The courtyard was paralysed. In the eyes of the residents, both those born in the house and those who had come later, Michal was a living foundation whose eternal presence transcended logic. She had seen many births and deaths and from her rug she had conducted the throbbing pulse of the life of the house. Yehuda's adoration gave her an aura of saintliness, and his despairing cry thus took on the force of an omen announcing a catastrophe of unnatural dimensions. Alarmed by the wails of their mothers the little children began howling like lost souls. Neighbours came running at the sound of the screams and hurried off again to bear the solemn tidings to the sons and other relations of the family. Aziza too tore the collar of her dress and beat her heavy breasts with her fists. Toya, eager to demonstrate her identification, stood in front of her and zealously punched her bud-like breasts with her little fists. Three men lifted the huge water jar and the men who had gone down only that morning ascended from the pit. Death, like the sandstorm, bestowed a kind of immunity. Ezra blinked in the sun, and Toya stared at him as she went on beating her chest. As chance had it, Ma'atuk Nunu and his father Abdallah met on the doorstep, and they seemed more upset by the meeting than the death itself. Abdallah averted his eyes from his son and fixed them on the fallen glory of his palm tree spreading over the sky of the courtyard, and his face twisted and his lips quivered in silent pain. In order to shake off his own grief, he said to Yehuda in a rather aggressive tone: "Man, it's not right to sit hugging her like that. Leave the deceased, may she rest in peace, alone."

Miriam fell on Victoria's neck weeping and shrieking soundlessly. "We're always running down your mother, and look how she's screaming and writhing on the bench because of Grandmother."

The true sorrow, said Victoria to herself, would descend on the courtyard when her father came. The sorrow of giants was hard to bear. And Rafael would not be taking his place in the prayer quorum, and perhaps the prayer for the dead should be said for him too. Miriam smelled good hanging round her neck like that. And her mother was only pretending, pretending out of fear and envy with the pathetic slyness of a persecuted child. But still, it wasn't like her to shed crocodile tears and put on such a show of hypocritical grief . . . Behind Miriam's shoulder she turned her head to look at her mother again. Miriam couldn't understand why Victoria suddenly pushed her away and hurried out of the arcade and out of the courtyard into the alley.

Jamila took one look at the distress on the girl's face and before she could open her mouth she said: "My daughter, do I need an invitation to come and wail for Michal?" And she beat her withered breasts with such a thump that it seemed to shake the air reeking with the excrement of goats and chickens. "Not only me, I'm bringing two strong young wailers with me, and we won't take a penny for it either. But it isn't done to wail now, my soul. Only when you come back from the cemetery." For Jamila was also a professional wailer, and no ordinary wailer either, but one famous for her rare ability to shed copious tears for knaves and scoundrels too.

"That's not what I came for," said Victoria shyly. "My mother's just gone into labour." She refrained from adding that because of the uproar no one else had noticed.

Jamila tightened the kerchief round her head, extracted a box of snuff from the pocket of her gown, took a pinch, sniffed, and sneezed like a horse in the gloom of the room. Then she tapped a bony finger on another tin box, took out a cigarette, and went to the kitchen, where she lit it from the fire burning under the pot, for it was not her way to waste matches on cigarettes, and all the time it was evident that the old witch was making an effort to suppress her laughter. The very thought of receiving Izuri's seed from between the legs of his downtrodden wife, and going straight after that to sit in the middle of the same courtyard and tear out her hair and conduct the lamentations of her two assistant wailers, the very thought of it amused her. But in order to maintain her reputation as a famous wailer she should arrive at the house of the deceased fresh, at the top of her form.

Who knew like she did how to shatter the imaginary calm of the mourners and drip the meaning of death into every pore and orifice of their bodies, until even the most reserved howled like lost jackals? And to do this she needed every bit of energy at her command. Sometimes she had to beat her body until it bled. On the stage of bereavement, she had been heard to boast, there isn't an actress to touch me. But this Michal, however pure and saintly, wasn't a young bride cut down in the spring of her days, and Jamila knew her sons, stern, haughty princes, disdainful of the ground they walked on: it would be no easy task to pluck tears from those sober eyes. And if the birth was a difficult, complicated one? Najia littered like a mouse, but mishaps sometimes occurred precisely with these prolific mothers, and she was liable to miss the show of her life if she got stuck in Najia's worn-out womb.

Victoria suppressed an urge to hurry the witch up. Back in her own courtyard too, presumably, the women were vexed with Najia for giving birth so importunely. Being the daughter of an unpopular mother wasn't easy. Instinctively she guessed the old crone's difficulty, and she waited patiently for her to decide between life and death.

Fear triumphed. Izuri, noblest of Michal's sons, a man who rose gladly at dawn for the Prayers of Atonement before *Yom Kippur* and prayed religiously three times a day, succoured the unfortunate and found husbands for orphan girls, was known as a giant with a kindly soul. But Jamila was not taken in. Many years ago she had once had the opportunity to peep inside this soul. In the middle of the night his sister-in-law Aziza, lying next to her husband Yehuda who was sleeping soundly on his back, had shrieked that an unclean shadow was touching her. In long-johns reaching to his ankles Izuri had glided through the night sky like a bird of prey from another world, leaping from roof to roof, jumping over the gaping darkness of the alley, and landed on the roof of her house, where he made a bee-line for her son Nahum, seized him by the feet, dragged him out of his bedding, and ran with him like a fettered lamb to the balustrade, where he let his body down over the side and began to shake him, while the boy yelled and screamed: "It wasn't me, Abu Murad, for God's sake, it wasn't me!"

"So you know what happened!"

As she lay there Jamila knew that the soul of the giant was being bared before her. There was a strange fire burning in his eyes, and she knew that all her pleas for her son's life would be in vain. She waited in terror for the boy to fall to his death. But Izuri heard her weeping, a groan escaped his chattering teeth, and suddenly her son's face reappeared in the starlight, pale as death. Without a word Izuri dropped him onto the roof and hurried down the ramshackle stairs. She heard him fumbling with the bolt in the darkness, until he finally broke down the door and went out into the alley.

"I'm coming," she said to Victoria.

The house was in a turmoil. Her father and Eliyahu had been summoned from the shop, and the undertakers from the Burial Society were running around the house as if they were about to usurp it from its rightful owners. Miriam and Aziza busied themselves sombrely with mountains of fruit and vegetables and baked bagels for the blessings. Again Victoria saw that no one was paying any attention to her mother, even her father seemed to have forgotten her existence, and Najia lay in the arcade, writhing in her labour-pains. On important festive occasions, and Michal's death was certainly an important festive occasion, Izuri was accustomed to seeing Aziza directing the preparations while his own wife was pushed into a corner.

Jamila, who knew the house well, made straight for the basement and turfed the protesting Eliyahu out. And Izuri still didn't understand what was happening. He considered the problem of the draft-evaders and issued orders to use the stairs to the roof as little as possible, so that they could escape if the Turks raided the courtyard. Then he caught sight of Yehuda's grey face and pronounced: "You're not going to the funeral."

"I'm not going to my mother's funeral? Even if I have to be buried with her . . ."

"All right, calm down," said Izuri, afraid his brother's heart would succumb to the violence of his agitation.

At the same time he saw Jamila and Victoria leading his wife to the basement, and he understood everything. For a moment he was overcome with compassion for her. Even now, when she was about to give birth, nobody took any notice of her. In order to quiet his conscience he told himself that she was probably going to produce another female, who would be an additional burden to him in his old age.

They returned from the cemetery at twilight, exhausted and hungry. Yehuda was slumped on the back of one of the grave-diggers, who was doubling as a porter for the occasion. Delicious smells rose from the kitchen. Mattresses were lined up against the walls, and the prayer-books were stacked in neat towers. Jamila's two assistant wailers took up their places in the middle of the courtyard, after the removal of the great water jar, and Jamila herself crushed a cigarette on the top step of the basement, came out and sat down between them, surveyed the whispering men and women sternly, and said "Shhhh" with a sound like the rustle of a silk ribbon. The sound of the rending of the neckline of her dress silenced the last of the murmurs, and after her assistants had followed her example, the three women beat their breastbones rhythmically with their open palms.

Jamila had chosen her dress and her slippers carefully, and she had also painted her face with a mixture of ashes and coal-dust to create a spectral effect. Her stage-fright was not dispelled by the hard slaps on her breast. And before she began to wail for the deceased she said to herself I was right, may my name and memory be blotted out if I wasn't right. That creature who just opened his eyes in the basement could ruin the performance of the most experienced wailer in Baghdad. That greedy male child. She had hardly wiped him dry before he fell on his mother's nipple like a famished dervish, and how his face had shone in the darkness. And his hair, thick enough to be cut. And his eyes. Unbelievable that a worn-out old womb like Najia's was capable of producing such a beauty. And this gem had to drop into Izuri's lap on the day of his mother's death. Her two assistants had already loosened their hair and they were diligently scratching their cheeks and beating their breasts, flailing away like leather-tanners, glancing at Eliyahu sitting and staring into space, ignoring Yehuda who was too exhausted even to cry, and pinning all their hopes on Izuri, who was talking in the solemn whisper befitting a man who had just buried his mother. Wait, said Jamila to herself, you don't know yet what a calamity is in store for you. This man of all men, one of whose tears would be enough to plunge the whole courtyard into heartbroken grief, is liable to forget his mother entirely when he finds out what his wife has just given birth to in the basement.

But she went on beating her breasts and pulling her hair, together with her assistants. Their faces grew flushed and veins burst on their breasts as they raised their voices in a desperate lament while their audience looked on indifferently. What's the wonder, said Jamila crossly to herself, the smells coming from the kitchen are enough to wake the dead. Those men sitting on the mattresses and rush mats, and those women clustering behind them—did they come to condole with the bereaved? They could hardly swallow the saliva filling their mouths. But there was no cause for despair, and every reason to try and try again. Two years ago Michal had called for her and paid her handsomely in advance for her services. But the dead were dead, and you could trust them to keep their mouths shut for ever, or for the foreseeable future anyway. There was no need for her assistants to know that she had received her fee in advance, and Izuri too might reward her with his well-known generosity if she made a good impression on him with her performance. She did not have high hopes of Yehuda. He was too absorbed in his own sufferings, and too saintly to spare a thought for anything as mundane as money. And only a madwoman would pin her hopes on Eliyahu, a grave-robber like him. In her despondency Jamila filled with hostility towards her audience. She hated the smug men and women waiting to stuff their bellies with the funeral meats. "Wail, cry, pull out your hair," she urged her assistants as she noted a kind of lassitude in their movements. The clatter of plates in the kitchen was louder than their lamentations. "You call this lot mourners?" complained the younger assistant bitterly. "Not even Moses's staff would get a tear out of them!" Jamila was wounded to the quick.

Her eye fell on Ezra, whose stay in the pit had left its mark on him. He couldn't take his eyes off Toya's exposed breasts, which had been beaten so much they looked like roasted chestnuts. The little vixen could probably feel the boy's languishing looks on her cheeky little bum. And here Jamila's cup of bitterness overflowed. She leapt to her feet, a burning brand of fury, and cried: "Men, women!" A hush fell on the courtyard. "You've just come back from burying Michal. What are you worth now that Michal's left you? Because of her the walls bowed down when you walked down the alley. Now the pillar which supported you has fallen, and you're licking your lips in anticipation of a good meal. Her rug is still warm and you're chattering as if you were at a party."

With a hand smelling of fish and sesame oil Aziza wiped away a tear. Toya froze in her place. Yehuda sat up on his mattress, as if he had suddenly realized that today he had lost his mother, his head fell in bitter weeping onto Eliyahu's resisting shoulder, and then the women of the alley added their high-pitched keening to the lamentations of the wailers. Jamila celebrated her victory. At a wink from her the assistant at her side turned to stone, and immediately after began beating her breast with all her might, faster and faster, until her flailing hands blurred, her body spun, her head dropped and her long hair spread out like a black fan, and all the time she went on hitting herself, until after a few minutes she stopped acting. Her body was caught up in the giddiness of the trance. Her wails were those of a tormented soul.

If it's possible for a person to weep bitter tears and smile in elation at the same time, Jamila was that person.

When nobody was looking Eliyahu stuffed his nostrils with snuff. The sound of his explosive sneezing interrupted the spell cast by the wailers. Izuri surveyed the crowd and saw Victoria emerging from the basement, her face beaming and her eyes smiling. And he knew how attached the girl had been to her grandmother. A son, a son! A triumphant cheer welled up irresistibly inside him.

The next day the mourning turned to celebration. Even Yehuda did not see fit to spoil the joy. Izuri was in the seventh heaven of delight. He took Najia and the newborn baby up to the glassed-in room, and saw to it that his wife was supplied with a constant stream of sweets and almonds and little cakes, to improve the quality of her milk. The crowds of condolers came and went, the prayers and blessings were recited in strict accordance with the law, and he took part dutifully in all the rites, and immediately returned to the cradle to feast his eyes on the fair-skinned baby who was going to make up for all the failures which had preceded him. In his heart of hearts he was glad that apart from Rafael no promising lad had grown up in the courtyard. There was a curse on Michal's seed, the dynasty was sinking into a dreary anonymity. Now he was sure that Baruch—this was the name he had chosen for the child—would overshadow Rafael.

Victoria sank into deep mourning. With the loss of Michal life in the courtyard seemed to have lost its reality. In her grief for Michal she felt that she was mourning Rafael. She took no part in the festivities, the eating and talking of the condolers. In any case women and girls had to make themselves scarce when the men were praying, and she was constantly sent to help Miriam and Aziza with the cooking in the stifling heat of the kitchen. But she liked it there. Opposite the flames whose glow was swallowed up in the black ceiling she thought of Rafael. She was already beginning to think that they had all been murdered. At the sight of their father guzzling and stuffing his belly with a martyred look on his face she was filled with indignation. How she missed Rafael's clear, intelligent voice in this buzz of idle chatter. On one of the days of mourning she found herself sitting on Michal's rug, which no one had had the heart to fold up and put away, and looking down on those stupid men as they sat on their mattresses talking self-important nonsense about the war.

Abdallah Nunu was a regular guest. The day after Michal's death he had sent three men to chop down the fallen crest of the palm tree. He mourned the tree bitterly and he was consumed by anxiety. He was sure that a catastrophe was about to strike his house. But he soon recovered and it was evident that he enjoyed the company of the mourners in Michal's house. His beard was trimmed and dyed, he was elegantly dressed, and he had a lordly look in his eye, but there was something peculiar about his mouth, as if some other mouth was struggling inside it. For the first time in her life Victoria saw false teeth. From time to time Abdallah raised his voice, and immediately stuck his finger into his mouth to push the magic teeth back in place before they fell out into his lap. He appeared undisturbed by the fact that in the dead hours his son sat on a stool outside his shop with his eyes fixed on the door of the house from which he had been banished. The death and burial of his wife made no impression at all on him. The inhabitants of the courtyard welcomed him gladly, for he was fabulously rich, and who were they to judge God's chosen? Because of his connections with Turkish officers, Abdallah possessed obscure information about the war, and the men, who had never read a newspaper in their lives, swallowed his stories eagerly. On the fourth day he bit into a bagel, and suddenly he seemed sunk in deep reflection, while his audience waited in silent expectation. With a gesture of his left hand he bade them be patient, while he stuck the fingers of his right into his mouth, and two rows of youthful teeth fell into his palm. Men and children alike were riveted by the magical sight. Abdallah Nunu, whose nose had suddenly collapsed onto his chin, cleaned the false teeth with his fingernails, blew on them carefully, replaced them in his mouth, smiled with relief, and continued: "Yesterday my sister Hannah came to see me, stinking of sweat and tears. They conscripted her son Elias. They weren't interested in the fact that the poor wretch suffers from epilepsy, as you know. Why carry on as if it's a tragedy, I said to her. You deserve a rest from him. Who knows, maybe he'll find his niche in a kingdom that's like a sick man itself. The madwoman wanted to gouge my eyes out, and all because of a creature who's neither a man nor a monkey. I had no choice but to go to the Turks. And the bastards told me that Elias is as healthy as a bull, and certainly capable of polishing off a few Muscobites before he kicks the bucket. Don't ask how much gold I weighed on their palms, damn their names and memories, until they agreed to let that floor-rag go. In the end I found the Muscobite-slayer lying in a corner, drooling at the mouth, his eyes lifeless as a corpse. That idiot of a woman. What an idiot. A millstone like that around her neck."

From her place on Michal's rug Victoria also saw that what was going on between Ezra and Toya was no longer an innocent game. With melancholy sympathy she watched the diminutive woman and the lively boy moving towards each other as if propelled by some hidden force. They still had not exchanged a serious word, but their yearning was irresistible. They were afraid of the prying eyes, they stepped carefully. Aziza, suspiciously measuring the nut-like breasts, held her tongue, for nothing improper had yet been done, and it was inconceivable that anything serious would develop between the two. In the eyes of the bloated Aziza the skinny little Toya was nothing but a tadpole, in which nobody but a pervert like Dahood could take any interest. But when the condolers had gone home she said to her husband nevertheless that there was no point in provoking fate, and the draft-evaders should go back to their pit. Murad nodded his head vigorously, because the sudden freedom had put him into a panic. He helped his father to carry the water-jar to the edge of the pit, and went down. In the courtyard sliding into the dark night Toya stood with a storm-lantern in her hand raised above her head, tears streaming openly down her smooth cheeks. Ezra rebelled. "I'm not going down into that stinking pit. If they come I'll run away, and if they catch me they'll catch me."

From the side it looked as if Izuri was about to strangle the boy. "You're not Rafael and you're not Rafael's shadow either." The lad kicked and struggled to free himself and Izuri said: "One more move from you and I'll crush your bones, you little worm." But the boy's face did not turn blue. It seemed that the mighty arm encircling his neck was not squeezing, although it was tight enough to prevent him from escaping. Aziza melted. It was clear that this close contact between her son and Izuri gave her pleasure, and Victoria remembered the old gossip. Father's right, she said sadly to herself. Even Rafael had always known better than to let an argument with her father develop into a contest of strength. What chance did Ezra have against her father? For a long time he looked at Toya's face flickering in the light of the storm-lantern, and then he bowed his head and went down into the pit with the help of the hand which had threatened to crush his bones.

For weeks Toya would only come to life in the evenings, when the men in hiding were fed. In the daylight she tiptoed round the courtyard and listened. Victoria wondered whether the boy in his darkness and Toya in the sunlight were speaking to each other in a language as mysterious as the whisper of butterflies. Dahood the zither player's living declined as that of the wailers and the psalm-sayers in the synagogues flourished. His daughter and his two sons from a previous marriage went hungry with his mother, with whom they were living. For next to nothing he too, like Eliyahu, went to work in the family business, which was also close to ruin because of the continuing war. Dahood's bed was still on those nights, and Toya would sometimes stay downstairs for hours, singing lullabies to the baby she would never have.

In any case Aziza had something more urgent on her mind than Ezra's problems. During the week of mourning for Michal she had put the crowds of women visiting the courtyard to use. Miriam's breasts and womb were ripe for a suitable marriage. It would be a sin to wait until the end of the war which was cruelly devouring men. Better to take the risk of fishing some man out of his pit, or marry her to a cripple or a rich old man than let so juicy a fruit lose its bloom. A few matchmakers came and looked Miriam over with practised eyes. The family connections raised her value, and so did the hints that her father would give her a substantial dowry. Nevertheless prospective bridegrooms did not line up outside the door, for eligible men were few and far-between.

Victoria could hardly stop herself from seizing Eliyahu by the shoulders and shaking him, demanding that he stand up and fight for the rights of his son: for had not the three brothers agreed between them that when the time came Rafael should choose between Miriam and herself? She dragged Miriam up to the roof and her voice was full of anger. "That's it. You've already buried him. How do you know that he won't come back?" She could hardly bring herself to look at Miriam's face, and she looked instead at the empty hole the fallen palm tree had left in Abdallah Nunu's roof. Miriam too averted her eyes and gazed at the flat, distant horizon which was always shrouded in a haze of dust. "I'm sorry to have to tell you this, Victoria," she said. "Rafael has already decided. He chose me."

Victoria felt her throat constrict. With all her might she concentrated on the hole in the roof and said to herself that Abdallah had better stop it up if he didn't want his house to be flooded.

"He promised to send me an engagement ring from Basra, with a messenger, as soon as he got fixed up there. He arranged it with my mother and father the morning before they left. Months have passed and the ring hasn't arrived. He's dead."

They both began weeping quietly. Victoria pressed herself against the balustrade. She didn't want Miriam to touch her.

12

The fresh, bracing air dispelled her weariness a little. The pangs of hunger dulled—but what was this smell taking her back to the realms of her childhood, conjuring up the girl who knew how to navigate her life between the bitter days and the sweet ones? She still had two markets to cross, five alleys and two squares. She hugged the walls as she walked and tried to merge into the pools of darkness between the weak oil lamps. In the main street electricity had been installed long ago, and in the luxurious suburb of Batawin, too, those miraculous lamps shed their strong light on the broad, straight streets of the villas. Jews who had left the Jewish quarter had bought up palm groves there, and the houses they had built themselves were now surrounded by gardens and birdsong. Madwoman. Only a few hours ago she had been about to jump to her death, her husband had vanished into the distance, he was dying or dead, she had no roof over her head, an unwanted foetus in her womb, no idea of where her next meal was coming from, and the thought of a room of her own, however dilapidated, far from her mother, was nothing but a wild dream. And now, madwoman that she was, she felt a smile dawning in the depths of her despair, and she said to herself that over there, in that rich suburb, she would have a house all her own, from the basement to the roof. She must be mad. Not even her father, in his days of plenty, had indulged in such fantasies. But the smile was as stubborn as the foetus growing against her will in her womb.

Water dripping onto her from a line of washing soon woke her rudely from her dream and sent her scuttling across the alley to hug the opposite wall, but there too the water went on dripping, and she remembered that today was Thursday. But the

Jews did their washing on Wednesday. And besides, no sane woman hung out her washing in the evening in a land so blessed with sunshine. Dread crept into her heart. She had entered the kingdom of darkness and hidden powers, and something was playing tricks on her. In spite of her fears she gathered the courage to raise her eyes to the sky. The roofs almost touched, and in the narrow strip of sky not a single star shone. Rain, she said wonderingly. In a city watered by a mighty river people loathed the rain, it was nothing but a nuisance, or a danger. And now she clung to this loathing in order to drive out her fear. But the purified air seemed to wash her soul clean, it was the fresh smell of rain in the air which had conjured up the sweetness of her childhood and the nonsensical dream of a house in Batawin. And the spark of hope, like a stubborn ember, refused to die.

In the meantime she reminded herself to hold her head high as she emerged from the alley into a square whose empty space was pierced by the bright light of lux lamps burning in two teahouses. Someone might leave his tea and his hookah for the pleasures of the pursuit. Or perhaps she should bow her shoulders and try to slip past without attracting attention? The rain increased and she crossed the square safely. At least there was one thing to be said in favour of the rain, it cooled the men down. And again that spark of illogical mirth in her heart.

No, the lives of human beings were not ruled by logic, and they certainly weren't when she was a girl. Her father had gone out of his mind with joy at the beautiful Baruch. In the shop he sat on pins and needles waiting for evening, when he would be able to feast his eyes on the moon-faced creature, and circle the jar in the middle of the courtyard with the baby in his arms, murmuring: "My son, my soul, my precious," like a sentimental woman. While he did so he ignored Toya, who had put away her childhood games, turned her back on her conjugal duties, and taken up a permanent position next to the heavy water jar. From time to time she raised her head at the sound of a bird's wings flapping in the sky, and immediately lowered it again and pricked up her ears to listen for the longed for sign from the bowels of the earth.

Najia took fright at the look in Toya's eyes, and warned aloud: "Izuri, you're going round that madwoman in circles with the baby." And she pulled her dress down and spat on her breasts. Anyone who circled round another person was bound to suffer the fate of the fowl whirled round the penitent's head as a scapegoat for his sins on the Day of Atonement. Accordingly Najia hurried to the courtyard and threw a handful of salt onto Izuri and the apple of his eye to ward off evil spirits. She was so proud of Izuri's happiness that she had become almost bearable. And Izuri would laugh his gigantic laugh and throw Baruch into the air and give thanks to God, paying no attention to the whispers of the matchmakers in the arcade, and giving no thought to the fact that his daughter was nubile and needed a husband. Or perhaps he had not forgotten her, but was simply being sober and realistic. The men had disappeared like flies in a frost. In spite of the dowry promised by her parents, in spite of the family's prestige, in spite of the undeniable beauty of her corpulent flesh, no suitable husband had been found for Miriam. The name of a wheat merchant as old as Abdallah Nunu had been mentioned, but he was too miserly to cover his naked gums with magic teeth. A broad-shouldered young man from a wealthy family had been flaunted before them, but a short inquiry had shown him to be suffering from syphilis. A promising widower, childless and in his prime, had given rise to grave suspicions, since the Turks had not conscripted him, and, indeed, he turned out to be nearly blind even though his eyes were bright as a child's. Two impotent men with their eyes on the dowry had been rejected out of hand.

True, a fine selection lay hidden in the cunningly excavated pits dotted about the city, but what bachelor in his right mind would risk his life even for such an abundance of choice female flesh? They remembered Rafael and grieved for him again. A man without fear. Even without a dowry a man of his calibre was capable of facing an empire for the sake of breasts and buttocks and dimpled flesh like hers. But to tell the truth, most parents were not enthusiastic about a man like Rafael, preferring industrious and cowardly sons-in-laws, the kind that stayed alive. During all this time Miriam kept quiet. Although she was aroused by the very talk of bridegrooms and weddings, she cried out in horror when the name of Murad, Victoria's brother, was mentioned as an ideal husband, available for the asking, and as eligible as Rafael himself. She wept for hours, and Najia leapt to her son's defence in her own inimitable style: "She's drooling like a whore, her cunt's on fire, she can't wait for it. So why the tears? As if my Murad disgusted her!"

A few days after this, Najia was sitting in the courtyard and smiling at Baruch, open-eyed in her lap, the only creature in the world who loved the smell of her body, whose whole existence depended on hers. For a long time he looked at her face, until she was sure that he was telling her in his own secret language how much he loved her. Immediately she was afraid of tempting the Evil Eye, and the sight of Toya sitting next to the water jar like a child who had lost all her toys made things worse. Clearly this poor excuse for a woman would never produce a child of her own. What could have made her brother marry her? Her mother, or she herself, must have cast a spell on him and driven him crazy—even now, when he was obliged to abandon his zither and go to work like a miserable slave in the family business, he bought her expensive fruits, even in the middle of the week. Even at this very minute, leaning against the jar as if she were in a swoon, she was holding a red Persian apple and a yellow banana in her hands. A banana! Izuri had never given her a banana in her life, not even now that she has given him a child who rejoiced the hearts of all who looked at him. And the imbecile didn't even dig her teeth into the fruit. Najia had overheard the women whispering about Toya's love for Ezra imprisoned in the bowels of the earth, but she didn't believe in love, at any rate not in a love which would prevent a woman from eating a banana. "Get up," she said sharply to the child she could not regard as her sister-in-law, "go to the market and buy something to cook for my poor brother to eat. Others fall conveniently ill and lie idle on benches, while he breaks his back at hard labour, and when he comes home he finds his plate empty."

Aziza, refreshing a matchmaker with sweetened rose-water in the arcade, overheard and lost her temper. "Breaks his back! He should be grateful to Yehuda and Izuri. But for them he would be rummaging in the rubbish for watermelon rinds like a donkey. Hard labour in a shop that it's a pleasure to walk into! Bolts of satin and silk with cups of tea for the asking, and light snacks between rich meals!"

Toya took no notice. Stealthily she scratched the tiles, perhaps he would hear, perhaps he would sense her presence. Then she laid the apple against one cheek and the banana against the other. In the evening, when they took away the jar, she would give them to him. She kissed the skin of the fruit. If only she could creep into the core of the apple, and lie there all night, inside Ezra's body.

"I told you to go away."

Tears rose to the little girl's eyes. "What harm have I done you?"

"Your looks, witch. The baby's stopped feeding, even though he's hungry," she said and squeezed her abandoned breast, touched the pearly drops it sprayed onto the baby's forehead, put her finger to her mouth, and couldn't decide if the milk was sour or not. "Bitch! You can creep in anywhere, like the pint-sized worm that you are. What did you put in my food? You've poisoned my milk."

"Me, auntie?"

"I'm not your auntie!" The baby began to scream. "Listen! Just listen to what you're doing to him, you criminal. Go away, move your arse," she cried and hit the rush mat with her hand. "You're killing my son!"

Unwillingly Toya tore herself away from the jar, slipped across the courtyard like a melancholy shadow and disappeared behind the sack-curtain at the door of her room.

In the arcade the matchmaker smacked her lips to indicate

her enjoyment of the refreshing drink. Aziza sat with her hands folded on her knees, and waited sourly to hear what the vile creature had to say. She had been disappointed so often that her enthusiasm had cooled. At the beginning she had waited confidently for the candidates to flock to her door. And here was Miriam sitting by her side, a hardworking, intelligent, warm-hearted, sensitive beauty with a dowry, and strangely enough she herself was not insulted or cast down by the disappointments. The girl was a riddle. Aziza knew that her excitement grew from matchmaker to matchmaker. The descriptions of the proposed bridegrooms, even the lame and elderly ones, inflamed her imagination like dirty stories. Yehuda too was there, lying on a bench in the arcade, fanning his face with his right hand to chase the flies away and holding his heart with his left. He had stayed home from work that morning, and none of it meant anything to him, the war, the smitten men, the women giving birth, the business, his son lying under the ground, his daughter's body crying out for a man. There were already signs that the inhabitants of the courtyard were getting fed up with his sufferings and his weakness. Fickle creatures. On the one hand they hinted that he exaggerated his illness because he wanted to be pampered, and on the other they sentenced him to absolute rest. Rabbi Juri Chittaiyat was no help at all either with his charms or with his greasy recipes. How lucky his mother was, she had returned her soul to her maker without any suffering, it was all over in a second. The terror of the Angel of Death fell upon him.

"Listen to me, Abu Ezra," the matchmaker sang out in a voice drenched in rose-water. "Smile and the world will smile back at you."

Smile! As far as he was concerned Miriam could marry a camel, or even that Salman scuttling round the dark alleys like a rat in his eternal overcoat. Smile! There were days when he could hardly climb the stairs to his room. On every third step he had to sit down and pant for breath like a lizard. At his mother's funeral he had almost given up the ghost. Where was he going to get the strength for the hullabaloo Aziza was planning for Miriam's wedding? Who would hear his death-rattle in the midst of the carousing? And what if his heart stopped precisely at the moment the bridegroom embraced her virgin body? How pointless everything was.

Victoria tried not to feel resentful towards Miriam for forgetting Rafael. After a while she realized that she was jealous of her cousin, and she wasn't in the least ashamed of her jealousy. Her own father and mother had lost their wits entirely over a lump of screaming flesh. And so she escaped to the stifling heat of the kitchen, where she did not have to listen to the chatter of the matchmakers. So why was she trying to silence the bubbling of the pots and the clatter of their lids? After Toya had fled the courtyard with her apple and banana, she could no longer restrain herself. Flushed and sweating, wiping her hands on the dress encasing her thighs, she wreathed her face in smiles and sat down on a stool at the edge of the arcade.

"How old is he? inquired Aziza.

Practitioners of the art of matchmaking were not in the habit of going into petty detail. "A spring-flower like your daughter," said the marriage-broker, with a jerk of her chin in Miriam's direction, "with her wealth and breeding! Would I bring her a mouldy old husband?"

"There's a war on," Aziza quickly poured cold water over the woman. "Our wealth has dwindled. How old is he?"

The matchmaker's eyes gleamed, the right one with the cataract too. Despite the bristling hairs on the three black moles on her chin, and the gaps and the gold in her teeth, she radiated a repulsive, lecherous kind of beauty. "Twenty-one!"

Experience had made Aziza cautious. "Blind or lame, heaven have mercy on us?" she asked.

"God forbid!" the matchmaker fanned herself with the neck of her dress, displaying breasts which were surprisingly beautiful. Yehuda's clouded eyes remained indifferent, and as if to spite him for it she said: "Strong and healthy, with stomach muscles to make any woman happy."

Aziza ignored the question of how the matchmaker had obtained her information regarding the prospective bridegroom's stomach muscles. "The Turks haven't left any men like that above ground," she said.

"They've left him. An angel keeps guard over him. Longevity is written on his brow. How much?"

Aziza knew that this was only the opening move in the bargaining. "Twenty gold coins," she threw out. "Naturally clothing as required and the customary furniture."

"That's not money, not for a man in the prime of his youth like I'm offering."

The matchmaker's confident tone impressed Aziza. "What does he do for a living?"

"He's a blacksmith."

"A trade for Gentiles."

"He's got a flourishing workshop of his own."

"His face must be black as soot and his hair stinking of burned coal. No thank you, I didn't bring up my daughter to drown her in soot."

"For your information, Jews with heads on their shoulders are beginning to go in for those trades. The world is changing, Umm Ezra. I say a hundred gold coins, not a penny less."

"We'll talk after he's had a good wash, so we can get a look at his face."

The matchmaker's gold teeth were revealed in a broad smile. "Tomorrow before sunset he'll come with his family, and the parties will be able to look each other over." And like a pervert torturing a corpse, she exposed her insulted breasts to Yehuda again. "All I ask is that she make herself scarce when they come."

"Victoria? She's Miriam's cousin."

The matchmaker wiped her lower lip with her finger, and in this gesture too there was something provocative. "You know, a man's eyes stray, and sometimes they get stuck in the wrong place. Tomorrow they're coming to see your daughter, Umm Ezra, and nobody else's."

Aziza was insulted. "Miriam, get up!" she shouted. "Look at her body. And open the eye with the cataract too." She put the miserable wretch in her place. Up to now she had restrained herself and ignored the liberties taken by the impudent woman. But this was going too far. To take no notice of so many magnificent pounds of flesh and hint that the skinny Victoria held some threat . . .

The experienced matchmaker immediately shrank to her natural dimensions. "I see, Umm Ezra, I see. But fate is blind sometimes. Once I offered a great beauty to a wealthy merchant, and he caught sight of a scarecrow of a girl with a dry bum in the courtyard, and in the end it was her skinny lap that he dropped his fortune into. So it would be better if this Victoria isn't there. One day I'll find someone for her too. Some man or other always turns up. Who is she, did you say?"

"Woman, that's Izuri's daughter."

The matchmaker beat her breasts. "Oy, may my tongue shrivel up! Oy, may I lose the sight of my eyes! Forgive me, child. Izuri's daughter . . . Oy, may I be buried in an unknown grave! Victoria . . ."

But Victoria had already escaped to the kitchen.

The next day the house was in a turmoil. Najia did not notice that the baby was worse. Toya was sitting next to the jar again, quiet as a beetle. This time she was shielding two big pomegranates in her hands, and when nobody was looking she rubbed them against her little breasts. Frenzied preparations were afoot in anticipation of the candidate's visit with his family. Holiday dresses were dragged out of their chests. Victoria was caught up in the excitement, and she joined the women sweeping the courtyard and the arcade, and polishing chairs and tables and benches. There was a festive scent in the air. Najia, forced to move from place to place with the sick baby in her arms, protested bitterly. Toya walked on tiptoe, afraid that one of the women might covet her pomegranates. Dahood's status in the courtyard was shaky, and she was an easy target. Towards noon she dared to pipe up: "Perhaps we should bring Ezra up, to take part in his sister's joy." Najia pulled a disgusted face, and Aziza burst into peals of good-humoured laughter.

"Victoria!" Miriam's voice cried desperately from upstairs about an hour before the fateful guests were due.

Victoria hurried up the stairs. Miriam was wearing a new satin dress from the trousseau her mother had prepared for her. Her eyes were made up and her lips painted. Victoria admired the stunning dress. Her parents hadn't even had one miserable nightgown sewn for her.

"I'm scared, I have to pee every five minutes. What will I do if I have to pee exactly when they call me to come and show myself to them?"

"You'll hold it in," smiled Victoria.

"You're so clever!" And they both burst out laughing and hugged each other and Victoria breathed in the sweet smell of her cousin's flesh again. She loved her so much at that moment that she felt jealous of the strange man who was about to proclaim his rights over her.

He arrived a few minutes after the men returned from work, surrounded by an impressive entourage of parents, brothers and sisters, three aunts with eagle eyes and a few uncles out for free food and drink. The matchmaker led the procession, sniggering and winking coarsely as if to make light of the seriousness of the occasion.

But the groom and his three aunts were very serious indeed. With the gravity of doctors summoned for an urgent consultation they sat down and made it plain to everyone that they had eyes in their heads, and they were not interested in the groaning table or idle chatter, and in a heavy silence they waited for Miriam to appear. Victoria, who had disobeyed the matchmaker and was helping to serve the refreshments, found her jealousy turning to revulsion against the man who was neither tall nor short. In his appearance he seemed to embody the arrogance of her father, the egotistical harshness of Eliyahu, and the self-righteousness of Yehuda. She was already acquainted with Jews who earned their living by hard manual labour, porters and house-painters and carpenters, but they lived from hand to mouth and behaved modestly and humbly. This smithy or blacksmith, or whatever he called himself, presumably owed his arrogance to the money he had in his pockets. His fingernails were black, but there was a steely glint in his eye. The matchmaker had not lied. He really was young. Men of his age were dying all along the lines of the Turkish debacle, or rotting in hiding under the ground, but he had no fear in his eyes. It wasn't Abdallah Nunu's boastful boldness, or Rafael's daring defiance. It was something else. Judging by his trimmed beard nobody would have guessed then that he was even more god-fearing and observant than Uncle Yehuda. But it transpired that his God was more decisive, practical and efficient than Yehuda's, and it was to Him that he owed his self-confidence, and it was He who came to his rescue and saved him from the disintegrating Ottoman Empire until it collapsed like a house of cards. Thirty-five years later, too, when men of his age were brought to their knees by the State of Israel, which sentenced the generation of the wilderness to spiritual extinction, he refused to bow his head, maintained his self-confidence and self-respect, and exchanging his hammer and anvil for the holy books, he studied them diligently until he emerged in the black hat and black suit and black shoes of an ordained rabbi. And while others were ground to dust, he flourished and gained a position for himself in the fledgling state.

On that distant day he sat with his head held high in the arcade overlooking the courtyard, as if he knew in advance what the next four decades held in store.

A hush fell on the courtyard as Yehuda calmly descended the stairs, his beard as white as a prophet's. Behind him Aziza squeezed her mountainous flesh sideways down the narrow staircase, and extricated herself at the bottom with a triumphant smile. Then the women guests stretched their necks and the men rested their fezes on their knees in awed admiration as the walls of the staircase became a frame for the wonder of wonders gliding from step to step in glorious waves of flowing satin, not to mention the bangles and bracelets and earrings and gold necklace and diamond tiara, and inside it all a lavish abundance of solid flesh, of warm and promising limbs. Both men and women gaped shamelessly. But the prospective bridegroom did not bat an eye, as befitting a coldly calculating businessman. His muscles, which forged iron, and his looks, which withered tough working men, stood him in good stead to repress his surge of thanksgiving at the marvellous grace of God.

The deal was closed on the spot.

Yehuda, who was afraid that the miracle might slip out of his fingers, and his treacherous heart might fail him, was not interested in bargaining. He agreed immediately to a compromise of seventy gold coins, and with the careful smile of a man in daily communication with the Angel of Death, he gave in to the parents of the groom and added a few insignificant items as well, such as a double bronze bedstead and a wardrobe with two outside mirrors.

The visitors and the members of the family congratulated each other in a clamour of cracking almond shells and clinking glasses of arak. The noise was great, but Izuri silenced it immediately with his roar: "You idiot, the baby's dying!"

Najia's face twisted into an ugly mask of shock and horror, and she crawled away from her husband dragging her bum on the floor and supporting herself on her left arm, clasping Baruch to her breast with her right. The astonished guests left the arcade and crowded round to see what was happening. With a terrifying glare in his eyes Izuri pounced on them and yelled: "Go away! Leave the house immediately! My son is dying in the arms of this imbecile and I don't want anyone here."

Aziza accompanied her guests to the door with appeasing smiles and handfuls of sweets, promising them in an undertone that the engagement would be celebrated on Saturday night, and all the time she didn't take her eyes off Izuri. She was more worried about him than about the baby. Babies got born and died, and there was nothing anybody could do about it. But the pillar of the family and its main provider was a different matter.

Victoria stood helplessly watching as her father bent over her mother as if he was about to crush her between his gigantic hands. Mother and daughter screamed. Yehuda interposed his silvery beard like a grotesque screen between Najia and his brother's murderous rage. "Leave the poor woman alone," he whispered, trembling with terror himself, "she's upset about the child too."

"I wasn't going to touch her!" yelled Izuri. "I want to take the baby from her. He's dying, I tell you. Doesn't anyone understand?"

The long-suffering Najia clung to the mite as if he could shield her from her husband's frenzy and cried: "It's her, her! I'm telling you it's all that bitch's fault."

Everybody looked in astonishment at little Toya, and she raised her shoulder obstinately like a child and refused to leave the jar when Dahood told her to. He guessed what was coming and upbraided his sister: "You were born a stupid cow and you'll die a crazy bitch. What harm did she do you? All she did was sit there."

Najia raised a tearful face to her husband. "He woke up in the morning bright and fresh as a bird," she lied passionately and immediately believed in her own lie. "He sucked with a hearty appetite and slept like an angel, until that witch gave him the Evil Eye. She's eaten up with jealousy because she's barren."

"What are you talking about, barren?" protested her brother. "She hasn't even started her periods yet."

"And maybe she'll never get them either, that little bitch on heat. She'll be dry and empty for ever. That's why she killed the baby."

"Get up!" Izuri screamed at Toya.

Toya curled up like a worm fighting for its life.

"Izuri," pleaded the wretched Dahood, who had been attached to the household on sufferance, as a poor relation.

"Get out of my sight," the master of the courtyard barked at him.

Dahood retreated like a cloud before the wind. Izuri's shadow fell on Toya, who suddenly pounded on the jar with her little fists and cried: "Ezra, Ezra, come out! They're going to kill me!"

The startled Izuri stood rooted to the spot. Aziza growled: "Leave my son alone, Toya, none of this has got anything to do with him."

With finger and thumb Izuri encircled the child's stalk-like neck, collecting the shreds of his sanity to keep his slap from being lethal. The little girl fainted, more from fear than pain. Dahood skipped from his right foot to his left, wrung his hands and wailed like a woman. Izuri splashed water from the jar onto Toya's face, and when she opened her eyes and saw him bending over her she shrieked in fear.

"I told you," cried Najia. "I told you. Look at the foam on her lips. Look at her eyes."

"What did you do to my son?" demanded Izuri. The little girl was dumb.

"What should I do now?" Izuri turned to Aziza. After his mother Aziza was the woman he had most respect for in the courtyard.

Aziza took pity on Toya. "Leave her alone. Her husband's right. What does she need a baby for at her age? Why should she harm your child?"

"Aziza!" her brother-in-law insisted.

Aziza saw that something had to be done. "Smear the baby with her piss."

Like a terrified bird the little girl fled to the roof and threatened to jump to her death if they dared carry out their plan in public. Everyone looked at her anxiously and sympathetically, afraid that her shame might really overcome her fear of death. But Izuri's voice and eyes mesmerized her. He stood in the middle of the courtyard and commanded: "Toya, come down here to me."

And she came down quietly, and only when he pounced on her and picked her up and carried her to her room did she burst into tears. He left her there with three women and stepped outside. In spite of all their coaxing and urging she couldn't pass water for hours. Until Izuri, with his son dying before his eyes, lost patience and went back in and hit her on the head. In the courtyard Dahood stamped his foot and cried: "Savages, you're all savages!"

Half an hour later Toya passed water.

The sky grew red in the east, despite the sunset in the west. Soon the roaring of cannons became audible. And soon after that a sandstorm shook the house.

Abdallah Nunu knocked on the door and proclaimed like a herald: "The English have crushed the Turks. Tomorrow morning they're entering the city. We're saved, Jews, our sons are safe."

A few moments later the baby died. His little corpse was spotted with urine. Izuri and his wife wept with one voice. At midnight Dahood and Toya went out into the terrible storm. Abdallah Nunu took them into his home.

In the morning, as the storm subsided and the dust settled, the answer to their prayers arrived, like figures in a dream, many of them golden-haired, blue-eyed and pink-skinned. Their eye lashes were full of sand. They didn't break down doors or loot shops in the usual way of conquering armies, they didn't rape the women and they didn't even smile the smile of victors. They were very tired. With a messianic sense the Jews grasped that the end of centuries of darkness was at hand. The young men came out of hiding. Men and women streamed to the main street to see their saviours.

In the midst of the rejoicing Izuri buried the son to whom his soul was tied. For a day and a half he mourned him. His grief, like his wrath, was quickly over. Najia wore her blue mourning dress, and she remained alone in her pain. Aziza said defiantly: "Betrothals can't be postponed. The ceremony will take place as arranged."

And indeed, the betrothal took place on Saturday night. The courtyard was thirsty for release. Izuri drank a lot, not to the point of actual intoxication, but enough to blur the features of his wife sitting mourning in her blue dress in the middle of the courtyard.

"Enough crying," Aziza scolded her. "You take pleasure in spoiling every celebration."

The blue-garbed woman cried out in her bitterness: "My breasts are hurting from the milk and you're all guzzling and laughing. My son's dead."

"Izuri," Aziza incited her brother-in-law against his wife.

"Go away," decreed the male. "Go upstairs to cry, you were born to spend your life crying."

Victoria wept with her mother, but she was afraid to protest, lest they accused her of being jealous of her cousin. Miriam proudly wore all Michal's jewels, which had disappeared when she died.

Ezra was a real man: he smoked like a man, drank like a man, and was sad like a man. After he shaved, his eyes were big and prominent, and they searched everywhere. Suddenly he was too shy to approach the adults. From the little ones he learnt what had happened to Toya. His hatred for Najia devoured him like fire. He accompanied her to the glassed-in room and on the way he bent over her as if to whisper words of consolation: "May you be buried together with your lousy little bastard. May dogs suck the milk from your stinking tits, you bitch." None of the celebrating guests could understand why the woman disobeyed her husband and let out a piercing shriek of despair. Aziza clapped her hands together and Izuri ran up to the second floor and pushed his wife into the room and closed the door behind her.

The men in their cups wanted more merriment. "Where's Dahood with his zither?" someone called.

Toya and her husband were recalled from their banishment.

13

The streets became narrower and turned into alleys. From here on there was no passage for motor cars. Pedestrians, too, had to flatten themselves against the walls to let the beasts of burden through the narrow alleyways. In such winding labyrinths, on the sharp bends and between the close walls, the overwhelming human torrent subsided, the mob was not free to riot and rampage, and it disintegrated into thin trickles. These mazes had often protected the Jews from foreign invaders, who had wrought havoc with the Moslem population too. Owing to the proximity of the roofs they could flee from house to house, and in times of danger women, too, leapt across the chasm to the roof opposite. From a distance the houses looked like a strong, solid wall. Only from close up could you see that its parts were shaky.

Close to the twilight zone between the Jewish quarter and the Moslem quarter the charred remains of the benches and the burnt poles and pegs of the vast tent were still being crunched underfoot. Despite the shadows lurking at the bends in the alleys, which were beginning to take on menacing shapes, Victoria turned her attention to the aftermath of that long-ago fire. As she gazed at the blackened earth it seemed to put forth embers, and the embers gave off sparks, and the sparks united into flames. She had sat there with her family, halfway between the little aperture behind their backs, which emitted a cone of bright light, full of motes of dust and cigarette smoke and moths, and the screen in front of them which caught the light and shaped it magically into men and women moving about, laughing and plotting. The men on the white screen were all dressed like Rafael, and they did not look like inhabitants of Baghdad.

The spacious houses were adorned with trees, and the streets were as straight as those in the legendary suburb of Batawin on the southern outskirts of the city. She still remembered the little man on the screen, who went on sipping from his slender-stemmed glass, oblivious to the flames which had already caught hold of the edges of the tent.

Half the inhabitants of the courtyard were there, all of them sitting in the same row, crowding pleasantly together in the intimate darkness of the tent. Her father, who had rapidly recovered from Baruch's death, had shepherded the entire family to the first moving picture show to arrive in Baghdad, and he had even persuaded Yehuda to come along. The only ones left at home were Najia and Eliyahu, who had shed his other-worldly dervish airs and recovered his sense of hearing on the very day that the Turks had fled and the bugles of the blue-eyed, golden-haired soldiers had resounded in the city. In the excited dimness of the tent her father had delved under his *abbaya* and distributed fistfuls of sweets, pistachios and roasted almonds, which were passed along from hand to hand. Before and behind them rows of excited, anonymous faces shone in the darkness. A festive smell of feminine perfume hung in the air, together with the smell of the leather of new shoes and cigarette smoke.

The little man, sipping complacently from his wine glass, had no idea that he was taking part in a vile, ungodly abomination, and of course he could never have guessed that Moslem fanatics were about to set the tent full of people on fire. It took the spectators themselves a while before they realized that the flames and the smoke and the smell of burning canvas were not part of the movie unrolling before their eyes.

A woman dressed entirely in transparent black lace, with arms so white they dazzled the eyes of the beholder, appeared next to the little man and held out her hand to him with an inviting smile. The man didn't waste any time, and in front of everybody he bent over and kissed the slender fingers which looked just like Nuna Nunu's. Above the man's head she smiled with a sly, scheming expression. And at that very moment the screen collapsed onto the first rows of the audience, as if the woman's designs had been realized. Tent, benches and screen all burst into flames, with a roar which mingled with the shrieks of the people being trampled underfoot. Agile men leapt over the heads of the stunned spectators. Others ran right into the jaws of hell to save a wounded old man. A wild-eyed, screaming man carried a child in his arms as he searched desperately for his other children.

Suddenly she found herself alone between the burning benches, a scream in her throat.

A similar scream froze in her throat when Rafael smiled at the guests invited to their wretched wedding party and closed the door of the room behind them. In the room they stood facing one another, only the smell of the new wardrobe separating them. In a moment he was a stranger. No longer the Rafael who had grown up with her in the courtyard, the Rafael made fascinating by all the yearning of her adolescence. Now she was afraid of him. Perhaps because of the European suit and the bare-headed curls parted in the middle, the cheeky moustache over the feline smile. At any moment, it seemed, he would devour her. But wasn't that what she had wished for all these years—for him to devour her? She had never believed that she would win him, sure that Miriam's fat would tip the scales, and on the night of Miriam's marriage she had wept, not only for the death of her little brother, but also because her cousin's marriage to Gurji the smith was tantamount to an admission that Rafael had perished on the way to Basra. She was beside herself with joy when he had returned with his family months after the end of the war, his mother silent as ever and his two married sisters with babies at their breasts. It was as head of the family that he came home, and as a gesture of magnanimity that he allowed his father to go on living with them in the basement. His sisters and their husbands rented rooms in other courtyards. For days she didn't sleep. She waited for a sentence, a word, a sign from him. Miriam was already taken. Politely he rejected her father's offer of a job in the family business until he found his feet. He had no desire to spend any more time in his father's company than he had to. It was enough that he was forced to endure his presence in the basement. Izuri tried to persuade him. Yehuda's condition was getting worse, Dahood had gone back to the zither and was much in demand at the celebrations Baghdad was now full of, and Ezra was studying to be a pharmacist in Beirut. With absolute frankness Izuri told him that the business was declining and that he and Murad needed Rafael's energy and initiative. But Rafael stood his ground, and opened a modest fabric shop of his own.

Victoria found herself waiting all day for him to return from the shop. The courtyard was desolate without him, after Miriam's marriage she saw herself as lagging behind. In the courtyard people had begun to pass spiteful remarks about how she was missing her chances, the best years of her life were passing her by. Her father didn't lift a finger and her mother, instead of applying to a matchmaker, was preoccupied with her fruitless search for Salman and his coat, both of which had disappeared as if the earth had swallowed them up, like the Ottoman Empire itself.

Miriam grew greedier as her pregnancy advanced. The lustful glint died in her eyes. Victoria did not blame the hard-looking blacksmith for slaying Miriam's tender, thrilling butterflies. Like many other women, Miriam herself believed that desire was only an illusion, doomed to disappear on their wedding nights. With a kind of sadness Victoria understood that this was the price you had to pay if you didn't want to be left behind. When Hanina accosted her next to the great water-jar, which had been returned to its place in the niche in the wall, and whispered into her ear: "Rafael wants you, do you agree?" she went red and her head nodded as if of its own accord, and she was ashamed of this alacrity of her head, and grateful to his quiet mother for her affectionate smile. A moment later, still in the throes of her excitement, she thought of the price: the burning coals would turn to hailstones.

This feeling too, of the loss of her youth, separated her from

Rafael in the transparent darkness of the room on her wedding night.

And then there was the insult. In spite of Baruch's death, Miriam's wedding had been celebrated lavishly. The women had clustered round the balustrade of the roof, while others laboured in the kitchen, and boys carried trays and bowls to the men seated at the tables. Dahood had appeared with his band, and Toya skipped about among the guests, and refused to help the women with their work. She had been exaggeratedly made up, and Ezra had taken leave of his senses and danced on the table, balancing a bottle of arak on his head. In honour of the occasion Aziza had asked Abdallah Nunu for his dentist's address, and the latter had made a set of false teeth for Yehuda. The father of the bride thus appeared at the party in the guise of Methuselah with a young man's grin. Najia had refused to take off her blue mourning garb, which had not been washed since the baby's death. Victoria suspected her of tearing the dress at the hem and shoulder and scattering ashes from the kitchen fires on it every morning as a protest against the cheerful atmosphere reigning in the courtyard. She had smeared her face with a paste of brown mud, until she looked like a corpse startled from its grave. For a moment Yehuda forgot his heart and said angrily: "What's this, woman? Show a little consideration."

"Salman's dead," she said. "He's gone."

"What Salman? What are you jabbering about? Go away." He was sure that she had gone mad.

In the middle of the party Najia went up to the roof and skulked behind the women looking down on the men below. Suddenly she shouted loudly: "Abdallah Nunu's riding his Nuna by the light of the stars!"

A hush fell on the celebrants, and the embarrassment increased when Abdallah was discovered sitting among the menfolk, while Nuna shone in all her radiance among the women. Izuri didn't know how to cover up his shame, and he smiled apologetically at the guest, who showed no signs of distress, with only the almond crushed to dust between his fingers disclosing what his calm face concealed. Nobody paid any attention to Dahood, who tossed off a glass of arak and resumed his strumming with a sombre expression in his eyes. In the tumult nobody but him had noticed the absence of Ezra and Toya, and consequently he was the only one who realized his sister's mistake. The beggars came and in exchange for a penny or a piece of meat they capered about like monkeys, adding laughter to the merriment. Victoria's pleasure in Miriam's joy was unclouded. In the generosity of her heart, or for fear of the Evil Eye, her aunt Aziza had sewn her a pretty dress for the occasion.

And it was this dress which she wore a few months later to her own wedding. There were hardly ten men for a prayer quorum, and the party resembled a wake more than a wedding. There was only one table, and it too was shamefully mean. Her mother insisted on adding another year to the year of mourning, even though her belly was swelling again. Victoria wondered why her father had given her such a pauper's wedding. The dowry offered to Rafael, too, was the dowry of a guttersnipe. Rafael kept quiet, even though he knew the size of Miriam's dowry. He, who had returned from exile without a penny, and supported his brothers and his mother, stood proud as a prince in the transparent darkness of their room and ignored the insult he had suffered at the hands of her parents. The shame filling Victoria's heart to overflowing, too, stood between them at the moment she had awaited so eagerly.

He shut the door and he didn't open his mouth. Her fingers were frozen, and although her knees had turned to water she was afraid to approach the bed. The few men outside were kicking up a racket as if they wanted to shatter the oppressive gloom in the atmosphere. Someone called out with the licensed impudence of the occasion: "Get it over with, man, and come out already!" His mother and Aziza, but not her mother, waited outside the door to examine the virgin blood on the sheet.

If only they would all disappear and leave the two of them alone! But at the same time she was afraid of being alone with him. And the tears were about to flood her eyes. The ghost of a smile smouldered sardonically on his delicate lips, and a malicious voice echoed inside her head: I suppose you're sorry you didn't come back sooner. A blacksmith with an iron face snatched those plump dimples away from you.

And he still hadn't taken a step towards her. He went up to the oil lamp and instead of lowering the flame he turned it up. Victoria wanted to push her fist into her mouth to stop herself from vomiting. Rafael took off his jacket and undid his bowtie. Nobody else in the alley wore such a dandified tie, she said to herself, as if a part of her mind had split off and was watching the proceedings with a sarcastic sneer. And still he said nothing.

Something like a whirlwind gathered force at the bottom of her back, and shook her until her teeth chattered shamefully. She couldn't hear what he was saying, and trying to suppress her terror she cupped her ear with her hand to make him repeat it, while at the same time the detached part of her mind asked: Why him? Nobody in the courtyard loved him. They all feared him, suspected him, admired him, boasted about him, were silenced by his presence, dwarfed by his stature. Even her father folded his feathers when they stood face to face. But apart from Miriam and herself nobody really loved him. Why had she given her consent at the first whisper from his mother?

The bed sighed when he sat down on it to take off his shoes.

Up to now she had grown up as the rejected daughter of a disturbed mother, and now she was going to be the slave of a man the courtyard idolized. And the detached part of her mind continued: You've forgotten Eliyahu. Everyone's afraid of his father's harshness, and the father himself bows his head at the piercing look of his son.

And if he unsheathed his talons and dug them into her flesh . . . Miriam had described the horror of it to her. How Gurji had jumped on her like a sledge-hammer. That plump body with its supple bones and eager flesh had been transformed in an instant to a shapeless mass of pains. "That accursed thing of his split me like a watermelon," she said and patted her private parts underneath the rustling fabric of her bridal gown. "Grunting like a dog he was. It hurts, Victoria, and it's as disgusting as having shit in your eyes."

And the detached part of her mind asked if he had been so silent with the singer he had run away with to Syria too. And with Rahma Afsa too. And what did they do while he sat taking off his shoes? Did they get their whore's pay for the shit that filled their eyes? And why were Toya's eyes shining when she returned with Ezra from Abdallah Nunu's roof? And where did that smile on Nuna's beautiful face come from?

And another strange thought astonished her: she was desecrating her father's honour. From infancy she had been trained to hide her limbs and cover her legs to the ankles. Izuri was fanatical about modesty. And now he was sipping arak with the men waiting behind the door.

"So they haven't explained anything to you?" asked Rafael again. His lean body bent down to take off his socks. How practical and businesslike he was. His hands gripped the belt of his trousers as if he was about to whip out a knife. Aziza thought that her mother had done her duty by her daughter, and her mother didn't even know what there was to explain. Perhaps they had explained it to her once and she had forgotten the explanation. With the obedience of a tamed animal she had learnt to adapt her body to the needs signalled by Izuri's body. Victoria was too shy to ask Miriam what she was supposed to do. Now she didn't dare admit her ignorance, or pretend to knowledge she did not possess. In any case she wouldn't succeed with a shrewd customer like Rafael. She was speechless.

"What's wrong?" The question sounded like a hoarse squeak in her ears.

Rafael sat down on the bed again and pulled his folded trousers over his loins. "You should enjoy it too. God created a lot of nonsense, but he never did anything better or more beautiful than this. I haven't got the time to sit down and tell you about it now. I know you, Victoria. You yourself will want what I've got inside what you've got, and you'll want to keep it there all the time. But those drunks outside don't know how to wait like human beings. They're losing patience already. Soon they'll start laughing. Then they'll pretend to be concerned. Come here."

It was hatred which melted the paralysis that had her in its grip. Hatred for her mother, hatred for her father, who had insulted her so shamefully, hatred for this man who was shattering her youth, hatred for Miriam who had jumped at the blacksmith and let him go. God! The detached part of her brain laughed out loud. What did God have to do with the cannon lying in wait for her under those neatly folded trousers? He spoke about enjoyment, and look at his naked feet! There were, indeed, a few experienced women in the courtyard, women with dirty mouths, who talked about a great flame. But she had never heard a man talk like Rafael. And the detached part of her brain made fun of her. What choice have you got? The minute that door closed behind you, you turned into dough to be kneaded as he sees fit. And she clenched her teeth angrily and said to herself: Let him knead. He wouldn't see a tear or sense her agony.

The bed groaned again as he stood up, this time without his trousers and with laughter in his eyes. He saw her staring for a split second at his penis, and the laughter turned to a lewd smile. Victoria remembered the vulgar matchmaker sitting between Aziza and Yehuda in the arcade. Her voice too had dripped with rose-water like Rafael's voice now, and her movements had hinted at a shameless excitement. And the detached part of Victoria's brain laughed in her face: What's all this maidenly modesty, miss? A carrot or a cucumber were enough to fire your imagination, just because they looked like this cannon.

Rafael tried very hard to be gentle with her, but he didn't know how to be gentle with a girl who had grown up with him like a sister, and had suddenly turned into a woman who was standing before him petrified with fear. When he approached her his penis leapt out of his control and rode before him like a creature with a life of its own. Any gesture of appeasement or reassurance would seem false with his cock so impudently and inconsiderately rampant.

His slender fingers closed resolutely round her wrist. And Victoria, true to her vow, yielded like a lump of dough. He laid her on her back on the bed and bent over her with the lightness of a shadow. She closed her eyes and hunched her head between her shoulders and bit her lips so that he would not hear her scream when the blow fell. His fingers brushed her belly like feathers. Something unexpected happened to the dough. As if it had been thrust suddenly into a blazing oven and risen. Her bare thighs tightened as if to protect the gate of a threatened city, and to her alarm she felt her buttocks lifting from the bed as if to bid him do his worst and go away, and she was ashamed of this sudden boldness of her bum. She closed her eyes and turned her body sideways, as if to hide at least a little of her nakedness. Suddenly the heat of his body over her was gone. A wind came and blew the feathery fingers away. She opened her eyes in surprise. Was it all over? Her relief was mingled with a desolate feeling of emptiness. She saw him going over to the oil lamp and lowering the wick. The light grew softer, and he and his penis flowed back to her in the velvety light.

"Haven't you finished yet?" she said and she was ashamed of the jarring sound of her voice.

Never in her life had she heard such a laugh, the laugh of a gleeful child, coming from the throat of a grown man. And the delighted laughter spilled onto the bare skin of her belly, and it had quivering lips, this laughter, like the petals of the lemon blossom, and it turned her onto her stomach and kissed her on her bum, until she forgot her hatred and her shame and suspected that it was about to lose its innocence and childlike clarity. And the laughter grew teeth and bit her nipples, and the dough which had risen and hardened now crumbled and dissolved into radiant drops of mist shining in the dim light of the lamp. And deep in the heart of the mist a surprising pain was born, more like the piercing scent of almonds than an actual stab.

When the detached part of her brain regained consciousness she felt an icy cold gripping her, because the laughter had disappeared and without it she was utterly naked, and instead of the laughter the smiles of Aziza and Hanina flickered above her as they examined the sheet underneath her body and covered her with loving hands. She didn't have the strength to get up, and the two aunts let her be and went quietly out of the room. And Victoria floated in the dim light of the lamp, an abandoned boat in an endless lake without sounds or smells. Her face flushed as she realized that neither weariness nor loneliness had defeated her. She longed for his touch, for the laughter biting her nipples. Her belly quivered with fierce joy and she wanted to shout out loud: Miriam, little Toya's right, you've been cheated, Miriam! For the first time her hands cupped her breasts without shame, even with pride, and a new, triumphant laughter was born inside her. Rafael was hers. She, who didn't have a single dimple, she had won him. She, who had worn to her wedding a dress made for the weddings of others. She, whose father's table had been bathed in tears on feasts and holidays too. She, who had not been showered with jewels or given a bed of burnished brass.

And then came the jealousy.

The bastard was a witch doctor. He had not learnt his magic touch from books of wisdom like Rabbi Juri Chittaiyat. Like Jamila, who practised witchcraft, he had acquired his skills in the places of abomination. Those same lips which had pricked her nipples erect must have played with the whore he eloped with to Syria, too. He was the only man for whose sake Rahma Afsa broke her rule and went to bed with on her holiday. Up to now his behaviour with the girls in the courtyard had been irreproachable, he had looked down on them with the patronizing airs of an older brother, and gone elsewhere to satisfy his desires. What would happen if Miriam overheard his secret laughter? She was in the third month of her pregnancy now, guzzling chickens and fish and mutton in spite of her nausea, and getting fatter every day. What would happen when she found out that no cook had ever concocted a dish to match Rafael in the heat of his randiness? And if he whistled in the direction of Nuna Nunu's roof? She remembered the dusty procession returning from Basra a few months after the end of the war. They were like skeletons from the dysentery and the malaria. They had nothing but for the meagre bundles on their emaciated shoulders. He walked at the head, and in spite of his pitiful thinness his eyes glittered as if he had defeated the Ottoman armies single-handed, and he was bringing them the tidings of peace and plenty. Cries of excitement went up from the roofs and the windows at the sight of this resurrection, for they had all been given up for dead. Eliyahu closed his eyes in resignation. He had enjoyed having the whole of the basement to himself. Victoria was too excited to take in the reactions of the others. She remembered Miriam crying "Hoi!" and that was all. It was hard to tell if her cry was one of joy, or sorrow at her haste in agreeing to be the anvil to Gurji's hammer. For a long time Miriam avoided looking at Rafael, and it was clear that she felt resentful towards him. But the girls who had ripened during the years of the war gaped and gawked. Nuna Nunu painted her face and hurried to their courtyard, where she stood next to her father's gleaming dentures and stared shamelessly at Rafael. She herself told him that she had been widowed.

Later on that night she let him enter her again, despite her pain, and forgot her anxieties. Like a man emerging from the desert he drank from her jar again and again. When she thought that he was asleep she lay on her side and looked at his delicate face. He had stripped her naked under the blanket, and so she remained, naked in bed for the first time in her life. Her knee accidentally touched his, and her desire flamed. He opened his eyes and smiled at her as naturally as a man smiling at himself in the mirror. "I told you so," he said tenderly, and she couldn't open her mouth because of the whirlpool surging inside her and crying out for him.

And Rafael was swept up in this whirlpool of hers. The days to come were like the voyage she had been taken on in her childhood. Yehuda was not yet ill then, and he and her father had taken all the inhabitants of the courtyard on a steamship to visit the grave of Ezra the Scribe, may he rest in peace. Rafael was inside her and she was wrapped up inside him, and the faces and quarrels, the sunsets and sunrises seemed to exist not inside her own courtyard but on the banks of a river, gliding past and disappearing into the horizon and leaving vague impressions behind them. During those days she was hardly aware of anything but the sounds she heard inside her. She ate when she was hungry, smiled a lot, answered questions, listened to what was said to her, and all the time she kept her head cocked alertly as if listening for an important and precious event awaiting her beyond the passing moment. And Rafael did not disappoint her. He always waited for her.

The detached part of her brain did not sink into total oblivion. Somehow it went on registering what was happening around her. In her great happiness she did not want to be bothered by trivialities. And in this new spirit of forgiveness and dreamy, floating mood she listened to her father apologizing for the miserable wedding he had given her. Izuri, who was not accustomed to justifying himself, piled explanation on explanation. The detached part of her brain told her that she should pretend to be embarrassed in the face of his embarrassment, but she just smiled and smiled. "For years I thought about who I would invite to your wedding. I planned a feast fit for a king. You're your father's good little girl. You supported me and were a mother to your brothers. And you of all people didn't deserve to be married like a poor orphan. Up to a year ago I could have thrown such a party for you . . ." And Victoria smiled from her ship of happiness and the detached part of her brain scolded her and said, say something, maybe he's going a bit too far, but you don't have to be nasty. And she said nonchalantly: "It doesn't matter, Father."

"It's eating me up. I don't know what's happening to us. There's plenty of merchandise and plenty of customers, I get a fair price and everything goes into the till, and nobody gets their fingers into it, and all I have to show for it is a big deficit. I'm like a man delivering ice to people in the sun, they refresh themselves and I remain thirsty. We're almost bankrupt, and I can't tell Yehuda because of his heart. Eliyahu's hands are clean, he doesn't dare go anywhere near the till. The creditors are at the door. I'll die of shame before I go to jail."

For a moment she stopped sailing. His suffering touched her. She had forgiven him long ago for her pauper's wedding, but in her heart she resented him for spoiling her happiness. Since that magical trip to the grave of Ezra the Scribe, how many times had she set sail? But the resentment soon passed, and so did the pity, and her father turned into a lonely palm tree waving its fronds on a distant river bank. Rafael overshadowed him. She was impatient to get back to his smell, his touch, his whispers, and in order to get rid of her father she said the first thing that came into her head. "You guard the till, and Eliyahu wouldn't go near it. No, he doesn't steal money. But perhaps he conspired with the night guard to steal merchandise from the warehouse."

Izuri's eyes opened wide in horror. "That's it," he said.

The next day Hanina was turned out of the basement. She and her children left carrying the wretched bundles they had brought with them from Basra. Rafael rented a room for them in another courtyard. His father disappeared into one of the pleasure groves. Because of Toya Dahood did not join him there with his zither. Ezra lay in waiting for her, and she waited for him like a sunflower for the sun.

During the course of that enchanted voyage they passed other landscapes, other things happened. The river reached the courtyard. Until then water had been transported from the river in tins, on the backs of donkeys. Now the authorities installed purification plants and laid down pipes, and running water flowed in the courtyard from a private tap. The children were beside themselves with joy at the sight of the water pouring out so abundantly in the summer heat. They blocked the drain with rags and opened the tap as far as it would go. Then they sat in washing tubs and set sail with deafening yells. Eliyahu's family's abandoned basement was flooded, and the children stayed away from its door, afraid of being swallowed up in the darkness from which suspect noises and squeaks emerged. And they abandoned their tubs and fled in all directions when a drove of wet mice came hopping up the steps, threw themselves into the water, and began to swim resolutely across the courtyard, their noses sticking up, like a miniature armada intent on invading the house and driving the inhabitants out.

On the second floor Victoria shook Michal's rug, her only inheritance from her grandmother, and burst out laughing at the sight of the children running away from the mice.

"May God sew up your lips for ever, you bitch."

Her mother sat with her legs crossed in the middle of the lake, as if the water and the mice and the shrieking children had startled her from her slumbers. She was still wearing her threadbare mourning dress. Her belly bulged above the waterline, and Aziza and other experienced women were of the opinion that this time she would not be blessed with a son, since her stomach was a little elongated, and she vomited morning and night as when she was bearing a girl. Najia believed them and acquired a new habit. At moments of despair or sorrow or anger she no longer slapped herself in the face as before, but dealt a vicious blow to her stomach instead, as if all the troubles in the world had come to settle in Izuri's miserable seed. His business was failing, his strength was failing, and he was no longer capable of producing anything but females.

The basement and the drain were full to overflowing, the water went on standing in the courtyard, and Najia did not budge from her place. The women and children began to bail the water out in pails and throw it onto the dust of the alley, until neighbours unable to afford the municipal water rates came and took it away to wash and do their laundry in. The lower half of Najia's body emerged inch by inch as the water receded. Twigs and mud and cooking ashes clung to the bottom of her dress, and as she sat there she looked like a strange plant sticking up from a dry river bed when the flood waters ebbed.

She fixed her eyes on Yehuda who was lying on a bench in

the arcade, until he blinked in inexplicable fear. For a number of weeks now he had been lying there on the bench, unable to get up and go to the lavatory without assistance. He would ask Aziza to take him there, and squat over the open hole still clinging to her hand and refusing to allow her to close the door, because there was no window in the lavatory and he was afraid of the dark, and Aziza would stand there pulling a face because of the stink. It was terrible to see his dignified grey beard in that foul darkness.

Like Victoria, Yehuda too was on a voyage, and he looked out with terror on a world which was slipping away from him. It was spring in the courtyard, a spring of rounding breasts, of maturing boys and girls, of pregnancies and births. How shocking it was to die in the springtime. Enviously he spoke of Michal and the sturdiness of spirit which had enabled her to give up the ghost with dignity. For a day or two he would keep his resolution to be brave, but the results of his tremendous efforts were negligible. He was sunk into himself and took no notice of the world around him. When Aziza told him that he was about to become a grandfather, all he could think of was that the grandson would live while he would be wiped off the face of the earth. So what was there to rejoice about? Aziza was tireless in her efforts to cheer him up, she told him that Ezra was doing well at school, and that he would soon travel to Beirut and acquire wisdom and knowledge there and come back with a pharmacist's diploma. He stared into space and said nothing, and wondered why she couldn't understand that by the time Ezra returned from Lebanon he would be dead and gone. Rabbi Juri Chittaiyat had recently sentenced him to a diet that was no better than fasting, and it annoyed him that he couldn't stop thinking of forbidden foods. He no longer filled pages with Arabic in Hebrew script. In his present condition they were afraid to tell him that Abdallah Nunu was dying, he was grunting and snorting like a slaughtered sheep, and they had removed the youthful dentures from his mouth in case he choked on them. His son Ma'atuk had almost entirely deserted his shop, he walked up and down the alley in front of his father's door, until Nuna collapsed because of her brother, and Hannah, the dying man's sister, saw fit to set her grandchildren on their crippled uncle and chase him away as if he were a dog. But it was impossible to keep a secret for long in the courtyard, and in the end Yehuda found out. And the Angel of Death, who was stretching out his claws for their sinful neighbour, was creeping up on him too, on Yehuda, who had tried so hard all his life to keep sin from his door. When Najia fixed her eyes on him, and he saw her growing out of the muddy floor in her mourning dress, his terror tricked him into imagining that he was seeing the Angel of Death face to face.

"Get her away from here," he groaned. "How long is she going to stink in that rotting dress?"

Najia patted her belly, got onto all fours, and finally stood on her feet. "I had a rosebud and it was plucked," she said, "and he, who was born dying, cries for himself in his old age. Aziza, everybody dies. Tell him not to make such a fuss about it."

"Mother," called Victoria from the second floor.

"Shut up," snapped her mother. "Everybody dies. Everybody. You've wrapped a snake around your neck and you're drunk on it. But it doesn't change a thing. Everybody's going to die."

Nobody knew what she had discovered that morning in her prowlings round the markets and bazaars. There were places in the city where swarms of flies made the air quiver over stinking rubbish heaps. Where residential courtyards, stores and workshops threw out their garbage to rot in the sun, where men turned their backs on the passers-by to urinate. Peasant women bringing their wares to town to sell also squatted there and spread their skirts to do their business with reflective expressions on their faces, paying no attention whatever to the milling crowds. Nobody troubled to remove the garbage. Ants, mosquitoes and flies, birds, mice and rats, cats and dogs rummaged in the rotting mounds. And sometimes hungry people too, or compulsive rag collectors. For a long time now Najia had been searching for Salman. In her despair she accosted strangers and asked about him, and they shrugged their shoulders as if to say that they themselves wondered where the tramp had disappeared to. Her pockets were as heavy as her breasts after Baruch died, and she wanted to invest her money, and also to know, if only approximately, how much interest her savings had accumulated, especially since she had forgotten the sum he had mentioned at their last meeting. Round figures were what she liked—and so did he. Anything else confused her. She peered into synagogue doors, questioned waiters in tea-houses, and pointed at the little bundle of rags in her hands, saying that she had made a vow to bring him food. Once she wandered as far as the vast mounds of ashes thrown out by the public baths, and once someone told her in a joke that he had seen Salman going down to the river on a khamsin day, where his heavy coat had made him sink like a stone, and she was furious with the joker for making fun of her.

Early that morning she set out to scour the stinking rubbish heaps, undeterred by their foul miasma buzzing with bees and flies. And behind a narrow alley near the Abu Sifein market her eyes lit up. On top of a huge pile of rubbish rose Salman's coat, the collar raised as if to protect him from the icy cold in the middle of summer, one sleeve in the garbage stewing in the sun, the other shielding his private parts. She knew his deplorable habit of going naked underneath his coat. "Salman!" she cried with a pounding heart. Suddenly she felt the fog in her brain clearing, and with a piercing pain she realized how few were the moments of happiness in her life. "Salman," she said, her voice full of joy, "don't you recognize me? I'm Najia, Izuri the son of Michal's wife." As the fog cleared tears of sorrow for some irretrievable loss rose to her eyes, together with a feeling of warm affection for this man who had come back to life, the bearer of glad tidings. When she was a few paces away from him a cry of terror escaped her lips. Several hours later, when she thought about what had happened, she remembered sensing something strange when her eyes first fell on the coat, but her joy at the meeting was so great that it fuddled her wits. As a woman who had been mercilessly beaten since childhood, she was always on her guard and ready for anything, but not for this: instead of a human face a black crow rose from the stiff collar, beat the shimmering air with its wings and flew up over her head. The coat itself was empty, a scarecrow in which the crow had taken shelter. She fell on it and tugged at the stiff sleeve. The sleeve ripped off and Najia recoiled in horror as if she had desecrated a corpse. After a moment she overcame her fear and tore the lining. With the grief of bereavement she beat her belly before the orphaned coat.

As the water in the courtyard subsided and she sat planted in the mud, no one imagined the extent of her terrible grief. Apart from the loss of the money and the gold, Salman was the only person in her world she trusted completely. Victoria saw only the empty despair in her mother's eyes, and she hurried downstairs to hold her back as she rose to her feet, in case they blamed her for Yehuda's death. Apparently the happiness radiating from her daughter was too much for the wretched woman to bear. As soon as Victoria touched her shoulder her eyes blazed. "Get away from me, you with your whorish smile."

But Victoria wasn't smiling at all. At any rate, not an external smile intended for others.

"He climbs on you like a leech and you dance like a fool. Wait, wait for the tears."

Victoria did not protest. She knew that the tears would come. But the knowledge did not spoil her happiness.

"I'm not moving from here," hissed Najia. Her arm trembling with rage, she pointed at Yehuda's bench and said: "What does he want of me? I've died a thousand deaths in this cursed house—did anyone whisper a kind word to me?'

In spite of her pity and sympathy, Victoria was too absorbed in herself during those days to be able to touch the loneliness of Yehuda's fears and the bitterness of her shunned mother. Najia shook off her daughter's hand and went on sobbing quietly like a branch which continues to tremble after the wind has subsided.

14

A few weeks after the wedding he began wearing glasses, and his appearance became more dignified and impressive. The girls breathed deeply in his presence and unconsciously thrust out their breasts. As a result of the British occupation Baghdad raced into a new era whose coming Rafael had anticipated many years before. And he now gained the reputation of a man who was at home in the new world unfolding before them. A year after she had given birth to Kilmanteen, the lamp still trembled in Victoria's hand when she went down at night to open the door for him. He was always the last to return from the theeayter. Other latecomers would bang on the door in a panic and call in trembling voices for someone to open up, for fear of the sinister forces swarming in the darkness. Rafael would clear his throat at the bend in the alley, and the sound of his elegant cane tapping on the door was calm and confident. On the narrow stair she would hold the lamp up before him, her head held high and her shoulders steady, with not a tremor to betray the wild churning in the pit of her stomach when his hands cupped her buttocks from behind. How naive Toya's childish fantasies and Miriam's tales of lust now seemed in her eyes. At first she had been sure that Rafael was pushing her down a slippery slope of wanton lewdness. The first time he asked her to strip herself naked in front of his glittering glasses, she had thought him a crazy pervert, and she had refused and blushed and persisted in her disobedience, and he had sent out his fingers, ten messengers which burned her like coals, and they had slowly peeled off all her clothes, until she felt that she could bear it no longer and in another second she would scream. He pulled up an empty tub and stood her in it and crouched down and turned it round, licking like a hungry baby, like a predatory cat, with tongues of fire. Once she had melted like a wax candle and bent over double and he had come at her from behind like a searing wind in summer. He would rub the bristles of his beard over her thighs, her hips, her breasts. One night her eyes rounded and she bit her lip and dug her nails into his back and pulled him into her and sobbed in shame, and her flesh exulted. "Now I'm a whore, are you satisfied?"

His tongue glided over her sweating face until it wiped away the shame. But as soon as they were dressed and he put on his spectacles her fear came back. She examined his plate seven times over to see if it was clean before she dared to serve him his food. Sometimes she furtively wet her finger and wiped away a minute speck. She was so frightened that her fingers lost their dexterity, her feet got caught in the hem of her dress, words grew jumbled on her tongue. For more than fifty years this fear accompanied her, until it disappeared into the mud of the immigrants' transit camp in Israel. In the storm of the flight from Iraq and the ruthless process of absorption in the new country the stunned men collapsed, and the women were forced to stand up on their hind legs.

But in those distant days of happiness Victoria looked down on the parched courtyard from above, from the best room in the house. Rafael's business prospered, and the young couple moved into the glassed-in room which had one whole wall of glass windows. The windows of the other rooms had nothing but wooden shutters to close them on winter nights. In the courtyard new names were born. In defiance of all the predictions, Najia gave birth to a boy, Fuad, who was dark-skinned and cried all day, and did not console his father for the loss of the beautiful Baruch. Miriam gave birth to her first-born, Naim. Kilmanteen did not detract from Victoria's happiness. She was sure that sons would come later. Ezra's eyes clouded before the journey to Beirut. It was hard for him to tear himself away from Toya. From time to time they bribed children to stand guard next to the stairs and went up to the Nunus' roof in the heat of the day.

The closer the time came for him to leave for Beirut the worse the lad's sufferings grew. Aziza lamented: "The child's shrivelling up. Skin and bones because of that minx. Someone should talk to him."

"Idiot, what are you wasting your tears on?" Rafael whispered into his disciple's ear. "Just as Jerusalem glories in her rabbis, Beirut boasts of her whores. You've never had a whiff of merchandise like that in your life. All shapes and colours. Someone like Toya would have to wait in line for months before they let her serve a glass of arak in a self-respecting brothel there. You'll hardly be able to close your eyes at night, your nostrils will be so full of the smell of the sea and the blonde Christian women." And in order to illustrate his words he did the boy a favour and took him to the theeayter for the first time in his life. A few days later Ezra gave Toya a page full of black lines and got into a car and disappeared into the dust of the desert. Toya, who had never set foot in a school, was unable to read a word of it, and she went out to the row of request-writers in front of the government offices in the Sarai and came back with her eyes shining. She shut herself up in her room, folded the letter up into a little ball, sewed it a purse of silk and hung it round her neck like a charm, and she never took it off, not even when Dahood crouched over her body.

In the tremendous shake-up of British occupation the Jewish community seemed to wake from its slumbers. The twentieth century invaded the city with a glitter of electric lights and a roar of racing motorcars. The Jews burst out of the cramped Jewish quarter and spread south along the Tigris, chopped down palm trees and planted fine houses and flowers in their place. Rafael's exotic suit became the garb of many. The men discovered the power of the written word and invaded the outside world with the determination of mountain climbers. Business prospered and affluence changed their way of life. Victoria's father changed his gown and *abbaya* for a European suit, and began to sport an elegant cane, like Rafael. He and Yehuda liquidated the bankrupt fabric shop and rehabilitated the little exercise-book factory abandoned by Eliyahu. This factory would still be supporting Murad fifty years later, when he remained stranded with a handful of stray characters after all the other Jews had left and the city was shaken by one military coup after the other. His cowardice was so intense that it paralysed him, and the mass exodus to Israel left him behind.

It seemed to Victoria that Rafael himself was performing the miracle taking place in the city, with the same mysterious power that aroused her body and thrilled her soul. She applied in secret to Rabbi Juri Chittaiyat and asked his advice about how to preserve her happiness. Strew salt against the Evil Eye, he advised her, and give a lot of money to charity. Rafael was making more than Izuri and Yehuda put together. By offering an exorbitant rent for the window-room, and on other pretexts, he supplied them with funds for the exercise-book factory and helped them until they could stand on their own feet again. Now she could smile at her mother's abiding hatred for Rafael, and even forgive her for the wounds of the past. Rafael loved her. Rafael slid his thrilling eyes over her body, touched with magic fingers the secrets of her innermost fantasies. He had always loved her. He had never desired any other woman. He had only gone to them because she was still a child and a virgin, and this was his way of waiting for her.

Even without the advice of Juri Chittaiyat she became more generous, and her sensitivity to injustice increased. When a cry of pain rose from the courtyard she put Kilmanteen down in her cradle in the window-room and hurried to the gallery railing. With the heavy hands of a blacksmith Gurji was raining blows on Miriam's head and mercilessly slapping her face. Yehuda sat up on his bench in the arcade and thumped his knees indignantly. The smith's pointed beard quivered with rage and a fire blazed in his eyes. "Thief, you've emptied the purse again!"

Blood poured from Miriam's squashed nose. Her vast body was trapped between the kitchen door and the stairs, and with her hands she shielded her milk-swollen breasts from her husband's fists.

"Aziza," wailed Yehuda, "Aziza, he's killing our daughter. Where are you?"

Aziza interposed herself between her daughter and her son-in-law. "Villain, leave her alone!" The blacksmith's fingers dug into his mother-in-law's fat shoulder until she screamed in pain. "Heathen, criminal," she shrieked. "Take your hands off my daughter."

His hand came down hard on Miriam's cheek. Her bracelets clattered, and she collapsed onto the ground. Victoria's heart bled for her cousin. "Do as you're told and leave her alone!" she commanded from the second storey in Michal's deliberate, authoritative tone.

The pointed beard rose towards her. "She steals from the purse in secret. It's Friday today and I haven't got any money left to pay the workers' wages, Jews with families who have to bring bread home for the Sabbath. And what does the stupid cow spend the money on? On mountains of almonds, dishes of sweets, buckets of meat. God almighty, she's a whale, not a woman!" And he kicked his wife's leg and strode out of the courtyard with flashing eyes.

Miriam rolled over onto her back and tried to get up, but she let out a scream and remained lying on the floor. Her leg was on fire, but she was so fat that she couldn't reach the place where it hurt.

"He broke my leg," she groaned.

Toya burst into tears and Yehuda growled: "God damn him to hell."

Victoria sent for Juri Chittaiyat to mend the break.

In the afternoon heavy clouds darkened the sky and the glass panes of the window-room rang with the rolls and claps of the thunder. Rafael sat in the tub and his head was a snow-white halo of fragrant Palmolive lather. With his eyes closed he laughed at Victoria's fear of the thunder, and she mastered herself and poured hot water on his head and enjoyed feeling frightened so close to his naked body with its mysterious power to move her. On Friday nights he was all hers. No café, no club, no theeayter. Kilmanteen, undisturbed by the thunder and lightning, gurgled behind her as she washed him. The clouds went on spattering the window panes with crystal, and she could already smell the arak he would soon be sipping. The table was laid for the festive meal, and her skin prickled in pleasurable anticipation of what would come afterwards.

"At Uncle Yehuda's it's like a wake," he said as she washed the lather off his back. "Tell them not to worry about Ezra. Lebanon really is a Paradise."

From the day of his return from Basra he had not spoken to Yehuda directly. A barrier of chilly silence had arisen between him and his uncle's family, leading Victoria to think that something must have happened between them. She could understand it if Rafael was angry about Miriam's marriage while he was away, but she couldn't make out why Yehuda and Aziza should have a grievance against her husband. The relationship between Rafael and her father, on the other hand, was close enough to arouse Yehuda's jealousy. Their uncle made a number of attempts to come down off his high horse and break the ice, but Aziza's withering looks nipped any attempt at reconciliation in the bud. Victoria asked Miriam what it was all about, but she couldn't get an answer. Rafael too evaded her questions, and tried to make light of the whole affair.

"It isn't because of Ezra that they look so glum," she told him. "Gurji broke Miriam's leg."

Until the day Raphael died he was afraid of catching cold, and he never gave up his belief that it was exposing your naked body to draughts after bathing which made you catch cold. Consequently he was unhappy about bathing in hot water in winter, and he racked his brain to find a system of dry cleaning instead, but he never succeeded in coming up with anything that could save him from steaming water and dangerous draughts. In his old age he ridiculed the idea of the skeleton holding the scythe as symbolizing the Angel of Death. In his opinion it was the icy draught cutting through the clouds of steam which was the messenger of death, and he would curl up like a foetus in the hot tub until Victoria wrapped him in a big towel.

But now he leapt to his feet with the water streaming down

his flushed skin, just as it was streaming down the window panes outside. She caught her breath at the sight of his copper-coloured penis. But his eyes were clouded with a stern, remote look. "My glasses," he commanded.

"It's cold. Dry yourself first."

"My glasses. So that swine broke her leg," he said and set the glasses on his delicate nose as if he were girding a sword. "Where is she?"

She shrank at the harshness of his voice. "In her parents' room. Juri Chittaiyat has seen to her leg already. I sent for him myself," she said meekly, so that he would see how devoted she was to Miriam.

"I'm going down there," he said and hastily pulled on his clothes and went out into the lightning and thunder without waiting for his hair to dry. Victoria snatched Kilmanteen from her cradle and ran after him into the rain. In the corner of the room sat Toya, splitting golden dates and extracting the pits, which she replaced with roasted almonds. Her fingertips were sticky with the juice, and her mouth was evidently full of saliva, but she self-sacrificingly fed the titbits to the wounded Miriam, and the black silk purse trembled on her slender neck. Miriam lay stretched out on her parents' bed, while her father sat on a pillow with his back against the mouldy wall and his beard floating over the open page of a book. Aziza walked to and fro with little Naim sunk in the deep groove between her breasts, patting him on the back and whispering fervent curses. Victoria sat down gingerly on the foot of Miriam's bed and reached hesitantly out as if to touch the wounded leg, but then withdrew her hand again and stroked Kilmanteen's forehead instead. Yehuda, she saw, ignored Rafael completely, while Aziza shot dark looks in his direction, and Rafael, to her astonishment, hung his head as if he had crushed Miriam's leg himself.

"How are you?" he whispered in the general direction of Miriam's bed.

Yehuda lifted his beard from the holy book and Miriam immediately hid the smile with which she had welcomed Rafael.

"You dare to ask her how she is?"

Victoria gaped. It was rare for Yehuda to speak to anyone in that tone. Rafael took off his glasses and polished them on the hem of his Sabbath robe. It took a while for him to control himself, and all the time he looked at Yehuda reproachfully. In the end he dropped his eyes and said to the floor: "Toya, please leave us alone."

Toya almost burst into tears. When arguments broke out on the roof or in the courtyard everything took place in public, nobody was ever asked to leave. She stood up and looked around in vain for a sympathetic face, and then she stole out of the room with a feeling of disgrace.

"The letter," growled Aziza, with her hand shielding Naim's head as if to protect him from a ghost. "We know that the letter reached you. Abu Ezra paid a fortune to find a messenger who was prepared to risk his life and travel for days and nights through the thick of the war to go look for you in Basra. We heard that he was seen there. He didn't die on the way and he must have given you the letter."

"What letter?" demanded Victoria at the sight of the tears glittering in Miriam's eyes. Her question died away in the air as if she wasn't there in the room. Her heart told her that they would like her to go away.

"The messenger arrived and he gave me the letter," said Rafael and his glasses glinted.

Yehuda snapped the book shut. "And . . .?"

"We humbled ourselves and asked you outright," said Aziza. "You've been dear to us since you were a child. Even a dog deserves an answer."

Miriam sobbed out loud. "Stop it!" she hushed her parents, unable to bear the shame. "Stop it!"

"I swear on the Torah . . ."

"Don't swear a false oath," Yehuda's voice cracked like a whip.

"I swear on the Torah that I answered." Rafael's voice was firm. "And not only that, but I'd like to ask you: where's the engagement ring I sent? Pure gold, twenty-four carats. I ordered it specially from the goldsmith Zaddik Bulbul. Ask my mother. Ask my brothers."

"We never saw any letter or heard of any ring." Aziza's hand fell from Naim's head.

"And what do I see when I return? You sold her for a song. Like damaged goods you handed her over to a blockheaded blacksmith. Nobody in the house heard me say a word. I swallowed the insult and I kept quiet even when I saw her belly swelling with that animal's seed."

Miriam let out a wail. For a moment she forgot her broken leg and tried to sit up and hold out her arms to Rafael. And she immediately collapsed with a cry of pain.

"May God forgive us," said Aziza. "May God forgive us."

Yehuda rose to his feet. "She's a married woman now. It's a sin to look at her."

The rebellious Rafael had a ready retort: "A cat can look at a king."

Victoria fled with her face burning. Back in the room Kilmanteen burst into tears. Victoria thrust her nipple between the baby's soft lips and said crossly: "You were born by mistake, I wash him and soap his balls by mistake. Miriam's husband fucks her by mistake." A smile broke through her tears. Then she was overcome with pity for Miriam. Miriam had never made a secret of her love for Rafael. She hadn't hidden it before and she wasn't hiding it now. And she wouldn't hide it in the years to come either. Not even after she opened her womb to the blacksmith's hammer and she gave birth to his sons and daughters. And not even after they had all crowded into airplanes and floated over the clouds to Israel. And she went on loving him when she lay dying, sixty years later, in a bleak old aged home on the outskirts of Petah Tikva. Rafael was a ray of light touched by many eager hands, a ray of light which flooded many women's nakedness. But Victoria knew with absolute certainty that apart from the innocent exchange of looks the two of them never touched each other until the day they died.

But when they went to bed on that Friday night she turned her back on Rafael and laid her head on her arm folded on the pillow, and stared at the still wall with the shadows from the wall of windows frozen on it. Up to now they had had a number of quarrels. And more than once he had raised his hand in threat. But in bed he was always gentle and considerate. Now he slowly lifted her nightgown to light a fire in her loins. Her body did not respond. And then he sent his "goodwill ambassador" between her thighs. This was a name he had picked up in the Arabic press, of which he was a keen reader at the time. And his member bore this imposing title proudly for many years of distinguished service, until when he was eighty-six years old it finally gave up the ghost, to his bitter lamentations. But on that distant Friday night Victoria was immune to the blandishments of the ambassador, and in the end it was obliged to admit defeat and lay between them disgraced, like the envoy of a vanquished power.

Now Rafael opened his mouth and said: "What do you want, it's fate. I grew up without a father. Your mother hates me, and your father picks on me as if he was Pharaoh and I was Moses contesting his crown. Yehuda and Aziza were like a father and mother to me. In Basra we ate our fingers with hunger. When we finished a meal we didn't know where the next piece of bread was coming from. And suddenly a special messenger arrives from them: Will Rafael, who hasn't got a shirt to his back or a roof over his head, will this pauper Rafael be so kind as to marry the apple of our eye and be our son-in-law and receive a dowry of three hundred gold coins? For one gold coin I would have been ready to wash the filthy arses in all the public baths in Basra. And where were you? Why did your mother and father keep quiet? I admit, I replied at once. With part of the money the messenger gave me I ordered a ring and I sent it with another messenger. But my messenger either got lost on the way or cheated me. God decided that Rafael would be Victoria's."

It wasn't his speech which caused her to open her gates so enthusiastically. It was the shrinking goodwill ambassador which aroused her passion. On the summer nights on the roof there was no escaping the sounds of tearing and brutal conquest by the men, the whimpers of pain and mutters of protest from the women. She had been sure that a full measure of violence awaited her at the hands of the husband she was so in awe of. And he was sometimes violent with his parents, his brothers, and with her too. But in the heat of his passion he was a cooing dove, a gentle shower, a ripple of silk, a whispering breeze, a glowing fire on a frosty night, an enchanted horizon beyond the daily grind. On that night she went more than halfway to meet him. With the tip of her finger she revived the shamefaced ambassador, and Rafael, with all his experience in the pleasures of the flesh, was astounded at the wantonness which could lie buried in chaste and modest souls. And as he plunged to the depths and soared to the heights he said to himself that he had found his heart's desire. This was the oasis he had longed for in his wanderings. A competent woman, an exemplary mother, a loyal wife, and a saucy lover. In his heart he almost vowed to be faithful to her for ever.

On Sunday Yehuda had one of his good days. He got up and washed himself, strapped on phylacteries and prayed, as energetically as a man in the best of health. The pains disappeared and the oxygen streamed into his blood, until it seemed to him that he still had plenty of good years ahead of him. He announced that he was going to the factory, and when Izuri and Aziza tried to stop him he put his hand on his heart and smiled at his brother and said: "I feel as if a holiday's been declared here inside me. I haven't been to the factory for a long time, I'm ready for a bit of work."

"God's helping us. We've already begun to return the loan to Rafael. Stay at home. Rest. There was frost last night and there's an icy wind outside."

"Izuri, let me leave."

"Listen to your brother," begged Aziza. "Stay home a few more days."

"I thought of going from the factory to Abdallah Nunu's

doctor. You remember how he nearly died last year and the doctor put him back on his feet. They say . . ." With the words still in his mouth he noticed the silence that had fallen on the courtyard, and saw Toya emerging from the sacks covering the entrance to her room, hesitating, and then crossing the courtyard on tiptoe, averting her eyes from his. He saw his son-in-law the blacksmith make for the outer door without looking at anyone. "Izuri," he whispered fearfully, "you're hiding a catastrophe from me."

From the depths of the arcade Najia's voice rang out triumphantly: "Father of our children, Fuad's first tooth has come out!"

Izuri pulled a face. He could hardly hide the revulsion he felt at the sight of his son. His lips were so dark, they always reminded him against his will of the dead Baruch's fair face. "Abdallah Nunu is dying," he said to his brother.

"You buried him last year too. He'll live."

"This time it's final. Perhaps he's already dead. His son's besieging the door, begging anyone who comes out for news."

Yehuda's lips turned white. He and Abdallah Nunu were both cursed by the same curse. They had both tried to cheat death with false teeth, with charms from Juri Chittaiyat. Perhaps the Angel of Death was summoning them even now to a meeting. Izuri and Aziza helped him back to his bench.

Murad, who was already married, came out of his room and stood before his father. He had already acquired the art of bookbinding, and now he was no longer dressed like a salesman but like a worker. Sliding down the stairs from the roof came Nissan, Victoria's younger brother. He was as fat as Miriam, and as spiteful as his mother. "Abdallah Nunu's kicked the bucket!" he cheered. "Nuna's tearing her hair out, and Ma'atuk's banging on the door! It's a madhouse!"

Izuri looked from Murad's fallen face to Nissan's excited grin, and then at Najia offering her other breast to Fuad's greedy lips. Victoria looked down on the courtyard from the second storey. In spite of the lines of defeat etched on her father's face, he still maintained his position as ruler of the courtyard. After Izuri and Murad left for work, she came down with Kilmanteen to visit Miriam. When Nuna's scream split the air Miriam shuddered convulsively. God, how terrifying it is to be so happy, said Victoria to herself and stroked Miriam's hair.

The Nunus' house was wide open. Jamila dropped in to make a preliminary tour of the premises and check out the best place to stage her performance. Abdallah was worth a fortune, and her hopes rocketed sky-high. On the threshold Ma'atuk Nunu covered his face with his six fingers, as if to wipe away the weariness of standing watch all night long. In silence he watched the undertakers from the Burial Society bringing the coffin, and then he went back to measuring the narrow space between the alley walls with his eyes, his hands crossed behind his back, underneath his hump. When Victoria came out of the house their eyes met. This time there was no melancholy in his eyes, only an obscure passion, which made Victoria so uncomfortable that she blushed and turned her head away. His father had only just died, and already he was planning his revenge, and at the same time sending lustful looks in her direction. She walked past him into his father's house. Nuna's three sons were already boys, alike as three fronds growing on one palm tree. The palms of Nuna's hands were painted with henna as usual, her eyebrows were plucked. Yesterday's make-up, which she had forgotten to remove from her eyes, emphasized today's grief. She had already taken off her diamonds and gold bracelets, and she stood at the door of the room where the undertakers from the Burial Society were purifying her father's body and choked on her tears. She was so beautiful, and her suffering touched Victoria's heart. The inhabitants of the alley forgave everything and offered their condolences. Toya pushed her fist into her mouth as the undertakers carried out the coffin and stood it in the courtyard, where they waited for the relatives and neighbours to gather for the funeral procession. Nuna shrieked as her brother crossed the threshold for the first time since he and his mother were banished from the house. He was bowed down under the weight of his crooked back. He walked deliberately to the coffin and announced in a voice hoarse with cigarette smoke and exhaustion: "There won't be any funeral." And he twisted his neck and looked up at the clear, empty sky and went on: "He'll stay here in the sun until he stinks and the worms eat him."

Chills ran down the spines of his audience. "Dirty dog." His aunt Hannah, whose epileptic son was cowering in the corner of the courtyard, rushed at him. "Hunch-backed bastard!"

The three palm fronds who had been cherished and pampered all their lives were at a loss. They fixed their eyes on the silent coffin, as if they hoped against hope that Abdallah would burst out of his wooden prison and teach their uncle a lesson.

The eldest of the undertakers, a hopeless drunk in his leisure hours, rebuked Ma'atuk: "Jew, what you're saying is against the law."

"Go home," said the hoarse, monotonous voice. "The carcass will rot here. There'll be no funeral."

Hannah went berserk. She rushed over to her son Elias and shook him by the shoulders until he stopped trembling and then she dragged him to the coffin and spat at Ma'atuk. "My brother was right. You're a monster."

"My father's dead," the monotonous voice reminded her, "and from now on I never want to see you in this house again. Get out at once."

She fell silent. His hands were still clasped behind his back. The fear stole into her heart that he was hiding a weapon behind his back and that he might use it. She opened her mouth to make a crushing retort and shut it again. In the end she turned to the coffin and addressed it instead: "You see? You hear?"

For some reason it seemed that Abdallah was smiling behind the pale wood. The bizarre situation probably amused him. Jamila's wailers considered an honourable retreat. Even if they tore their breasts to pieces and pulled out all their hair nobody would pay any attention to them now. And who would pay for their wailing, for their blood and their sweat? The distraught Nuna, the murderous sister, or maybe Ma'atuk, on whom death had bestowed such an advantage?

After a while they sent for Izuri. "My son," said Izuri and

touched Ma'atuk's shoulder. "There are duties we owe to God, and duties we owe to the living and duties we owe to the dead, and you are transgressing against them all."

Ma'atuk was stunned. No man had ever called him "my son" before. Because of his hump he had been seen as a kind of old man even when he was a child. Due to the respect he felt for Michal's son, Victoria's father, he took a step backwards and spoke with his eyes on the ground. "Now he's in the hands of God, answering for the nights of pain and shame he caused my mother. What's lying in front of us here is nothing but flesh rotten with guzzling, Abu Murad, and as for the duties we owe the living, my dear neighbour, I've already spoken to a lawyer and he's probably on his way to the police right now."

His Aunt Hannah leapt into the air and slapped herself in the face. A groan of horror ran through the crowd. Izuri's eyebrows shot up. "Would a Jew incite the police of the goys against his fellow Jews?"

"The charge, Abu Murad, is against a corpse, which no judge could possibly put in prison. The police will search the house and examine the double books where he kept his accounts. I don't know how much money he left behind him." And he fixed his eyes accusingly on his aunt and said no more.

"May your name and memory be blotted out, hater of Israel," said the aunt, breathing heavily. "Abdallah, do you hear him?"

The hunchback looked at the coffin and a murmur of expectation ran through the crowd. Even Hannah, whose question had been rhetorical, was alarmed at herself. Like all the members of her generation she believed that inanimate objects were inhabited by spirits, that demons ran about under the ground, that at night the dead came out of their graves to play tricks on the living or to bemoan their fate. Nuna Nunu shuddered in horror: what if the dead man really came back to life? She would have to submit to a man who had been a corpse, who had already been ritually purified and wrapped in a shroud.

Ma'atuk was ready to face his maker at that very moment, if need be, and the idea of meeting the father whose mocking smile had already been wiped off his face held no fears for him.

He stepped up to the coffin and pounded on the lid. Jamila, who was experienced in magic and witchcraft, shouted: "Pregnant women outside!" But everybody stood rooted to the spot, and not a single woman moved, even though the thumping sounded as if it was coming from inside the coffin. And as if borne down by the weight of his hump, Ma'atuk knelt beside the coffin and said in his hoarse voice: "Nuna, listen to me. It's God's questions he's answering now, and so he has to tell the truth. Would you like everybody here to hear his confessions, my dear sister? Nuna, half of everything. And I mean everything. Fifty-fifty."

The crowd was spellbound. The sophisticated saw themselves as spectators at a riveting play. The naive saw themselves as witnesses at a just trial. Both felt respect for the hunchback now. Both considered his words to be reasonable. Victoria saw that even her father appeared to have forgotten himself and he was nodding his head gravely. White bubbles escaped from Hannah's gaping mouth. "He's a leper, don't listen to him."

Nuna took no notice of her. "The books are in the basement," she whispered, "under the firewood. His bookkeeper's name is Menashe Karkukli and he'll do whatever you ask."

"Ah," said Ma'atuk and rose to his feet. "So our father used a crook to cook his books. Nuna my sister, from now on we won't need Menashe Karkukli or Aunt Hannah either. Trust me. Everything will be divided equally." And with the six fingers of his left hand he motioned the undertakers to set out on the funeral procession. He himself walked at the head, after the coffin. The cantor sang psalms and Jamila began to set the stage for herself and her assistant wailers again. The dense knot of people unravelled into a winding thread as the cortège made its way along the alley. Victoria's eyes were full of tears, but her heart was glad. "He got what he deserved," she said to herself, and she didn't know which of the two she meant: the dead man who had been disgraced or the hunchback who had come into a fortune.

Nissan tugged at his father's sleeve. "Father, Auntie Aziza says you mustn't go to the cemetery. Uncle Yehuda . . ."

"What happened?"

"It's like . . . He's making a loud snoring noise and Auntie Aziza . . ."

The giant looked at the plump, inarticulate boy. He remembered Rafael at his age. Ezra was getting an education from the Frenchmen in Beirut. His son Murad stood at his side, and his shadow on the ground looked to him like a dull, dirty puddle. The funeral procession passed on, and Victoria followed her father and brothers home with Kilmanteen in her arms. Rabbi Juri Chittaiyat was already standing next to the bench with his hand on the sick man's brow, his lips muttering ceaselessly and his eyes closed, but from the expression on his face it was evident that he himself did not have too much faith in the efficacy of his prayers.

Yehuda did not die that day. The next day an outlandishly unfamiliar figure appeared in the courtyard—the doctor. His gleaming bald head made an impression on everybody. His gold pince-nez were a startling innovation. It was the first time in their lives that they had ever smelled shaving-lotion on a man. His lowered voice, too, his "hmms" and "mmms", aroused their awed respect. It was Rafael who had brought this medical man in his elegant suit and imposing pith helmet to the courtyard. The men stood in the first row, the women behind them, with the children crowding in the rear and at the sides, and they all held their breath as the doctor bent over and opened his black bag. When he pressed his stethoscope to Yehuda's chest and bent down to hear, the audience stiffened in suspense, and waited for the words of wisdom that would no doubt follow this mysterious transaction between the healer and the patient. But they were bitterly disappointed. A little note was handed to Rafael and that was all, without any interpretations, and not a single word of encouragement, the absolute opposite of the treatments favoured by Rabbi Juri Chittaiyat, who believed that words had it in their power to overcome diseases. The doctor rose from the stool and waved away the men and women crowding around him, as if he were shooing chickens from his path. Then he skipped between crawling infants, jumped over puddles and left the courtyard with Rafael, abandoning his patient in a state of heavy depression without even the consolation of a warm, human touch. But Victoria's heart swelled with pride. It was obvious that the doctor regarded only Rafael as his equal. He took her husband by the elbow as they went out of the courtyard entrance, and from the alley she heard his quiet voice talking to Rafael.

From her bed inside the room Miriam called out: "What's happening? What did the doctor do? Is Father feeling better now? What potion did the doctor give him?"

Gurji remembered the peace-offering he had brought his wife and hurried to her side with the big kerchief wrapped around six bananas, four red Isfahan apples and a few handfuls of sweets.

Despair stared from Yehuda's eyes. The visit had been difficult for him. As long as the doctor was there he had felt as if he were in the hands of a machine which although there was no telling what it was going to do to him, nevertheless gave him a sense of security with its silent efficiency. But now that he was gone all he had left was the evil omen: to the charms and false teeth with which he and Abdallah Nunu had attempted to cheat death there was now added the visit from a doctor who had studied in England, making the resemblance between himself and the dead man complete. The sunlight had already retreated behind the roof, the gloom was beginning to creep in from the corners, and he was very afraid of the dark. At his request they helped him to sit up and leant him against a pile of cushions, and all the time he kept his eyes fixed on the light of the lamps. "Come and sit down beside me, my brother," he said. Izuri sat down on the stool which had been vacated by the doctor.

"That's it," said Yehuda and tried to be brave. "I'm going. The factory is in your hands, Izuri, and you'll look after my wife and son . . ." Fear overcame him and pushed his wife and son aside. "I'm so frightened, brother."

The presence of death poured fire into Rafael's veins that night. Victoria was inhibited but his passion was infectious and she allowed him to gallop to his heart's desire over and over again, trying her best not to whinney with him. When he calmed down she smoothed her hand over his face to wipe away the sweat, like she did with Kilmanteen when she was breast-feeding her. His skin was dry and pleasant to the touch, as always. Even in the heat of the Israeli sun and the stifling closeness of the tent in the transit camp many years later, his face hardly perspired. Only in his last moments the sweat poured out of him, and she was there, her calloused hand ready to sorrowfully wipe away the sweat and the fear.

On that night in the courtyard he couldn't fall asleep. After his body was satiated, he crossed his hands under his head and gazed at the moonlight dappling the windowpane room. "Yehuda is dearer to me than my own father," he said and coughed.

Victoria laughed. "You're Yehuda's son, and they say that Miriam is my father's daughter. I wonder whose daughter I am."

"You're your father's daughter, you love passionately and hate passionately."

"I hate?" She was astonished.

"Wait. You haven't had a chance yet. You're not forgiving like Miriam."

"You'd prefer me to be like Miriam."

"Miriam's Miriam, and Victoria, I'm happy to say, is Victoria."

Her nipples stiffened against her will. She pressed her thighs together to stop the shameless quivering. Talk, talk to him, she said to herself in order to distract herself. "Your brother Asher came when you went out with the doctor to buy the medicines. He saw the commotion in the courtyard and he got a terrible fright. I fed him."

"What did he want?"

"A little help. He's found himself a bride. A girl with a pauper's dowry. I think he's in love with her. He kept on saying that she was a rose."

He coughed again. "He should have come to the shop."

"I don't mind if you help your family. When my father appealed to you you weren't stingy."

Rafael bent over her face and kissed her eyes, and she soared sky-high. And that quiver again. He lit a cigarette and coughed and cleared his throat.

When he was still a boy he used to clear his throat too, with a clear, delicate sound like the last note of a yearning love song. At night, in the darkness of the alley, he would clear his throat until his mother or one of his sisters woke up and opened the door. Miriam would lie awake listening for that sound, and sometimes she would get there before them. Victoria would stiffen with anticipation and suspense at the sound, but she never dared to get up and open the door for him. But from the day she married him it was her role and hers alone to respond to his signal. Sometimes, especially at twilight, when the remains of the dying light shrouded the courtyard, Victoria would see the shadow of a mute longing in Miriam's eyes.

Rafael's voice was steeped in memories. "I never wanted to be rich for myself. Life's too short to waste on money. But still I always had a dream. I would see the ashes of the cooking fire in my mother's hair . . . You know that we used to steal firewood from you? Because of the hunger my brothers did things I'm ashamed to tell you about."

"So it was your mother, not Aziza, who stole my mother's gold from the walls."

"That's not all. In the winter frost we would be blue with cold. My mother would steal clothes from your washing lines and dye them for us in secret. Dye them and cry. I swore that one day I would buy her a tiara fit for a queen."

"It really is beautiful, the one you bought her."

The cough ran down his body like a wave. Victoria was surprised. Like her father, Rafael was wonderfully in control of his body. Other men were not ashamed to sob. Sometimes they extorted pity with their moaning and groaning. But her father and her husband hid their wounds. Perhaps it was for this reason that Rafael's cough seemed to her to be stronger than he was.

"You've caught cold," she said, "because of the way you ran to Miriam on Friday night straight from the tub into the rain."

He lit another cigarette. "It's older than that."

"You have a fever."

He laughed. "Because your arse is driving me mad. Thank the Lord for creating the female arse to give a man's hands something to take hold of."

"Don't take God's name in vain," she protested, but the itch between her legs was already out of control. She was waiting for his fingers. In the moonlight she saw his eyes gleaming, and she moved so that her back was resting on the mattress and waited for him. His body was so warm in the white light. She closed her eyes, she felt the need to explain and apologize for the tempest sweeping her away. This time Rafael did not carry her to the heights. There was a kind of hesitancy in his body. And then a decision: "I think I should go down and see how Uncle Yehuda is."

The tempest swallowed itself. She forgave him for making excuses. "Aunt Aziza is looking after him and I think you should sleep."

The next coughing fit took him by surprise, his body convulsed, his knees touching his stomach, and the bed beneath them creaked.

"You're ill."

"Nonsense."

He poured water from the jar next to the bed and drank. His eyes were open and far-away as he pinched her thigh. His voice was faint. Victoria stayed awake until his fingers slipped and his eyes closed.

Yehuda's recovery the next morning boosted the reputation of modern medicine in the courtyard. Thanks to a few clear drops and a few pills Yehuda sat up, his feet groped for his slippers, and he succeeded in standing up by himself before Aziza noticed and hurried to his side. They both smiled proudly as he took a few tottering steps in the arcade, breathing easily. The iron fist which had gripped his chest had disappeared, and hope sprang up in its place. "I've been reborn, I'm alive!" he cried. Aziza spat in four directions and made haste to sprinkle salt against the Evil Eye. Yehuda sent Izuri to work with the joking remark that if he didn't hurry he would go and open the factory himself. At midday he announced that he wanted to go and pay his respects to the Nunu family. The women remaining in the house could not dissuade him. Aziza and Victoria accompanied him, both in order to support him and in order to satisfy their curiosity about what was going on in their neighbours' house. Miriam stayed behind with the two babies, bemoaning the cruel fate that had laid her low just when something so interesting was happening next door.

As the visitors entered the courtyard they were startled to see Ma'atuk lying at his ease on the central mattress, as complacent and at home as if he had never been banished from his father's house. His shop, which now seemed very wretched and ridiculous, was closed as a sign of mourning, and his wife and children had already been installed in the big house. Nuna had accepted the situation gracefully after the initial shock, and she even seemed pleased that another man had appeared to take over the running of her life. Victoria examined the exquisite beauty whose face was now unpainted. She was about thirty years old, almost ten years older than Victoria, but she refused to grow up. A Kurdish maid bent over her and said in a sweet, wheedling voice, as if her mistress was five years old: "Nuna, my eyes, you must drink hot tea. It's very cold today."

Nuna nodded her head. "Yes, you're right, it's really icy today, I should have something hot to drink." She did not snigger at the sight of her brother's six fingers, or recoil from his hump. She looked up at him as if he were her father, her husband, her new lord and master. "Bring some for Ma'atuk too," she whispered into the servant's ear. The Kurdish woman smiled a servile smile. Abdallah, who had made a fortune in the cattle trade, had trained the people about him to act like animals. The few he did not succeed in taming he had sent away. Victoria saw that the faces of Nuna's sons were stupid too, even though their beauty pierced her heart.

Hannah and her invalid son had disappeared. They had been banished in the dead of night, never to return. Ma'atuk Nunu, who had not yet adopted the airs and graces appropriate to his new position, scrambled to his feet when he saw Yehuda in the doorway. Obsequious and ingratiating, like a poor, penniless grocer, he led the important guest to a padded wicker armchair.

Victoria and Aziza did not disguise their astonishment when Toya emerged from the kitchen behind the Kurdish maid with the tea, and offered the guests peeled apples and bagels as if she were a daughter of the house. She was wearing a velvet dress from Nuna's wardrobe, precious earrings twinkled on her ears, and her whole appearance radiated an air of triumphant well-being, as if she was where she wanted to be at last. She almost bowed down worshipfully to Nuna. Laying the tray with the refreshments at her feet, she gazed at the beautiful face and smiled admiringly. The black silk purse swayed like a pendulum on her pure breast as she knelt and stroked the toes of Nuna's little feet. The two of them barely suppressed their gleeful peals of laughter. It transpired that Dahood had been out working with his band, and Toya had spent the night at the neighbours' house.

Yehuda saw none of this. Delighted to be there, the dying man who had come back to life sat in his armchair and tried to engage the ignorant grocer in learned conversation. Aziza felt no resentment at the sight of Toya's enjoyment, she herself would have been happy to help their neighbours with the refreshments if not for Miriam lying at home with her broken leg and the two babies to look after. She hinted to Yehuda that this was not the time for Talmudic subtleties, and rose to her feet. Outside Yehuda flourished his cane and announced with a smile: "Tomorrow Izuri won't be able to stop me from going to the factory."

They found Miriam lying on her father's bench in the arcade and sticking her tongue out at Najia. She had dragged herself on her backside with Naim and Kilmanteen from the dark room to the sunlit arcade. Najia had picked a quarrel with her and accused her of being a liar like her mother, and claiming that her leg was broken simply in order to make that poor blacksmith crawl: "Sweets, bananas! What next? Can't a husband teach his wife a lesson any more? What's the world coming to?"

"Why not?" smiled Miriam. "Even if Izuri broke your back you wouldn't get a shrivelled-up raisin out of him. That's what's eating you, aunt. Ask Victoria, go on, ask her."

"What can she tell me? The silly fool's laughing now because of the heat that's warming her. She doesn't know yet what kind of a frying pan she's fallen into. Let her wait until the oil starts boiling."

"If only every daughter of Israel had a frying pan like hers. Right, Victoria?"

Victoria didn't know if Miriam was laughing or crying.

Aziza came to the defence of the blacksmith. "And what's wrong with your Gurji? He's got a pair of shoulders on him like Samson himself, touch wood."

"So all that's missing is for someone to gouge out his eyes," said Miriam.

"May your tongue shrivel up," said Aziza in horror. "How can you talk like that about your husband?"

"Mother, he broke my leg and at night he wanted . . . he wanted . . ."

Victoria didn't know where to hide her face, as if she herself were lying on the bench and pouring out the pain of her life. "I'm going up to bathe Kilmanteen."

"Victoria," sobbed Miriam, "may I die this minute if I've got a grudge against you. It's fate."

"That's what Rafael said, too."

Miriam was moved. "Really? Is that what he said?"

Victoria kept quiet. In vain she sought for some glib, light-hearted word to conclude the painful conversation. Like her father, she had no talent for joking.

"Wait. Don't go up. There are two bananas left. One for you and me and one for my mother and father."

Najia pushed her nipple sullenly into the swarthy Fuad's mouth, and racked her brains to remember when she had last tasted a banana. Perhaps when she was a little girl, when her brother Sabah, God rest his soul, had hidden the red kerchief behind his back and smiled and said: "Guess what I brought you." And ever since then nobody had wanted to brighten her eyes with the light of anticipation. And now nobody paid any attention to her prophecies. With a mouth full of saliva she saw Yehuda's transparent fingers peeling the banana until it looked like a yellow flower, and holding it out to Aziza, who broke off half and put it in her mouth, while her face melted in delight. Najia's eyes returned to the banana peel dangling over Yehuda's fingers. And so she was the first to realize the significance of the muffled clatter which echoed dully in the courtyard. Miriam stared at the floor as Victoria and Aziza bent down to pick up the lower set of dentures which had dropped out of Yehuda's mouth. For a moment the women sitting in the arcade couldn't understand why Najia was shouting: "Yehuda's dead!"

15

The rain stopped. After crossing the familiar al-Hanuni market, already deserted in the darkness, she took off her veils. A light breeze washed over her face. After a few minutes she reached the alley of her father's house. Sadly she remembered how jubilantly she had left it only a year ago. Rafael had stood in the middle of the courtyard supervising the three porters headed by one-eyed Kaduri. The furniture was moved to a spacious two-roomed apartment in a strange but well kept-up house. With every chair and bundle of clothing they took out of the glassed-in room, she felt as if the bonds which had tied her there for too long were being sundered. Now she was sailing off with Rafael to a different landscape, a new era. Her shoulders would no longer rub against her mother's in the narrow kitchen. From time to time she would visit her father's house bearing gifts. And they too would come to visit her, the guests of a woman whose husband was universally admired. That morning her father left in a hurry without saying a word, as if to avoid the parting from her. From the day Yehuda died he had become more pious, even though he did not give up his modern attire and other secular ways. That morning he rose early and strapped on his phylacteries and ate a hurried breakfast in silence. He regarded their move to another house as an act of betrayal: she was abandoning him to a widowed sister-in-law who had stopped smiling, an embittered wife and a flock of children who brought him no joy. Victoria had hoped for a fond parting and a kind word. However, she comforted herself with the thought that someday soon he would forgive her and come to visit her. But until the day he died, forty years later, he never set foot in any house she lived in, and he even refused to visit her in the miserable tent in the transit camp in Israel.

On that morning she stood in the courtyard, Kilmanteen on her hip and Suzanne in her arms, dimly expecting some sort of ceremony to mark her parting from the house where her grandmother, her father and uncles, her husband, herself and her two daughters had been born. It hurt her that everybody behaved as if it was just another ordinary day. Miriam roped in her husband and another couple of men and made haste to move her furniture into the window-room. Aziza, who was very hard of hearing now, was moved into Miriam's cramped room. Ezra, who had married and bought a pharmacy in al-Rashid street, the main street of the town, had disappeared from the courtyard long ago. The black silk purse had dropped from Toya's neck, and Dahood was up to his old tricks again.

Najia disappeared into the kitchen in order not to see her daughter's happiness. It was early in the morning, the meat had not yet been brought from the market, and she sat idle in the dark kitchen and scratched herself. Victoria looked silently at the eroded walls, and suppressed a strange urge to go up to one of the cracks and poke her fingers in it and find a gold coin and display it to her mother. When the work was done Rafael swept his arm round the courtyard and called out in his clear voice: "Goodbye and good health to you all!"

Nobody came out to say goodbye, but faceless voices replied through the walls and doors. To Victoria it seemed that the house itself was bidding them farewell, and for some reason this pleased her. For a moment she looked into her little brother Fuad's eyes as he stood there staring at them with a bewildered air, and then she walked wordlessly out of her old home.

In the new house they were met by her sister-in-law Flora, the woman Asher had married for true love and with the help of Rafael's money, a short, energetic young woman, buxom and full-bodied. Grateful for Rafael's generosity she immediately offered her help. Miriam had warned her against her sister-in-law's enthusiasm, but Victoria thought that it was Asher who was prompting his wife to dance attendance on his brother and keep in his good books, until he could stand on his own feet and establish a business of his own. The two rooms were on the second floor of a house where five more families lived. Flora showed the porters where to put the children's beds and where to put the wardrobe. Her bum bounced on the double bed to test the springs, and she and one-eyed Kaduri burst out laughing. She was a high-spirited, laughter-loving woman in a community which regarded hilarity with contempt. People said behind her back that she drank in secret, in male company. Victoria preferred not to listen to the gossip. The black gaps between Kaduri's rotten teeth were exposed when he laughed and his brown eye winked as if to encourage the white eye to join in the laughter. The laughter was foolish, but Kaduri himself was far from foolish, and it was this which made the spectacle so repulsive. Now Victoria saw that her sister-in-law was indeed drunk. Her face burned as if she herself was an accomplice in the disgraceful deed—to lead this poor stinking old man on and make fun of him purely for the pleasure of it. Rafael sent the candied-turnip seller and occasional porter away with no more ado. "Flora," he said curtly, with his eyes flashing behind his spectacles, "go downstairs and wash your face at the tap."

"What about my powder and lipstick?" she said with arch defiance.

"Bugger off."

She immediately resumed the role of a little woman who had tripped up on heels that were too high for her. She crumpled her silk *abbaya* in her lap like a rag, her eyes dimmed and her voice choked. "I cooked lamb with mint and garlic for you. I put it in a new pot I bought specially for you as a gift. There's red rice boiling too on a low flame," she said without moving from her place.

Rafael took her by the hands and led her out to the gallery overlooking the courtyard, rubbed his hands together as if dusting them off, and said: "In my house you don't behave like a whore."

She nodded her head, said: "Yes, yes, yes," and went downstairs smiling faintly and tapping her heels. Victoria tried to hide her jealousy, just as she tried to hide her bitterness thirty years later, when her sister-in-law turned her home in the north of Natanya into a thriving gambling den, while she and her family were wallowing in the misery of the immigrant transit camp. But on that day, in the middle of the nineteen twenties, Victoria saw herself as a lady standing by the side of a man whose star was rising, while the wretched Flora retreated to the dank room below where Asher lay in bed doing nothing.

Her jealousy grew a few months later when she heard Rafael's angry cry from the next room: "Not here, not now!"

For a long time Flora urged her to let her teach her the art of make-up. "I wish I had your body, your beautiful neck and hair. What's the crime if you add a little shadow to your eyes and a shine to your lips? Make-up is an art you should acquire if you want to keep your man. What's the difference between your mother and, begging your pardon, someone like Rahma Afsa? Your mother dresses for your father as if she's in perpetual mourning, and Rahma Afsa wears holiday clothes every day of the week. That's what men like, a holiday in the middle of the week."

On the day that Rafael's second brother, Yehezkel, was to be married, Victoria yielded to Flora's blandishments and allowed herself to be led into an expensive haberdashery shop next to Arrozdibek, where she bought a pretty box of powder, a scented lipstick in a refined shade, and black khol, which reminded her of the sooty kitchen ceiling in her father's house. She was carried away by Flora's exhilaration and by the effeminate behaviour of the owner of the shop. The bright colours captivated her, and also the reckless impudence of her sister-in-law, who offered to sew the smoothly shaven and slightly rouged proprietor a black tunic decorated with pink lace. Victoria, accustomed to men who took pride in appearing tough, was amused to see the delighted smile spreading over his face at this suggestion. In exchange he offered to fit her out personally, on the spot, with a pair of gorgeous silk panties which had just arrived from Paris. Flora licked her lips and retorted that she had no need of half a man to teach her how to put on panties and take them off. And by this time Victoria's head was in such a spin that in addition to the cosmetics she bought a soft leather handbag, silk stockings, a vial of perfume, and a couple of petticoats described by Flora as "whorish", and was even tempted by a saucy hat with a veil which was "out of this world". When she heard the sum total of all her purchases, she pushed the luxuries heaped on the glass counter away in alarm. "No, no, it's a fortune."

"Go on, buy it," Flora coaxed her. "Your husband will be happy to have a woman and not a washerwoman. I'll cut off my hand if he doesn't lick you when he sees you with all that on you."

Victoria would have far preferred to be joking with the simple Miriam than with this worldly woman. If Miriam had been there she would have replied that Rafael licked her without whorish petticoats too. But then she thought that she wouldn't have said any such thing to Miriam. The truth was that from the day she married Rafael she and Miriam had stopped joking together. She had seen very little of her cousin lately. Miriam was immersed in her gluttony and the gloom of Gurji's daily routine. Yehuda's death had affected his son-in-law profoundly. His heart was set on abandoning the smithy and devoting himself to the study of the Torah. Miriam was beside herself. "Isn't it enough that my mother's living on Izuri's charity? To be a rabbi! You've got the soul of a beggar. Look around you and see the fortunes men are making. A rabbi! You're not going to sentence me to a life of poverty."

"Take it, take it," smiled Flora.

The parcel was wrapped and the shop owner changed his coquettish simper for the smile of a polite tradesman waiting for his money. Outside Flora opened her bag and extracted two pairs of panties. "The black ones," she explained with mischievous frankness, "are my commission on your purchases, and the yellow ones I pinched just for the fun of it. In any case that poor creature's not going to have any offspring to leave his money to.

Wait for me this evening. I'll come and make you up before Yehezkel's wedding party."

Now she had just finished washing in the one room when she heard Rafael's angry cry from the other: "Not here, not now!" She was already standing in front of the mirror and waiting for Flora, the cosmetics in her hand. When she opened the door between the two rooms she wanted to close her eyes at once. The two of them were locked together in the hatred which springs only from love. Little Flora had shrunk even further, and the expression on Rafael's face was one of disgust. They didn't see her. Flora was hanging round Rafael's neck and now she slid down, her fingernails tearing his shirt and his skin, leaving tracks of blood on his chest. In her horror at the sight of the blood Victoria cried out, and the two of them turned to look at her, but not before Flora, who was beside herself with rage, had punched Rafael on his bloody chest. Taking no notice of Victoria she yelled: "Not here, you bastard! Not now! All of a sudden you're a monk!"

Victoria's thoughts were in a turmoil. Why didn't her husband kick the loathsome little monster? He should have ripped the arse off the whore. And what panties was she wearing now? The black ones she had earned as her commission or the stolen yellow ones? He must have gone to bed with her already. But when? Where? And was Asher so blind? While I was sitting in the tub the bastard felt like a quick fuck . . . She took a kind of perverse pleasure in the words, which she was not accustomed to pronouncing even in her thoughts. Rafael's hand landed on the woman's cheek and Victoria came to with a start. "Get out of my sight," he whispered, fighting a moist cough which grew worse and worse until it was greater than Flora's rage, deeper than Victoria's confusion, more terrifying than the red rivers pouring down his chest—the cough of death. All three knew it, and they were paralysed. Blood, said Victoria to herself, he's coughing blood. Flora shuddered. Only a moment ago her flesh had yearned to touch the flesh of death. And Rafael said to himself that they would go on living.

After the festival of *Sukkot* they came down from the roof and went back to sleeping in their rooms. The watermelons in the market were already hollow and had long ago lost their juicy taste. In the morning Rafael would cram six handkerchiefs into the pockets of his suit. Even on the days when his eyes were glittering with fever he forced himself to go to the shop. The days were growing shorter and he would come home before sunset with all the handkerchiefs soaked in pieces of his lungs. Victoria was well aware of the dimensions of the catastrophe. Only very few people survived the disease. And she was surprised at herself for not trying to influence God. After all, she could have fasted, made vows, and performed pious good deeds. She explained it by saying to herself that Rafael himself had fed and supported his family, married his sisters and brothers, and not only contributed generously to saving young men from military service by paying ransom money to the authorities and young girls from spinsterhood by providing them with dowries, but also gone knocking on the doors of the wealthy in the street of the banks. And he was always ready to go without his own meal for even the meanest of guests. So what difference could her good deeds make? There were days when she wanted to shout like Flora, bastard, bastard, but she could not avoid acknowledging that he himself was incapable of nursing a grudge. Without losing his self-respect he found ways to her father's heart, and even though he knew that her mother hated him implacably, he responded willingly to Victoria's requests and went shopping himself for the gifts she bore her. Instead of imploring God, therefore, she protested to him as indignantly as if He were flesh and blood, and she would hurry to divert her thoughts from Him lest her bitterness turn to blasphemy.

But she worshipped Rafael as if he were God.

At first she tried to believe that she herself might vanquish this death that had descended upon her disguised in robes of red. She took care to provide Rafael with five hearty meals a day, guarded him from draughts, and was ready to sacrifice her life for his. One night when he was sleeping she bent over him and breathed in a lungful of his breath in the crazy hope that death would leave her husband alone and set his sights on her instead. Once death roared and buffeted his body like a sandstorm. His head shook on the pillow and his face turned red in the lamplight. With her fingers she wiped away the blood congealed on his lips and raised them to her mouth, about to lick death in. His eyes, flooded by his coughing, stopped her. "No!"

She got up and wet his face which refused to sweat with a cloth dipped in vinegar, and she washed his lips with rosewater. Then she laid the finely carved head on her breast and rocked it gently and sang to him as if he were a baby, trying to subdue the new wave of coughing rising and swelling in the depths of his chest. "Vixen," he murmured. "Your nipple's erect and the goodwill ambassador thinks he's been invited to a banquet. Look, feel." She drew down his pyjama pants and looked. "That's the last thing that will die in me," he boasted.

"You haven't got the strength now. You mustn't tire yourself."

Her voice grew husky. Her cheek touched his head and she slid onto her back. And he was wild and tender and she loved his fingers lighting flowers of fire in her body. Her hands stroked his back and the touch of his velvety skin maddened her.

Afterwards he said in his clear voice: "Let's sleep." But they didn't sleep. For a long time he was silent, and for some reason it seemed to her that his eyes were full of tears. She didn't dare raise herself to look. When he spoke his voice did not betray a hint of tears, it even held a mischievous note. "Imagine if you were in bed with the blacksmith now, and Miriam was getting the blood."

"You're not blood, you're Rafael."

"Miriam got the best of the bargain. Her table will always be laid. How are you going to manage when you're a widow?"

"You won't die."

"Rafael's not afraid of death."

Fear showed its face little by little.

Rafael's partner suggested renting a bigger shop in a central location in the fabric bazaar. Rafael avoided giving him an answer. In his heart he wondered what the point would be. He wouldn't be there to see the new shop bringing in profits. Ezra, whose pharmacy was flourishing, set his heart on taking a trip to Egypt. Rafael was not enticed by the urging of his friend. What would happen if a curtain of blood came down between him and the Sphinx or the belly-dancers? Acquaintances spoke of renting a summer cottage on the banks of the Tigris next summer, and he asked himself if he would last till then. When he saw the pretty faces of ten-year-old girls he said to himself that by the time they ripened his flesh would be eaten by worms. With growing rage he asked if he would smell the scents of the coming spring, if he would taste the first apricots on the feast of *Shavuoth*. The cobbler who made him new shoes boasted proudly that he would be able to wear them for years. When he crossed the bridge Rafael threw them into the river without taking them out of their white cardboard box. His elegant suits, too, would be cast into the river by Victoria, in the custom of widows grieving for their husbands. He already saw life with the eyes of a tourist passing through a beautiful but alien land. Victoria's declarations of love jarred on his ears. She would go on eating and sleeping and crying and laughing and perhaps she would even go to bed with a new husband while his memory would be wiped off the face of the earth. Victoria's buttocks and breasts ceased to whet his appetite. Making love wore him out, and sometimes angered him. He already saw himself as a shadow passing over the landscape, with others usurping his place. He had always enjoyed drinking in moderation with friends, now he poured half a bottle down his gullet of an evening, until his eyes glazed.

And another passion gripped him. His mastery of Arabic, which he had acquired by his own efforts, increased by leaps and bounds, and he became a voracious reader of the world literature which was then being translated in Cairo. Of all Victoria's rivals, the printed page was the most constant and stubborn. When he hid his face behind a book, she ceased to exist. Sometimes he would tell her about a moving passage, but he always remained behind the screen. To his astonishment, Rafael discovered that the spiritual giants of every age were, like himself, preoccupied by thoughts of death and sex. The puritanical translations emanating from Moslem Cairo called it love, but he was sure that in the original the writers had written about the honey and the gall he had tasted in the company of the nightclub singer from Damascus, about Rahma Afsa's thrilling laughter, about the blazing lust of his brother's wife, about Victoria's surging billows and dove-like cooing, about Miriam's melancholy yearning.

And about death. Even after the pious filter of the free translation the experience remained in all its sublimity. The authors knew how to write about death as if they had personally experienced it. In any case, they were very good at describing the thoughts and feelings which preceded it. And he realized that none of them believed that there was actually anything beyond the dark threshold.

And there was something else which the books gave him. He regarded himself as bold and intelligent, the finest fruit produced by the courtyard in the last two generations. It seemed to him that he knew everything and was capable of anything. And now these giants of the spirit came and taught him a lesson in humility. They spread a vast world of profundity and imagination and wisdom out before him, and he stood amazed and awed like a dweller on the plains looking for the first time upon the sublime glory of the mountain peaks. It grieved him to have discovered this humbling knowledge precisely on the brink of death. For however salutary the lesson was, it could not prepare a man for his death. Victoria did not hide her tears from him. At first her weeping pleased him, but later on it disturbed him, especially when he lay awake at night staring at the ceiling, buffeted between rage and terror. He suspected that it was herself she was weeping for, and there was a grain of truth in his suspicion. She felt as if she had been betrayed by him and God. In the society in which she grew up there was no such thing as public welfare. Women who had known affluence were utterly impoverished by widowhood. When the breadwinner died there was no bread. Children whose future had seemed assured were obliged to beg for food. Her daughters would grow up to be servants in other people's houses. And she herself would be a bitter, lonely outcast. Women would hide their riches when she passed, they would turn their backs on her, close their doors to her, afraid that she would cast the Evil Eye on them and their good fortune. Miriam, for instance, who was so jealous of her today, would she be afraid of her when Rafael died? And how would Flora greet her? Surely not with tears for the loss of her lover. And she would be forced to return to her father's house, to the mother who hated her, with two babies in her arms. She had no doubt that her mother would make her pay for every smile she had known with the detested Rafael. And she would eat the bread of charity and suffer in silence.

After lighting the seventh *Hanukka* candle he wrapped a woollen scarf around his neck, put on his heavy coat, and set his hat at a jaunty angle on his head. "It's a long time since I visited the theeayter."

That day she had baked *salona*, one of his favourite dishes, scrubbed her body in a steaming tub until it shone, and sprinkled a few magic drops behind her ears and in the cleavage between her breasts.

"It's freezing cold even inside the house. You know you mustn't catch cold."

"I'm reading a story now that takes place in Germany. A beautiful, rich young woman gets the same illness as me. You know where her devoted parents send her? To a snow-capped mountain."

"If the Germans are crazy, that doesn't mean you have to go out on an icy night. The puddles in the streets must have frozen over already."

"The doctors abroad recommend fresh air. There's a lot of oxygen outside. That's exactly what a person in my condition lacks."

Oxygen. She pulled a face. He must have picked the outlandish word up in his books. Its sound and smell disgusted her. "I suppose they serve the guests in the theeyater with that oscagyn on trays." She realized immediately that she had pronounced the word wrong. In her embarrassment she felt that the smell of her sweat had overpowered the scent of the perfume. "Go, go to your theeyater and ask the naked dancers to give you a double dish of that bloody oxygen, may the devil take it."

He glanced at the beds where the two little girls were sleeping, and went out into the dark, cold courtyard. The sound he made when he cleared his throat was as clear as in the days of his frisky youth. In this courtyard too, the outside door was bolted from inside when night fell.

"Don't keep me standing and knocking on the door until the dead wake in their graves."

She stood in front of the wardrobe mirror and wiped the lipstick off her lips. "Go already. When did you ever have to knock twice on the door?"

She pricked up her ears. She didn't want to accompany him downstairs and bolt the door behind him right away. Let him put a little distance between them first. She looked ugly to herself now, and her face would probably look twice as ugly to him if she was holding the lamp and lighting its downcast features from below. She didn't hear the scraping sound of the outside bolt being dragged shut. In the courtyard she heard the sound of hammers beating. She flew downstairs without taking a lamp, running and jumping down the stairs. The hammers were beating inside him. She pushed her head under his armpit and straightened up with him. Even as fragments of his lungs sprayed from his mouth he took care that no speck should sully his expensive jacket. He caught the blood in a handkerchief and put his hand in his pocket to draw out a clean one.

"Lean on me," she murmured.

"I haven't got the strength to go upstairs." Blood spurted as he spoke.

"I'll carry you on my back. Don't talk."

With one hand she clasped him to her back and with the other she clung to the wall and commanded her leg muscles to mount the thirteen endless steps. Rafael struggled with his coughing on her back and tried with the last vestiges of his strength not to bloody her braids. She laid him on the bed and rushed to warm a glass of milk for him, and in the meantime she went back to him and wiped his face. He had already stopped coughing and his face was burning. He noticed that her lower lip was grey, while the upper lip still bore traces of the lipstick she had not had time to wipe off. He tried to smile and say something affectionate, but the words seemed meaningless in his condition. The smell of burnt milk and a quenched, kerosene-soaked wick spread through the room. When he drank the milk he wanted to tell her to get undressed herself before she undressed him and helped him to put on his pyjamas, but he said nothing, for this too seemed senseless to him in his condition.

"In my condition." How repellent and bitter the words tasted. Among the books he devoured were some which described the coarseness of soldiers as they lay dying. They swore and cursed everything men held holy.

How he longed to curse now. How did the writers know what dying men screamed on battlefields as they gave up the ghost? Perhaps they copied from one another and the first had taken it all from his imagination? Would a writer have described him as a coarse warrior? But what did he care about all this when he was dying?

"What are you thinking about, Rafael?"

The tone of her voice maddened him. "I won't die like a dog."

"I'd give my eyes for you. You're dearer to me than my soul."

"Jamila's mutterings didn't stop the blood. One doctor prescribes fatty foods, another absolute rest. And their medicines are as much help as Juri Chittaiyat's prayers. Something in the city air is suffocating me. The owner of the shop next door, on the left . . . two weeks ago he looked fine. He laughed and said that he and I would live to bury all the healthy merchants. And now he's dead, deceased, finished, buried, gone. His wife's wearing a blue dress, his sons are growing beards."

She drew his hand towards her and kissed it.

"Don't agitate yourself, my soul."

"Don't agitate myself!" he repeated furiously. "I'm alone, Victoria, alone opposite . . ."

A chill ran up her spine. Her body felt leaden. Rafael was afraid. Rafael, who had got the better of fighting armies, who had crossed borders and come home safe and sound, who wasn't afraid of the dark or demons or murderers.

"Your crying's getting on my nerves."

"I won't cry any more," she sobbed. "Sometimes when I hang out the washing on the roof I talk to God. The days you gave me were the best days of my life, Rafael. And sometimes when I'm standing there on the roof I think the white clouds are the hem of God's robes, and I want to climb up and kiss them. He was so good to me when he returned you to me, Rafael. How can I not cry?"

"I'm not dead yet."

Her eyes clouded over. "You'll live. Neither God nor Satan will take you away from me."

"I listen with a third ear to the words the doctors don't say. I know that they themselves don't believe that I'll live more than a few months."

"Send them to hell, those doctors."

"And on the other hand I know that all consumptives don't kick the bucket."

"You'll be one of them. You'll get well. As soon as this damned winter's over. You'll see how you'll feel on Passover."

"Not here."

"Where?"

"In Lebanon. Well-known doctors have set up hospitals there that work miracles. Like in Germany, the hospitals are in the hills."

"So you'll go to Lebanon. What are you laughing at?"

"Those hospitals are for princes and millionaires."

"You've been earning well and we've saved. So we won't buy a villa in Batawin. We'll eat humble food. My needs are modest. Get rid of this curse in Lebanon and come back healthy, and then we'll start saving again. They'll look after you there, and your partner will transfer your share of the profits to us here."

"I've already made the calculations."

In spite of her innocence she felt as if a hidden hand was leading her astray, to an unknown destination, and she was silent.

"I didn't want to depress you. Our savings are a drop in the ocean. And the whole of my share in the business will only be enough for a few months."

"And how will you manage after that?" And in her heart she asked: "And what will I and the girls live on?"

"The furniture and the jewels. Everything, Victoria. After that I won't shrink from begging for charity. There are Jews everywhere in the world. They won't throw me out of the hospital. Why don't you say something? You said you'd give your eyes for me. What good are eyes to a corpse?"

"You're not a corpse."

"I suppose you'd prefer me to be buried tomorrow. Some widows get an inheritance at least. That's what you don't dare to say. And the bastard is plotting to rob you blind first, and leave you a widow afterwards. Rafael was a bastard when he lived and he'll be a bastard when he dies. That's what your mother will say to you when you go back to her destitute with our daughters. That's what you're thinking about now, and not about Rafael, for whose sake you wanted to climb up to God. You'll have to think twice before you ask her for a dish of rice. You won't be able to dream of a new dress when she herself goes round in rags. So why doesn't God do you a favour and take Rafael before you fall into your mother's vengeful hands . . ."

His prophecy came true, more grotesquely than he could have imagined. Najia grabbed hold of a frying pan and banged on the sooty side, dancing and singing like a celebrant greeting a bride on her wedding night. It was terrible to see her mimicking with clumsy movements the familiar dance. Her hand grew black as she beat the frying pan and her skinny bum skipped as she stumbled and steadied herself again. Thus Victoria with her two terrified children re-entered the courtyard of her childhood, as Najia capered to and fro and the residents clustered round. At that hour there was nobody there with the authority to order the mother to stop abusing her daughter. Miriam had gone to pay a visit, Toya escaped to her little room, and Aziza, who was almost deaf by now, was a widow who lived on Izuri's charity and tried to avoid getting into arguments with her sister-in-law.

"Why are you dropping your eyes? You won't find any gold on the floor," sang Najia. "Lift up your head. Where's that haughty nose-in-the-air? You always came here like the Sultan's wife showering your bounty on the poor. So your wandering Bedouin's left you and taken off for whorehouses far away. Sit down, daughter, sit down. You must be tired. Sit down on that chair and dazzle our eyes with the earrings and bracelets he bought you." In spite of the evening chill her face was bathed with sweat, and she wiped it with her soot-blackened hand. Kilmanteen and Suzanne saw their grandmother wearing a black mask of soot, and they started screaming. Najia gasped for breath. "Ah, ahhh, ahhhh," she groaned. "Oof, how happy your father will be when he sees you close to his bed. How miserable he was, how he suffered to see you with the Bedouin. He was always jealous of him. Ah, ah, ahhhh."

The two little girls clung to Victoria's skirts and bawled, their eyes fixed on their grandmother's black face. Victoria bent down and picked them up. There was a wretched bundle of clothes at her feet. She wondered when Miriam was coming back.

"Ah," the sooty face exulted. "I suppose you're looking for some hole to crawl into. You wouldn't want to creep in between your mother and your father. No, you've got more sense than Nuna Nunu. Over there." She pointed to the abandoned basement which had become a wood cellar and a refuge for mice and snakes.

For two months Victoria lived like a servant in her father's house. The factory had fallen on hard times, and apart from

Miriam and her blacksmith the rest of the clan went short. Izuri knew that his wife tormented Victoria. Sometimes he slipped her a coin, but he was afraid to give her an affectionate look. True, he was capable of beating his wife to a pulp, and Miriam and Aziza entreated him in secret to do so, but he knew that in his absence Najia would get her own back on Victoria and make her life a misery. In fact, he had almost stopped hitting his wife, and he would control himself with a groan of rage, in order not to give his wife a pretext for avenging herself on Victoria. But all in vain. One day Najia's fury boiled over. "Look how I'm trembling. Damn you, I dreamt that your father beat me black and blue. That criminal is killing me in my dreams because he wants to live with you."

"Am I to blame for your dreams?"

"After that I couldn't sleep a wink. My heart's still beating."

"I'll go and be a servant in strangers' houses," threatened Victoria. "I'll find myself a hovel to live in."

"Forget it. You want him to go running to you without my knowledge. You're not budging from here. You had to go and marry a dying man. Why don't they bring us news of his death already? Maybe we'll find some old man to take pity on you."

And then she caught her in the corner of the roof, next to the corrugated tin partition. "So you're vomiting now! Who got you pregnant, your father or the Bedouin? Just like your husband, to knock you up with another brat and go off to kick the bucket at the ends of the earth. Another daughter, I'll bet. He fucks and fucks and he can't produce one son. What a man you found yourself."

Victoria knocked on Jamila's door. The wailer, matchmaker and fortune-teller mixed her a powder and ordered her to take it three times a day. She also recommended taking long, hot baths and skipping with a rope like a little girl until she was exhausted. The foetus reacted with indifference to all this abuse. It was tied to her with fateful bonds. In her despair she beat her fists on her belly. In vain. Her nausea increased and at night she would run out of the basement and vomit directly into the drain in the middle of the courtyard. A few weeks before Passover an icy cold invaded the town. Victoria bathed her face in the dark with the freezing tap water and shivered all over. Her fingers were blue with cold and her ears were numb. The little girls too were coughing. Daughters were a curse. And she herself was a living proof of it. Healthy, with a head on her shoulders, but unable to go out and earn a living like a man. She ate the bread of charity and was showered with abuse. Even when Rafael was struggling with death he had still managed to marry his younger brother and support his mother. Even when he was almost dying he had gone on providing for his wife and children. They were right, those mothers who left their new-born daughters next to open doors on freezing nights. They were sparing them a lot of suffering.

"Is it a cat?" The frightened voice belonged to Miriam, who had come out onto the middle roof from the glassed-in room. On frosty nights she was too lazy to go down to the lavatory, and she would squat on the roof to pee. "God in heaven, what a fright you gave me. It's you."

"Yes," said Victoria in a dull voice. "You're pregnant, I didn't mean to frighten you." She did not mean to sound resentful, but from the day of her return to the courtyard her cousin had avoided her like the plague, as if she herself was suffering from the dreaded disease. She would carry her pots quickly from the kitchen to the window-room, before the aroma could reach Victoria and her children. Painfully she remembered the days when Rafael's abandoned family had gone hungry. It wasn't out of hard-heartedness that people had shunned them, but for fear of the Evil Eye. Victoria and her girls didn't actually go hungry. The leftovers from the food Victoria cooked for others was enough to feed them adequately.

"Excuse me." Miriam ran to pee. She had always had difficulty keeping it in. When she returned her head was outlined against the stars. "Victoria, swear to me, if you need anything . . ."

Victoria's feet were freezing in the darkness of the courtyard. "I don't need anything."

Miriam hugged her shoulders. "The cold's killing me," she said and ran inside.

That night Victoria left the basement door open. It was so cold that the little girls curled up into balls under their blankets. Victoria didn't have the heart to remove the blankets. But she herself lay exposed and breathed in the icy air, waiting for the lethal coughing to start. The air flowed freely into her lungs and its bracing cold actually made her feel better. Damn it, she grumbled. Even Rafael's breath had not infected her. She was strong and healthy, like her mother, her father, and Grandmother Michal. Sentenced to a long life. But not little Suzanne, whose coughing grew worse. She woke up, and fell asleep again. The accursed foetus too was apparently from the same sturdy stock as herself.

In the morning her father put a coin in her hand and strode off to the factory, with Murad and Nissan behind him. In the arcade Murad's young wife, Clarisse, sat and sullenly pushed the milk bottle into the resistant mouth of her baby. She was a very fair-skinned woman with a face as blank as a fish's. Suzanne's cough reverberated in the basement. Why shouldn't I ask her for a little milk, said Victoria to herself. Anyway the baby only drinks a quarter of the milk Clarisse boils for him.

"Give me back the whore money your father slipped you," demanded Najia.

Victoria's eyes were fixed on the arcade. "Leave me alone," she sighed.

"Give it back."

The baby's mouth pursed. Clarisse squeezed his cheeks to make him open his jaws. The practised baby cried with his mouth clamped shut.

"You think I'm stupid. I know why you left the basement door open last night."

Victoria couldn't believe her eyes. Clarisse put the bottle down and picked up a hand enema.

"You're inviting him to steal into your bed in the dark."

Clarisse stirred the milk in the saucepan next to her.

"On my oath you're right. He's dying to screw you."

The baby was dear to Clarisse's heart. He was the only creature alive capable of bringing a spark of life to the mask of her face. Sixty years later Victoria sat in the dim, heated room in Ramat Gan and bit into an apple from the Galilee and watched a scene from a Japanese play on the television. The actress's face, painted white, flickered on the screen. "It's Clarisse!" she cried. Rafael did not react, for he did not remember Murad's wife. On that distant morning Clarisse looked at her son with piercing eyes, but her face revealed nothing. Deliberately she screwed the white tube onto the enema.

"Get this into your head. I lie awake at night and listen even to his dreams. If he gets out of bed I'll be right behind him."

Clarisse opened the little blanket and undid the nappies, dipped the tube into the pan of milk at her side and sucked the milk into the enema, and pushed the end of the tube into the baby's rectum.

"What powder did Jamila give you? You and your father won't succeed in putting me to sleep so that he can run to you with his pants down. I don't eat from a separate plate. I put a double portion on his plate and then I eat the leftovers. I stay awake every night, and I'll go on staying awake," the exhausted Najia said emphatically.

A dreamy, satisfied expression spread over the baby's face as the warm liquid flowed into his intestines. She's insane, said Victoria to herself. Clarisse used to be the most rebellious woman in the alley. At night she would shriek and scream and bare her claws at Murad's approach. In daylight she glared at him, and he waved his arms like a soldier putting his hands up as a sign of surrender. In a world where men ruled Murad stood out like a strange traffic signal.

"Give me back the money he gave you."

"The girls are famished for a little milk and I've got nothing to dress them in."

"Then get out of my sight. I'm throwing your rags out together with your brats. From the day you returned your father hasn't looked at me, as if I murdered his mother. How much do I have to suffer because of you, how much?"

That was the day when Victoria decided to commit suicide by jumping off the bridge into the swollen river, and she wrapped herself in an *abbaya*, hid her face behind two veils and abandoned her children. In the meantime she was angry with Rafael too. He should have known that he was carrying death inside him. Why did he marry her and give her two babies, and how could he have made her pregnant again before he took all they possessed and went to a distant grave?

In the evening she returned hungry and exhausted from the bridge suspended over the raging river, from the markets and dark alleys. Walking down the alley in front of her she saw Ma'atuk Nunu, who had been trapped a few hours before between the carts galloping over the bridge. His clothes were tidy now, the *abbaya* covered his shoulders and there were no traces left of the humiliation he had endured. She slowed down to allow him to reach the entrance to his house before her. Ma'atuk Nunu had made a fortune. He had founded a company for exporting the fish of the Tigris and the Euphrates to Palestine, sold his father's cattle and mules to buy trucks for transporting wheat, bought up land in the south of the city and built apartment houses, far from the Jewish quarter. Victoria heard that he had suggested to Nuna that she emigrate to Palestine with her sons and start a new life there. In the presence of witnesses he had promised to support her in style for the rest of her life, even after she remarried. Nuna had agreed, and she was waiting for the end of the seasonal sandstorms in order to set out on her journey on the festival of *Shavuoth*.

If she had jumped into the river there would have been nothing left of her by *Shavuoth*. Without tears or undue emotion she wondered what Rafael's grave looked like. She had fallen so low that there was no real sorrow left in her for her lost love.

Ma'atuk Nunu indeed reached his house before her, but from the way he was standing she realized that he had seen her and that he was waiting for her to catch up with him. An unpleasant flush spread over her face. Had he seen her watching his humiliation on the bridge? And perhaps he had been following her because he had guessed her intention to put an end to her life? Retreat was impossible. The silk *abbaya* was already folded over her arm, and the veils were cupped in her hand. All she could do was quicken her step as a sign that she was in a hurry to reach her father's house.

"A word with you."

She stood still. Because of the hump he was obliged to twist his neck and look up at her sideways. It was a terrible effort for him to look up into her face. She towered above him. His hands were outside the *abbaya* and they moved over the wool like two combs with six teeth each. For a moment their eyes met and she saw that his eyes were beautiful, big and brown, and they held a melancholy smile. And she was ashamed, as if the moment had contained an undertaking or a promise. She conjured up Rafael's princely features, his supple body, his presence which made the air around him quiver. But the memory was like rummaging through a dead man's clothes.

"I know everything, I hear everything."

The cripple had a pleasant, melodious voice too, and it gave her an illogical feeling of security. In the continuous roar of her world crashing around her Ma'atuk's voice had the gentleness of a lullaby.

"My mother went mad when my father threw us out. Sometimes she crawled round naked and bit the wood of the bench like a stray dog. I wept with shame. Nobody understood why I didn't want to sleep on the roof in the stifling heat of the summer. Do you know that the hunger in winter is worse than the hunger in summer? I could have gone to my father and fallen at his feet and cried that I was willing to carry chamber pots in his house if only he would take us back, to stand outside Nuna's bedroom door and sing them serenades."

"I know." The desperate beggarwoman consoled the cripple who had come into a fortune.

"It's no good for you to stay at your mother's."

"I've got nowhere to go. How will I feed my children?"

"You left the house hours ago. When I went to the synagogue I saw your sister Nazima running to Rabbi Juri Chittaiyat."

"Suzanne!"

"Perhaps it's better this way."

She stared at him. Didn't he understand that she might be to blame for her daughter's death?

"Listen. I've set up a big cigarette factory. I've got dozens of women working for me. They roll the cigarette paper and glue it together and afterwards expert workers fill the rolls with tobacco. They do it at home, in their spare time. Every Thursday the rolls are counted, and my bookkeeper pays them. You won't get rich, but you'll make enough for a room in a modest house and a dish of rice. Go to the poor child. May God give you strength."

The next day the baby girl was buried. The mound of earth above her grave was very small.

16

Sixty years later three of her sons sat back in their armchairs after the lavish Passover meal and lit cigarettes. The other two brothers and their sisters protested against the poisoning of the air. The hair of the men was grey, and the necks of the women were gnarled as walnut shells. The three-bedroomed apartment with its two toilets which she had bought not long ago in Ramat Gan was much bigger than the octogenarian couple required. But this evening it was swarming with daughters-in-law and sons-in-law and grandchildren and great-grandchildren. The spring breeze brought with it the sounds of the wild animals in the nearby "Safari" park and the singing of the scrupulous who had not yet finished reading the Haggadah. Even in his venerable old age Rafael was not overly observant, and at the sight of the exhausted great-grandchildren he was ready to give up the reading after the festive meal. Every corner of the apartment was brightly lit, every globe shone with a power greater than that of all the oil lamps in her father's house put together. The windows were open, the blinds raised, and the conversation flowed in the spirit of goodwill displayed by those who have eaten their fill. Victoria suffered from high blood pressure, rheumatism plagued her joints, every vertebra in her spine played a different note of pain, and from time to time a hot flush flooded her face. Nevertheless she stood up briskly and placed a bowl of apples and pears on the table. Her eyes were still sparkling, and she didn't need glasses. One of her grandsons sat on the arm of his father's chair and described the telescope orbiting in space to search for supernovas and black holes in unimaginably remote reaches of the heavens, and spoke knowingly of distant galaxies as if they were familiar buildings at the end of the neighbourhood. Victoria paid no attention, and ignored the quantities of leftovers her daughter-in-law ruthlessly threw into the garbage can. Her eyes darted between the great-grandchildren romping round the rooms, this marvellous mix of Iraqi, Egyptian, Polish, Syrian, Dutch and Bulgarian genes. Green eyes in swarthy faces, golden curls above velvety brown eyes, north Atlantic sturdiness touching the subtlety of the Nile valley. A pair of green eyes and flaxen braids clambered onto her swollen knees, a little dress displayed ivory thighs. The little mouth brushed the quivering flesh of her arm. "It's nice and soft," chimed the bells on her knees, and her great-granddaughter buried her fragrant face in the slack muscles. With dreamy movement she raised a tiny finger to stroke the deep lines furrowing Victoria's face, and said as if summing up the stormy experience of a lifetime: "I love you." And for emphasis the golden curls nodded vigorously on Victoria's slack breasts, until her eyes filled with stinging tears. She was already older than Michal when she died. She bent down and planted a grateful kiss on the little girl's head.

"Mother, we're talking to you."

She looked up. The smiles and satisfied expressions vanished. The words flew in the air like a spray of spittle. The brightness of the light hurt her eyes. A long moment passed until she sensed that she was being called upon to account for herself to people who were settling a hard and bitter score.

"I didn't hear you," she confessed.

"We were talking about the transit camp," grumbled her youngest son, who more than all the others resembled his father. "Everyone was put through the mill in those days. And nevertheless people came out of it as teachers, professors, even generals in the army grew up in immigrant transit camps. How come none of us have a college degree?"

But they were all living in the lap of plenty and affluence. It was enough to look at the apartments they lived in. Year after year she fondled their healthy children, many of whom were outstanding students. Wordlessly she turned to the silent Albert, whose cheek was resting on his granddaughter's head, expecting him to explain to his brothers, in his usual reasonable way, the turmoil of her life. But he was silent.

"That's what you feel, that you were left behind?" she asked in bewilderment.

"And how we do," another son snapped, and blew out an angry cloud of smoke.

For four days she had slaved over the cooking, from dawn to late at night. For two weeks she had been sweeping Rafael along in her excitement, in her joyful anticipation of this family gathering. Why should they want to spoil it now because of the flooding rain and mud, the burning summer heat in the canvas huts of the transit camp forty years ago? She had never met a professor and she didn't know any generals in the IDF, but the tents of the transit camps had also nurtured a generation that populated the slums of the margins of the cities today. Drug pushers, prostitutes, thieves, murderers, jailbirds, they and their fathers before them had all received their first lessons in the transit camps. All these years she had been proud of the spotless records of her children.

"So it's my fault?"

"And how," said the son who imported ornamental fish from south-east Asia.

"How old were we?" the designer of the lampshades much in demand for fashionable salons wanted to know. "Just kids. You pushed us out into the squalid labour market between Tel Aviv and Jaffa. In the evening we were so tired we didn't even know we were missing out on our youth. Instead of going out to breathe a bit of fresh air in our spare time you forced us to grow chickens and beans round the tent."

"We had to exist, to save ourselves from hunger," she defended herself. "There was no choice."

"And did the few miserable pennies we brought home save the situation?"

"That's how the most glorious carpet begins. Thread by thread," she said and kissed the forehead of the little girl who had fallen asleep on her lap, stood up and carried her to the door of the living room, which she opened without asking for assistance, with her elbow and her knee and all the obstinacy of her eighty-five years. She laid the child on the bed and covered her, and collapsed on the bed beside her, scarcely able to restrain her tears. The galling taste which she remembered from sixty years ago returned to her mouth.

Thread by thread.

All alone she lived in the strange courtyard with Kilmanteen and the feeling that she was to blame for Suzanne's death and the knowledge that she had wanted to kill the foetus inside her and the gnawing hunger and the memory of her husband who had betrayed her and given up the ghost, and with the typhus epidemic, and with the menacing jaws of the world-wide depression which threatened to swallow up every act of charity.

Thread by thread.

One cigarette paper after the other. On a round wooden stick she would roll the thin paper and smear glue on the edges and stick a cardboard tube in one end and arrange the narrow cylinders of paper in the boxes. One box after the other. Towers of boxes. From the moment she could see the paper and the glue in the dawn light until darkness fell. Sometimes she would pop out into the courtyard to "steal" a few rays of light from the neighbours' lamps. She didn't have the heart to light her own lamp, because the kerosene cost more than the wages she earned for her work. She grew thinner but her belly swelled. She denied herself to feed Kilmanteen the food of the poor, a porridge made with date-honey and sesame seed paste. Strictly doled out. Sometimes her nostrils were assailed by the stunning smells of frying fish or roasting mutton, and she would ignore them, just as she suppressed the fire burning in her passionate dreams, just as she denied her longings for a kind word.

Sometimes her little sisters Salima and Nazima visited her and wanted to help her. They had quick, clever hands and they would surely have been a help to her, but she was afraid her mother would demand payment with interest in return. In any case she was grateful for their company and for the fact that they played with Kilmanteen. Sometimes they even slipped her a dish of rice. Her father did not show his face. He considered her a traitor for leaving his home once more.

Every day a messenger came to collect the boxes. On Thursday afternoons she would present herself in Ma'atuk Nunu's spacious office, which was situated in the big khan, next to the offices of the wealthy merchants. A safe, an accountant, a softly humming fan revolving on the ceiling, businessmen coming and going, Persian carpets absorbing the sound of their footsteps, a gigantic desk, a personal servant bringing trays full of little cups of tea and coffee, the rustle of banknotes and the aroma of the tobacco from the hookah mingling with the smell of the nearby river, the fawning of the creditors and the flattery of the brokers, the striped English suit instead of the *abbaya* and the gown. It was a different Ma'atuk. He seemed a little more erect, his hump was swallowed up in the dimness between his armchair and the wall behind him. There was a note of calculation and impatience in his tone, the tone of a man whose time was precious, who gave orders, made decisions and closed deals worth large sums of money. At the entrance a Circassian doorman sat on a stool, frightening in his huge moustache and heavy turban and the dagger stuck in his broad sash, and Victoria would quake at the sight of him, even though he was a God-fearing fellow and lowered his eyes modestly whenever a woman walked past him. In this office Victoria would forget Ma'atuk's miserable past in the alley and her knees would tremble when she stood in front of the big desk. His excitement on these occasions did not escape her. She would greet him in a weak voice, and he would return her greeting in a faltering whisper. She was always careful to wear a veil, so that nobody but Ma'atuk would recognize her. For the sake of her father's reputation she did not want it bruited abroad that Izuri's daughter was working for her living, dependent on the cripple for her bread.

On their last meeting only Ma'atuk himself and his accountant had been present in the office. Despite the black veil her eyes were still dazzled from the glare of the sun outside, and

Ma'atuk's face was a blur. "Today there was a driver who transports merchandise to Palestine in my office," he told her. "Nuna sends regards to all of you."

"I wish her good health," she replied with polite reserve.

"I saw to it that each of her sons has a profitable business." For the first time she heard him laugh. "You won't believe it, my sister has found a husband!" Behind the veil Victoria's eyes opened wide in wonder. Ma'atuk didn't know how to laugh. The sound was repellent. "Would you believe it, there's hope even for a widow of her age in Palestine. The driver met him, he's quite well off, touch wood. They've invited me to visit them. Maybe it's worth a trip to see that peculiar country. I recommend it to you too, as soon as the news comes at last and your widowhood is officially established, go there as quick as you can. Why should you suffer here?"

He was her benevolent guardian angel, even though he never instructed the accountant to add one penny to her wages. But for that beggarly wage, she sometimes thought bitterly, perhaps she would have removed Kilmanteen's blanket on a cold night, sought other ways of killing her foetus, gone out of her mind. On Friday nights when she lit the *kuraya*, she would thank God and Ma'atuk. Now her face paled behind the veil. He had no right to talk about Rafael like that. With her eyes closed she took the coins from the accountant and stumbled out of the office, whispering to herself: "May your name and memory be blotted out, crooked hunchback that you are. Is that the way to talk about a man fighting for his life? What harm did Rafael ever do you?"

It may be that during that time nothing of her former love for her husband was left in her heart. Much resentment against him had built up inside her, and jealousy of other women too, even of Miriam who was brutally beaten by the blacksmith. Why couldn't Rafael have been satisfied with a modest death, like the other consumptives in the city? Months had passed since he had disappeared into the Syrian desert. No news had come from the Lebanon mountains. In the depths of her heart she believed that he was dead. But how dared the hunchback speak so impudently of widows and bridegrooms? There was a stinging feeling in her eyes and all of a sudden the longing for Suzanne hit her like a blow. She had a birthmark like a tiny star behind her right ear. When Victoria pressed her lips to this little star, the baby had tilted her head towards her, shivering at her mother's ticklish breath and purring like a kitten. Now her feet carried her through the stinking squalor of the slums. Outside the brick buildings she passed the mud huts of poverty and disease like a black ghost in her *abbaya* and veil, on her way to visit the little mound of earth. She remembered only the general direction. And she couldn't find it. Perhaps she lost her way among the graves, or perhaps the rain had washed it away. It was the last light of dusk, and everything was still and dry. Not a living soul, not a bird or a blade of grass. At the thought of the loneliness of the little girl whose grave had disappeared her own loneliness turned her heart sour inside her. The darkness gathered between the graves. Suzanne, her lips whispered. And she immediately took fright at the accusing silence of the dead. She hurried back to her room in order to free her sisters who were looking after Kilmanteen and send them home.

Victoria was ashamed of her mother, revolted by her disgusting appearance, shrank from her touch, but she did not hate her. Once she saw Yitzhak Alima trying again and again to balance the tray of bread on his son's head. The boy with the watery eyes and the swollen lips stretched and shrank alternately under the tray without understanding what his father wanted of him. They stood there barefoot and up to their ankles in the freezing puddles left by the rain in the night, while the baker tried painfully and patiently to get the boy to balance the tray, miserably aware all the time of the passers-by sniggering at the sight of his attempts to instil some sense into that vacant head. Finally the father shouted in a voice hoarse from the smoke of his ovens: "Go to hell, you idiot! Your grandfather's already blind, your father's old, your mother's half paralysed. Who's going to support you? Who's going to put a shirt on your back when we're gone? Nasty children are already waiting for you round the corner. They'll knock you on the head, they'll throw stones at you, and you'll laugh and cry and run away like some poor lunatic. Idiot, listen to me, you're not crazy. You've just got clouds in your head and rags for hands. Look, son, even monkeys can learn, even dogs. Surely someone like you, even if God made you a little crooked, surely you can learn to put the tray properly on your head, lift this hand and then that hand and hold it on both sides. Yes, you donkey, hold your head up straight, so all the pittas don't fall off the tray. Don't tell me you don't know where the Nunus' place is, or Michal's family, and you've already been to Juri Chittaiyat's plenty of times too. All you have to do is stand outside and call them. They'll come themselves and take. I'll collect the money myself at the end of the week. You have to learn, you hear me?" The boy smiled in delight at a splinter of glass which had caught a shining sunbeam. "No, no," groaned Yitzhak Alima as the pittas fell into the puddle and floated off in all directions like pale flowers. The boys watching from the side bellowed with laughter as the baker hit his son and the lad sank to his knees and sat down in the puddle and tried in vain to trap the elusive sunbeams in his hands. Victoria was filled with pity as the father kicked his son and sobbed, and then shielded him with his body from the taunts of the boys, and then hit him again, this time on the face, and then wiped away the blood streaming from his nose with his blackened baker's hand.

She remembered this puddle one day when her eyes fell on her mother making her way slowly across the courtyard, in the shadows of the washing hung up to dry, evidently too shy to ask anyone for the whereabouts of her daughter's room. At that moment Victoria forgave her everything, and her throat choked up at the sight of the lost expression on the ravaged face. Her *abbaya* had slipped off her head and off one of her shoulders. In the middle of the courtyard she stopped and stood there helplessly. It was a khamsin day, and Victoria had set up her work-table in the doorway. Inside the room she was boiling a cup of milk for Kilmanteen.

"Ah, there you are," muttered Najia, and the lost expression vanished from her face. She dropped onto Michal's rug which Victoria spread out for her and examined the stack of cigarette paper boxes. "You must be rich by now. You were always quick as the devil. Ma'atuk Nunu isn't tight-fisted with you, I'm sure. Ever since you were five years old he's had his eye on you, but you preferred the dying Bedouin. What are you smiling at?"

Victoria couldn't believe that she was actually glad to see her mother. "I'll make you some tea."

"A good thing you remembered to offer. It's a long way and my mouth's dry," she said and recoiled as her granddaughter made a sudden movement in her direction. Her nostrils flared at the smell of the boiling tea. "And a bit of bread and cheese," she called to Victoria as she bent over the kerosene cooker.

"I've only got dry bread from yesterday."

"Bring it. I haven't had breakfast yet."

Victoria served the refreshments.

"And how's the pregnancy?"

Victoria's eyes widened in astonishment. Again she remembered Yitzhak Alima's tears. Even in her childhood she couldn't recall hearing such an almost affectionate tone from her mother. Her heart instantly froze within her. Something must have happened to her father. But she was afraid to ask in so many words, lest her question was wrongly interpreted. "How are things at home?"

"I'm pregnant again," Najia stated with weary indifference. "Three or four months after you. Who knows?" Previously she had thrived in her pregnancies. Now she looked limp and wilted.

"Are you ill?"

"Just tired all the time. And all for what? I thought that if I gave him sons maybe I'd get a kind word from him. Today he looks at me as if I've grown a boil on my belly."

So my daughter will have an uncle younger than she is, thought Victoria. And she'll grow up without a dowry. The first hunchback that comes knocking on the door will be welcomed with open arms.

"Get up," said Najia.

"Where are we going?"

"You're coming home."

Victoria was startled by her own composure as she heard herself saying: "You've heard news of Rafael's death."

Najia wiped her lower lip with two fingers, to indicate her disapproval. "I told you, I'm tired all the time. I wouldn't have dragged myself all the way here on account of that Bedouin. I'm worn out. This pregnancy's killing me. Who knows what I've got there inside me? I haven't got the strength to get up and I haven't got the strength to sit down. You have to come back. Everything's upside down at home. Your father hardly gets one hot meal a week."

"Mother, you threw me out."

"So make a bonfire and burn me. If you didn't want to run away from home, would I have been able to throw you out? Now the stink of hunger coming from your mouth is so strong you can smell it miles away. Look at your daughter, skin and bones."

Victoria couldn't suppress her pain. "My other daughter died of cold in your courtyard."

"You can thank God for it. Who needs daughters, they're a catastrophe. Look at me, look at yourself. Anyone would think we have a party every day to celebrate the fact that we were born. Get up already."

"I have to think about it."

"Only the rich have time to think. Yallah, get up."

"No, I need a few days to think."

"I want more tea."

"I'm out of sugar."

"So go and ask the neighbours. Listen, when you give birth you won't have to worry about nappies. I put a bundle aside for you."

The courtyard to which Victoria returned was not the same one she had left. The decline had set in after Michal's death, and Yehuda's death had accelerated the process. After twenty-five years of living with Najia, Izuri had grown indifferent to dirt and neglect. Aziza had aged overnight. In order to make room for Victoria she was evicted from her room. However, since she needed supervision she was not banished to the basement but put in the arcade, where she lived without any privacy at all. True, it was summer, and people hardly used their rooms, but nevertheless the move broke her spirit. Her belongings were heaped up in the arcade, on display to every prying eye. There was no room there for her big bed, and she spread her mattress on the bench where Yehuda had breathed his last. Izuri scrupulously presented her with a share of the profits every week, but she had lost all interest in shopping and cooking, and she gave the money to Miriam and ate at her table. Her contact with her surroundings diminished as her deafness increased.

Something had collapsed inside Najia. Despite her pregnancy she looked and behaved like a worn-out old woman. She went on pushing coins into cracks in the walls, but she immediately forgot all about them. She went on grumbling and complaining to herself, but it was as if the other residents of the courtyard lived their lives in another world. From time to time Izuri and her sons would hit and curse her, and she would cry and curse and then calm down again, like a cripple resigned to his fate. Almost all her teeth had fallen out, and she stopped annoying others and gave Victoria a free hand with the housekeeping.

Ezra had become a well-known figure in the night-life of the city thanks to his impressive pharmacy in al-Rashid Street, and he was a respected customer at every notorious theeayter in the town. Apart from Victoria and Miriam he was the only one who mourned Rafael's absence. The brief period of time from his return home to Rafael's falling ill had fanned the flame of his longings to participate in Rafael's nights of passion and realize his ideal of "manhood". A wife, a child and a pharmacy were not enough to satisfy him. In any case, he kept away from the courtyard. He was now a man of the world, and he looked down on his old home as a backward, disintegrating, confining place. From time to time he sent a messenger with a gift for his sister and a few coins for his mother.

Izuri had exchanged his *abbaya* and fez for a suit and cane, and discovered the delights of night-life outside the house. On his return from the factory he would bathe and eat, and set off for the club. There he met middle-aged men like himself, took part in relaxed conversations and watched backgammon games. He no longer roared for Najia like a cat on heat when he got into bed. Her last pregnancy had destroyed the vestiges of his lust. Aziza too, who spent most of her time lying on the bench like a rag, no longer fired his imagination. Clarisse, his young daughter-in-law, had the face of a Shi'ite mullah. He wondered how Murad managed to light a fire in such a creature without risking scratches and bites.

Miriam's belly swelled together with Najia's, Victoria's and Clarisse's, and she sank between the pots and pans and grew so fat that she panted for breath with every step she took. After months of beatings she had learned to fight back. As a daughter whose father had never raised his hand to her, she refused to submit to the fate of a battered wife. After every quarrel she would retaliate with a surprise attack and drop heavy objects on him in his sleep. And one night she sat on him and buried his head under a hundred kilos of flesh and accumulated rage. Her mighty buttocks almost smothered him. His legs kicked in the air as his blacksmith's fingers tried to tear out lumps of her flesh, but the heavy bum did not budge from his nose. "Listen here, Gurji," she panted like a bellows. "If you ever raise your hand to me again I swear to you that you won't live to see old age or be a rabbi in Israel. Now you're still strong and in a minute you'll throw me off, but one day you'll be ill and tired. I promise you that when that day comes I won't move from your mug until the undertakers come. What will they do to me? No judge will believe that a woman murdered her husband with her bum." And she raised herself slightly to allow him to breathe and immediately came down on him again and continued her lecture: "You fly into a rage and accuse me of stealing from you. A woman who takes money from her husband's wallet isn't stealing. Rafael, may he come home healthy, let Victoria take money from his pockets without checking up on her. And that's all I've got to say." And she wriggled about until she squashed his nose and lips and rose to her feet. After that he never hit her again, but he cursed her with venomous eloquence, his mouth like an overflowing sewer.

Dahood explained to his wife that his mother was now too old to look after his children. Toya gladly took in his two sons and his daughter Layla. The sons were older than she was, and Layla only a little younger, and the four of them united into a merry band of pranksters in the house where laughter had almost died.

The imposing Nunu home too grew quiet and subdued after Nuna and the children left. From the day Victoria returned to the courtyard she naturally stopped working for Ma'atuk. Every week her father gave her a full coin for looking after the family, and it was more than enough. She was glad to be free of the embarrassing obligation to present herself at Ma'atuk's office. She remembered the warmth shining from his eyes and the emotion in his voice when he addressed her. He had never looked down on her, in spite of her humiliating situation. It wasn't his deformity which made her despise the bold and enterprising hunchback, but his stinginess. If only he had really taken care of her needs when she was slaving for him, perhaps he would have earned her affection. When they encountered each other now in the alley he mumbled a faltering greeting and she murmured coldly in reply.

She lived quietly then, without stormclouds gathering over her head, and she was content that it should be so. Kilmanteen regained her strength, and Victoria began to save for the dowry of her child who would grow into a fatherless girl. She calculated that she would give birth close to *Rosh Hashana.* Sometimes, when the last rays of the sun faded from the courtyard, in the melancholy dusk before going up to the roof to sleep, she would think of Rafael. It was as if the river had swallowed him up. From the day he had left town she hadn't heard a word. Since she had parted from him at the door, her imagination sometimes played tricks on her and led her to believe that he was hiding somewhere nearby, leading a different life, evading his responsibilities as a husband and father. Had he reached the hospital in Lebanon safely? During the period when she had run from doctor to doctor with him, visited amulet-makers and healers of various kinds, she had met others in the same situation. In the past month alone she had met three women wearing the blue garb of mourning. In moments of grace she longed to touch his grave, to fondle it, to whisper something to him, to tell him that little Suzanne with the tiny star behind her ear had died and her grave had vanished as if it had never been.

One day she overheard Miriam saying bitterly to Gurji in the course of one of their frequent quarrels: "What you've got in your whole body isn't worth what Rafael's got in his little fingernail. Don't you dare sully his name, I'm warning you. People like him weren't born to live on the dungheaps of this world. You've forgotten his eyes, you don't remember his voice."

Victoria never heard a finer eulogy for her husband.

But she refused to accept his disappearance from her life. And at the same time she was afraid to think of him too much, thoughts which disturbed her peace of mind and fanned a flame in her flesh. She had never spoken to anyone about Rafael the man, but she listened to other women comparing the feats of their husbands, and she would smile and say to herself, what do they know, what do they know. The treacherous Flora would have been only too happy to have a heart-to-heart talk with her. She ran into her several times, and Flora was very cordial, but she did not dare bring up Rafael's name. The more she tried to forget him, the more he invaded her dreams, and sometimes he gave her so much pleasure that she woke up with an acute feeling of loss and longing.

One day she was standing at the door and waiting impatiently for Nazima and Salima, who were dawdling far too long over the shopping. They had run out of oil and the salted slices of aubergine were lying limply in the bowl next to the waiting frying pan. Her eyes rested on the little girl dressed up as a woman in an *abbaya* and veil, who emerged round the bend in the alley and approached their house. When she removed the hood of her *abbaya* Victoria cried out in surprise: "Toya!"

"Shhh!" The little woman silenced her and dragged her back into the sweltering kitchen. "Smell me, go on, smell me!"

It was hard to smell anything in the air of the boiling kitchen, full of the aromas of cooking and frying. "What am I supposed to smell?"

"I poured a whole bottle of scent over myself, I covered my body with a kilo of scented powder. I've been to see Ezra."

Victoria blushed. Her voice was faint with excitement. "You're still seeing each other."

"God damn his eyes, how I missed him! And him? As if nothing had ever happened between us. You know that him and Rafael get mixed up in my dreams?"

Victoria felt a stab of jealousy.

"So today I went to his pharmacy. You've never seen anything so clean in your life, even the walls stink of medicines. I think it's even infected Ezra. He pretended he hardly knew me. I told him I had a rash on my back. I'm standing there trembling with excitement and he tries to rob me blind for a stinking powder I wouldn't even use on rats. There never was a man like your Rafael and there never will be."

The diminutive woman's face expressed neither pain nor sorrow. For this astonishing little Toya, for her chestnut breasts and childish voice, a Druze in Israel would one day convert to Judaism, thereby cutting himself off from his community and forfeiting his place in the orderly cycle of reincarnations promised by their religion. As she spoke she bit into a piece of meat, nobbled a burgul *kubbeh*, and stole a handful of hot rice straight from the pot. When Victoria stood up Toya measured her swollen belly and touched the taut skin under her dress with her slender fingers. Victoria did not recoil, she found Toya's touch enjoyable.

Darkness gathered in the courtyard. Birds caught the last rays of the sun and flashed in the air. Kilmanteen lay on Salima's lap and dissolved into laughter when her aunt's head touched her bare stomach. A strange man appeared at the courtyard door. Aziza woke from her slumbers and cried: "Yehuda, you've come!" Her feet fumbled for her slippers and she tried to rise from the bench and serve Yehuda his supper.

"I'm looking for Victoria," said the stranger.

Aziza said sullenly: "Damn you, you're not Yehuda."

Victoria stared at him. He was wearing a light jacket over his striped robe. There was something different about him, his Arabic was not the Arabic of the Jews of the town. Her knees turned to water. His face was grave. The evil tidings have arrived, she said to herself. For a long moment she was silent, as if she were waiting for someone to stand up and say: "I'm Victoria." Then she approached the stranger and nodded her head. He was holding a folded piece of paper in his hand, white in the gathering darkness of the courtyard.

"So why did I think you were Yehuda?" muttered Aziza in the arcade.

Victoria took the letter and asked herself what she was going to do with it. In the entire alley there was nobody who knew how to read Arabic. She would go to Ezra. He would come there himself to sit *shiva* with the family. She pulled a chair from the arcade for the visitor with the aplomb of a practised mourner. When he sat down she gave him a fan and went to fetch him a glass of cold water in the courtesy usually offered to summer visitors. Without turning her head she knew that the residents of the courtyard had emerged from their corners and were encircling her and the stranger in a hoop of tense expectation. Why were they so silent? Why didn't someone stand up and break the silence? Why didn't some other throat utter the scream of despair? Where was Miriam?

The stranger drank thirstily, as befitting a visitor who had travelled across the desert. The handkerchief peeping elegantly from the upper pocket of his jacket seemed inappropriate to the occasion. And she was outraged to see that he was appraising her with a blatantly male eye. The smile on his lips seemed at odds with his mission. In her confusion she clasped the letter to her breast, above her swollen stomach.

"There's a picture inside," said the stranger and held out his empty glass to Toya, for her to fill it again. "Child, I'm so thirsty."

Toya took the glass with ostentatious womanly dignity, and he seemed momentarily taken aback.

Victoria took out the photograph and saw a great stone building unlike anything in Baghdad, which was built of burnt bricks, with lawns, flowerbeds, and a wood. On the left, in the background, something immense topped with white lather rose into the sky, and she guessed that it must be a mountain capped by snow. Then she made out a hammock slung between two trees and on a chair beside it with a book in his hands a man dressed like the stranger—a light jacket over a striped robe. At first she couldn't understand why she was escaping to the building and the trees and clinging to the mountain, avoiding the face of the seated figure. Because she knew at once that it was Rafael. That intelligent, reserved smile under those awe-inspiring spectacles.

"Is that all that's left of him?" At last she opened her mouth. And she waved the photograph foolishly. And immediately she wished that the earth would open and swallow her up, because she realized that she was smiling. The hoop tightened and thickened around her, and they all suppressed their avid curiosity to see the photograph and waited in a heavy silence to hear her scream of despair.

"He didn't tell me you were pregnant," said the stranger with unbecoming frankness, as if he hadn't understood what she'd said to him at all. "Altogether he kept the fact that he was married secret, and he made me swear not to tell anyone."

At the sound of his laughter Victoria wondered for a moment if he was completely sane.

"He's in demand with a lot of Jewish families in Beirut. You don't know how the Christian nurses spoil him at the sanatorium. But now he needs money, otherwise his position there will be very difficult indeed."

At that moment Miriam trumpeted from the door of the glassed-in room: "Victoria, Rafael's not dead. He's alive!"

Victoria looked up at her cousin and her eyes were flooded with tears.

The visitor pointed to the paper clasped to her chest. "You'll find the address of a merchant in Beirut written there. Send him the money and he'll take care of everything. I'm on my way home to Abadan."

Victoria was stunned. "So people really come out of it alive?"

"Look at me, praise God. They thought I wouldn't reach Lebanon alive. Two years there and look at me. Look!"

There was something improper in this appeal, and she lowered her eyes to the ground and refused to look at him. "When did you see him last?" Her face was burning.

"Six days ago. They say there's hope for him now. He arrived there like me, a foot and a half in the grave. Over there we became like brothers. It's wonderful there in the mountains, so wonderful that it's hard to go back to your family and work. And in southern Persia the air's more suffocating than Baghdad in the summer. It's hell on earth."

"Forgive me." She roused herself. "I'll set the table for you right away. You must be hungry."

The pounding of Miriam's feet was heard on the stairs. "He'll be our guest until he returns to Abadan."

"Thank you, thank you," said the guest and he took the scented handkerchief out of his pocket and touched it to his lips in the habitual gesture of a consumptive. "And how are the girls?"

"The little one gave you her years," said Victoria and disappeared into the kitchen.

But the money was not available.

The stranger stayed on for two weeks. Again and again he complained about going back to the daily routine and the necessity of earning a living. Izuri treated him well, took him along to the club, and in the mornings invited him to the factory, so he wouldn't be bored in the company of women and children. But the guest was content to wander the streets of the town and sit in the tea-houses lining the banks of the Tigris. He was an amiable man, his stories won the hearts of the residents of the alley, and Izuri presented him proudly to his acquaintances, as if he were an exotic bird who had flown into an old dovecote. At the same time, he wasn't free of suspicion. "What kind of a man is he?" he said to Victoria. "After such a long absence from home, how come he doesn't rush back to his wife and children and parents? He's a pleasant fellow, but he's got a touch of the crook about him, the same as your husband, if you don't mind my saying so. How do we know when that picture of Rafael was taken? Maybe that merchant in Beirut is conspiring with him to rob us? Maybe Rafael was buried long ago?"

But her heart told her that the guest was telling the truth. The luxurious atmosphere of the sanatorium in the photograph moved her. She could look into Rafael's eyes, she could touch his face glowing with idleness and gratification. Better an idle husband than a dead one, widows were shunned like lepers. Her loneliness was like burning coals. In any case, she did not ask her father to help her find the money. For all his European-style suits and clubs, the little factory brought in barely enough to feed all the mouths dependent on it. Other, more enterprising men of his position had already gone far, they were living in the new neighbourhoods in solid houses with electricity whose windows looked out on trees. And her father was still wallowing in the squalor of the alley. Ma'atuk Nunu had already rented his spacious home to twenty poverty-stricken families, and bought himself a mansion in the suburb of Batawin.

During the stranger's stay friends and visitors began dropping in of an evening and holding modest parties. First to come was Ezra, who questioned the stranger discreetly. He knew Beirut well from his student days, and the two of them sang the praises of the enchanting city until they both got drunk on Izuri's arak. The pharmacist didn't so much as glance at Toya, who was trembling with excitement. Several times she snatched the tray from Victoria's hands and served the men at their table. In the end Ezra looked up at her in surprise and said: "Are you still living here?" And when he was completely drunk and his eyes were red and his mouth wet, he smiled at her as if she was incorrigible and shook his head and said: "Toya, Toya, is that it? Have you decided never to grow up?"

Toya ran away.

Dahood, who was sitting at the table and strumming his zither, looked at his wife and burst out laughing. "Come here, Toya," he said and lifted her into the air and kissed her on the buttocks. "I'd lay down my life for this chirping little bird," he said to Ezra in drunken camaraderie.

The day after the stranger left for south Persia, Victoria went to the pharmacy in al-Rashid street. "Well, what do you say?" she asked her cousin.

"I made inquiries through a friend in Beirut. Here." He showed her a piece of paper.

"What is it?"

"A telegram." Victoria blinked. She had never heard the word before.

"Everything's above board. Rafael's alive and the merchant in Beirut is an honest man."

"So he really needs money."

"He needs it. Go to his mother, to his brothers. He showered a fortune on them. Let his mother sell the jewels he bought her. Asher would be a beggar if it wasn't for Rafael. Go and sit in his shop and don't budge from there. It's up to you. You're the only one who can help him."

In fear and trembling she set out on her sacred mission, and returned empty-handed. Ezra contributed something from his own pocket, and then made the rounds of the wealthy merchants, as Rafael himself had done many times before him, to ask for charity to save a Jewish soul. Because of his reputation as a playboy, his harvest was poor.

17

Over a thousand years of destruction and crowded building had left the Jewish quarter without a single flower or blade of grass. Here and there an old palm or stubborn jujube tree rose from a courtyard, but they did nothing to vary the landscape or announce the renewal of the changing of the seasons, and people recognized the time of year by the heat of the sun or the nip of the cold in the air. There was no such thing as a calendar in the entire alley, and the only signposts were the length of the days and the Jewish festivals. By the glinting of the tin balustrade on the roof, which caught the golden rays of the sun, Victoria knew that in spite of her condition she had succeeded in getting her father's family ready for the Sabbath. The aroma of the cooked dishes rose from the pots and the bowls, the bedclothes were spread out on the roof to air, soon the courtyard tiles would be washed and shining. And nevertheless the delight she had once known in these pre-Sabbath hours was not there. Apart from the gratification and measure of pride she felt at having done her duty well, there was nothing. Her mother, in her difficult pregnancy, lay like a limp rag next to Aziza's bench and watched the energetic young girls preparing the house for the Sabbath apathetically. In ten days' time they would celebrate *Rosh Hashana*, said Victoria to herself, and put off thinking about Rafael until she went to bed. By then her body would be so numb with exhaustion that the pinch of the memories would not be so vicious.

Her brother Fuad fell with murderous savagery on Nissan, who was older than he was, and the latter fled to the roof. Victoria grabbed the cooking board from Fuad's hand and scolded him. "We have an important guest in the house," she said and pointed to a man in a white shirt and cheap blue trousers. "He's an emissary from Palestine, and father has invited him for the Sabbath, and it's not nice to behave like that in front of him."

"The stinker bit me on the bum," growled the child and ignored the guest who understood no Arabic, but was making an evident effort to absorb everything with his eyes. "Look, look." He picked up his gown, pulled down his underpants, and displayed two rows of tiny, bleeding holes.

"I'll slip you a sweet peach later," she said to appease him.

"Give it to me now. You're busy all the time and you never remember."

Suddenly she clenched her lips. Not now, she tried to calm herself, not on the Sabbath eve. She noticed the emissary looking at her. Her father's business was showing signs of recovery, and he had begun inviting passing guests for the Sabbath. She tried not to blush at the emissary's stares. Didn't he know that it wasn't done to stare at a woman in the home of his host? In any case, the woman had no option but to ignore such looks and keep her mouth shut, for complaints were liable to be interpreted as boasting, and proof that she wasn't as virtuous as she should be: if she noticed lustful looks it meant that she had invited them. In her heart she admitted that the emissary's looks pleased her even though they aroused her indignation. Afterwards she wondered why Ma'atuk Nunu and the consumptive from Abadan and the emissary took such liberties with her. She wasn't Flora, or Toya. Perhaps the fault lay with her, with the way she bore herself, and not with them. Rafael's look was different, though, it caressed you lightly and moved on, and you were left wondering if he was really interested in you or not. But now she had to bathe and light the *kuraya*.

Another contraction took her by surprise.

Victoria was an expert at distracting herself by now. She gave Fuad, whose father hated him, a peach in secret, and saw Toya crossing the courtyard with her step-daughter Layla devotedly dogging her heels. The iron in the diminutive woman's hands smelled of burning coals. She filled her mouth with water until her cheeks were swollen, raised herself on tiptoe and sprayed a fine mist onto Dahood's robe. The material hissed at the touch of the hot iron as Toya smoothed it along the stripes, her doll-like buttocks sending signals to the emissary from the Holy Land. Victoria smiled faintly. Toya's tricks never failed to amuse her.

And again she jerked her head as if someone had hit her hard on the back.

God, how I love sharp peppers when I'm pregnant, she said to herself as if to deny what was happening. When the men and boys left for the synagogue she went to her room and sat down in the tub and washed herself at her leisure. Kilmanteen and Layla struggled with the door she had barred with a chair and squeezed through the narrow opening they had succeeded in making. The two little girls sat on the bed hand in hand, their shoulders touching, and watched her with wondering eyes, and Victoria delighted in the sight, as if it held a guarantee that her daughter would never know loneliness. She had not yet accepted the thought that Rafael was coming home alive. And even if he did come home, he would be as confused as the man from Abadan. And the latter was a tame pigeon compared to the restless, ebullient Rafael. And perhaps Rafael would settle down in Lebanon and refuse to part from the mountains. Why should he return to the grinding poverty of the alley? If only she could be cured of this pregnancy as if it were a disease. If only her belly would collapse like an empty gourd. But her huge belly, strewn with soap bubbles, captured the imagination of the two girls.

"Mother, I want to touch your stomach. I like feeling the baby."

The baby, said Victoria to herself, it's going to be another girl, another catastrophe, dust and ashes, mourning and lamentation.

Layla approached her, with Kilmanteen clinging to the hem

of her dress. Tears welled up in Victoria's eyes. It isn't a game, children. Nevertheless, the fingertips stroking her swollen stomach comforted her. Who said that every female was doomed to miserable slavery? But immediately her face fell. Her battered mother, Aziza who had been left to her own devices, Miriam suffering the blacksmith's insults, Toya who was a plaything in the hands of Dahood, whether he was drunk or sober. Clarisse's stony face, married off to a numbskull. Even Nuna Nunu—what had fallen to her lot after living in the lap of luxury? Exile in a distant land. And what would have become of her if she had been the one to get tuberculosis instead of Rafael? How much would her husband have been ready to sacrifice to save her life? She would have choked on her blood and died long ago.

No, I won't give birth tonight, she commanded herself. It's forbidden to light a lamp on the Sabbath. And there's a strange man in the house. Not tonight. On Saturday night or Sunday. And she put on her dress and braided her long hair.

"Mother, Layla doesn't believe that Suzanne's lying in her grave. She says that it's impossible for anyone to lie under the ground for so long."

"We all end up under the ground," said Victoria.

Her mother hit herself on the forehead and ran to vomit in the lavatory. Salima and Nazima took revenge for Fuad, and administered a sound thrashing to Nissan, who was trying to peep at them as they bathed. Miriam's face was wet with perspiration. In view of the heavy khamsin the Sabbath table was laid on the roof. Aziza was left below with a heaped plate next to her bench.

After midnight Victoria sat up in bed. Next to her lay Kilmanteen and Layla, their foreheads touching. At the end of the roof Dahood snored, dazed with arak. The sleepers lay abandoned in the starlight, desperate for a breeze to lighten the stifling heat. The mosquito net sagged limply over Miriam and Gurji's broad bed. A tired moon sank behind distant roofs.

Who could she call?

Aziza was sleeping the sleep of the deaf far below. Toya was trapped between Dahood's knees. Many men, from Indonesia to Iraq, sleep with a pillow between their legs. Rafael liked sleeping that way too. Little Toya served as Dahood's pillow. Her childish face was buried deep in his paunch, his arm lay limply on her head.

"Miriam."

The mosquito net didn't stir.

"Miriam."

Miriam's face, a squashed, doughy moon, peeped out of the white drapes.

"Miriam, I think it's happening."

"Now of all times," whispered her mother. "You chose a fine time."

"Someone has to fetch the midwife," said Victoria.

"I'm not waking your father," said Najia. "He drank a lot and he has to get up soon to go to the synagogue."

Miriam clucked her tongue. "A pity you didn't say something before the Sabbath began. We would have left a lamp on downstairs."

The emissary's eyes glittered on a mattress set apart, next to the balustrade. He had evidently guessed what was happening. Victoria was ashamed, but she had no choice. "Somebody has to do something."

They shook Murad awake.

"What's the matter with you?" he said angrily.

"You must fetch a midwife for your sister."

Murad shuddered. "I'm not going out alone in the dark. And who can I fetch?"

"Even Jamila," whispered Victoria. She knew that the old woman was almost blind.

Nissan pretended to be sleeping. His eldest brother's fear infected him. How many of the men were pretending to be asleep, Victoria wondered.

"I'll go," volunteered Sa'id, Dahood's eldest son. Miriam's husband Gurji went down with him.

Miriam held Victoria's hand. The moon disappeared and it was pitch dark. "Where do you want it to be?"

"Let's go down to my room."

"It's black as hell in there."

"Anyone would think it was a party." Najia's voice rose hoarsely. "Light or dark, what's the difference?"

Victoria got out of bed without waking Kilmanteen and turned with Miriam towards the stairs which were swallowed up in the gloom.

The emissary's hand groped for his cigarettes, but he remembered that it was the Sabbath and his craving for nicotine increased. Najia sighed and sprawled out next to Izuri again, and he flung out his mighty arm and drew her to him and went on sleeping. In the light of the stars Najia's eyes met Toya's. Dahood's finger groped to see if his wife's eyes were open. As the effects of the arak wore off life stirred in his penis, crushed between Toya and his legs. "If only we had a fucking mosquito net to cover us," he whispered. Exposed on the mattress spread out on the roof, with so many people awake around them, he refrained from mounting her and made do with her back, against which he thrust his erection. Najia and Toya did not take their eyes off each other. As Dahood pushed himself against Toya's bum, it seemed to Najia in the deceptive starlight that her sister-in-law was very close to her, and that her hand or foot was about to touch her. In any case, it was clear to her that her sister-in-law's flat stomach was mocking her. Her eyes drilled holes in Toya's face and she muttered: "May you both rot in hell."

Nissan whispered: "Take it easy, Uncle Dahood. Have pity on the roof." The proud mast collapsed, and Dahood cursed his nephew from the bottom of his heart: "May you go blind. May you marry a woman with the face of a policeman's boot, like your brother Murad."

Victoria and Miriam passed the bench where Aziza, protected by her deafness, was sleeping soundly, and groped their way to Victoria's room holding hands, like they did when they were children. The starlight did not reach the room, and the darkness was palpable. "I'm staying with you to the end," said Miriam. Victoria squeezed the fingers laced with hers gratefully. "The mat's rolled up next to the chest," she said.

Miriam spread the mat on the floor. "Wait," she ordered, "let me make sure that there aren't any scorpions first." And she stamped her heavy feet to and fro over the mat until she lost her way in the dark and shrieked in terror: "Where am I? Victoria, I don't know where I am!"

When they found each other Miriam helped her to lie down on the mat. The stabs of pain grew worse, and Victoria's anger grew with them. He knew he was ill, maybe he already knew in Basra. Why had he given her two daughters, and now another one? He sat there at his ease in the mountains, he lay there in a hammock, and the nurses thought he was a bachelor. And so did his wealthy patrons, the fathers of the virgins of Beirut. The bastard. Perhaps her mother was right. His seed was corrupt. Capable of producing nothing but daughters. He had fathered a daughter on Flora too—Rachelle was as like poor little Suzanne as two peas in a pod. How many daughters had he left behind him, from the coast of Beirut to the Persian Gulf? Even that whore, Rahma Afsa, who had grown rich from her conquests of the British who had conquered Baghdad, had returned to the bosom of the alley with a curly-haired black-eyed daughter. She wondered if they would all wear glasses one day like their father, and she almost smiled. A flock of bespectacled girls with the same face walking the streets of the city.

A renewed wave of pain wiped the picture from her imagination.

Outside the despairing cries of the purblind Jamila were heard. "Give me your hand, don't leave me, may your mothers weep on your graves. Where's the step? I'm lost in the dark. Are you sure there aren't any stairs?"

With the onset of old age the inhabitants of the flat city, surrounded by broad plains, were plagued by the fear of stairs. In summer the very old renounced the fresh air of the roofs, and in winter they froze to death in the ground-floor rooms. Jamila brought with her to the delivery room an archaic fear of heights. She smelled of urine and sweat and chicken-shit. She had long abandoned all her occupations and lived off the crumbs thrown her by her daughters-in-law.

Sa'id and Gurji deposited her in the doorway and turned towards the roof. "Where are you running to?" she called after them. "And if there are stairs?" Miriam's hand pulled her inside and closed the door behind her. Jamila crouched down next to the mat. The name of the woman in labour had slipped her memory. "Izuri's daughter, I heard your husband kicked the bucket. Who's going to pay me?"

"I've saved money," groaned Victoria.

Jamila's fingers, stiff as twigs, felt her in the suffocating darkness. "You're ready, my daughter." A surprising note of compassion crept into her voice. "You could have given birth by yourself. Press down a little. Where are you, Yehuda's daughter? Look how I've forgotten all your names. Here, hold on here. Listen, Najia . . ."

"This is Victoria, Najia's daughter," Miriam corrected her, afraid that the midwife was losing her grip of reality.

"It's been a hard winter. The grave-diggers got rich on the sudden frost before *Pesach.* Why didn't you invite me to wail for her? I still know how to cry."

"She isn't dead yet. She's lying in bed upstairs next to her husband."

"What greed. It's seven years already."

Miriam wanted to rebuke the old woman and tell her to concentrate on Victoria, but she was afraid of angering her.

"Here it is," exclaimed Jamila in relief.

A midwife's fee for delivering a boy was far greater than for a girl, but the humility of old age had taught her to be content with whatever came her way. "As long as you've got your health, nothing else matters," she consoled the mother, as one woman to another.

Victoria had already heard this sentence twice before. She said nothing, and she felt nothing either. Emptiness rang in her ears. She heard the familiar screams of the newborn baby. When Miriam picked her up and wrapped her in a rag and hurried with her to the middle roof to abandon her there behind the big trays of tomato paste drying for the winter, the beaten Victoria did not protest or ask any questions.

"And now who's going to take me home?" asked Jamila in a tone of defeat.

Victoria tried to suffer the blow in silence, to be practical and tell the old woman that she could stay there until morning, but tears choked her throat.

"Why doesn't Yehuda's daughter come back?" said Jamila.

Victoria had no expectations left. A tiny spark of hope had stolen into her heart in the last month of her pregnancy. Perhaps it would be a boy. A boy would bring Rafael home, if he really recovered. A boy would prevail over the snow-topped mountains. Even if death won, her son would be a support to her in her old age.

Soundlessly she wept, and she felt her body sinking into an abyss of emptiness. For a moment she opened her eyes, almost joyfully. Perhaps it was death. Jamila had stopped touching her. Perhaps she had despaired of her. And she went on sinking even when the door opened quietly and Miriam put a clay cup to her lips and raised her head and commanded: "Drink."

"I can't," now she was sobbing aloud. "I give birth and murder the fruit of my womb. I'm a monster."

"It's God's will."

"A while ago I went to the bridge to throw myself into the river. I was afraid for myself, Miriam."

Miriam was horrified. "Have you gone crazy?"

"Bring the baby back. Not even Rahma Afsa abandoned her baby girl. And look how the cats fight for their kittens. I'm a criminal. Miriam, bring the baby back."

"So that she can grow up to be humiliated? And what if Rafael doesn't come back? By the time she grows up your father will be a doddering old man. Who's going to provide her with a dowry? Will you go to Murad? To Nissan?"

"Bring her back."

Jamila raised her head. "What's that madwoman yelling about?"

Victoria and Miriam kept quiet. On the middle roof Clarisse was shouting for her husband in her harsh voice. "You've brought me to a house of savages!" On her way to the lavatory she had stumbled over the whimpering little bundle. "Damn that Victoria, may her name be blotted out, may her womb shrivel up for ever."

"Miriam!" cried Victoria. "If you don't go and fetch her I'll get up and do it myself."

They were both terrified of Clarisse, afraid that she would incite the alley against them. A moment later she sounded a different note: "Victoria! Victoria!" she cried exultantly, as if the stone mask had turned into a pealing bell. "Victoria! Victoria! Murad," she went on raising the rooftops with her ringing new voice, "go and wake your father. Abu Murad, get up, you've got a grandson!"

A strange paralysis took hold of Victoria. She felt as if she were rising above the mat, and floating over the worn tiles of the courtyard, up the stairs to the miracle taking place there on the middle roof. She discovered that she was unable to move her legs, and she covered her face with her hands and barked like a wounded dog. She heard the pounding of feet running down the stairs from the upper roof. Creaking beds. Children's shouts. Neighbours' congratulations.

"Victoria." She heard Clarisse's voice. "It's terribly dark, I'm afraid to come down the stairs."

"Miriam." Victoria couldn't stop her barking sobs. "Run to her. She might trip up there. My legs have folded up. My head's buzzing like a beehive."

And they brought him to her, still wrapped up in coarse rag, still naked and covered in the slime of his creation. In the total blackout of the Sabbath she removed the rag, wiped his body on the hem of her dress, cleaned his face with hers. He put his tiny mouth to her ear and whispered his bitter protest to her. It seemed to her that she wouldn't have the strength to contain the wave of joy engulfing her. She asked God and Rafael to pardon her. The miracle of the baby's touch brought the life back to her legs. They moved. Only words failed her. Her mouth kept producing the strange barking sound. The door of the room was jammed. Women, girls, children, and behind them the men. Her father's excited voice silenced the uproar: "Let me see him."

And before her lips touched his face she made up her mind that he would be called Albert. From then on the words "Albert" and "miracle" were synonymous in her mind. She wanted to compensate him for the moments of the eclipse of her sense when he was abandoned on the roof. How could she have gone on living if Clarisse had not arrived in time? In return for her discovery, she rewarded her sister-in-law with decades of loyalty. In the wall of hostility surrounding the strange woman, Victoria made a single breach of sympathy.

The inhabitants of the courtyard began to treat the emissary from the Holy Land with admiring respect. There were those who attributed the miracle to his presence among them. Up to then, nobody had shown any interest in the reasons for his appearance in Baghdad, some of them thought that he was collecting charity for some Yeshiva or other in Jerusalem. When they returned from the synagogue and sat down to a festive breakfast, Izuri spoke to him in a Hebrew derived from the Bible and the prayer book, but the emissary's Hebrew was foreign even to those who prayed in the holy tongue. So their surprise was great when he explained that he had come there to teach the Jews of Baghdad Hebrew. Murad, who knew the prayer book by heart, rose to the defence of his city. "Baghdad, thank God, is blessed with yeshivas and rabbis, and they all know Hebrew, God save them. This isn't a village in Kurdistan."

"It isn't that Hebrew I've come to teach," explained the emissary, "but living Hebrew. A Hebrew you can talk in, read a newspaper in, write a letter in."

"We should learn to do all that in our mother-tongue first," said Dahood. "Suddenly I feel like a blockhead. Rafael and Ezra read the newspapers, even my son Sa'id turns the pages of books, and I stand and stare like a donkey."

The emissary didn't understand a word and Izuri translated the gist of it for him. The emissary's eyes lit up. "That's the point," he said to Dahood. "You're a foreigner here, like the Jews are everywhere in the diaspora. By teaching you Hebrew I'll be preparing you for immigration to Palestine."

Dahood couldn't believe his ears. "I saw you yesterday licking your lips from the fish. You polished off a whole dish of dates. What harm have we done you, that you want to cart us off to a land of hunger? They sent Nuna Nunu over there because of what happened with her father. That was the only place where they had a chance of finding a husband for damaged goods like her. And besides, what will I do with my zither in Palestine? It's my living and I love it and it makes people happy. Who'll listen to it over there? Translate, someone, please."

There were no volunteers for the job. Izuri, who was a perfect host, tried to distract the guest from Dahood's angry voice by inviting him to stay with them until his grandson's brith.

Even after giving birth Victoria did not miss a day of work. Her mother was worn out. No one urged her to rest. To tell the truth, she herself was eager to parade her happiness in the courtyard. Albert was attached to her as firmly as if he were a limb of her body, until it seemed that her inner pregnancy had been transformed into an external one. From time to time she lifted the lace and feasted her eyes on his face. Not only did he resemble Rafael, in her opinion he was even handsomer than his father. And he would be tall too, very tall, that was obvious. Up to now her father boasted of being the tallest man ever born in the courtyard. Let him wait until Albert grew up. In his shade she would never know hunger. Although she was exhausted and had no appetite, she sat down at the table because she wanted to dazzle them all with the new light which had been born in the dismal courtyard, but she didn't listen to the conversation. How was it possible to take an interest in anything else?

"Victoria, you're not listening to your father."

She roused herself. She could almost have wept with joy.

"I've invited our guest to stay with us until your son's brith. I've never told you how much I owe you. If I've still got a family . . ."

"Enough, Father."

"Next Saturday the whole alley's invited. Let them all see how Izuri celebrates a brith."

"There won't be a brith," she whispered with her eyes downcast.

"He looks healthy to me, touch wood."

"He's healthy, and how he's healthy, *tfu tfu*," she said, "but there'll be no brith until his father takes him in his arms and lays him on his lap for the circumcision."

Izuri replaced the eleventh egg in the bowl. He would polish off about twenty eggs at breakfast on the Sabbath. "I don't understand. All that's come from there is a photograph. For the money we sent we haven't even had a thank-you. Who says he'll recover from his illness? And if he recovers, how do you know that he'll come back? Your mother talks a lot of rubbish, but this time she's right. Rafael's a Bedouin."

"Albert will bring him home."

And Victoria blushed. It was no easy thing to disobey her father. Albert's birth was no miracle compared to the miracle of what she was doing now. She tried to stop the snake of her pride from raising its head but it was stronger than she was. Victoria with Albert was not the Victoria before Albert. Now she could say without any hesitation that it wasn't only her father's family she had saved from the gutter; she had saved Rafael too. And she pressed Albert's head to her face and fled from the table.

The self-confidence she drew from Albert's existence was stronger than her guilt at the way she had treated him during the first moments of his life. When her mother broke her promise and refused to give her the bundle of nappies for the baby, Victoria tore up sheets for nappies. She was already seeing herself as invincible. When she sang to Albert, she was really singing to herself. She hardly parted from him.

"Write," she said to Ezra, as she sat opposite him in the pharmacy after the holidays, "write: Rafael my husband, you have a son whose face brings a cry of 'Praise the Lord' to the lips of everyone who sets eyes on him."

The shining pharmacy with its glass cupboards and strong smells, its delicate scales, filled her with awe. On the other side of the glass door carriages, grand motorcars and pedestrians in expensive suits streamed past. Outside the world bustled and roared, but inside there was silence, and the whisper of Ezra's pen on the paper. Albert lay in her lap and she rocked him slightly with her hand on his stomach so that he wouldn't slip off her knees, God forbid.

"Write: I hope the money reached you and that your health is improving. The man from Abadan told us that you are recovering, thank God."

Ezra's important expression impressed her. Not a trace of the mischievous lad was left. When he sat like this at his heavy desk holding the pen which gave birth to the words on the sheet of paper, and knitting his brows under the electric light, who would have dared question him and say: Why did you abandon your mother? Poor Toya. What chance did her chestnut breasts and childish buttocks have against the rows of jars holding the wisdom of the wide world? The bold, sensitive Ezra had disappeared. His movements were now deliberate, his words measured. A trace of red in his eyes bore witness to over-indulgence in drink, and his moist, fleshy lips hinted at his dark nights. He wasn't a good-looking man, but he wasn't ugly either.

"Write also: I didn't want to grieve you in the last letter, but now that Albert, may my life be a ransom for his, has been born, I can tell you: the Lord giveth and the Lord taketh away. Suzanne . . ."

The carriages, the motorcars, the crowds of people. They had streamed like this a few months ago, on the narrow bridge. She clasped Albert to her breast in horror. If she had thrown herself off the bridge he would have died with her . . .

"Write, it's important: Father says you don't need to worry about earning a living. The factory supports a number of souls and it will support us too. Father will be happy if you go to work for him at a weekly wage which will be as much as he can afford."

Albert's tongue stuck out between his crimson lips. Rafael and her father flew out of her head. She took out a full breast, and the touch of the soft lips sent a shiver down her spine.

"What else?" urged Ezra.

Neither of them was embarrassed by the bare breast in the sterile pharmacy. They had both grown up in a courtyard where countless breasts had been exposed to public view, and droves of babies had been suckled in broad daylight.

"Write to him: I have been given a room for nothing, and we'll go on living there until we can stand on our own feet."

Half an hour later she listened as Ezra read the letter aloud to her. What a disappointment! Despite the flowery Arabic she understood almost everything. She had swept into the pharmacy on a wave of enthusiasm, sure that her arguments would prevail over any other considerations in Rafael's mind. With Albert's presence to sustain her, she had no doubt that Ezra's letter would melt the heart and elevate the spirit. She couldn't blame her cousin. The words were almost her words, the ideas were her very ideas, but the result! Something had been spoilt, she said to herself in distress. The photograph brought by the man from Abadan was in her handbag. Mountains terrible in their splendour, a forest such as she had never set eyes on before, a hammock such as the weary might dream of. And his eyes encompassed this enchanted landscape as he drank in the pure crystalline air. How wretched and disappointing the letter seemed next to the photograph. Rafael would be insane to exchange the tranquillity of those summits for the stench of the alley. How could this pathetic verbiage entice him from the Garden of Eden? He had seen for himself how the consumptives in Baghdad faded away. Almost up to their last day they were obliged to keep their noses to the grindstone to support their families and save them from starvation.

Ezra, on the other hand, clucked his tongue in admiration at his handiwork. "You don't get a letter like this every day," he said. At about this time he had bought himself a gramophone, and he now scattered various pearls culled from Egyptian love-songs, such as "beloved of my heart", among his lines. His lips grew wetter. Victoria transferred Albert to her other breast and covered his face with the white net so that Ezra's body odour would not reach his nostrils, in case he had picked something up from the women he spent his nights with.

"Wonderful, eh?" said Ezra and lit a cigarette which he extracted from a gold case. Victoria watched his fingers folding the sheet of paper with the precision of a pharmacist. He wrote down the address with a sweep of his pen. The letter would cross frontiers. The Beirut of his student days was no doubt filling his heart with memories and longings. His tongue licked the glue on the envelope sensuously and was suddenly arrested. Neither memories nor longings were causing him to forget his tongue on the paper, but something happening behind her back. She turned her head and saw her sister-in-law Flora standing on tiptoe at the door, her eyes and hands and lips engaged in a mute dialogue with Ezra's protuberant eyes. It was all so clear that Victoria blushed. "Come in, Flora. We were just writing a letter to Rafael. Come in, we've already finished."

Flora smiled. The woman who was to become the owner of a flourishing gambling club in Israel preferred from the start to play with her cards on the table. Obscure situations were not to her taste. She took a wicker stool, sat down next to Victoria, lifted a corner of the net and looked at Albert's face. "His father's son, his father's son," she murmured. "*Tfu!* Keep him safe from the Evil Eye."

For many years Albert was to enjoy crumbs from the table of his father's charms. Women with a soft spot in their hearts for the father avoided using the son's name. For them he was always "Rafael's son".

After a moment Flora stood up and went into the little chamber next to the medicine-cupboard where Ezra made up the prescriptions. It was clear that she was at home in the pharmacy. She emerged shortly with a glass of water in her hand. Victoria understood the hint in this display of domesticity and stood up to leave.

"I'll put on a stamp and send it myself," said Ezra. Flora's free and easy behaviour was evidently making the mischievous boy from the courtyard uncomfortable.

Albert grew and put on weight. At the beginning of winter Miriam gave birth to a daughter. During the festival of Hanukkah Victoria's mother entered labour and gave birth to a boy. For four days they searched for a name, vacillating between whether to choose a name from the Bible, the source of the names of generations of their forefathers, or whether to compromise with the new reality which was invading the alleys. In the end they decided that the name Victoria had given her son, even before his ritual circumcision and initiation into the covenant of Abraham, was good enough for his new-born uncle too. And in order to distinguish between the two Alberts, Victoria's Albert became "Albert Toria", and her brother, Najia's son, "Albert Jia". No reply came to Ezra's letter.

18

Victoria waved the little dress she had just finished sewing, and at the sound of her call Kilmanteen came running and pulled it on until her head poked out of the little collar. A melancholy face on a stalk-like neck. Her daughter's eyes were big like her father's. "Shall I wear it now?" The question expressed a wish. The little girl's manner made her shaky status in the courtyard evident. She had made the mistake of rubbing up against Izuri on two or three occasions, just as Miriam's son rubbed up against his father. Her grandfather pinched the coat over her skinny shoulder between his fingers and pushed her away from him as if he were brushing away a spiderweb. And he shook his son Fuad off in exactly the same way, only Fuad refused to learn the lesson and came back for more. Nissan, Nazima and Salima had learned from early childhood to efface themselves in his presence, but to hurry to him when he demanded service. When Izuri held Albert Jia in his hands, at first so as to see how much he weighed, and then as if examining some suspicious new invention, he ordered Salima to take her brother from him and wiped his hands, and this was the end of his physical contact with the son of his old age. Victoria wondered if her father had ever loved a living soul in his life. The two women who had stirred his passions as a youth squatted in the arcade, Aziza a huge lump of flesh giving off a bad smell, and her mother breast-feeding Albert Jia with her head nodding like the heads of the wailers during an interval in their performance. It was only rarely that her father called "Najia! Najia!" now at night, and at the sound of his summons she still dragged her body to his bed in mute submission. Even her malice had disappeared, and it was a long time since he had beaten her about the head, because he had resigned himself to her stupidity, and his daughters took care of the housekeeping. He was about fifty years old, still an impressive figure of a man with his strength in his loins but no smile on his lips. Sometimes he paused for a moment next to Victoria and looked at Albert Toria with a youthful look, and his lips moved under his moustache. A week before he had slipped a coin into his cradle and whispered: "Don't expose his face too much. The Evil Eye is all around." Victoria blushed to the roots of her hair with happiness.

"So I'll just wear it for a little while," said Kilmanteen, her eyes two lakes of hope. "I'll go for a little walk in the courtyard in it."

"Soon it will be Passover. It's the only new dress you've got to wear for the festival," explained Victoria. The little girl resigned herself and hid her disappointment and went to play with Layla. Victoria's heart soured within her. Because of her guilt it seemed to her that her own childhood had been happy compared to her daughter's. Months had gone by without a word from Rafael in reply to the letter Ezra had written for her. Her father advised her to recognize the facts and resign herself to her fate. Albert Toria had to be circumcised, because if anything happened, God forbid . . . he was still a heathen. But Victoria decided to go on waiting.

"Will one of you shift her arse and bring me breakfast," said Najia and jogged Albert Jia on her skinny knees. "Salima, I'm dying of hunger."

"Breakfast now?" her daughter said in surprise. "It's almost noon."

"I'm hungry, and I don't remember eating breakfast at all."

The mountain of flesh moved on the bench. "You forget on purpose," her sister-in-law Aziza grumbled. "You always blamed me for everything. Was it my fault that Izuri beat you for the clothes that disappeared from the washing line?"

Najia pulled a face. "What do I care now about clothes that disappeared twenty years ago?" And again she turned to the sunny courtyard. "At least a cup of tea and a piece of bread." Salima ignored her in the usual way that old people are ignored when they make nuisances of themselves. She was busy trying to persuade Victoria to let her undress Albert Toria and wash him.

"Why isn't it possible?" Aziza shrieked at Najia with an ancient rage. "I'm telling you that she used to steal your clothes from the roof and dye them black or brown. For years they dressed themselves at your expense, and you got it in the neck from Izuri on Friday nights. And if you ask me about the gold you used to hide in the holes in the wall . . ."

Najia put her fingers in her ears with demonstrative fastidiousness. "Miriam, please come and shut your mother up. Her mind's rotting, God forbid it should happen to us."

"I haven't got time for your squabbles," said Miriam's voice from the glassed-in room. "Lying there on your mats all day and talking nonsense."

Nissan, who had played hookey from the factory that day, saw this as a sign that Aziza was now fair game. He stole to the foot of the bench, with his brother Fuad on his heels. Naim, Miriam's eldest, handed them the box of matches and watched fascinated as his cousin stuck a match between his grandmother's exposed toes. Aziza's suspicions were aroused. "What are you doing there, you dogs?"

The grandson knew his grandmother's weakness. "We brought you *halva*."

Because of the rheumatism her legs were painful at night and numb by day. Her great paunch separated her eyes from the three boys busy at her feet. Nissan lit a match and set it to the match sticking between her toes, while Fuad and Naim hid him from view.

"A scorpion," roared the old lady. "A big scorpion bit me. Like a red-hot poker."

"Rascals," Salima scolded the malevolent imps. "Wasting matches like that, and at night there's nothing to light the lamps with."

"A scorpion!" Aziza's scream silenced the courtyard din. Miriam pounded down the stairs with a sound like rolling thunder, and the three miscreants fled to the alley. When a slender figure hesitantly entered the courtyard a moment later, she thought that one of them had returned to tease her and she grabbed him by the collar and got ready to slap his face.

"What do you want of me?" asked Juri Chittaiyat's grandson sullenly and turned to Victoria. "Umm Albert, your husband has come home, the Lord be praised," he said proudly and waited in silence for his reward.

"What?" grunted Miriam.

Victoria paled. She was speechless. She saw that the boy was panting for breath as if he had been running.

"Did you see him with your own eyes?" demanded Salima.

"At the entrance to al-Shorja market. A Kurdish porter is dragging a box behind him. He told me to run here and tell you so you wouldn't get a fright when you saw him."

"Victoria," Miriam burst into tears. "Rafael's alive. Oh God, he's come home."

Victoria was still unable to talk, or to cry like Miriam. She saw Aziza's wide-open mouth and forgot what she was screaming about. Panic seized her. I'm paralysed. I can't stand up. Rafael's coming back to a crippled woman. She snatched Albert and clasped him to her bosom and she didn't know if she wanted to protect him or be protected by him. If only he had let them know a day before, half a day. It was midday, the courtyard had not yet been washed, the children were running about, almost all of them barefoot. Albert was like a flower in a vase, Kilmanteen too was more or less decently dressed. And she herself! She was seized by the sense of worthlessness common to women in the east. The man was the peacock of the family. Especially when he was a man of the world like Rafael. To be caught like this, now of all times, in a plain shabby dress, slightly soiled, and scuffed slippers on her feet. With all the morning's work ahead of her she hadn't even combed her hair properly. Her face was crying out for a little care. One of her molars had been extracted a month ago and she had to be careful when she smiled, and especially when she laughed. For a moment she wanted to shout for someone to shut the door of the lavatory that served dozens of people, most of them small children and old people with poor eyesight, until it was no more than a filthy hole, invading the courtyard with gusts of foul, stinking air. And again she remembered the picture of the mountain and the green forest, the book lying on his knees and the gaze encompassing the enchanted view.

"Why doesn't he come already?" said Miriam. Juri Chittaiyat's grandson was still waiting for his reward.

"I'm telling you it's a scorpion!" yelled Aziza.

"Mother, it wasn't a scorpion," said Miriam impatiently. "They burnt your foot."

"Burnt?" said the old woman in bewilderment. "Who would want to burn a foot?"

"Stupid cow," said Najia with crushing superiority.

Rafael entered the courtyard. His eyebrows were covered with the dust of the Syrian desert and he was obviously very tired. He sent the porter away, gave the rabbi's grandson a few coins, and stood in the courtyard in all his glory, his head bare and his curls parted down the middle with waves on either side. His glasses in their black frames glinted in the sun. His blue suit emphasized the suppleness of his body, and the tip of his cane tapped lightly on the ground as if to measure the depths of the swamp he had landed in. Victoria remembered the doctor who had visited Yehuda before he died, the way he too had looked around him disdainfully as if unwilling to sit down or touch anything. But this prince had been born right here, and he hadn't belonged to the élite of the courtyard either. And now he was putting on airs. Then her heart failed her. Her husband had returned from the valley of the shadow of death, he had risen from the grave.

The cane tapped twice towards her. "Hello, Victoria."

Her face flamed. She didn't dare open her mouth for fear of producing an incoherent stammer. The courtyard saw every movement, heard every word. "Praised be the name of the Lord for bringing you safely home." A fire burned in her throat, sweat dripped from her armpits. Why didn't he take off those glasses that froze her blood? In the end she realized that it was only in her imagination that she had returned his greeting. That faint smile was still playing on his face, the indulgent smile of an adult encouraging a tongue-tied child to talk. Kilmanteen clung to her tightly. Speechlessly Victoria held Albert out to him. Her heart pounded. What if he rejected him after touching him? Her father had touched Fuad and Albert Jia and pushed them away.

"Is this our son?" asked Rafael and hung his cane on his arm and held out both his hands.

"This is Albert," she said and breathed a sigh of relief.

Her hands supported the baby's neck and buttocks and were loath to part from him. Rafael crossed the heavily drawn line dividing the sun from the shade in the courtyard. His fingers touched hers as he took Albert from her hands. He stepped back into the sun and examined the little face in the harsh light. The baby closed his eyes against the glare, and as if remembering something important he opened them again and fixed them on the glinting glasses. Rafael stood with his back to Victoria, and suddenly he bent over and she hurried to his side in an obscure fear and saw that his face was bare and his eyes were gazing without a trace of arrogance and the glasses were clutched in Albert's fist.

"Naughty boy," Rafael exulted in the tone Victoria had been longing to hear for so many months.

He rescued his glasses carefully from the little fingers and fell onto a nearby chair without first looking to see if it was clean, and laid the baby on his knees and began to take off his nappies.

"What are you doing?"

Miriam burst out laughing.

"Don't worry, we examined his prick a hundred times because of that blind Jamila."

"He'll be cold outside." Victoria's voice trembled.

"I brought him a suit. Open the box."

Albert enjoyed his freedom and kicked his laughing father's

chest, but the suit was too small for him and his limbs refused to be crammed into it. A shadow darkened Rafael's eyes. "What's this?" he asked with a lecher's suspicion he didn't bother to hide.

But Victoria answered him firmly and confidently. "Count the months. He was born big," she said proudly, "and as Ezra wrote you, we still haven't had him circumcised. We waited for you."

With his own hands he swaddled the infant. Then he put his hand on his daughter's head and looked into the shy eyes fixed on his face. "And you, Kilmanteen, I bought you a silk dress, my girl." Over her head his eyes met the little eyes of his mother-in-law, and he was surprised to see how mild the hostility reflected in them was. His attention was immediately turned elsewhere. "Who's that lying there?"

"My mother," said Miriam in an embarrassed mumble.

He gave Albert back to Victoria. "Aunt Aziza?" he said, shocked. "Left outside in the winter cold?" He pulled a fine woollen shawl intended for his wife out of the box.

The old woman recoiled in horror from his glasses. "It's him," she cried. "The Angel of Death's at the gate. You're in a hurry to get rid of me and that's why you've fetched the doctor."

"Aunt Aziza, I'm Rafael, not the doctor."

"I'm not deaf, I can hear that you're the doctor. Go away. Enough that you robbed me of Yehuda. I don't want your poisoned pills and your cursed potions."

"Look, see what I brought you from Lebanon."

"I'm perfectly healthy, and I'm not a child to be taken in by your tricks. I'm very hungry and nobody gives a damn."

"Damn your souls for not believing me that I'm hungry too," complained Najia.

"What's going on here?" Rafael turned to Victoria as if she was to blame for the old-age and decay which had invaded the courtyard. "What happened to her room?"

"We're living there. The window-room belongs to Miriam and Gurji now."

"Don't worry," Najia spoke to him for the first time in years.

"The frost is over and she'll live another year at least. Look how worried he is about her. Anyone would think she was his mother."

"If only someone would bring me a plate of beans with a little onion," said Aziza cajolingly.

"Listen to her," grumbled Najia. "All the time you thought that I was the crazy one."

Rafael moved away from the arcade. "I saw strange faces in the Nunus' house."

Toya's little head popped up over the second-floor railing. "Ma'atuk moved into a rich man's house. Those people are renting the rooms." Rafael smiled at the childish face. He hasn't changed, Victoria said to herself. That's how he smiles whenever a woman's voice takes him by surprise. With her eyes downcast she plucked up the courage to ask: "How are you?"

"Tired and dirty from the journey. The doctors say I'm almost well." And he jerked his head in the direction of Najia and Aziza and lowered his voice: "And I'm ashamed to say that I'm hungry too."

"Go and lie down to rest in the room. I'll heat up water for a bath and bring you food."

She gave Albert to Nazima and Salima and went to fill a big basin at the tap. Nissan helped Rafael to drag the box into the room. In the kitchen she lit twigs under the basin and collapsed onto the cooking board. She was full of bitterness. Not one look of affection, not one warm word. Not a smile. He addressed her in the same way that he used to address his mother when he came home from work. She had been afraid of him too. His glasses were cold. And his suit was remote in its elegance. Now it was her duty to take the steaming water and pour it over his naked body. And she would soap his back too. She would touch his flesh. In the light of the flames she saw her toes sticking out of her slippers. The toenails were coarse. Almost black. A person needed to be in a good mood to look after his toenails. How could she have guessed that he would suddenly turn up after the long silence of the grave? And how was she going to get into the same bed as him tonight? She had seen the women winking at each other in the courtyard. She needed time to think, to prepare herself, to run to the bath-house. It was late. Past midday. She had been sleeping alone so long. There was a shameful down on her legs. Her breasts were full of milk. Her hair was rusty. She had almost grown used to the idea that he was under the ground. Then she mocked herself: What makes you think he's so eager to drown himself in your body? Don't forget, he made himself out to be a bachelor over there in the mountains. He had probably come home satiated, after tasting the best the beaches of Beirut had to offer. And perhaps he would run off this very night to the theeayter with Ezra. Heavy clouds were covering the sky. Soon it would pour with rain. He probably hadn't recovered completely yet, he would be afraid to go out in the rain and postpone his revels to another night.

Ezra came post-haste with bottles in his hands. Dahood removed the zither from its case and sent Toya to help prepare refreshments. Izuri caught three chickens in the courtyard with his own hands and sent Nissan to the ritual slaughterer. Clarisse, who didn't love anything, escaped to her room where the door was almost always locked. Under the pots the flames roared, and the aromas coming from the kitchen were so delicious that Aziza rose from her bench and undid the kerchief on her head and scratched her balding head and wondered aloud: "Who did you bury today? Who are you sitting *shiva* for?"

Flora came with her husband and laid the festive table in the arcade, after banishing Aziza to one of the rooms. The light from three big lamps gleamed darkly in Flora's hair. Her eyes flashed. Ezra took a few staggering steps towards the arcade. Already drunk before the party began, he gave the high-spirited woman a hard pinch. "Bitch, what rooster did you fold your wings under lately? Isn't Ezra good enough for you any more?"

"Go and sit with Mother for a bit," said Miriam rebukingly. She didn't see that his mind was on other things. A sly smile appeared on Flora's face. "Be careful," she said, glancing at Rafael rather than her husband. The two of them, Asher and

Rafael, were approaching each other along the balustrade of the middle roof, Asher's arms open to embrace his brother, and an expression of resignation on Rafael's face. Ezra was furious. "Wait!" he said and pointed to his fly. "You'll still come begging, but you won't get any, not even if the worms are crawling out of your eyeholes, you bitch." Flora's laughter rang out in the courtyard, the pure laughter of an innocent girl who had forgotten herself for a moment. This virginal laughter defeated the pharmacist, and he retreated and spat sullenly on the ground.

Victoria looked at Toya bowed over the fire next to her with her head hanging. "Stop eating yourself up," she rebuked her gently. "Wash your hands of him. He's not worth your heartache."

Miriam was jealous of this intimacy. "What are you two doing, fawning on each other like a couple of love birds?"

Victoria waved her hand with a smile. Suddenly she was happy. She was an important, privileged member of the courtyard again. Toya came to her for comfort, Miriam was jealous of her favours. The whole house was in a turmoil because of the return of her breadwinner. Suddenly the smile froze on her face. "Where's Albert?" She saw her sisters, who were supposed to be looking after him, going from the basement entrance to the water-jar niche. She rushed into the courtyard.

"There he is." Kilmanteen pointed to the landing at the bottom of the stairs.

With two bounds she reached the stairs and saw both Alberts, her son and her brother, greedily sucking her mother's teats. A talon of jealousy clawed at her chest, and her indignation flared, as if Albert Toria had betrayed her on purpose, in order to torment her. He screamed in protest as she snatched him from her mother's breast. Quickly she pulled out her own fresh breast and stuck it into the screaming little mouth, with the blank stare of a person who had been close to catastrophe in her eyes. At her back she heard her father's chuckle. "Your mother's milk isn't polluted."

Her frown melted a little. She stroked the baby's sweating

forehead and murmured: "Traitor, you're a traitor like your father."

An hour later there was a holiday atmosphere in the arcade. In the light cast by the three big lamps on the lavishly laid table, dozens of people pressed into the narrow space, united in the joy of the meeting, and listened open-mouthed to the story of Rafael's resurrection. The money they had collected after the man from Abadan's visit had evaporated very quickly in the luxurious sanatorium. Rafael had captured the hearts of the nurses, but they couldn't help him when the management were about to throw him out, and he threw himself on the mercy of the director. From the day I arrived here, he said in the office, I've only seen two or three patients walking out of the gate on their own two feet. All the others were taken out in coffins, surrounded by grieving faces. He himself, so he had heard, was regarded as a particularly severe case, an incurably ill man whose days were numbered. They were only treating him for show, because there was no point in wasting drugs on him. He wasn't complaining. He was grateful for the pleasant room, the intoxicating air, the good food, the books in the library—all these things made his last days bearable. He was ready to give up his expensive room and move into the servants quarters and even to work a little. Bury me here, he said, in one of the pits behind the hill. I've heard that the doctors need corpses for research. So I'll sell you my body in advance. I have nowhere to go. I'm a man who leaves no impression behind him. When I'm in front of people's eyes they love me, when I move on it's no catastrophe. That's the curse of a man who wastes all his substance on others. When he's left without a penny nobody expects anything of him. He's wiped out before he dies. At the most people remember his sins.

Rafael stopped talking. Victoria was taken aback when she realized that up to now she had never seen things from his point of view. She remembered the diamond-studded jewel he had given his mother, and how his mother had refused to give it up and contribute it to the costs of his treatment. Rafael knew that his audience was spellbound. Tears ran down Miriam's fat cheeks unchecked. Toya bit her lips. When he repeated the word "sanatorium" their heads jerked back as if at the beating of a giant gong. Out of habit he wiped his dry lips with his handkerchief. Flora made haste to peel an orange, divide it into segments and display them on the palm of her hand. Her tongue ran slowly over her upper lip. Ezra handed him a glass of arak, and when Rafael took the arak she began to feed him the segments one by one, and he took them absent-mindedly without looking at her. Izuri found the woman's behaviour insufferable, and he cleared his throat and coughed as he did when he was disturbed while strapping on his phylacteries. At first Victoria suffered agonies of jealousy, but then she saw the remote look in her husband's eye, the same look she had seen in the man from Abadan's eyes. He was still somewhere else. And she understood that there was no place now for her or for Flora in the desert of his loneliness.

In a humorous vein he went on to say that all his words had fallen on the floor of the office like flies killed by the cold. Next to the director sat three doctors. One of them, with a red face, said that Rafael was right: there were a lot of germs floating around the sanatorium, and this was precisely the reason it would be better for everyone concerned if he left before he returned his soul to his Maker. They had the good name of the sanatorium to think of, and it was important for a few of the patients at least to survive. This doctor was a Lebanese who had studied in Vienna, and it was the first time that Rafael had ever met anyone for whom hatred of Jews was a religion. Curiously enough, the anti-Semitic doctor breathed new life into him and he left the office with his head held high. Rafael decided to turn his back on the sanatorium and apply to his fellow Jews for help. He would ask no more of the Jews of Beirut than a piece of bread and a roof over his head in his last days on earth. He would look for lodgings close to the entertainment district. He was still a young man in his prime, and he was shedding the leaves of his life while they were still green. Surely he was entitled to feast his eyes on young flowers before he expired, rather than choke on the smell of the dying. The Jewish merchant in Beirut promised him that his body would not be left to rot in the streets like the carcass of a dog. When his time came he would be buried in hallowed ground and given a proper Jewish funeral.

Victoria drank in Rafael's words with all her being, until it seemed to her that she was filled with the same pride as he, the empty pride of those condemned to death. She noticed that her father was smoking a lot and listening intently to Rafael's every word, and she began to suspect that Rafael, who did not usually talk about himself, had some hidden purpose in telling the tale of his adventures in a foreign land to so many listeners. The three strands from which he was weaving his story, too—death, the obligation of Jews everywhere to help one another, and his profound loneliness—also seemed directed at her father's ears. The two of them hardly ever addressed one another directly, especially when they wanted to wound or to express affection. It was clear that they were attracted to one another to the same extent as they repelled one another. Just as they refrained from emotional embraces, so they did everything in their power to avoid open conflict. Both of them sought a language or a means of communicating their repulsion and their love, and they did not find one. Sometimes, for lack of any other alternative, they used her: "Tell your father," "Tell your husband." And she lacked the malice, the daring and the impudence to do as they bid her. It was Albert who in time to come received the ungrateful task of the courier delivering their messages. "Tell your father," "Tell your grandfather." And he too did not understand at first how the left hand of either one of them wanted to tear the other's head off, while the right hand wanted to clasp him in a manly embrace.

On that distant evening her father drank glass after glass of arak, without bothering to help himself to the refreshments on the table, but smoking between sips. Rafael's eyes strayed to the little handkerchief whose one tip was between Flora's teeth and the other between her fingers. Unconsciously she pulled the handkerchief in a spasm so violent that Rafael stared, marvelling at the strength of the flimsy material, which finally tore with an obscene squeal.

Rafael exerted every ounce of his strength not to cough and spray his Jewish blood in front of the anti-Semitic doctor. The storm gathered in his chest, and as he stood next to the door he doubted whether he would have the strength to turn the handle.

"Just a minute," one of the doctors called as he stood in front of the door with his back to them.

A sigh of relief swept through the audience. "He must have been a Jew, that doctor," said Murad, who had escaped the loneliness of his wife's room and stolen furtively into the arcade. It was a doctor who had studied Rafael with interest during the interview and encouraged him with smiles and nods to make his plea, but there wasn't a single Jew in the whole of the sanatorium, neither among the staff nor among the patients, explained Rafael. And then one day a magnificent limousine had driven up from Beirut with a young woman of about eighteen, her father who was smoking a fat cigar, her red-eyed mother, and a pile of luggage containing expensive dresses and precious jewels. They were from Australia. Rafael didn't understand their English, but the whole hospital was thrown into a furore when the father's voice was heard in the lobby. In the evening the parents returned to Beirut, and a few days later Rafael saw a Magen David on the girl's breast, and he knew that she was Jewish.

Victoria buried her head in Albert Toria's body in order to hide her embarrassment. How had he discovered what was hanging on the breast of an English-speaking girl in another room of the hospital?

"Was she pretty?" Ezra asked the question to which Victoria already knew the answer.

"Her hair was silky gold," Rafael closed his eyes, "and her skin like a sun-kissed peach."

Victoria could not hide her hostility. "And what happened to her in the end?"

His glasses stared into her face and her blush deepened. After a few weeks had passed her parents came in a bigger black limousine, whose back seat was long enough to hold a coffin.

Four women beat their breasts like wailers. Because of Victoria's jealousy the nameless girl became a dear daughter of the courtyard who had just lost her life. And that doctor, Rafael continued his story, even though he wasn't a Jew but a Christian, was a human being. He followed Rafael into the corridor and led him to a chair and put his hand on his shoulder until the coughing stopped.

"God will reward him." Miriam wiped her eyes with her fist. Victoria was there in the cold corridor too, and she blessed the doctor for his kindness. With that feverish Rafael in the cold hospital corridor she might have been able to talk, but to this Rafael lighting a cigarette over the laden table she was afraid to say: Don't smoke so much after everything you've been through. Ezra, her father, Dahood and even Nissan followed his example and soon a dense cloud of smoke was hanging over the arcade. Instead of accompanying him to his room, the doctor led him to a bench in the spacious gardens surrounding the sanatorium. There are some things, said the doctor, that money can't buy. You can't be tall if you were born to be short. There are things that you have to accept. But there are other things, no less important, which even if you can't buy them with money, you can achieve them with courage.

"I'm ready," Rafael interrupted the doctor in a firm voice.

The doctor said in surprise: "You know?" And indeed, Rafael had seen a considerable number of beggarly patients in the expensive sanatorium. They arrived shrouded in a heavy silence, and when they disappeared, in the same heavy silence, the doctors looked glum.

"But you don't know the nature of the experiment we're conducting here."

True enough, even the lips of the friendly nurses were sealed, and Rafael had not succeeded in getting a word out of them.

"We pierce the flesh with hollow needles, penetrate the chest cavity and puncture the lungs." Through these hollow needles, the doctor explained, they fed compressed oxygen into the lungs. Up to now all the unfortunate wretches who had participated in the experiment had died. Had anyone volunteered for the experiment knowing in advance what lay in store for them? The doctor squirmed on his seat. "As a rule the families volunteered the participants. It isn't easy to keep a tubercular patient in a poor household. And it would be cruel to frighten the poor creatures before the end. The nurses didn't tell you because they themselves don't know all the details."

Rafael said that he would volunteer and there was no need to obtain the signature of his family.

"I have to tell you frankly once more that nobody has survived the experiment to date."

Rafael asked what he would get in return.

"Free hospitalization until you recover."

Or until he died, including the funeral expenses.

The doctor nodded.

"And what happened then?" asked Murad when Rafael's silence lengthened.

"I'm here," said Rafael.

During her lonely nights Victoria had bitterly resented Rafael for running off to Lebanon and leaving her destitute. Sometimes he seemed to be like a drowning man who dragged everyone around him down to the depths. Only her mother had dared to denounce him openly. But Victoria knew that many others had the same thoughts. Even his own mother. She had said so in so many words when Victoria asked her for the diamond-studded tiara to help pay his medical expenses in Lebanon: "If I had given in to his father the way you give in to him, we would have all been dead long ago." And she had not tried to persuade her mother-in-law, because in spite of her belief that perhaps he might come back to her, especially after the birth of Albert, she could not completely suppress the thought that perhaps his mother was right, perhaps there was no hope for him and conscienceless doctors were robbing him of his money in vain.

And here he was. He had gambled with his life and won. Played with death and come out the victor. And it was her victory too. The love which had turned to cold ashes inside her revived. Those big eyes, that delicate nose, his shapely lips, his dexterous fingers, his spellbinding tongue. He had come back to life. Let Flora sit next to a mountain of oranges and feed him segment after segment until the world came to an end. Where was Rahma Afsa? Where had the singer who snatched him away to Damascus disappeared to? You only had to look at Gurji's face to understand Miriam. God forgive her, she too was declaring her love for Rafael in her own way.

And nevertheless her distress did not disappear. It seemed to her that the more her admiration grew the more her desire withered. He seemed to her now pure spirit. She almost fainted at the thought of this quintessential spirit bearing down on her this very night and taking off her clothes. If only she could have gone on sitting in this magical warmth and drinking in the sound of his voice and feeling Albert's soft breath on her breast. She couldn't stop worrying about what she would do with Albert. Up to now she had never been separated from him at night. He slept with her on the clumsy bench. Rafael had come back unexpectedly, and apparently trivial things sucked her thoughts into giddy whirlpools. Even for Rafael's sake she would not banish Albert to a cold, shabby, unravelling mat. And on the other hand, it would be a shameful thing to force a man who had just returned from such a luxurious sanatorium to spend his first night at home on so coarse a bed. Suddenly she realized that she was ashamed to confront him with her poverty. Rafael was entitled to something better. A little devil sang in the secret of her heart: You're afraid of him, of your own husband. You've borne him three children, and you still behave like a foolish virgin.

"How are you going to earn a living, Rafael?" said Ezra. "Your wife ate dirt while you were away. Have you got any ideas?"

Rafael gave him a long stare. "I've just escaped from the grave and I'm not even fully recovered yet."

"Come to the pharmacy. Work as much as you can. Maybe one day we'll be partners."

Rafael expressed his thanks with a noncommittal smile.

Victoria saw that her father was listening intently. Flora was bored. She stood up and disappeared into the thick darkness of the courtyard. Victoria was probably the only one who noticed the bottle she concealed under the jacket of her suit.

"So you'll come on Sunday and begin work with us."

Victoria's throat contracted. Her father had said with us and not for us.

"And how long are you going to stay stuck in this hole?" said Ezra. "Ma'atuk Nunu has already escaped from the dirt. Look for a bigger house and I'll join you. I abandoned my mother," he added with drunken tears. "We should all be together again."

19

The Jews uprooted more palm trees and spread out boldly along ruler-straight streets on the German model, surrounding themselves with spacious parks in the English style. Not everyone could afford to jump straight into a private, one-family villa in the prestigious new suburbs, but those who were on the way up leap-frogged year by year into bigger, newer apartments, in better neighbourhoods, which had been evacuated by those fortunate enough to take up their abode among the palms. As a rule they all moved into their new homes together at the end of the festival of *Sukkoth*. The entire community would scurry about like a frenzied anthill. Wagons, donkeys, mules and porters trailed along the streets and alleys carrying wardrobes, beds, jars of preserves and bundles of clothes, with columns of sweating women, stern-faced men, and noisy, romping children bringing up the rear.

The courtyard waited from Passover to *Sukkoth*, and then joined in the carnival and set out with its children and chattels for an imposing new house in the fabric bazaar. Different smells, different sounds, no longer a dead-end alley but a street leading to other streets. The new house was an anonymous door in a long row of doors, and it shattered the old feeling of permanence where time held no sway. In this new era many people believed that there was nothing too precious to leave behind in order to seize hold of something new. Without sorrow Victoria left the house where her father and her husband, she and her children had been born. Since Rafael had returned and become a partner in the exercise-book factory, she had accumulated a considerable amount of property: a big iron bed, a wardrobe, a table, chairs, a carpet, a silver *Hanukka* lamp, clothes. Rafael walked in front of the cart and she carried Albert in her arms behind it, with Kilmanteen hanging onto her skirts. Also in the caravan escaping from the alley were her father and his family, Miriam and her family, her brother Murad and his household, Ezra, who had joined them, and Dahood with Toya and his three children.

In the commotion of the move Aziza had almost completely lost her hearing. Again and again they explained to her that no catastrophe had occurred, they were simply moving from the old ruin into a house "where you could breathe". But she waved her hand in disbelief. "I hear noises in the night too. And they're not demons or ghosts. Listen to me, we had good times in this house. It's foolishness to leave it for lies." She clung to her bench and refused to leave the house. She snatched the bundle of old clothes Miriam was about to throw into the mouldy cellar and cried: "Izuri, they're throwing your brother's clothes away. Say something!" Some people laughed spitefully. Only Izuri's vigilance stopped the boys from tormenting the confused old woman. He was moved by the tears streaming down the wrinkled face, and he had to suppress an urge to wipe the sunken cheeks with his big hand and tell her that sooner or later everybody was obliged to leave their youth behind them. He was the only one to understand her feelings, and also her longing for his dead brother. In the caravan she stumbled and protested and wept. He looked down at her and the black tassel of his fez trembled. Because of his wife and children and grandchildren he was afraid to walk beside her and support her on his steady arm. But he helped her to catch up with the cart and to hold onto the side, so that she could drag herself to the new house with its help. Her fingers slipped off. Nissan pretended not to notice her and jostled her and kicked her leg with his new Sabbath shoes. His father hit him on the chest and he lost his breath and fell back to the end of the column, with the big bundle of clothes on his head giving him the appearance of an industrious ant. Then Izuri slipped his hands under her armpits and lifted her onto the cart. Her legs swung between the back wheels grinding the dirt of the road, her kerchief slipped and revealed her balding scalp, her huge bosom fell onto her thighs and her head wagged to and fro with the pounding of the horses' hooves as if repeating the same question over and over again. Izuri walked behind the cart, and she saw him taking one step after the other towards her and never catching up, and she sat opposite him and waited for him, looking with the yearning of years into the eyes of the youth who was as tall as a giant, and a reckless, immodest smile dawned on her puckered lips, and in her withered body an astonishingly youthful cry echoed: Izuri, we're wasting time! She had put a silver coin into Jamila's hand so that she would weave her web of black magic well: a fatal stumble, a malignant disease, a death while giving birth. But the sudden death did not come. The magic had bestowed eternal fertility on the loathsome creature instead. How deeply Izuri's cry at night had cut her heart: "Najia! Najia!" That other cry she longed to hear: "Aziza! Aziza!" had been throttled at birth. And Izuri hobbled slowly in time to the cart, like a manacled giant in a convoy of convicts, unable to take his usual energetic strides, and Aziza's face in front of him was a disintegrating ruin of a once handsome house. Once upon a time that dark maw surrounded with wrinkles had whispered things it was worth living for. Those slack folds of fat were once firm and scented with the perfumes of India. His brother Yehuda had never been jealous of him, because he had never even noticed such things. Or at least so it seemed to Izuri. But jealousy had dug its claws into his own flesh on the summer nights. Mosquito net touching mosquito net, a sky strewn with stars. He and she eternally imprisoned on the ocean of a single roof. And the closeness was crushing. The neighbouring net quivered, and there was no telling if it was a gust of wind or flesh opening like a screaming wound. Then Izuri learned to shout: "Najia! Najia!" in order to avenge himself on Aziza, in order to embarrass his brother. Afterwards he would fold his arms under his head and look at the sky.

Three days later Victoria was beside herself with happiness. She stood in the doorway of her new room on the second floor, with Albert in her arms, and breathed in a lungful of the intoxicating air. "It's rain. The first rain. Smell it," she said to the infant who had suffered from the sweltering summer heat. It was already night. In the lights coming from the doors and windows of the rooms the rain looked like thin threads dropping from the blackness of the sky and disappearing into the darkness of the courtyard below. She passed a hand wet with rain over the baby's face, and he closed his eyes and pursed his lips as if making up his mind whether to cry, until she could no longer restrain her laughter, and she laughed at the rain and the perfumed wind and the fine room with the spotless ceiling decorated with plaster flowers, and she pressed Albert's face between her head and her shoulder, and bit her lip to stop herself from biting him. She could hardly restrain herself from digging her teeth into his flesh. "There'll be no more khamsins, the summer's over," she announced gladly, even though she herself detested the rain and the cold.

And indeed, he began to flourish as soon as a cool breath of air penetrated the nets on the roof at night, and the blazing heat of the sun abated. In the first khamsin at the beginning of summer, when people were blessing the bountiful watermelon crop, and bands of boys were going to swim in the Tigris, Albert had hung his head like a wilted flower, while Albert Jia celebrated his freedom from his nappies and made a bee-line for the sun. Her mother fell on her. Her son was lying in her arms as if there was no life in him. It was her punishment for Suzanne. The cold had killed her daughter and the heat would kill her son. His lips fluttered on her nipples without the strength to suck. His arms dropped and his eyes closed. At first she did not make the connection between his condition and the heavy khamsin, and she ran with him to Juri Chittaiyat, who wrote a few lines on a piece of paper and instructed her to soak it in water and give the water to Albert to drink. Albert got worse. It was the weird Clarisse who opened her eyes. "The child is sensitive to heat. My brother's the same. He can dance naked in the hail and he turns into a rag when the dates ripen on the palms."

"What should I do?"

"Wrap him in damp cloths."

"He's so small. He'll catch cold."

"I told you. Types like that you can lay on ice."

Victoria was insulted. Her Albert was not to be dismissed as a "type". "And your brother," she asked, "how did you look after him?"

"My mother used to run with him to Abu Sifein and they would lie him under a nanny goat and milk her straight onto his face and he would revive."

Without her *abbaya* Victoria ran to the little sheep pen in the middle of the Abu Sifein quarter and took off his clothes and his body was bathed in the rich jets. His skin gleamed and became smooth and slippery and his lips parted and he even drank, and Victoria cried and all around her the sheep bleated and the goats sneezed.

Thirty years later Albert stood on the verge of the beautiful spring of Nun near the village of Migdal north of Tiberias. The spring had carved out a round pool and the water burst forth into a canal built of black basalt rock and ran from there to the fields of the village. Albert spread a measuring form on his thigh, and as he wrote down the coordinates of the spring and the flow conditions, he explained to the new apprentice in the hydrological service how to set the current meter in the canal in order to measure the discharge of the spring. A few steps away from them sat a Moslem shepherd of about nine years old, with whom Albert had already struck up a friendly relationship. For some reason the boy's parents had delayed his circumcision, and he needed to hear Albert's repeated reassurances that the circumciser was not a monster, and the unavoidable rite was not as horrific as his friends had made out in order to torment him.

The new worker stood in the canal in rubber boots, the upper half of his body naked, slapping his back and chest to kill the horseflies sucking his blood, and wherever a yellow fly met its death a rose of blood blossomed. He had just been discharged from the army, and in spite of Albert's eccentricities he found the work interesting. From time to time he bent down to bathe his fly-bites in the spring water and as he did so he glanced angrily at the shepherd boy who was taking Albert's mind off the job and keeping them there longer than necessary. In the end he could endure it no longer and he complained aloud: "That goddamn stink!" As if the smell of the sheep-pen coming from behind the eucalyptus grove was to blame for all the afflictions of this godforsaken hole.

Albert's nostrils flared and his look grew remote. "It's a wonderful smell," he said.

The apprentice pulled a face. Albert did not tell him that he had been born on the banks of a mighty river, far away from the little grocery store of Migdal, and even if he had wanted to he would not have been able to tell him why whenever he came to measure the discharge of the spring of Nun he felt as if he had already been in this beautiful place a long time before. He did not remember when he had learnt to delight in the smell of sheep and goats. Sometimes he liked to joke that in a previous incarnation he must have been a shepherd.

Inside the room at whose door Victoria was standing and touching the first rain of the season Rafael was busy polishing the *Hanukka* lamp and other silverware and a strong smell of Brasso filled the room. From time to time he would bring home some astonishing new invention from abroad. For generations his forefathers had resigned themselves to scratching the bites of the clouds of mosquitoes and flies, but Rafael had bought a spray-gun of Flit, which resembled a miniature cannon, and he fired it ruthlessly at the pests until the floor was black with their corpses. This new toy had captured the hearts of young and old alike, and one Friday Najia had wielded it furiously at a swarm of flies buzzing round the fish waiting to be fried, with the result that everyone who ate the fish spent the whole of the Sabbath running to the lavatory.

The *Hanukka* lamp shone and Kilmanteen hugged her knees and sat next to her father and gazed at the gleaming silver. Victoria's room was neat and tidy, their dinner was simmering on the little kerosene cooker, and the furniture gave off a new smell of bright, solid domesticity. Rafael had put his intelligence and ingenuity to work on the little exercise-book factory, and they now produced thick book-keeping ledgers too. Michal had been forgotten, and from now on the family was known as Mujallid, in other words, bookbinder. Her father rewarded him handsomely, although the silence which cried out for closeness still stood between them.

Albert's lashes fluttered on Victoria's cheek and sent a delicious tickling sensation through her body. She gave all the credit for their good fortune to Albert. At the age of fourteen months Albert Jia was already an obedient plaything in his hands. Recently he had learned to walk by his own unaided efforts. He could even curb his uncle Fuad's violence. Her brother would gaze at him admiringly, allow him to clamber onto his back and take him on tours around the house. She was always vigilant, and she hardly ever let him out of her sight. Rafael scolded her, and said that she was turning the child into a sissy, like her brother Murad. His words hurt her. For two whole days she fasted and cold-shouldered him, until he unbent and turned on the charms of the goodwill ambassador. And as she was stroking his dry forehead, in her customary caress after she had taken her fill of him, he whispered in his jasmine-sweet voice: "I love him no less than you do, but the world's a hard place, and he has to grow claws of his own. You hardly let him learn to crawl, he was always in your arms. In life anyone who doesn't know how to run is crushed underfoot." And that was exactly what she feared. Perhaps it was from his father that he had inherited his wanderlust, which drew him to the darkest corners of the house, the haunts of snakes and scorpions, and to the smells and lights of the street. In the end she let him walk by himself, but first she tied two gold anklets with little bells on them to his feet, so that she could hear him wherever he was. Sometimes the bells would ring from the laps of the girls in the courtyard, who liked to wash him and lick him with the flame of their tongues. Once she heard the chimes from her father's lap, and saw Albert Jia sitting on the floor and looking up in mute longing. Hardest of all to bear was his craving for her mother's breasts. He would clamber onto his grandmother's bony knees, and he and his uncle would each nestle up to a different breast. For about two years they drank from this fount, and Najia never pushed him away. When he approached her, a strange gleam would brighten her eyes, as if Albert Toria did not belong to the same race which had tormented her all her life. Sometimes Victoria suspected jealously that her mother was sending him secret signals that only he could hear, and he would come and suck the marrow out of her bones, and then he would pass his lips over his grandmother's wrinkled cheeks and look into her eyes until at last he plucked a rare smile from those melancholy lakes.

"Victoria," said Rafael's voice from the room which smelled of polish and new furniture.

A shiver ran up her spine. She knew that tone. Where she came from a man did not call his wife in a tone like that, half in wonder, half in lewd invitation, as if asking and answering at once, and she knew to the roots of her hair that tonight he wanted her with a smile, with laughter, with consuming passion. As she crossed the room on her way to the cooker her thigh brushed deliberately against his back.

She didn't remember when she slid into the shadows of a delicious sleep. The mattress was transformed into a cradle rocking her to sleep, and she closed her eyes and gave herself up to the fragmentary memories of her earliest childhood. She heard the match grating in Rafael's hand and she wanted to tell him to take care of his health and not to smoke any more that night. At the sound of the second match she woke up, and found him lying on his back, one hand under his head and the other bearing the cigarette to his lips, his eyes on the plaster flowers on the ceiling. The pungent smell of their lust lingered in the air. She turned over onto her side in the foetal position Rafael liked so much and waited for him to finish smoking and encircle her body with his and stroke her belly and squeeze her thighs between his until they both fell asleep. Kilmanteen was dreaming a sweet dream and murmured gently in her sleep. Albert moved in his sleep and his head bumped against the bars of his crib. At the first cry she leapt out of bed and came back with her nipple in his mouth. "You're wide awake."

She paid no attention to the fact that she was completely naked, and he looked at her and thought of a mountain brook dashing between rocks and gurgling over exposed roots. "You remember Shaul the peddler?"

She knitted her brows.

"The one who took us to Basra in the war in his cart."

"Yes. He didn't come back," she said. "His wife died, and even his children forgot him."

"I couldn't understand why he was afraid to come back with us. He wasn't afraid of the cannons and the bands of robbers during the war, but he was afraid of going home to the alley, to his wife and family. The man who used to travel to remote villages with his mule and his wares and sleep under the open sky was afraid of going home and stayed behind in Basra. Maybe he's still there."

Albert fell asleep on her breast. Suddenly she realized that she was naked and she felt shy. She took a thin blanket and wrapped it around herself and her child before taking him back to his crib. There was a vacant look in her husband's eyes. "Why are you suddenly talking about Shaul? You understand him instead of sympathizing with his poor wife."

"Yes," he said without hesitation, "I understand him."

"The man from Abadan was afraid of going home too. Rafael, why did you come home from Basra yourself? Why did you come home from Lebanon?" she said and turned onto her back. The stiff flowers on the ceiling were not as white as they had seemed up to now. The house was not so new. Other people had lived in this room before them. What had become of them?

"I was born with the soul of a vagabond, like Salman," said Rafael. "He had no family or place to call home. All he had was a coat. A coat to carry his food in and all his earthly possessions."

"In the end they found his coat on the rubbish tip with a crow sitting inside it. His body was never found."

"And we, who are always running home, who knows what will become of us in the end? Look at Aziza. She carried a whole family on her shoulders. And now it makes no difference to her if she's living in a pigsty or a palace. She's forgotten all the things she was once prepared to die for."

"You should have stayed in Basra, like Shaul. The man from Abadan would have been willing to stay with us for ever, if my father hadn't thrown him out."

He smiled nastily. "So he had his eye on you."

"I'm not Flora."

"She's a leech."

"And you're still going to bed with her."

"I came back from Basra for your sake, for your sake I gave up the shade and sparkling water of Lebanon. For your sake I buy new furniture and stay here stuck between four walls. For your sake, Victoria, damn you, I chose life imprisonment with hard labour. At least you could appreciate it. At least you could paint your face like Flora and kneel down and worship a man's balls. At least you could say thank you . . ."

The first time she didn't realize what was happening. The second time his hand came down on her head she was stunned. Through the fear a dark rebelliousness flickered inside her. His hand hit her like the crack of a whip. She was stronger than he was. She could have locked him in her arms and thrown him down into the blackness of the courtyard. But fear prevented her from defending herself, and she choked on her tears.

"Rafael," she whispered, "you'll wake Albert. You'll frighten him."

Like an animal which had scented blood Rafael went on raising his hand to her in the years to come, in the days of hardship and the days of plenty. It was only in the muck of the transit camp in Israel, twenty-five years later, when everything was lying broken and crushed around them, that she stood firm against his blows. When he refused to take the hint, she was torn in two, one Victoria hit him with her fist and sent him flying onto the wretched iron bed, banging his delicate head against the canvas wall, while the other Victoria saw what she had done and was as horrified as if she had burnt a scroll of the Law. Israel did not welcome him with flowers. It saw him as a member of the generation of the wilderness and diminished his stature and thrust a hoe into his middle-aged hands and sent him to clear a field of thorns in the blazing summer heat. Victoria felt as if she were joining forces with those who had passed this sentence on him, and smashing his image with her own hands. It hurt her to see him submit to his fate with the proper humility, his only protest a prolonged hunger-strike. In the transit camp she found her feet willy-nilly, like a sailor on a ramshackle ship, and jealously guarded the few life-belts for the many children. Unexpectedly, Rafael did not drown in the mire, and in the end he rose from the depths, although his wings were clipped. He was still the same Rafael, studious and hard-working, but from the day she sent him flying onto the blazing canvas wall he never soared again.

But on that autumn night of love in Baghdad she was the wounded one. For the first time in her life she felt that her body had been violated. She pulled the thin blanket off the bed and sat on the Persian carpet and stopped her ears to his pleas. The smell of sulphur and the cigarette smoke exacerbated her nerves until she rose to her feet, picked up Albert and made for the door.

With a cigarette stuck between his lips he lashed out with his clear voice: "You're not leaving this room."

And with the same sullen rebelliousness she returned to the carpet, all her resentment at her mother's submissiveness bursting into her throat and choking her.

The next day the people in the courtyard guessed that they had quarrelled. She cooked and prepared his meals, and looked out of the corner of her eye to see if he was eating enough. She was anxious about his health, and afraid for him when he and Ezra went to the theeayter in the evening and stayed out until late at night. On the evening of the second day he took his elegant cane and accompanied her father to the club.

Anxiously she saw that he had left half his food on his plate, as on the previous day. She felt her head in order to remember the blows and fan her fading rage. On the third day she was annoyed with him for not going out of his way to appease her. In the afternoon Miriam told her that Flora had been seen not far from the factory, lying in wait to catch him when he came out. That night he didn't leave the house. He didn't touch the stuffed vegetables she had prepared, and he and Ezra joined her father, who set a bottle of arak on the table. Dahood strummed his zither and sang, and Toya noticed for the first time that Ezra had very big ears and his eyes had grown old before their time. "Look at your husband," she smacked her lips next to Victoria's ear, "at least five years older than he is and still a boy, a gorgeous boy." And Victoria suppressed a proud smile.

On the fourth day the sky clouded over again and groans came from Aziza's mattress, who spent all day lying in her room and didn't even venture into the courtyard any more. Miriam brewed her a sweet-sour herb tea and said that she feared the worst. The violent Fuad took the end of a rope in his mouth and went down on all fours, and Albert Toria pulled the other end and led him thus from the basement door to the stairs, with Albert Jia wailing behind them. Izuri watched the scene without a word and thrust the pointed toe of his shoe into Fuad's buttocks, who rolled over onto his back. Albert Toria shot a bemused look at his grandfather for spoiling such a wonderful game. Izuri breathed onto his face and he took fright and fled to Victoria, the golden bells on his ankles ringing like the cries of a startled bird. Victoria picked him up and looked at her father rebukingly. Izuri gave in and smiled at her, and she showered kisses on Albert's face.

That night she surrendered to the coaxing of the goodwill ambassador.

When Aziza died the sorrow was measured, and in order to make up for the lack of pain they held a big funeral, and sat *shiva* with exaggerated solemnity. Autumn lingered, full of the smell of the end-of-season dates. Straw mats and mattresses were spread out in the courtyard under the crystal sky for the mourners and the condolers. The door stood open from morning to night. In honour of the deceased the men stayed home from work, even though most of them were not obliged to do so. The only one who grew a beard was Ezra, and the four-day-old stubble was enough to cure Toya of the vestiges of melancholy in her heart.

Among those who came to pay their respects were relatives, neighbours, friends, and the usual rabble who went from wedding celebrations to wakes for a plate of rice and a piece of bread. The latter would cut their condolences short and fall on the refreshments like a swarm of locusts, devouring everything they could lay their hands on. Nobody took any notice of them, and they only stayed long enough to fill their bellies, and made off muttering a hasty salutation. They knew each other and on the threshold they would exchange information about which wake it was worthwhile attending and which miserly funeral meats it would be better to avoid. Perhaps because of the endless stream of uninvited visitors the members of the household did not at first pay much attention to the stranger standing at the door and making a request so strange that those who heard him thought a madman had landed up there by mistake and took no more notice of him. After about half an hour Nissan announced in a worried voice: "There's a Shi'ite mullah at the door demanding that all the women be removed from the courtyard."

Everyone was thunderstruck by this announcement, and Nissan was cross-examined to make sure that he wasn't pulling their legs, after which speculation was rife before anyone went to the door. For some reason Najia was the first to go. A short scream escaped her lips and she came back with an even more obscure announcement than the previous one: "Amalek, God forbid, is waiting outside, in Haman's hat and the black *abbaya* of the Angel of Death. And his eyes!"

"Rafael," called Izuri, "where are you?"

"He's busy now," called Victoria, for Rafael was in their room with a lather of shaving soap covering his face.

Stumbling from the amount of alcohol he had consumed on the sly, Ezra went to the door, with his black beard and his protuberant bloodshot eyes, and returned with the same peculiar announcement: "It's true. The Shi'ite has come with an important message and he won't come in as long as women and girls are walking around the courtyard with their faces exposed."

"Does he want us to wear veils inside the house?" demanded Miriam indignantly.

"Who does he want?" asked Izuri.

Ezra cupped his hands round his mouth and yelled: "Rafael, someone's here for you from el-Kazamiya. He's come in a special car to take you, but it can't get through the alleys and it's waiting for you next to al-Shorja market. Come down!"

Rafael came out to the second-floor gallery with his face shaven on one side and lathered on the other. Victoria was alarmed. Her man was shrouded in mystery, who knew if he wasn't being called to reckoning for some sinister deed? This was the first time she had ever heard of a motorcar being specially sent for someone. Nissan and a few other boys were already racing to al-Shorja to see the motorcar stuck there. Izuri was uneasy about the whole business too. What was a Shi'ite mullah doing coming to a Jew's home instead of his place of business? Then he remembered that the factory was closed.

"Rafael," he called, "come down to see what he wants."

Rafael wiped the lather off his face with a towel and came down to speak to the mysterious messenger, after which he said to his father-in-law: "He may be only a messenger but he's an important man and he shouldn't be left outside until I finish shaving. He won't show disrespect for a house he's been sent to ask a favour of, and if you ask him in you must consider his religious feelings and get the women and girls out of the courtyard."

Izuri's curiosity got the better of him and he clapped his hands and ordered all the females over five years old to hurry up and retire to their rooms or to the second-floor gallery. Dozens of hidden eyes watched in suspense as Izuri strode proudly to invite the messenger to come inside. The black *abbaya* was indeed immense, and the man was as tall as Izuri. On red pumps he walked as if he were floating, his neatly groomed beard hennaed orange, his soft white hands showing his Persian origins. His big green eyes were lowered modestly to the ground and the turban wound round his head added a haughty dignity to his appearance. Izuri led him to an almost new chair, and the two of them laid their hands on their hearts and greeted each other again with impressive formality. The Shi'ite's turban turned around and responded with strict but somewhat reserved courtesy to the greetings of the other men, too. It was clear that in his eyes speech was a sin to which he had to resign himself. He pressed his knees together and fixed his eyes on a distant point on the wall. In the memory of the hiding women he went on sitting there without moving for decades to come, especially because of his turban and *abbaya*. He didn't bat an eye when Izuri cleared his throat. The head of the clan immediately remembered that not only was it impossible for him to instruct one of the barefaced women to offer the guest a glass of cold water and peeled cucumbers, as was customary when someone came in from the sun—he could have surmounted this obstacle by serving the Shi'ite with his own hands—but that a pious Shi'ite like him wouldn't touch food which had been handled by a Jew, since this was considered a sin. Izuri's eyes flashed, and his soul protested. He was a Jew of the old generation, and he drew pride from the depths of his faith. He was ready to face threats of violence in a spirit of sacrifice, just as he was ready to endure the depredations of floods and plagues. On more than one occasion he had swallowed his pride and continued on his way after some knavish official had slapped his face and spat at him. He had accepted in advance the price he had to pay for being a Jew. And precisely because of this acceptance he had cultivated a feeling of superiority in compensation. A man did not sting a scorpion, or bite a snake, or a dog. The stingers and biters were invariably the lower forms of life. And consequently it followed that his persecutors must be inferior to him, which was why they needed to bite and sting. And therefore the Jews were the elect of God's creation, and every other creature had been brought into the world for the sole purpose of testing and trying the Jews and their superior virtues. They could wear turbans as big as millstones and wave crosses studded with diamonds—they would always be as loathsome as pigs to him. He was higher than any Gentile king.

When Rafael returned a few hours later from his mysterious journey in the grand limousine to the holy Shi'ite shrine in the south of the city, he was a different man—his eyes were shining, his lips were smiling and altogether he looked like a dreamer who kept pinching himself to prove that he wasn't dreaming. Rafael told them about a different courtyard, in which there were no women, with streams of turbanned worshippers coming and going. Many men, a sea of *abbayas* and pious poker-faces, had been sitting there and waiting since the early hours of the morning, in sun and shade, filling the stairs and the second-storey gallery surrounding one big room, all their eyes directed in awe and suspense at this room, which was also full of people, those who had been fortunate enough to be received into the presence of the leader. It was far from certain that all those waiting would be received by the great leader, but nevertheless they sat without moving or uttering a sound. Most of them had come from far away with their bundles in their hands. They looked enviously at the men emerging from the inner sanctum as if seeking the effects of their audience with the leader on their faces.

"And who is this leader?" asked Dahood.

"Al-Jamali," said Rafael with undisguised pride.

"Oh-ho!" cried Dahood. "As rich as Croesus and up to his elbows in politics too. Even the English are prepared to pay a lot to be in his good books."

"And I," said Rafael, "a Jew up to his elbows in the glue of the bookbindery, follow the messenger, and the crowd of Shi'ites in the courtyard parts like a black sea, and your humble servant passes through it. Inside I'm trembling like a leaf and I make an effort not to show it."

He was still excited and he smoked one cigarette after the other, and the girls ran to serve him with one cup of strong tea after the other.

"On the way I tried to persuade the messenger to tell me what they wanted of me, but his lips were sealed. Not a word. When I entered the room al-Jamali stood up to receive me. In the silence that fell I could hear my heart beating. I thought that in a minute they would realize their mistake and chase me out of there in disgrace. The man crossed the room to meet me and put his hand on my shoulder and asked me if I was Rafael the son of the esteemed Eliyahu. You hear—the esteemed Eliyahu. I said that I was he. And he said: So then you are the one who was brought back to life and came home healthy. I said that I was still recovering and I had not yet fully regained my strength."

So go on smoking, grumbled Victoria to herself from her place by her father's side, and run to the theeayter every night, and jump on Flora whenever you get the chance. Still recovering indeed!

"How would you like to go back there at my expense and receive a salary to keep your family in comfort, until you come home completely healthy? he asked me. Yes, gentlemen, that's what he said, word for word."

Victoria saw a new storm gathering on the horizon of her life. "So tell us already what he wants you to do for it," she called out.

"His son and heir is ill with tuberculosis. He wants me to accompany him to the sanatorium, and stay there with him so he'll have a friend who's familiar with the strange place and who'll bring him luck too."

This son was the same Fadl al-Jamali who in time to come became the Prime Minister of Iraq.

In time to come. In time to come, after they had spent five

years in the squalor of the transit camp, they regarded the ugly cubes of the public housing estates as mansions, with running water and inside lavatories and a solid roof over their heads. Now it was possible to buy a radio. Rafael spent long evenings sitting and listening to Radio Baghdad and heard barking officers crucifying his friend in the show trial after the coup. Like himself, Fadl had been saved from tuberculosis, and lived to endure this humiliation at the hands of the brutal army officers. Rafael, who had suffered sorely in Israel, was no longer envious of his friend who had risen to such great heights.

On that distant day in Baghdad they went to bed late. Rafael was still wildly excited. Layla and Salima spread their bedding out together and begged Victoria to give them Albert for the night watch. At first she refused, but they pleaded with her and clung to the hem of her dress, and Layla swore that she would "keep him in between her eyes". They were crazy about the smell of his body, they said, and Victoria looked at them compassionately and said to herself, you don't know yet, you don't know anything yet. The room was desolate without him, but he was delighted to wander to new pastures with his little bells tinkling, and this hurt her too. Her body was indifferent to the overtures of the goodwill ambassador.

"So we're opening a new business, an escort service for the dying."

"Six months, woman. And the reward is so great, and it all comes straight to you."

"You want to escape from home."

He was silent. And the goodwill ambassador came back to life. She didn't like the smell of the cigarettes and the arak which he had sipped in secret with the grieving Ezra.

That night she became pregnant again.

20

The debilitating Khamsin had already lasted four days. The temperature was almost 50°C in the shade, and the tubs of washing steamed under the open sky. People knocked the brass knockers on the doors with handkerchiefs wrapped protectively round their hands. Men's feet swelled in their shoes and socks. Householders sprinkled their floors with water and prayed for a stray gust of wind. Above the river a thick haze formed, and at a distance of a few paces from the bank skins peeled from the intensity of the dry heat. Women did their chores like sleepwalkers or bared their teeth like animals. Quarrels between men grew more violent.

Fuad kicked the plate with his dinner on it and let out a hoarse bark. His big eyes bulged from their sockets. "Please keep quiet," said Victoria. "I can't hear Albert because of your yelling."

"Yes, shut up." Najia drew courage from her daughter, irritated beyond bearing by the rash which had broken out on her body on top of everything else.

Fuad went berserk, ran to the kitchen, grabbed a hot pot and threatened his mother with it, screaming: "You dare tell me to shut up?"

Nissan warned him: "I want to eat. If you throw that pot at Mother you'll be in big trouble."

Fuad butted his fat brother, felled him to the ground, and kicked him in the groin. He took no notice of Nissan's screams, his only aim in life was now to attack his mother, who had fled to the arcade in the meantime shielding her head with her arms. Victoria boxed him hard on the forehead and the pot fell from his hands, scalding his bare feet with the hot, oily liquid. He let out a blood-curdling bark. Victoria barred his way, and something which went back to his infancy penetrated the fog of his frenzy and stopped him from hurting her. His eyes turned into narrow slits, the veins swelled in his nostrils and spittle flew from his mouth.

Layla tugged at Victoria's dress. "There's a visitor asking for you."

Victoria shook off her hand. "What visitor? I'm looking for Albert."

Albert Jia emerged from the late Aziza's deserted room. "He's in there," he said fearfully. Victoria raced to the room. The child was lying next to the wall in a limp, lifeless ball, his lips as white as the flaking walls he had been gnawing. His mother and father did not know that he suffered from low blood pressure, and this was why he raided the salt jar in summer and scratched at the whitewash which contained salt. And because they were ignorant of the cause of his behaviour, they were ashamed of it and tried to hide it. Now Victoria carried him into the courtyard. "Water," said Fuad in a sober, sensible tone. "Pour water onto him, Victoria. He's not dead."

"Hurry up and take him to the tap," said Salima.

"The tap water's boiling," said Toya, "dip his head into the drinking-water jar."

Albert's head rose above the cold water in the jar and he opened his eyes in bewilderment as if he had just woken from a confusing dream.

"What did you see?" wept Victoria. "What happened to you?"

"Run with him to the sheep-pen," said Fuad.

"The visitor," whispered Layla. Victoria saw a slender figure in a black silk *abbaya* and a veil. How could she bear the heat in that get-up? Fuad took Albert from Victoria's hands.

"A few words," said the woman in black in a regal tone, her voice firm and steady despite the terrible heat and her heavy garments, the voice of authority. Victoria was confused. "You're in a Jewish house, why are you wearing a veil?"

"Never mind, come into the arcade for a moment."

"I have to take the child to the sheep-pen . . ." But Salima, at Fuad's instigation, had already thrown a basin of cold water from the jar over Albert, who shrieked, and Fuad rocked him in his arms and reassured Victoria and hinted that she should turn her attention to the visitor.

"I can't even offer you cold water," apologized Victoria. "We have to change the water in the jar."

"I didn't come here for a drink of water."

Her arrogant manner annoyed Victoria, but not unduly. From early childhood she had been trained to recognize that some people were superior and others inferior. "So why did you come?" she asked directly.

"I wanted to know if there was any hope of your husband returning alive, or if he has already passed away, God forbid."

Victoria was speechless. "Who are you? Why don't you take off your veil?" she said at last.

"I wanted to inquire about your husband and it's a matter between you and me," said the woman deliberately.

"My husband's alive and I have to run off now with my child."

"When will he return?"

"Why won't you tell me who you are?"

"It doesn't matter."

Victoria refrained from telling the woman to go to hell, but decided not to waste words on her and present a poker-face.

"My son has a big shop in the textile market," said the woman.

"May God bless you with prosperity."

"He already has, we were born with money."

"That's obvious."

"I had no intention of offending you, my dear. Only to say that as far as health is concerned He wasn't so generous. My son is sick."

"My husband is occupied with another patient," said Victoria shortly, afraid that the woman was here on some new mission, to take Rafael away from her again. "I hope your son recovers."

"There's no hope of recovery. He was born with it."

"You shouldn't talk like that. You should put your faith in God."

"My brother and I have always faced facts, and believe me it makes life simpler."

"Do I know you?"

"I've known you since the day you were born," the visitor said deliberately, as if her age gave her an additional advantage. "Pardon me, where is your toilet? A punishment from heaven. I try not to drink but it doesn't help."

"Over there," said Victoria, almost pityingly.

The old woman stood up. "Rest assured that we pay handsomely."

"But I don't understand what you want of me."

"Your husband's intelligence and resourcefulness are worth more than their weight in gold when a man lacks good health. I want him to be my son's partner."

"We haven't got a penny. And he doesn't consult me in such matters."

"Nonsense. Every woman has a dream that can only be realized with money. Every man has a finger that a woman knows how to touch with her own finger."

Victoria thought about the house set among the palm groves that would be all hers.

"Don't wait for me to come out of the toilet, my daughter. Run along with your son."

Albert was already riding on Fuad's shoulders. "Will you please put your shoes on?" she said to her brother. Fuad liked going barefoot in summer and he would curse furiously when he trod on broken glass or burning cigarette stubs. "Then give me the child," she said.

"Victoria, even if I walk on coals Albert will stay on my shoulders. I promise you." To be on the safe side she walked behind him, ready to catch the child. On the way she stopped an ice-cream seller and bought a double portion for Fuad and a portion each for Albert and herself. She wasn't being exactly truthful when she told the visitor that she didn't have a penny. It may have been true in comparison to the old woman's wealth, but as far as she was concerned she had never had so much money in her purse in her life. And permission to do what she liked with it. A messenger from al-Jamali came every week to her father's factory and left a handsome sum for her. She contributed generously to the common table of her father's family, and bought material and sewed dresses for her sisters. The rumour reached Rafael's mother Hanina's ears, and she turned up and sat in silent expectation. His father had reverted to his old tricks and disappeared. There wasn't a grain of rice in the house. Victoria responded unwillingly; she hadn't forgotten the diamond-studded tiara her mother-in-law had refused to contribute when she herself had gone begging for help to save Rafael, especially now that he had indeed been saved.

They remained in the sheep-pen for hours, and it was already nearly evening when they set off for home, the hour when people escaping from the stifling heat of their houses were sitting outside on their steps. Victoria's dress was soaked in perspiration, she breathed heavily and dragged her feet. Her belly stuck out in front of her, and she said to herself that this was her most difficult pregnancy yet.

About three weeks later she came home from the market on Thursday, with a porter behind her carrying the baskets of fruit and vegetables and meat for the Sabbath, and Albert laughing and shouting in front of her on Fuad's shoulders. From the distance she saw that something had happened at home. Women she encountered on the way stared at her. A young woman suckling a baby at her breast called to her from one of the doorways: "Congratulations, your husband has returned home safe and sound."

"Give me Albert," she said to her brother with her knees trembling, but Fuad had already charged ahead, and she was obliged to take her last steps without Albert to protect her. Her stomach was huge, and she was embarrassed by her old dress and her uncombed hair. At the entrance she caught up with her brother and took Albert and clasped him to her belly. His shining eyes would make up for her dishevelled appearance.

Her anxious calculations were in vain. Rafael's neck, face and head were covered in lather, and his hands groped blindly for the beaker with which he was drawing water from the pail standing next to him. He had stopped washing himself naked in public, like many men did, long ago, and now he was busy scrubbing his body upstairs in the room deserted in the sweltering summer months. Victoria wondered who had hurried to serve him. Even in the boiling khamsin he demanded very hot water, and he had certainly not entered the kitchen to light a fire under the cauldron himself. In Baghdad no man with any self-respect ever set foot in the kitchen. Next to the door Ezra was sitting on a chair and conducting an animated conversation with him, and when he saw her he cried in an unnecessarily loud voice: "Rafael! here's Victoria with your Albert!" and immediately retired with demonstrative consideration. Victoria understood that he wanted to warn his friend, whose eyes were closed under the lather, not to say anything not intended for her ears.

She took the beaker and poured water over her husband's head. In the stifling heat of the room the water enticed Albert, and he lifted his foot and stepped into the tub with his father. Rafael undressed him, and his laughter resounded between the walls. She had never heard him laugh so happily. He kissed the boy between his eyes and the laughter rang out again. And Victoria knew that this time he was home for good. The distant look in the man from Abadan's eyes was gone. He embraced the wet Albert and said: "Victoria, the child really brings us luck. I'm completely healthy."

"*Tfu! Tfu!*" Victoria silenced him for fear of the Evil Eye.

"The minute I got Ezra's letter telling me about his birth I believed that I would live."

"Enough, enough."

She was overjoyed. How happy she was that her husband saw the child as a talisman, a kind of good luck charm. It had always seemed to her that Rafael attached more importance to worldly success than to his home and family. In this he differed from her father and the other men she knew, who accepted their lot in life. Albert could act as a steadying anchor for him if he believed that he held out an assurance of success. She stepped out onto the gallery and called down to the courtyard: "Layla, Salima, go up to the roof and sprinkle a lot of water to cool the floor. Spread out the mattresses to cool too." She wanted to include everyone in her happiness. Tonight her father would not go to the club and Ezra would not slip off to the theeayter. They would hold a big party on the roof. Miriam joined in her joy. "I'll send someone to the fish market. Maybe there's still something left there. It's already late. How much should I buy?"

"As much as you like, Miriam. The more the better."

Two tables were pushed together and they ate their fill, together with the neighbours and friends who arrived to welcome Rafael home. After twelve years of wandering the Bedouin had finally pitched his tent in Victoria's courtyard. She was too realistic to believe that he would ever be satisfied with the role of a tame husband and father, but that evening she dismissed her doubts. A moon sailed in the heavens and a wind blew up, ruffling the mosquito nets and bathing the faces of the people sitting round the table. Najia sat apart in a corner of the roof, like a dark stain absorbed in itself. From time to time she raised a hand as if to scratch her head, and then lowered it again as if she had changed her mind. Her lips muttered ceaselessly, but nobody heard her talking to herself. She showed no signs of the senile feeble-mindedness which had come upon Aziza in her final years. She grew more silent and withdrawn, demanding less and less of her little world. Sometimes she scratched in the cracks and holes to bury a coin she had saved, but the passion for hoarding had left her. She was exempt from the duties of keeping house. Victoria and her two unmarried sisters, Salima and Nazima, took care of their father and brothers, and she was free to wander at will and soak up whatever sights and experiences the streets of the city had to offer. She never confided her adventures to a single soul. Sometimes, in a burst of energy she would invade the kitchen and cook a special dish for which everyone complimented her. But on the whole she maintained her isolation and obeyed Izuri's rare calls upon her silence. She tried to keep out of the way of Nissan's and Fuad's blows, and defended herself against her daughters' scoldings with transparent, childish lies. On that evening she was glad the people sitting round the table were occupied with each other. And she was startled when she noticed someone approaching her.

"Come and sit with the others for once like a human being." Despite the censorious tone of Victoria's voice it was obvious that she was in the seventh heaven of delight. She handed her mother an aromatic plate, and Najia took it and shovelled the food into her mouth in stubborn silence. "It wouldn't hurt you to smile a little," said Victoria. "Life's not all black."

Najia stopped chewing and looked at her daughter's radiant face. A knot of words was trapped in her throat. How could she say everything in one clear sentence? From the inchoate muddle one lucid phrase emerged clearly: "You're dear to me." But she said nothing, words which sounded fine to her were always received by others with revulsion. "Go back to the table," she said to her daughter.

A spirit of mischief descended on Ezra, and he decided to make his blacksmith brother-in-law really drunk, pressing glass after glass on him and singing the praises of the excellent arak. Gurji's beard swayed more solemnly with every sip, but a sly smile appeared at the corners of his mouth. He knew only too well that in the end Ezra would fall to the ground in a drunken stupor, while he himself would remain sober.

Toya didn't take her eyes off Rafael's face. She did this with great charm, and from time to time she gave Victoria a smile full of goodwill. Albert Toria fell asleep on Salima's chest, and his breath made her nubile nipple prick up. The girl's eyes clouded and her slender neck bowed like a stem until her cheek rested on the infant's head. Layla whispered: "Don't be a pig, give him to me for a bit."

Izuri concluded his speech: "We're waiting for you at the factory. Nobody has taken your place."

"Thank you, uncle," Rafael replied politely.

"But first you should hear what Victoria has to say."

Rafael did not hide his astonishment. "Has the world turned upside down in the months I've been away from home? Do women decide now what the man does for a living? Yes, woman." He turned to his wife, his tone one of flirtatious amusement.

Victoria blushed, tongue-tied. She was incapable of opening her mouth in front of so many people, especially with Rafael's eyes fixed on her like that, after so long an absence. "Let Father tell you. He knows everything."

"A goldmine," said Izuri. "You remember Hannah, the late Abdallah Nunu's sister?"

"I remember," said Rafael with narrowed eyes. He remembered Ma'atuk Nunu's crush on Victoria. Everything to do with the Nunu family and its two estranged factions disgusted him.

"You must remember her son Elias too," said Izuri. "He has a big shop in the textile bazaar. God sometimes likes his joke. What good will all his money do him? He's lucky to have a mother like her."

"Another woman who supports men," said Rafael with a sneer.

But Izuri said enthusiastically: "She's a demon. The eyes of an eagle. She manages everything shrewdly behind the scenes. She came to see me and she even dressed up in a veil and paid a visit to Victoria."

"What did she want?"

"She wants you to go and work with her son. She's offering you a partnership."

"A partnership," sneered Rafael. "And where am I going to find my share of the money?"

"The old woman says that your luck and talents are enough."

Rafael's face hardened. "And why didn't Ma'atuk Nunu come to Victoria himself?"

"What's the one thing got to do with the other?" said Izuri in surprise. "They quarrelled and split up, don't you remember? He threw her out of the house after all the years he spent in banishment because of her. It was her who incited Abdallah to throw him and his mother out of the house. There's no contact between them today."

But Ezra understood. "Rafael, wash out your mouth before you say another word."

"Did you keep watch over her?" said Rafael between clenched teeth. It was obvious that he had hardly heard a word Izuri said. "The hunchback has been lusting openly after Victoria since he was a child. Did you follow her every time she left the house in an *abbaya* and a veil? The first time I was away she worked for him, this time they dump a bag of gold in my lap . . ."

The blood drained from Victoria's face.

"Lechers like us suspect even our mothers," said Ezra, his face white with rage. "You should be ashamed of yourself!"

Izuri's nostrils flared. "Rafael," he whispered, "do you suspect Victoria? Beg God to forgive you."

Dahood hit the zither with the palm of his hand as if he wanted to clear the hot heads with the booming sound. "The old woman has been taking an interest in you. She hears the stories they tell about you in the market, how you went to find your grave in Lebanon and overcame the Angel of Death. It makes an impression on people. Someone like you brings luck. You heard for yourself, there's no connection between that family and Ma'atuk Nunu. While his mother was tightening the swaddling clothes to straighten his back, his Aunt Hannah was inciting her brother to drown him in the tub, to throw the child and his mother into the street. She herself bought the powder and scent for Nuna. That bitch hated her sister-in-law so much that she made her brother and his daughter into what they became. Sometimes God knows how to punish people for their wickedness. Maybe that's why her son Elias was born an epileptic, God forbid it should happen to us. Listen to me, Rafael. Don't turn your head away after slinging mud like you just did. The witch is getting old. And she's apparently sick. Every five minutes she has to pee. She chases men out of the public urinals so she can squat there. They say she's got cancer in her cunt. Who knows why she chose you, maybe it's just your good luck."

Rafael and Izuri snarled at each other like a pair of angry dogs and withdrew into hostile silence. Nobody expected them to bury the hatchet there and then. Wounds of honour take time to heal.

As expected, Rafael's star rose in the business world and consequently Victoria's star rose in the courtyard. Again the dream she was ashamed to tell even Rafael about blossomed in her heart. A new house, really new, with the smell of fresh paint on the walls. Windows open to a lovely garden and a roof overlooking palm fronds and pomegranates. Where had she seen such a house? Perhaps on one of the excursions with her father, in the days when he would take a large flock of children out for long Sabbath walks. She would have a salon for visitors with embroidered covers for velvet armchairs. There would be a whole kitchen for her exclusive use. Sometimes she would see the house when she closed her eyes at night and fell asleep with a smile on her face. She had no idea how much her dream would cost and whether it would take one year or ten years to come true. Every week Rafael put a sum of money in her hands. "Spend as much as you like." She knew that he gave her less than a quarter of his profits. He was extravagant by nature, and ever since his miraculous deliverance from death he was not interested in saving. She would put something aside, and the more her savings grew, the less bold she became. What was all her hoarded money worth? A basement? A cubbyhole of a kitchen? Would she be able to hear the birds singing from its windows?

The inhabitants of the courtyard treated both Rafael and Victoria with a certain obsequiousness, but they all knew where the fount of plenty originated. In the eyes of many of them the rich were ipso facto beautiful, wise and powerful. Consequently, when Rafael announced that Hannah and her son Elias were coming to call on the second day of *Rosh Hashana*, the courtyard filled with awe and busy preparations—washing and polishing and instructions to the children not to shout or snatch food from the table. The common lavatory was available for use up to a certain hour only, after which it was subjected to a special cleaning and disinfection and declared out of bounds. Those in need were required to go to the neighbours.

They hardly remembered Elias from the days when they lived next door to the Nunu family. Dahood's words about the mother, too, seemed to smack vaguely of envy and self-righteousness. Victoria herself did not have much to tell the curious women. Evil tongues tended to describe the mother and son in an unfavourable light, and Rafael did nothing to correct this impression. Accordingly, everyone was astonished at the sight of the couple entering the door and crossing the courtyard to the arcade with a regal dignity beyond their wildest dreams. The old woman came without an *abbaya*, holding a purse of fine leather in her hand. Her steps were measured and her chin held high as a cantor's on his way to the Ark of the Law, and everything about her radiated an air of authority and refinement at once. The figure of Elias was no less impressive. He was taller than Rafael, his face smoothly shaven, a red carnation in his buttonhole and a patrician's smile on his lips. He was fifteen years older than Rafael, and the years added dignity to his appearance.

Rafael led his guests to the wicker chairs and prompted Albert, standing there in his new sailor suit: "Say hello to the Uncle and Aunt." The child went straight up to the old woman and seized hold of her leather purse with the glittering buckle, as if intent on retrieving stolen property. With equal determination the old lady and the child tugged at the purse, until Rafael was obliged to drag the little boy away and exchange embarrassed laughter with Elias. Through the sailor suit Rafael could feel the roar gathering inside the little chest of his son, who kept his eyes fixed on those of the august visitor. Victoria hurried up with a tray of tall glasses of lemonade, and the tinkling of the glasses as they trembled and touched each other betrayed her nervousness. Kilmanteen, as shy as her mother, clung to her skirts. With two fingers Hannah took the glass and said: "*Merci*."

Elias saw Victoria biting her lip in confusion as to the right response to this polished piece of French, and came tactfully and courteously to the rescue, smiling at Kilmanteen and calling out: "What a pretty little girl!" Then he drew a pipe and a flat tin of tobacco from his pocket. The aroma of the tobacco was intoxicating.

Rafael handed Albert to Victoria, whispering: "Calm him down. A devil's got into him." Victoria overcame her embarrassment and took the boy from him. Albert was not a bad child. Something evil about the old woman must have upset him. To be on the safe side, she felt in his pocket for the turquoise bead, the garlic and the gall nut. They were all there. The salt too. Elias was a confirmed bachelor and the old lady had no grandson. Now Victoria remembered the epilepsy, and if not for fear of Rafael, she would have fled the courtyard with Albert. In the meantime her father entered the arcade and greeted the guests. An adolescent embarrassment took hold of Hannah, who had known Izuri for decades, and she fiddled with the buckle of her purse in confusion. Her simpers pleased the grandfather, but not the grandson. Everyone in the courtyard, to Victoria's pride, spoke admiringly of Albert's precocity in talking, but now he seemed to have lost all powers of human speech and he growled like an angry puppy.

"Umm Albert, why are you leaving us?" The old woman's voice overtook her as she tried to escape. "I see your husband once a week at least and your father is like a brother to me. We came especially to see you."

Albert found himself led towards the old woman again and he began emitting ferocious noises again and struggling on his mother's swollen belly. Rafael saw her distress and took the boy from her and seated him on his knees, where he sat still, well aware of the restraining power of the arms embracing him, until Rafael thought he had fallen asleep, and he bent over to examine his face and met his blazing eyes. "I don't know what's got into him today," he apologized to his guests.

"A beautiful child," the old woman whispered in a melancholy voice.

At the sound of the old woman's tone Victoria glanced

quickly at Elias. He was indeed a well-built man, but she noticed the twitch under his left ear, and the way his knuckles whitened as he gripped the stem of his pipe.

"Victoria my daughter," Hannah turned to her hostess, "tell those girls that we don't eat people."

Their party dresses bloomed in the sun, their pert breasts stuck out with spring-like impudence, the freshness of their youth sent out signals in all directions. It was Izuri who realized what was going on, and he made haste to reply: "A cheeky, lazy lot." He waved his arm in dismissal and they fled like a shoal of brightly coloured fish.

"Izuri," the august guest sighed, "I've already told you we didn't come to grab. But I have to tell you that even from a distance you can see that they're as pretty as Victoria."

"Lazy legs, clumsy hands and chattering tongues, that's what they are, Umm Elias. Victoria is half a punishment too."

"I hear only her praiser."

"That's just it. May God forgive me for saying so, but He could have tried a little harder and made her a boy." And without meaning to he added: "A man deserves a real support when he grows old and tired."

The aroma of Elias's pipe spread through the arcade again. They sipped their drinks in silence. Married women served the fruit and roasted almonds soundlessly. The young girls hid their faces and from time to time their peals of laughter invaded the courtyard. Hannah got up to go to the lavatory and came back with a sombre face. "Abu Murad, I won't embarrass you by asking you to present the girls. If anyone asked me, I would have been prepared to give the whole thing up as a rude joke on the fast of *Tisha B'Av*."

"God save us!" exclaimed Izuri, scandalized. "Woman, it's *Rosh Hashana* today."

"The head of the year is also the tail, Abu Murad. We run and run and arrive at the same mud we thought we'd extricated ourselves from. You can relax, we already have a girl. The problem is that she's too young, too clever, and very, very beautiful. You were once a textile merchant yourself. You know the danger. Most of the customers are women and girls. The girl came in and he's already so besotted he can't tell day from night. Rafael saw her, he can be my witness."

Victoria stole a glance at her husband's profile.

"Right, Rafael?" the old woman insisted.

"Right," said Rafael unwillingly over his son's blazing eyes.

"I've already made inquiries. She's got an older sister and they're fatherless. What do I need with a daughter-in-law who's so clever and beautiful?"

"It's not done to take the younger sister before the older one," said Izuri.

"Abu Murad, money buys everything."

The old woman's brutal practicality wounded Izuri's sense of justice. "What's all this got to do with Victoria?"

Victoria was indignant. Her husband, not her father, should have been speaking to the frightening old woman on her behalf.

"I want her to go with Rafael to the girl's house to ask for her hand from her mother. Elias has lost his head completely. He's lost his appetite. He stands and stares at the walls like a zombie. That a man should snivel over some female at night! What have we come to, Abu Murad? Pardon me," she said abruptly and stood up to go to the lavatory.

After the festival of *Sukkoth* Rafael and Victoria went to the girl's house. It was very rare indeed for them to go out together. In the world Rafael roamed outside the house there was no place for her. She was thus very excited and very careful not to stumble or give the man walking by her side any grounds for disappointment. All the way there he didn't speak a word, and her heart told her that he would have preferred to carry out the mission on his own. How come he didn't ask anyone where the girl lived? Could it be that he already knew . . .?

Three women were sitting and waiting for them. The mother Tova, the elder sister Rivka, and Naima, the intended bride. The house was small but all theirs, and it shone with cleanliness. The touch of clever hands which knew how to cover up the wounds of poverty was evident. The three knew the purpose of the visit in advance, but their faces were reserved and expressionless. Victoria asked herself why she had come. The two sisters, Rivka and Naima, were alike as a perfect work of art and its almost perfect reproduction. The same hair, the same almond eyes, the same sensuous mouth, the same stunning figures. It was the younger Naima who was the perfect one, and she who looked them straight in the face with the challenge of a gambler. The older sister lowered her eyes modestly and shyly.

As she served the dates and peeled cucumbers the mother said in an expressionless voice: "Abu Albert, your man is almost fifty, and she is not yet sixteen."

"True, he is rather old, but why exaggerate? Victoria has seen him, and he's no stranger to your daughters either." Smiling faintly at the younger girl he added: "They came several times in *abbayas* and veils and looked their fill. A handsome, impressive figure of a man, and anyone who's seen him will tell you that he's fit as a fiddle. I know young men whose teeth have fallen out and whose backs are bent, and anyone who feels like it can kick them around because they haven't got a penny to their name."

"The coffee's getting cold, Abu Albert. Fit as a fiddle, you say. God forbid it should happen to us, what I've heard about him, God forbid."

"We've been working together for months. It's never happened once in the shop. In the morning he comes to work bursting with energy. Sometimes these afflictions come and go. Look at me. I was almost given up for dead myself."

"In my experience misfortunes and afflictions don't go away. Taste the Turkish delight. Naima made it with her own hands in your honour."

"And don't forget the money. He'll shower gold at her feet," the cunning merchant stressed.

Victoria's throat constricted. This was how she would have had to put Kilmanteen on the market when the time came, but for those miraculous needles which had punctured her husband's lungs. And what would have happened to Albert? An apprentice to some harsh tailor or shoemaker. She forgave Rafael for her suspicions and upbraided herself for the anger at him for being ashamed of her and not exchanging a word with her all the way.

"I thought I was bringing you good news," said Rafael, "and here we sit picking nits and turning scratches into wounds."

"That's no scratch he's got, Abu Albert. And the money's not in his pocket either. Most of it's in his mother's name."

Naima's expression was not in the least innocent in Victoria's opinion. It was clear that the girl was eager to have the deal sealed and signed as soon as possible. In Baghdad gramophones had recently made their appearance, and they brought with them the voice of Egyptian singer Umm Kulthoum sighing shamelessly over her loves. Victoria had never in her life heard a woman singing thus about love. Was it possible that this young girl too had been afflicted by the sickness of Umm Kulthoum and lost her head completely? Rafael's partner was certainly an impressive figure of a man. Or perhaps the girl was frightened by the fate of her nubile sister, who had no suitor due to her lack of dowry. Or perhaps she was simply a good soul, willing to sacrifice herself to save her family from poverty? But in spite of everything it was somehow hard to feel sympathy for her.

"Naturally Elias won't ask for a penny. On the contrary, he'll pay all the expenses, and also help with the dowry of the elder sister when she finds a husband, God willing. And you yourself won't be left out in the cold either. Presents . . ."

"What good will presents do me, Abu Albert? We are speaking of my daughter's life."

"And she is silent," smiled Rafael.

Even then Naima did not show the proper embarrassment.

The mother groaned. "The foolish girl agrees to everything with her eyes closed."

"A rich husband is the best insurance against the vicissitudes of fate."

"His mother asked a lot of questions, and I'm not deaf, Abu Albert. Rivka, give our guests tea with cardamon, the way you know how to make it. His mother didn't hide her suspicions.

She's afraid we're scheming to lay our hands on his property. You knew her brother Abdallah Nunu. They're frightening people, Abu Albert. Where's the tea, Rivka? Umm Albert, you haven't touched a thing. Don't insult us. At least a sip of rose-water. The mother doesn't want to bring a strange woman into the house. You know what happened to Abdallah's poor son-in-law . . . The only property his mother registered in Elias's name is his part of the shop. You look as if you've got a head on your shoulders, Abu Albert. Don't be offended if I tell you that that woman has hidden many things from you. She's quite capable of transferring everything to her niece Nuna and her two sons in Palestine. Nuna belongs to a family that doesn't like strangers.'

Victoria saw that Rafael was taken aback. The cunning merchant's smile was wiped off his face. He forgot his manners and turned directly to the girl: "Did you know about this?"

The girl nodded her lovely head, excited by Rafael's surprise.

Victoria's suspicions turned to painful certainty. Her hand shook slightly as she replaced the glass of rose-water on the tray. In the dead of night she had fled the courtyard when the big flood came. She remembered the first jet of blood from Rafael's mouth. She had stepped onto the bridge with the intention of putting an end to her life. She had buried her little daughter. She regarded herself as a woman who had experienced a great deal in her life, who had known suffering and hardship. And tasted happiness too.

Until the last days of her long life she would never forget the ordeal of Naima. Sandstorms, two world wars, many births, and the upheaval of moving from one country to another—everything paled in comparison to the bitter sediment left by the days when this girl overshadowed the skies of her life. She was not surprised when she discovered not long after the wedding that it was not Elias's wealth which had captured Naima's heart, nor the fear of her sister's fate which had swayed her decision. The girl had agreed to the marriage on one condition only: Rafael would be her lover.

21

Wednesday. Victoria sorted out the dirty washing next to the tub. All around her in the courtyard the other women's tubs sprouted mushrooms of pure white foam. Albert's pillow case. Stained with sweat and dry tears. Her heart swelled inside her. The child was crying in his dreams. Kilmanteen's dress. She outgrew new clothes in a matter of months. The delicate girl would grow up in a different world, in a house surrounded by its own garden. She would hold books in her hand, read the newspaper, and not stammer like she did before an audience of four people. In Batawin electric lights turned the dark of night into the bright light of day. Linda's nappies. She put them to soak separately in a small basin, so that their smell would not cling to Rafael's shirts.

The locks of the houses in Batawin were so small that you could carry the keys in your coat pocket. In the frosty nights she would not have to get out of her warm bed to open the door for him after his nights of revelling. She would have a servant too. That was an accepted thing nowadays in families of their standing. She would take a young girl and train her and keep her in the house until she got married. Rafael's seed was sprouting inside her, and the house glad with birdsong would hum with many children's voices. Rafael's underpants. Crumpled and shapeless after lying for a few days in the laundry basket. Ezra, in spite of his red eyes and wet lips, was still the same clown as ever. Last Saturday he had told them something he had read in a magazine. Women in France examined their husband's underpants before washing them. What could a man's underpants reveal? Rafael's looks revealed more.

His partner Elias's wedding night. A frenzy of restlessness

took hold of Rafael at the banquet preceding the consummation. As if he were the best man, brother, father and groom rolled into one. Now that she thought about what had really happened, it seemed to her that he had not been running around as restlessly as she had thought then. It was only the nervous darting of his eyes which had given her that impression of ceaseless movement. The bridal gown, white as the foam in the tub, expressed her innocence and the innocence of the beautiful Naima. Her lips smiled bravely, but her eyes were as terrified as those of someone being led to a dangerous operation. Flora and her husband Asher were there, and Ezra and his wife, all Rafael's guests. On the consummation night everybody ate standing up. Everything was done in haste in order to concentrate attention on the couple about to be united. The mother of the groom abstained from the refreshments served at the big table. Her lips were two tight lines of bright lipstick, and her eyes darted about like Rafael's. She received the congratulations of the guests with a scornful expression, as if waiting for a cheap joke to be over. The tears of the bride's mother were not tears of joy. The groom trembled. In a tone of patronizing contempt Rafael told Victoria that in spite of his age Elias had never known a woman. It was cold in the house, in spite of the many guests, but the groom was bathed in sweat. The girl he loved so much had become his opponent in a contest whose rules he did not know, and he was afraid. If only he could have taken her tender hand in his and walked with her hand in hand to the end of days. How much he loved her when they were surrounded by people, and how he feared the terrible moments when they were alone together. Again and again he cross-examined Rafael about what he had to do in the moment of truth, and he couldn't understand why his partner evaded the issue and denied him the comfort of a single word of reassurance.

Flora pushed herself between Rafael and Victoria. Perhaps she was pretending to be drunk. The drumstick she was holding in her red nails dripped sauce onto her chin, and she giggled and said without taking any notice of Victoria: "And if it turns out that his peg can cleave a rock? All this time you've been so complacent. Tell your little chick to look at his hands. In spite of his illness he's got strong hands. I couldn't resist tormenting your brother a little on our wedding night too. Because of his fear of me he slapped my face and ripped me open like an animal. Don't despise frightened men. Look at his trousers. Thank God, they're bursting at the seams. And your little chick . . ."

Rafael's face was frozen. Without blinking an eye he absorbed his sister-in-law's blows. Perhaps he needed her insults to keep his sanity. He smoked without stopping, until Victoria almost took pity on him. At any rate, she loathed Flora then more than she hated him.

Flora took a piece of baked fish. "And supposing he doesn't slap her face, and his rooster faints without a crow. She'll have to get undressed anyway. He'll see her naked. He'll touch her there with his finger. And you, have you ever touched her at all? You see?" she said and threw a little bone onto the floor. "You see? In spite of all your schemes he's beaten you to it."

The guests were bursting with all their guzzling. Someone clapped his hands. In a heavy silence the couple were led to the bridal chamber on the second floor. Rafael threw a cigarette stub into a puddle of pomegranate juice and lit another. The corner of his mouth twitched in a kind of spasm. In the hatred of her love Victoria wanted to yell: Scream, cry, howl! The silence continued. People looked at each other and the routine jokes called for on such occasions died on their lips. Flora shattered the silence by a loud ululation such as those uttered by celebrating women from the common people. "Is this a celebration or not?" she announced and suckled the juice from a piece of orange and ululated again, forcing two or three other women to join her. Rafael and the mother of the groom closed their eyes in disgust.

They waited for an hour. Malicious whispers spread. Anxious whispers too. The red line on Hannah's face opened and turned into a mouth again. "Pardon me." And she hurried up the stairs to the second floor, and then there was a scream and the door to the bridal chamber opened and the bride appeared like a ghostly apparition on the gallery overlooking the courtyard. Her hair was dishevelled, her gown was crushed, and her screaming mouth said: "He . . . he . . . his tongue . . . his mouth is full of foam . . ."

"My baby," her mother wailed from below.

Naima recovered somewhat at the sound of the familiar voice. Her eyes focused. She even noticed the presence of the guests. Her hand went up to her ruined hairdo, and she was about to call the monstrous event by its name, when Hannah's hand slapped her mouth and she dragged her back into the room from which she had just escaped.

Shortly afterwards, Hannah came out and ordered the guests to disperse. Rafael hesitated. Victoria moved off with the others and he lit another cigarette and left with her. In the street Flora was about to accost him, and he stood still and fixed his flashing glasses on her without saying a word, until she hung her head and gave in to the pressure of Asher's hand and walked away with him.

What more could his underpants possibly tell her? Ezra and his stories. But she examined them nevertheless. Her right hand threw the little ball of pink cloth into the tub and her left caught it before it fell into the water. She spread Kilmanteen's panties out on her knee. She lost the thread of her thought. The black stains were dry blood, and they shouldn't have been there. Something had gone wrong. The child was only eight years old. Victoria decided not to call the little girl. What could she say to her? What could she ask her? Now she noticed Albert Toria and Albert Jia playing on the middle roof with other children. Their cries floated over the courtyard. Only Kilmanteen's voice was missing. But she was always like that. The seed of the deprivation and misery of her childhood. Restrained in her unhappiness, reserved in her enthusiasms. And what a rare soul she was. She had almost neglected her in her unbounded joy at the birth of Albert. The little girl had never complained.

On the contrary, she had taken Albert under her wing. She was as shy as her mother. They would speak to each other for hours in broken phrases. Actually, she couldn't remember when she had spoken to her last. Suddenly she realized that lately the little girl had tended to withdraw into herself. She was alarmed at any loud noise. And she was pale and had no appetite. Victoria made haste to examine the dress whose hem was already in the water.

Oh God, it wasn't a period.

She pushed the panties down into her lap and bowed over them, rocking to and fro as if she were soundlessly lamenting. In horror she looked around her at the tubs radiant in their white blossoming. The women and girls were absorbed in their chatter and work. They were all squatting with their knees apart. It was hard for Miriam to breathe in this position because of her fat, and she kept on straightening up to catch her breath. Layla, Dahood's daughter, skipped from tub to tub and finally sat down next to Salima, and the two of them put their heads together in adolescent whisperings. Najia retired into a distant corner and picked nits with black fingernails. In this ancient task too her yield was meagre, and in her despair she tugged furiously at her hair.

Rafael?

Just like Abdallah Nunu?

But Kilmanteen was not like Nuna Nunu. Victoria was always vigilant. Even in the dark room at night. Once his finger had brushed the sleeping little girl's forehead, and suddenly he had pulled the blankets up and covered the small body. Could he have seen Victoria looking at him and had second thoughts?

Where had he done it, and when?

She bit her lower lip. Idiot. It must have been after the last wash, in other words after last Wednesday. When did you fall asleep at your post last week? She thrust the tortured panties to the bottom of the tub and stood up breathing heavily. The women's arms stirred the mountains of foam with rhythmic, sensuous movements. First Victoria went to the lavatory to put them off the scent. Then she stole up to the middle roof and pulled Kilmanteen out of the bevy of children. The two Alberts wanted to go up to the upper roof with them, but she instructed them to go on playing with the other children. Kilmanteen's hand fainted in hers. The little girl had guessed why she was being led upstairs. Tears fell from her eyes. She was afraid to cry aloud, and she didn't beg for her life, even though she was sure that her mother was going to punish her severely, perhaps even throw her off the roof into the alley and kill her. With every step her guilt grew. At the top of the stairs she couldn't deny it any longer. "Don't kill me, Mother. I didn't do it. It was him."

"Who?"

"All the time he forced me to wrestle with him. He's so mean. And it hurts awfully, Mother."

"Who?"

"Uncle Nissan. Here on the roof on the Sabbath, when it started raining hard. Under that bed. It was freezing cold. And he had eyes like a devil. I was afraid even to scream. Don't kill me, Mother. I swear to you. He pulled my hair and said he'd push a dead mouse into my belly if I told on him."

Victoria clasped the child to her.

"You'll never kill me, Mother, will you?"

"I'll never kill you."

She returned Kilmanteen to the playing children and went down to her mother, who was sitting and combing her hair with a wooden comb.

"Mother, Nissan, may dogs maul his corpse . . ."

"What's he done?"

"Talk softly so nobody will hear. I'm going to kill him. He raped Kilmanteen."

"He's scum like the rest of them."

"That's all you've got to say."

"What do you want me to do? Rend my clothes?"

"I told you, keep your voice down."

"And how are you going to kill him without everyone finding out?" inquired Najia, still combing her hair and cursing the lice for evading her.

"Rafael will tear the house down if he finds out."

Terror came into Najia's eyes. The comb stuck in her scalp and her hand froze, while her face twisted in pain. "God save us." And she shifted about as if seeking a refuge from the wrath of Rafael, who would roast the boys alive for the slightest affront. "What a grave you've found for yourself, Nissan," she lamented. She resigned herself to the situation immediately, and went back to combing her hair. "As far as I'm concerned he can kill him. The animal."

"And you think that's the end of the business?"

"You won't let me scream. I'm afraid of your husband. I'm scared of Nissan, may his name and memory be blotted out, and I'm terrified of your father. Look, what's this blood on the comb?"

"Just let me catch him," said Victoria and bit her lips and pinched her thigh with her nails and stamped her foot until her knee hurt. But she nearly burst out screaming anyway. Kilmanteen's fate was sealed. At so tender an age she had lost her chance in a society which sanctified virginity above all things, considering it more important than status, beauty or wealth. She was already an outcast. The more furious she was with Nissan, the more she feared Rafael. Rightly he would accuse her of the worst of all sins: you abandoned your daughter. Even whores guarded their daughters' virginity to preserve their value on the marketplace. When the time came they displayed the maidens proudly. While she, Victoria, daughter of the strict Izuri, had destroyed her daughter's future. How was she going to hide it from him, how? He was so clever. He fixed her with his flashing glasses and read her thoughts. If he suspected anything he wouldn't let her go. He had tied Asher's feet and hands and poured boiling water over him when his first watch had disappeared, and all Asher's shrieks didn't help—his body was scalded and his skin blistered. Rafael had fended off the people rushing to the aid of the boy. "The watch is rubbish," he growled. "It's a matter of principle. Nobody steals from me."

And now his daughter had been raped.

How could she hide it from him, how?

She was sorry she had told her mother. How could a crime like this be concealed in a courtyard where the deepest secrets were put on display? The women must already be wondering why she had left her washing. They must have pricked up their ears when she pulled Kilmanteen up to the roof. They would whisper, sniff, poke and pry. There would be no peace until the truth came to light.

Making her face as expressionless as possible she returned to her tub, and on the way she caught sight of the silk *abbaya* at the door. A light gust of wind wafted the scent of a perfume unusual on washing day in her direction. Victoria continued on her way to the tub.

"It's you I've come to see." Flora folded her *abbaya* and sat down next to her, trembling with excitement.

In the heavy silence which had fallen Victoria hinted that the visit was not welcome. But Flora was not the woman to pay attention to hints. Her knee touched Victoria's knee, and Victoria moved her stool away from Flora's with a jarring scrape.

"Your house is falling on your head and you occupy yourself with washing. I can't touch other people's shit and piss today. I'm burning up, and you sit and play with rags?"

Victoria's blood froze in her veins. How did she know, this man-hunting bitch on heat? Unwillingly she turned to face her agitated sister-in-law.

"Rafael's made her pregnant!" she cried for all ears to hear.

Even though she was immediately aware of the severity of the blow, she breathed a sigh of relief. Miriam wiped her hands on the hem of her skirt, slid her vast body between the two sisters-in-law, and listened quietly in anxious concern. Flora was annoyed at Victoria's frozen, unresponsive face. She leant over Miriam's breasts and said: "My blood's boiling, Victoria. The way that little slut's playing with him!"

"Nobody plays with Rafael," Victoria hissed, alarmed at the sound of her own voice.

"Then she put a spell on him."

Unusually for her Flora was sloppily dressed. She must have

been in such a hurry that she didn't have time to make herself up properly. Actually, she looks nicer like this, said Victoria to herself, and was immediately disgusted with herself for having such frivolous thoughts at a time like this.

"She goes to the shop every day."

"Who?" asked Miriam.

Flora was glad of the presence of an intelligent witness who paid the proper attention to the painful facts. "I'm talking about Naima, Elias's wife—at least that's what's written on the marriage certificate."

"I wouldn't mind paying a few visits there myself." Miriam tried to laugh. "What a shop! The muslin, the satin, the silk, the colours. A sight for sore eyes. And anyway, her husband's the senior partner."

Under other circumstances Victoria would have thanked her cousin for her attempts to cover up the truth.

"So I've got news for you, Umm Naim. She runs there precisely on the days when her husband's sick in bed."

Victoria's hands stirred aimlessly under the foam. She wished her sister-in-law would evaporate.

"And he's away often," said Flora emphatically. "He hardly leaves the house. His fits, it shouldn't happen to us, are getting worse. Suddenly he's lying writhing on the floor, and go catch his tongue before it chokes him. And the bitch was prepared to go to bed with that semi-corpse simply in order to get her hands on Rafael."

"So make up your mind," said Miriam, "who's playing with who?"

"I don't know. I said maybe she's put a spell on him."

"Flora, Victoria and I have known him since the day we were born. No spell would work on him."

"So why is he running after that yellow scorpion?"

"First you said she was running after him."

"Stop driving me crazy, Miriam."

"You've been crazy for years."

Flora burst into tears. "Rafael is a sickness with me."

Miriam giggled. "He's a plague that all of us, God forgive me, are dying to be infected by."

Victoria glanced at her cousin—did she still love him so much?

Flora's face relaxed a little. It was good to talk to sister sufferers. "And you," she turned to Victoria, "haven't you got anything to say?"

"I understand that you run to the shop every day too." Her voice sounded hoarse and ugly in her ears.

"That little whore is killing me. Victoria, did Rafael tell you that Hannah threw Elias to the dogs and ran off to Nuna in Palestine?"

Victoria stared at her blankly.

"She sold all the property and left her son with only his share in the shop. And the epileptic knows exactly what the pair of them get up to behind his back. He's afraid to get out of bed and look in the rooms in the dark. Every now and then he calls out, and one of them answers that they'll be with him in a minute. Two days ago for example . . ."

"Flora," Miriam interrupted her, "how do you know all this? Do you live there?"

"Naima tells me herself. She's still a child in spite of everything. Her mother and sister don't want to have anything to do with her. And she's already pregnant like I told you. So we became friendly, her and me. She's dying to talk as much as I'm dying to hear. She invited me to visit them whenever I feel like it. She showed me the big bed in the spare room. The vixen is delighted to tell me all the details: listen and eat your heart out. She guesses, the little viper."

"What does she guess?" Miriam smiled.

"About my sickness, about that plague you mentioned." The two women burst out laughing.

Victoria waited impatiently for them to leave her alone. Fear of her husband, the man who thrilled their imaginations, dominated her feelings.

What would she tell him? How could she not tell him?

The secret which burned inside her for sixty-two years was never revealed to him.

At night the rain came down harder and she got up to help her son draw the blinds and close the windows in the elegant Ramat-Gan apartment. Her mind was on the reddish mound of earth heaped with wreaths and bouquets of flowers. A few hours before she had stood there in the drizzle, still unable to grasp the fact that this was all that remained of him. He was always so afraid of rain, detested cold weather. And now he was outside, in the cold, in a dark night full of thunder and lightning, and she was sheltered between warm walls. Her sons and daughters and their children had gone home to sleep. Only Albert would remain to sleep in her house for the week of mourning. Both of them felt a certain relief after the clamour of the large family that had gathered there after the funeral. Albert was already grey, a tall, thin man. Like his father, he took a book from the shelf to lose himself in it after all the commotion. He was more attached to his father than his brothers, and the emptiness of the loss had not yet taken on the shape of a specific pain in his heart.

"I'll make you tea," she whispered.

He wanted to sit alone. And actually he preferred coffee. But he gave in to the hushed voice of his mother, who was about to become a lonely old woman after eighty years of screaming babies and romping children and the concrete presence of a demanding and providing husband. He decided that it was better not to offer her help in the kitchen, even after she broke four matches next to the gas cooker. Today of all days she would be better off occupying herself with the little services she was accustomed to performing for his aged father before they went to bed at night, not missing the little chore of preparing the tea in the sudden silence that had fallen on the house. She sat opposite him as he sipped the scalding drink, too sweet and strong for his taste.

That day Rafael returned soon after the lamp lighter had

passed down the street, a few hours after all the merchants had gone home. His eyes were tired behind his glasses. He smelled of sex and lust and a stranger's sweat. Months afterwards she heard from his own mouth that they had left the sick man to his own devices and gone down to the basement to continue their quarrel. Rafael had demanded that she have an abortion, and she had defied him.

"Your father went mad. You see your brothers, you're so alike that people take you for one another despite the difference in your ages. The daughters he gave Rahma Afsa and Flora and me are as alike as the white chickens in the chicken coops here in Israel. Maybe he didn't want too many replicas in the alleys of Baghdad. They quarrelled and said harsh things to each other, and you know how lovers make peace in a cold basement. And he came back to me exhausted and reeking of that woman. And I trembled in his presence. Instead of tearing the eyes out of that fornicator, I was afraid that he might go too close to the child's bed and guess by her dreams what my brother did to her. I wanted to tear him to pieces, and I held my tongue. I couldn't meet his eyes.

"Today we live in other times. But then? How I feared him and hated him on that night."

"And Nissan?" her son asked.

She lay in wait for him before Rafael came home. He usually came back from the factory early to grab a bite before the common evening meal. She prayed that Rafael would be delayed to give her time to get her hands on her brother before he arrived home. She didn't know what she would do when the time came. But the desire for revenge drove her out of her mind. She suspected her mother of sending a messenger to tell Nissan that his crime had been discovered. And indeed he arrived home together with her father, keeping as close to him as his father's repugnance at his touch allowed. Her sisters served supper in the big room, and when she entered she found her brother sitting on the floor, a plate on his knees, his backside almost touching his father's toes.

Her rage at Nissan and the odours rising from Rafael's body kept her awake all night. Rafael tossed and turned in his sleep and he flung his arm out in the air, and before it could fall on her she caught it and put it on his chest. If he had washed at least before coming home, but in those days people bathed once a week in winter. Anyone who lived in a private house with his family could afford to bathe twice a week. Rafael brought the taste of his adultery home to his wife's bed. The goodwill ambassador sometimes called on her when it was still sticky from other missions.

Close to midnight he woke up and wanted her. She froze. Not on the day that her daughter's agony had been revealed to her. Not after Flora's revelations. Rafael opened his eyes in astonishment and felt her forehead. "Are you ill?" he asked in sincere concern. She clenched her teeth to stop her voice from betraying her tears. And in her heart she repeated, I'll kill him, just let me get my hands on him and I'll tear off his head. Rafael lay on top of her hardly breathing. Patiently he tried to carry her with him. And all she could think about was Nissan, how his blood would spill and flow along the cracks between the courtyard tiles.

Her heart beat wildly when she heard Rafael accosting her brother in the courtyard the next morning: "Nissan, just a moment." Nissan paled. With a generous smile Rafael turned to her father as he breakfasted on salt cheese, fresh pitta and tea. "Uncle, will you give Nissan your permission to begin work with me tomorrow?" he said loudly, so that she too would hear how good he was to her family.

"Just try to make a man of him," replied Izuri.

Rafael was in a merry mood that morning. "I'll send him back to you fried and roasted the first time he gets out of line."

Nissan needed a long moment to recover from the shock. As soon as he understood that Rafael wasn't joking or plotting revenge, his greed gained the upper hand: "How much will you pay me?"

"You won't be disappointed, believe me."

Decades later she became addicted to the movies shown on the television. She was an active participant, and from time to time she would raise her voice to warn the goodies against the baddies. That distant morning she stifled the cry of warning struggling to escape. From the courtyard Rafael lifted his face to her as she stood next to the railing of the second-floor gallery and his glasses coaxed her to say something about his good deed. Kilmanteen was standing next to her and she gripped the railing with her little hands and looked down at the heads of her father, her grandfather and her uncle. She didn't understand why her father looked so pleased with himself and Nissan looked so happy. Victoria's hand stroked the nape of the little neck tenderly. The child pulled her head away. She watched them showering favours on Nissan. The suspicion crept into her head that she was the sinner, not he. No doubt her punishment would follow soon.

22

A tiny spider emerged from a crack in the plaster and ran sideways, jumping over the other cracks, and suddenly stopped dead, as if trapped in the web of cracks. Victoria was worried.

"Mother, I'm hungry."

"Soon, my eyes," she said in a hushed voice, in order not to disturb Kilmanteen's sleep. The table looked festive. It was already three hours since the entry of the Sabbath and she and Albert were still waiting. The desolate festive table made her feel sad and lonely. Linda had already fallen asleep. Kilmanteen was delirious. She was so quiet when she was awake, so restless in her sleep. Victoria stood up and put her hand on her forehead. It was still burning. The spider was nowhere to be seen, and she couldn't understand why its disappearance filled her with dread. Again she wrapped Kilmanteen in a blanket and stood looking at the thin face, the blue veins branching under the transparent skin. No, she said indignantly. There's a limit. God couldn't do this to her. He had already taken his tribute when He took Suzanne. Perhaps He was only reminding her to count her blessings. They had plenty to eat and a roof over the children's heads. She should thank Him for his goodness and not complain. In the end He would leave the child alone.

The doctor had diagnosed typhus and prescribed ice packs on her head and liquid nourishment only. The rubber bag with blocks of ice clinking inside it looked like a grotesque hat on her head. She shook her head frantically and the hat slipped off. Many generations had believed that cold killed and heat revived. Victoria was afraid that her daughter would freeze to death. And instead her fever had risen and she was burning like fire. From the table rose the scent of basil leaves, rissoles and fried aubergines. The oil in the *kuraya* was almost gone and the Sabbath eve flames were fighting for their lives.

"Then I want to go to bed," grumbled Albert.

"Wait, maybe your father will come."

"Where is he?"

"With your brother," she said. After all, the foetus in Naima's belly would be his brother.

"Albert Jia's not my brother," he responded in a tone of superior wisdom. "He's only my uncle."

The brother she spoke of with melancholy humour would resemble her son Albert more than a brother. More than twenty years later she heard the sound of shoes squelching in the mud behind the door of the canvas hut in the transit camp. The rain swept the fields and flooded the floor of the hut. Inside they went barefoot so as not to wet their shoes. The legs of the beds pushed up against each other looked like the black legs of strange aquatic birds. The mice had already fled the hut, paddling frantically. "It's open," cried Victoria before the wet stranger could knock on the door. When the light of the kerosene lamp fell on his face she said in surprise: "You said you were on guard duty tonight." Then she saw that he wasn't wearing a black beret or an army uniform, and the hair above the rubber coat gleaming with rain was different. After a few moments of explanation, when the mistake was cleared up, the young man retreated down the dark paths of the transit camp. Rafael didn't even bother to look at his face. He was ill with asthma then and unemployed, and meetings with forgotten offspring did not gladden his heart.

Toya and Layla came in and went up to Kilmanteen's bed without saying a word. Toya whispered: "It doesn't look good. Has Rafael gone for the doctor?"

Victoria's laughter frightened Layla. "I'll take Albert," said the girl. "He'll sleep with me tonight."

"Goody!" cried the child, who was depressed by the dismal atmosphere. "I'm hungry and I want to go to bed."

"I'll give you supper and then we'll go to sleep," Layla

promised and hugged him tightly to her chest before leaving the room with him.

Toya, who had preserved a childish freshness and vivacity, lingered by Kilmanteen's bedside. "So he's with her."

Victoria distractedly pleated the corner of the little girl's blanket. This was the first time Rafael had neglected their Friday night dinner for another woman. She was too proud to pour out her heart to her uncle's wife, who was younger than she was. But she was burning with curiosity to ask Toya all the questions she would have liked to fling at Naima. It occurred to her that perhaps Toya too was jealous of Naima.

"She's so beautiful it's out of this world," said Toya.

"And she's got money too. Rafael has been transferring her husband's share of the profits to her every week since he passed away. Her mother and sister are living on her charity. They found a husband for the sister and she's paying for the dowry."

Toya sighed. In such matters you needed luck. How she had yearned to harness Ezra to her chestnut breasts, and all to no avail.

Victoria felt that she had said too much. When Linda woke up she opened the buttons of her dress and pushed her nipple into the baby's mouth before she could scream. It wasn't the same as the sensuous thrill when Albert closed his lips around her breast. Every feed gave her the same feeling of disappointment at the attempt to recreate a lost experience. Kilmanteen groaned in the furnace of her fever. With her free hand Victoria pressed the bag of ice onto her burning head. Toya didn't take her eyes off Kilmanteen. "Rafael's children are beautiful. Ezra's look like monkeys . . ."

Victoria looked at the *kuraya* which had gone out. Kilmanteen's suffering made her feel afraid, and hatred for Nissan engulfed her. If only Toya wouldn't leave her to visit a jollier place in the big house. Salima and Nazima were laying their father's table, and Dahood was singing and strumming on his zither while sipping arak with Ezra and her father. "Sometimes I think it would be worth trying a bit of magic," she said, mainly in order to keep Toya there.

"Don't believe in magic," stated the experienced Toya firmly. "It's a disease like any other."

"She's threatening to find another husband if he doesn't divorce me and marry her." At last she had succeeded in pronouncing the words, in revealing the stinging pain.

Toya's jealousy grew more intense. It had never occurred to her to make any demands on Ezra. And what was her reward? "And him?" she asked.

"I don't know. He's completely confused. Sometimes I hear him cursing, sometimes he just lies on his back and stares at the ceiling. And there are days when he rushes off to her like a whirlwind. Flora says that the little bitch is crazy too. Maybe crazier than him."

"And if he leaves you?"

Kilmanteen moved in her restless sleep. Victoria offered her other breast to Linda. Suddenly the thought hit her like a blow. Kilmanteen might die. This thought was so paralysing that she thrust it out of her mind at once.

"I don't know," she said. "I really don't know what I'll do if he leaves me."

Toya caught the imploring tone in her voice and blushed. Victoria was ashamed to ask her what she thought. She wanted to know how strong the power of love was. Toya had not left Ezra alone even after he married another woman. "Rafael's always returned," said Toya. "From Damascus, from Basra, from Lebanon. He always comes back. It seems there are men who turn the world upside down but always come home in the end."

"You think Rafael's so strong?"

"You're wrong, Umm Albert. Rafael and Ezra are great cowards, if you ask me. Dahood is the strong one," she said with a hint of pride. "He's capable of burning the nest on the tree and flying to another forest. Like they say he did in el-Kazamiya. Rafael . . ."

"She's devouring his soul."

"He's devouring her soul too. So what?"

About half an hour after her father answered the call of the synagogue beadle for the early morning prayer, Rafael came home. Befuddled with exhaustion and a little drunk he groped his way carefully through the dark courtyard. His body was crying for rest. With half-closed eyes he turned to his bed and all he wanted was to be left alone.

"Kilmanteen is very ill," she said.

"There's no improvement?" he asked, more wishful than questioning.

"We have to fetch a doctor."

His legs were about to collapse. He leant against a chair to stop himself from falling. The night before he had tossed and turned till dawn. At midday, when he returned from the shop, he had gone to call the doctor, and then washed himself quickly and gone to Naima. The sleeplessness was taking its toll, he wasn't a strong, healthy man who could go for days without sleeping. In his exhaustion he looked almost ugly and repulsive. "A doctor," he repeated, struggling against the drowsiness numbing his mind. "What more can a doctor do? He gave her medicine. She's got ice on her head. That's what he prescribed." He was ashamed to sit down on the chair, never mind sprawl out on the bed. "What else?" he asked helplessly and his eyes strayed to the untouched Sabbath table. The fragrant basil leaves had wilted, the slices of aubergine were oozing oil like brown tears. He loved Kilmanteen, he said to himself, no less than Izuri loved Victoria. Because of Albert and Kilmanteen and the swaddled little creature in the cradle, yes, and because of Victoria herself, he was adamant in his refusal, even though the girl's tears seared his flesh. In his own eyes he was a devoted father and a loyal husband. And he loved Naima so much. The sound of her steps made his life worth living, her blood flowed in his veins. The fragrance of her skin. Her tongue was so sweet on his. She cried out to him in all her scents and orifices. And his child was in her womb. "I won't kill myself if you don't marry me. Worse than that. I'll go and wash another man's underpants again. His sweat will be on my belly."

He was too tired to remember any more. And he didn't want

to remember either. All he knew was that he had come home, maybe for an hour, maybe for a night, maybe for the rest of his life. How could a man be so tired that he was indifferent to the dying of his own daughter? He wanted to cry for leaving Naima's sad house. His lower jaw trembled.

"You're drunk," whispered Victoria.

"You'll never have the chance to see me drunk." He was ashamed to reveal how exhausted he was. She might think it was from making love. But that night he and Naima had not been swept away. Their lovemaking was cold, deliberate, calculated as a chemist's scales. Everything was cast onto the scales and the scales were evenly balanced.

With the chill of the breaking dawn the wooden beams supporting the room made popping noises, like the creaking joints of a stretching body. Victoria was horrified to realize that she was quite capable of slapping his princely face. He wouldn't have the strength to react. Rafael didn't notice her lowering her blazing eyes, for fear of betraying her sinful thought. But he hadn't failed in his role of provider, she thought. Not only her mother but everyone in the courtyard said that the apple didn't fall far from the tree, and predicted that Rafael would behave like his father: he would spend his money on his mistress and return to Victoria, if at all, with a dirty garment on his back and nothing in his pockets, and she and her children would starve. And they were all wrong. Rafael came home every night. Sometimes at dawn, but he always came home. The more passionately he loved Naima, the more generous he was to his family. He doubled her weekly allowance, he bought the finest clothes for her and the children, he hung gold round her neck, until the women of the courtyard were jealous of her. And not only that, but something strange happened—he desired her more often than previously, and more voraciously. Sometimes she forgot her wounds, and sometimes they opened wide and demanded more.

He noticed Albert's empty bed.

"Layla took him to sleep with her." In the dawn light she saw that his eyes were glittering as in the days of his illness. It seemed to her that all he wanted was to curl up on his son's bed and go to sleep.

Kilmanteen woke up and opened bewildered eyes. Victoria raised her in her arms and the little girl whimpered faintly until she was silenced by her weakness. Her mother raised the glass of orange juice to her lips. "Why don't you drink a little? You haven't touched anything for two days." The child closed her eyes and plunged back into the unconsciousness of her sleep.

Damn you, Nissan, said Victoria to herself.

Rafael stood in the corner and took off his jacket and loosened his tie and removed his shoes. Then he stood in his pyjamas next to the big bed as if requesting permission to lie down on it. She saw that he was biting his lips. His legs were trembling.

"And the doctor?" she demanded. She could feel the rings of darkness behind his closed eyes. She was as tired as he was. She too had not slept for two days. "Rafael!" she cried.

Rafael fell onto his back on the bed and his bare feet touched the floor. Furiously she kicked his toes with her slippered foot. He didn't move. A long moment passed until she realized that he had fainted.

Kilmanteen took three days to die. Victoria entrusted Albert and Linda to Salima and Layla, and shut herself up with the little girl. When she saw that the Angel of Death was waiting for her daughter behind the door, she commenced a bitter argument with Heaven. She saw the doctor as a simple soldier in the ranks with no say in the matter. To God she said that He didn't understand, this was the second time that He had misinterpreted her thoughts. The first time she had wished for her own death, not Suzanne's. Now she mourned the little girl's virginity, but on no account did she want her to die. It was Nissan on whom He should wreak his wrath, not destroy this tender little body. The stars went out and the sun rose and her body grew thin with that of the child shielded in her arms, and she was afraid to close her eyes, in case the Angel of Death seized the opportunity to rob her of her daughter. In her mind's eye she saw herself neither sitting nor lying, but standing on her feet and facing God with the child behind her back. Wasn't it a crying shame to pluck this flower which He himself had made so beautiful? Hadn't they starved together, she and the child, in the freezing basement when Rafael was considered dead? Kilmanteen had grown up without a father. And now that the days of bread and cake were here, the ring of gold and laughter, now of all times the little girl was being thrust back into the dark basement of fear and loneliness.

Damn you, Nissan.

Sometimes she turned her head to look at the child, in her mind's eye, and implored her to raise her voice, too, and beg for her life. Why should God take her?

Let him take Nissan.

In the foggy background blurred figures moved, muffled voices were heard. Sensations of hunger and thirst and weariness passed through her body, but her clear-voiced vigilance did not abate. She was sure that she would prevail. She was strong enough to petition God to ensure that His own justice was done.

And the strength of her faith was matched by the devastation of her defeat. A little coffin and lips whispering prayers, and a hole in the ground in the same landscape where it had been impossible to find Suzanne's grave.

Rafael mourned his daughter, but he had grown up in a world which buried two-thirds of its children, and was grateful for the third remaining. He still had Albert and Linda and a fertile womb and the strength of his loins. It was forbidden to resent what had been taken away. Victoria's grief was exaggerated, even suspect. After the *shiva* she kept a semi-fast and shunned the company of the other women. When he came home from Naima in the evenings Victoria's silences weighed more heavily on his conscience than his mistress's loud scoldings. She shut her doors and allowed only Albert to penetrate the cracks. Her milk dried up and the famished Linda was nourished from any breast available and from cows' milk.

The apathetic Victoria allowed Rafael complete freedom, and he did not hesitate to use it. When they closed the shop in the afternoon he went to Naima's house. After a few weeks he realized that precisely Victoria's indifference led him to miss her touch. He was a gifted lover, and he never took a woman's response for granted. He needed to court her and win her heart with amorous caresses, to play on her body and fan her flame until she burned with passion for him. He had tired of Flora very quickly, for she had caught fire at the first breath. But now when he tried to court Victoria with his amorous ploys he was obliged to retreat in wounded pride. Victoria stared at him in outrage, and waited with withering restraint, and when he failed to recover she rebuked him with icy indignation. It was all wrong. All his tricks failed and the goodwill ambassador retreated in disgrace.

"Go to her and put it into her." She spoke not in anger but calmly and rationally, even with a measure of understanding, like a woman advising her neighbour how to treat an irritating rash.

He stood up and pulled on his underpants. "What do you know about her?" he growled. He himself understood that his question was stupid and spiteful, and he boiled with rage because she had brought him to such a pass.

"She's ready to burn her house down for your sake. Go to her."

"You'll still blame me for what happened to Kilmanteen."

"No. I'm just afraid of you, like a backward child who's been taught nothing but fear. Go back to Naima. She didn't grow up with you. She never learned to tremble in your presence."

"Remember—what happened to Kilmanteen was God's will, not the act of any human hand."

He couldn't understand why she froze. "Go!" she shouted.

His feet were nailed to the floor. She wasn't angry with him. He saw that her scream came from fear. Something of that strange fear crept into his own heart. "Am I a monster?"

"No. Just go now."

He left, but he didn't go to Naima. He went to sit in the al-Shaat tea-house on the banks of the Tigris, and saw two fishermen drawing their long net studded with flapping fish into their boat, and shouting angrily at a group of Jewish boys amusing themselves on a rowing boat and endangering their net, and he said to himself that once upon a time no Jew would have dared to laugh at the threats of Moslem fishermen. Then he drank his cooling tea and asked himself if his wife had gone mad. And he was ready to believe that he was bearing a heavy load of grief, and he admired himself.

With a strange stubbornness Victoria would take out Kilmanteen's clothes and wash them diligently, and not on Wednesdays, when everybody did their washing, but on Sundays. The little garments would sometimes flutter alone on the line for two whole days. Then she would prepare the coal iron and iron out every crease with great concentration and press the pleats to perfection. Sometimes she took a needle and thread and changed a button or added a white frill here and there. But for her elevated status in the courtyard the women would have been outspoken in their condemnation of this defiance of God. Since Rafael left her to her own devices to do as she wished, her father decided to scold her in his place, and told her that she must submit to the will of God. This display of the child's clothes at the front of the roof smacked of defiance and even heresy. "Take down the poor child's dresses," he ordered her. "Give them to the poor. Give them to me and I'll throw them in the river."

Tears welled up in her eyes and a new and unexpected wave of hatred for her brother surged up in her. She almost betrayed him into the murderous hands of her father and her husband. She wanted to shout: I want him to see her clothes until he dies like a dog. Instead she screamed: "Why me? What have I done?"

"And me? What have I done? I gave your mother nineteen children, and what did the Master of the Universe leave me? If I hung up the clothes of all those who have gone, the world would be full of clotheslines. And the ones I've got left apart from you, Victoria? May God forgive me. They're not worth even . . ." and he waved his hand dismissively and was silent.

Nissan kept to the shadows. He would leave for work before

Rafael and come home after his father. His mother had already completely forgotten his crime. Victoria heard the people in the courtyard praising the new Nissan, so quiet and industrious, and held her tongue. For many years her brother never looked her in the eye. He died at the age of seventy-one, sitting at his ease amid the bunches of parsley and spring-onions in a corner of the Carmel market in Tel Aviv, and until that moment he didn't even know that there was anything wrong with his heart. At his death he left grey-haired children and so many grandchildren he didn't remember their names.

Miriam silenced the gossiping tongues. Her cousin, she said, was entitled to mourn as long as she liked. Kilmanteen had sometimes slept with her when Victoria was in difficulties. Now she cooked for Victoria and looked after her children, and together with Salima and Layla she encompassed her in a circle of warm affection. Victoria was grateful to her precisely for not denouncing Rafael, unlike the others. In her mourning too Victoria did not forget their hypocrisy. The men were jealous of Rafael, the women of her.

It was Flora of all people who was responsible for her recovery. One day she burst into the courtyard with her usual tempestuousness, when Victoria was standing in the smell of smouldering coals and ironing the dead girl's dresses. Flora overturned the table and as the two women struggled the dresses were torn between their fingers.

"Madwoman, stupid fool," shrieked Flora with her hair dishevelled and the powder streaking down her face, a gold tooth glittering in her mouth and her silk *abbaya* lying at her feet in a black pool. "Who are you trying to impress with your insane grief?"

Victoria breathed heavily and looked at the tatters of Kilmanteen's dresses in her clawing fingers, and she fell onto a wicker chair. Flora loomed up as if through the shimmering haze of a khamsin and gave her a glass of water. "Drink," she said. And Victoria drank like an obedient child, and Flora took a silver case from her bag and pushed a cigarette between her lips, like a man, and lit it. The eyes of the women watching from a safe distance popped out of their sockets. This was the first time they had ever seen a woman of her age smoking in public. Flora crossed her legs and scattered the ash next to her chair with a practised tap of her finger.

"I'll bring you a mirror so you can have a good look at yourself. A brokendown old antique looks more attractive than you do. I've just come from there. She's having a party to celebrate her sister's engagement. That little brat's got more sense than all the rest of us put together. She twists you and your husband round her little finger. Her sister's laughing and she can't see that her fiancé's eyes pop out whenever he looks at the bitch."

Victoria listened in spite of herself. "May they all rot in hell. What do I care?"

"You were almost a widow. You think a divorcee's any better off? A widow may have a chance, but a divorcee? Hunger and cold and barefooted children. You'll have to send Albert out to break his back at the age of ten to support you. If you've made up your mind to be a deserted wife you shouldn't have brought him up the way you did. He won't have any teeth left with the blows that will land on his face. He'll learn to serve his masters the hard way. They'll have to break his spirit before he'll bring a penny home. Between one glass of arak and the next your husband found himself inside that bitch's cage."

"And her sister's fiancé?"

"That's just blackmail. To threaten Rafael. Her mother's putting pressure on her. She's demanding that she make Rafael divorce you, or she'll find her a husband. Listen to me, even though she's so clever, she loves Rafael like a madwoman. She's not interested in his money or the presents he brings her. It's the most dangerous kind of love. Are you listening to me? She loves him more than you do."

Victoria stood up without noticing that her hands were clenched into fists. It's not possible, it's not possible, she muttered, and she walked across the courtyard and found Albert playing with her two brothers and took his head in her hands and went on muttering to herself.

23

Rafael took to his bed. The courtyard was all agog. In the days of his consumption, when he was coughing up his lungs in bits and pieces, he would get up and go out to earn a living for his family. Now not only did he stay in bed all day, but they could hear his groaning through the walls. The adults hushed the children so as not to disturb his rest, and they too walked on tiptoe in respect for the man sick with the most fatal disease of all.

Victoria hovered over him day and night, soothing him with a cup of hot milk, listening to the sick, swelling heart. Her lids dropped, but she went on nodding her head as if she was still hearing the outpouring of words. Sometimes he would suspect her of only pretending to be awake and listening, and he would stop the rain of poisoned words and cry out in terror like a man abandoned in menacing darkness: "Victoria, can you hear me?" And she would take a deep breath and rub her eyes with the back of her hand and say: "I'm here, Rafael, I'm listening."

She kept her happiness to herself. In her mind's eye she would sometimes pat herself on the shoulder and exult: How lucky you are, Victoria. Like a babe in arms she fed him on this happiness, lapped him in her smiles, but at the same time she hid them from him, lest he think she took his hellish suffering lightly, and did everything in her power not to betray her feelings of triumph to him. Only the fear that he might not recover clouded her joy. Some people had died of this disease, and others had gone mad.

The residents of the courtyard did what they could to succour the couple. Salima and Layla took care of Albert and Linda devotedly. Ezra, the faithful friend, spent hours at Rafael's bedside, and he would drink straight from the bottle and offer it generously to his cousin fighting for his sanity. Najia ignored the ancient enmity between them and brewed a potion of camomile with her own hands to soothe his spirit. Flora appeared in the courtyard every day and slyly offered the cure at which she excelled. Victoria smiled in embarrassment. "I'm serious, Victoria," explained Flora, an old hand at diseases of this nature. "In the same way that the hair of the dog cures its bite, so the fragrance of the lemon expels the perfume of palm blossom from the heart." Victoria politely declined both her mother's camomile and the scent of the lemon blossom given off by Flora's practised body.

"Do you think she's arrived there already?" asked Rafael when he awoke from his delirium.

Victoria knitted her brow. "How should I know? You say that you have to cross a great desert to get to Syria, and from there you have to travel to Lebanon, and until you arrive in Palestine . . ."

His face was covered with an eight-day beard. His eyes were sunken. In her heart she was glad that her rival couldn't see him like this. Rafael had not gone to say goodbye to her. Perhaps he had done so in another place at another time. But he probably hadn't said goodbye to her at all. That was his way. But she, Victoria, had been there. Two hours before the time of departure. She wanted to see her enemy quitting the battlefield with her own eyes. In her *abbaya* and veil she stood at the corner of the alley opening into the big street. Men and rough women passed her and turned to look at her in surprise, wondering what a woman in a silk *abbaya* was doing there so early in the morning, and she had been obliged to walk to and fro so as not to attract unwanted attention. A horrible suspicion tortured her. The square was full of donkeys and carts and mules. Peasants who had already unloaded their wares sipped strong tea, horses munched oats, and peddlers shouted in the midst of the crowd. Those who couldn't afford to buy leaned against the wall and breakfasted on bread and onions. Flora had spoken of a motorcar, but there was no car parked there. But for the fact that Ezra had confirmed it, she wouldn't have believed that she was in the right place. Again she crossed the square and made up her mind to return home in a quarter of an hour, no more. The sun had flooded the roofs long ago and touched the windows of the upper storeys.

When the car finally appeared, arrogantly thrusting people and beasts aside with the roar of its engine, the hooting of its horn, and the reek of its petrol and oil, she still couldn't believe that she was actually about to witness the defeat of her rival. Instead of the joy and triumph she had anticipated, everything seemed so futile. The driver was a red-headed giant, hot-tempered and mean-looking, a ruffian who appeared to enjoy the terror he inspired. "Son of a sodomized whore," he bawled at his assistant, "wash the windows again and this time don't smear them with the stinking piss of your sister who fucks lame dogs." The assistant waited patiently for the storm to wear itself out, and then he sat down, humming cheerfully, next to a stall offering of a mixture of broad beans and onion wedges and breadcrumbs soaked in lemon juice. The driver turned to the other side of the square and ordered breakfast in the company of those who could afford to sit around a spit of roasting mutton.

A sudden gust of wind buffeted Victoria's *abbaya* and threatened to thrust her forward, and she was afraid that it would blow her like a black kite all the way to the empty car. At the same moment the witch appeared without a veil, her *abbaya* draped elegantly round her shoulders, with three porters carrying her luggage behind her, and the little bastard bringing up the rear in the arms of a strange man, and gazing curiously at the square with Albert's eyes. Victoria knew the man from Flora's descriptions—a shy man with broad shoulders, solid thighs and big hands, a provider and support who Naima's sister would be able to rely on for many a year. So the elder sister had finally found a real man. Strange, though, that her sister's fiancé was carrying the witch's child like a loving father, as if he himself was about to drive away with her. Victoria's heart understood the evidence of her eyes before her mind grasped it, and accordingly she was surprised to see that her rival's mother and sister were not there to say goodbye to her. Something collapsed inside her. Rafael too had not come to say goodbye to the poor girl. Naima radiated a touching, youthful loveliness, and she was leaving the city of her birth like a thief, with only a strange man to see her off. She was setting off alone, almost a child herself, with a baby, for a country full of greedy mosquitoes and angry Arabs. Now she was shaking her beautiful head. For some reason she seemed to be fasting. You could see the hunger on the faces of the fasting, even if they themselves did not sense it. Victoria was an expert on hunger, and the hunger suited her husband's mistress, it made her beauty even more bewitching.

The luggage was hoisted onto the roof and tied down securely. The red-headed driver and his assistant got into the car, and the driver hooted to frighten a donkey standing in the way, and the donkey bolted and overturned a vegetable stall. Rafael's mistress sat down in the back of the car with her tender neck bearing her head high. And Victoria's heart was touched with pity again. The pool girl had even forgotten her little son—she did not stretch out her arms to take him from the man. She sat motionless, indifferent to her surroundings, and then she shifted on the seat until her shoulder touched the other window. The fiancé looked round the square and got into the car and sat down in the empty seat next to Naima. The driver's assistant roared with laughter and made an obscene gesture at the owner of the vegetable stall, who was protesting vociferously about his spoiled wares, and the car drove off with a loud hoot on its horn.

Victoria was left standing open-mouthed.

A pallid light filtered through the slits in the blinds. Albert was busy relaxing his body, limb after limb, from the bottom up, before falling asleep. He tautened and relaxed his muscles, lingering from time to time over a strained tendon or dull ache in his bones. Thus he would patiently and carefully loosen the knot of tensions which had accumulated in his body, controlling his breathing until it was even, avoiding any unnecessary movement, making his heart beat quietly, purifying himself of sensations and emptying his mind of thoughts, and when he finally reached his head, in a blessed semi-consciousness on the very verge of sleep, he would pray that no cat would choose this moment to break into an angry wail or neighbour shatter the stillness with an irritating cough. Some forty years had passed since his experiences in the underground in Iraq, and the method was still proving its efficacy on the desolate white nights when both body and soul were exhausted in the arid urban desert. The sweetness of sleep encompassed him. On the edges of consciousness he heard the heavy rumbling of a truck, and his sleep was shattered when a rubbish bin slipped from a sanitation worker's hands, the driver stepped on the accelerator in neutral and the engine screeched.

Victoria was ready waiting behind the door, and she opened it with the freedom of a mother's demanding love. "You need more tea," she pronounced. He had hoped to resume his relaxation when the sanitation truck moved off, but his mother was standing there at the beginning of the *shiva*, unaccustomed as yet to her widowhood, and afraid of the loneliness threatening to engulf her days.

"I'll bring you a few biscuits."

He stood up. "Let's go to the kitchen." The kitchen table was very small. Their knees touched. She didn't pour a cup for herself, since she had already drunk her fill. The intimacy of the way they were sitting increased the feeling of bereavement.

"Do you understand? I stood there as if I was drugged. The minx had run away to Palestine with her sister's fiancé!"

Albert protested. "Where do you get the energy to talk about a thing like that now?"

Victoria took no notice of him. "I was trembling all over, as if I'd witnessed a murder. I looked at the tomatoes and turnips scattered on the ground and I said to myself, Victoria, you don't understand what's going on here. That trollop loves your husband, she loves him so much she was willing to be his mistress. Her mother and sister made her life a misery in order to save her from herself. The hussy was prepared to sacrifice everything for your father's sake. Flora told me that they'd offered her wealthy, quite attractive men, but she reacted as if she was blind and deaf. Her nose was full of your father's smell, damn him!"

"Mother, we're still sitting *shiva* for him. There isn't even a tombstone yet. His grave is full of this rain."

"Oy, I forgot . . . Forgive me. My tongue can't forget the bitterness of those days. His body was in the shop or at home, but his soul was over there, with that wicked witch. It wasn't Rafael. You spoke to him and he stared at you, forgive me, my son, with the look of a retard. For no reason his face would suddenly darken with grief and he would begin writhing inside his shirt as if he was struggling for his last breath. Out of love for that criminal he lost his masterful voice, his dignified bearing that sent thrills through me.

"The mother and sister, especially the sister, never left your father and Naima alone, they would shadow her footsteps, whisper in her ear that your father was playing with her, that he would land her with a bastard and never divorce me to marry her, that tomorrow or the next day he would find some other, more beautiful, woman and throw her to the dogs. They would follow her to their secret assignations and surprise them and make scenes. It's a wonder they didn't get heart attacks. Your father and Naima roamed around the town searching for a refuge for the love that was burning up their bodies, and the minute they touched one another those two women set up a hullabaloo. Your father was fading away, he had black circles round his eyes, his hands shook so much that his cup rattled on its saucer like castanets. I was sure that the TB would return or that he would go mad. And Flora, whose thighs were smoking and whose arse was in flames, would turn up every day in the courtyard and feed me the latest news, because she couldn't drink the poison alone. She thought your father would break. She was a constant visitor in Naima's mother's house, and she knew how to worm her way into the good graces of both sides with her flattery. Everything was open to her. And she told me that your father wouldn't be able to stand it for more than two months. If his lover fell ill he would go mad, forget his wife and children and run to her. He would crawl on all fours to the mother and sister and beg for the hand of that hussy or do something even more terrible—he would find a house and move into it with his fancy suits and live there in sin with her for the rest of his life.

"And so I stood there looking at the tomatoes and turnips and shouting to myself: Victoria, your salvation's come. Naima has renounced your husband! She's eloping with another man, who she may not even be attracted to. It's simply revenge against her mother, her sister, and especially your father. Until she got into that car, she and I could have torn each other to pieces. In those days a husband was first and foremost bread in your mouth and a roof over your head and a garment on your back and the respect of other people. Only after all that was he anything else. So I unsheathed my claws, I raised my voice. I fought, Albert, with all I had. And I didn't have much. A son and a baby girl and two little graves obliterated by the wind and the rain. And suddenly this ravishing beauty admits her defeat. Runs away and leaves your father tossing and turning on his bed and raising the roof with his groans. Let me give you another cup of tea. Am I boring you? It's almost morning and I'm ruining your sleep. But listen. The mother and sister searched here, they searched there, one day passed, and another day, until they realized that they'd been had for the biggest suckers in Baghdad. After a while news came from Palestine. The two women sat and tore their hair out. Naima had married her sister's fiancé. The mother and sister ran to the Rabbinate in Baghdad and they sent an urgent letter to the Rabbinate in Palestine, and the marriage was annulled. From the distance the hussy replied with a loud burst of laughter. She was a character, that Naima. She lived with the fiancé like man and wife even after the annulment of the marriage and cocked a snook at the whole world. And afterwards? She died after thirty years. We were already here in Israel. They started a big factory for radios and she rose to the position of shift manager there. Those were the days when a middle-aged immigrant like your father couldn't get a job sweeping the floor in a place like that. You should have seen her funeral. They took the bier to the factory and men and women filed past and paid their respects like they did with the coffins of kings in Baghdad. And the convoy of buses and cars that drove from the factory to the cemetery with their lights on. Not like your father's modest funeral. No. He didn't meet her here and he didn't even go to her funeral. The tables were turned. She turned into a mountain and he, begging his pardon, was like a mouse in those days. Flora came to the transit camp and took me to the funeral. Of course I talk about her with admiration. She was a woman who succeeded in a country that broke strong men. They say she read books, and even learned English. After forty years in the country your mother hardly understands her great-grandchildren's Hebrew."

The courtyard's sympathies were with Rafael. "Love is a grave disease," Dahood explained to Victoria as he sat with a bottle by Rafael's bedside. The last arrow Naima shot into Rafael's body was poisoned. The fiancé was contemptible in his eyes. Naima would ask him to overcome his revulsion for her sister's sake. And now she herself had taken him to her bosom. Victoria was sure that he would recover in the end and get over the blow, but he would be a different Rafael. Perhaps, she hoped, he would be a more domesticated Rafael, a more faithful, more considerate Rafael. Later on she said that he had always been domesticated, faithful and considerate in his own way, even in the days when he had been spellbound by Naima. There wasn't a man in the courtyard of whom she could say that he was a better man than Rafael.

One morning Rafael's outpourings came to an end and he withdrew into silence. Victoria told him in detail of the scene she had witnessed in the square, and he didn't react. For decades he never mentioned Naima's name.

At midday Miriam came in with a plate of soup she had prepared from the leftovers of the chickens they were cooking for dinner. Festive dinners were held almost every evening in order to cheer up the patient. Her daughter Amal, who was Albert's age, came in with her, clinging shyly to her skirts.

"Get up," said Miriam. "How long can a purse mourn for the money that fell out of it? If I know you, you'll still bring joy to the hearts of a lot of trollops, damn your soul."

"Miriam," he whispered in the fainting voice he cultivated in those days, "please leave me alone."

Albert's eyes flashed in the corner. He was sick and tired of the way everybody was pampering the grown man, and he shouted: "Go away, Amal! This isn't your room." Amal, gaining confidence from her mother's dress, put out her tongue at him. He rushed at her, but she was a tough little girl and not afraid of fighting with him. His charge was broken on her plump shoulder. He put his hands around her throat and she slipped her foot between his legs and brought him down like a practised wrestler, and they both rolled on the carpet. Amal's face was flushed. Miriam looked at the two of them and her throat constricted. Just like Rafael, she said to herself, exactly like him. In a hoarse voice she cried: "Yallah, get up! And I'm not inviting Flora to feed you either."

Before sunset Victoria went up to the roof to take down the washing. A light breeze soared up into the azure sky, and for a moment Victoria left the washing and lay down on the summer bed and stretched her neck and watched the birds still gliding in the last rays of the sun. The flocks bypassed the houses of the Jewish quarter and hurried towards the magic realms, where she had bought a new house, almost exactly like the one she had seen in her imagination. Behind it stretched green fields, and near its windows flowed the clear water of an irrigation canal. With her own eyes she had seen birds perching on clods of earth and drinking from the canal. Opposite the house the palm groves stretched as far as the horizon, and all around it was quiet, and there was no stench of urine and sweat and rotting fruit and mouse droppings, but the fragrance of the flowers of the fields. People strolled there at their leisure, enjoying the scented air. Four days after Rafael had taken to his bed she had gone out with Flora to meet the contractor Abu Hamid, and returned intoxicated to the delirium of her lovesick husband. Between one groan and the next he had agreed. "Pay him an advance and leave me alone," he said.

On the roof she held the clothesline with both hands. From the distance her body looked like another garment blowing in the wind. She was so happy. That night Rafael whispered his agony, and she turned around and cupped something in her hands in her sleep, and it swelled and swelled between her fingers. He didn't move away from her. On the contrary, his sighs subsided. In the morning there was still a shadow of a smile left in the corner of his eye. Victoria was radiant. The long winter hibernation had sloughed off her. He was still her husband. He was still in her house. She immediately hid her smile for fear of the Evil Eye.

24

At the end of his life, when he was ninety-two, he didn't know what to think. He was in "Beth Batya", a clean, efficient, modern institution, standing on the edge of a blooming orange grove. The smiling nurses whose voices murmured in the shining corridors did not expect a man of his age to return to the outside world after fracturing his thigh bone. The institution was grand, but the inmates were like the survivors of a column of ants which had been viciously sprayed with a noxious pesticide. About ten years before he had given up wearing the glasses which had made such an impression at the beginning of the century. All his friends and acquaintances had already given up the ghost, and it seemed that he was looking forward to seeing the dawn of the twenty-first century with liberated eyes.

He was aware of everything that was happening around him. He sat in a wheelchair and waited with all the other patients in their wheelchairs for the rooms to be cleaned before lunch. Opposite him a woman inmate sat up straight in suspect alertness and stealthily peed into the bulky nappy between her legs. The head of the old man sitting next to him dropped onto his shoulder and he cried out piteously as if his shoulder was about to collapse beneath the weight of his vacant head. Next to a giant potted plant a woman stared at the closed horizon and saliva dribbled down her chin. Rafael looked, and the stench of death rose into his nostrils from the spotless tiles. Here he was, at the very end of the corridor which began in running feet and strong feelings and ended in staring vacantly at a sick woman who had lost her wits, and opened her legs to display a hole as black as the memory into which all the years of passion had disappeared.

In the dining room an inmate whose daughter was trying to feed him a meat ball spat it out like a naughty child and began to whimper.

Rafael froze on his wheelchair and wondered why he, the delicate, sickly consumptive, should have outlived the group of old men who had become friends on the green bench in the avenue of eucalyptus trees in Ramat-Gan. They had all shrunk until they disappeared. Before he broke his thigh he had grown sick of literature, and developed a passion for history books and fried onions and black bread smeared with blackened oil. In the wheelchair these appetites too had faded. All that was left was a kind of dull ache in his leg and a kind of fear of the darkness which resembled the private parts of the old woman opposite him, and which was about to swallow him up. His sons shaved his brown face, but he was indifferent to them. They urged him to get up and take the glass of water on the bedside locker by himself, or at least to wriggle the toes of the broken leg. With the determination of healthy people able to walk about on their own two legs they explained to him that he was liable to get pneumonia, that he was in danger of dying if he didn't move. His eyes searched for the window, for the scraps of clouds disappearing behind the orange groves. His sons took on the dimensions of threatening figures, intent on forcing him to do things beyond his capacity.

"Why don't you say anything?" demanded Victoria, who had saved him from many deathbeds. Just as he had been saved from tuberculosis decades before the discovery of penicillin, just as she had saved him from malaria and typhus and asthma and disappointed love and the hardships of the mass immigration in the fifties, so she would bring him back to her this time too in order to repulse the loneliness threatening her nest. "Rafael," she cried, beside herself with fear disguised as insult, "why are you looking into the distance as if I'm not here?" She avoided looking at the window for fear that she too might see in the scraps of cloud what it was that was attracting his attention. Her fingers tore the peel off a tangerine and angrily ripped off the fibres, and she pushed a segment of the fruit between his pursed lips until he was forced to part his stony jaws. "Eat," she commanded. "It will make you strong. You're drying up."

The fruit turned into a lump in his throat that it was impossible to get rid of. How hard it is to go on where there's no strength left, he said to himself. But Victoria thought otherwise. Her busy fingers tore off another segment. Her face was flushed. She was encouraged by her little victory, her triumph over the scraps of clouds. "Open your mouth," she said firmly.

This time his jaws were locked.

For decades he had known how to hide from her in the crowded courtyard in Baghdad, in the house swarming with children in the wooded suburb, in the canvas hut in the transit camp in the back yard of Israel. And she had been searching for ways of knowing him since she was a small child. He was the only man she knew who could hide when he was present. When she asked him the first time, about sixty years before he broke his thigh, why he did this to her, his answer was strange: "I'm thinking." The other men she knew were obliged to think only when asked a question, or faced with a difficulty. Or so it seemed to her. And they generally thought aloud. But he thought for no evident reason. As if he were spreading inner wings and travelling to secret realms. Thus he would disappear in silence behind his books too, and his seclusion seemed to her to smack of something shameful.

The tangerine segment remained suspended in mid-air between them, his fingers were stiff in spite of the generous heating. Again the pain welled up in her. "Tell me, why won't you say anything?" The tremor of a person encountering an unknown darkness crept into her voice.

His eyes withdrew from the window. Now he closed his ears against the noise of the patients in the corridor. The disintegrating creatures who were once men and women all looked alike. A faint flush spread over his face, and suddenly he looked young and handsome in Victoria's eyes, as if he were about to be reborn. He went on ignoring the horrors in the wheelchairs around him.

He had told her a lot of lies in his life. He had lied about the other women, he had hidden money from her, he had hidden shameful intentions. And she had always loved the thin, brown man, whom she had never trusted, not now either, as his eyes continued to be drawn to the hostile darkness. And so she asked him suspiciously: "What are you thinking about now, Rafael?"

"I'm afraid, Victoria," he whispered.

She thought he was up to his old tricks again, that he was deceiving her. His handsome face was calm, his brow unruffled.

"What are you afraid of? Tell me," she encouraged him.

He closed his eyes. Her voice was an agonizing searchlight.

"You're hiding again."

"I'm afraid," he repeated with the patience of indifference.

She took his frozen fingers in her hand. Something horrifying flowed from his icy skin into her flesh. Immediately she repulsed the fear. "We're going to eat," she announced briskly.

He closed his eyes again. "I don't want to."

"The food will put you on your feet."

"I can't stand on my feet. I don't want to stand on my feet," he said with a clarity unusual in that institution.

She flared up. With a swift movement she stood up and banged her hand on the window sill. She saw the young nurses with painted lips and made-up eyes and fresh, smooth skin. With red smiles they shook the sheets and blankets, and their young hands invaded the privacy of the men's flesh.

"So you like it here!" she burst out. "Go on, say it, say that you like it here because of the nurses. You always wanted women to pamper you day and night."

"I worked hard all my life," he rebelled, with a sudden spurt of animation. "I've got enough money in the bank. You can leave me here."

She was used to not believing him. For about a week he lay in bed at home and she didn't believe that his thigh was broken. The children, too, who had drunk in their scepticism with their mother's milk, refused to realize that he was suffering. Sometimes he would become confused and complain of pains in the wrong leg. One of the daughters-in-law claimed that when nobody was looking he stood up and took a few steps unaided, without a single groan. He had already spun so many webs of lies around her that she feared she was losing her sanity. Women were drawn to him like wasps to date honey. And she always took him back. Her passion for him was like a smouldering ember which she never stopped fanning, but at the same time layers of resentment and suspicion accumulated in her soul.

When she turned her head from the window she saw that he had fallen asleep and his head had dropped backwards. At this moment he was so precious to her that she was afraid he would slip away from her in his sleep. Her heart went out to him: he was handsome as a bridegroom. He smelled good. Not the smell of old men. Not the smell of death. With her gnarled hand she stroked his white hair. She peered round the corridor, and for the first time in sixty-eight years she kissed him on her own initiative. And she blushed.

"Victoria, are you still here?" he asked when he woke.

"You've been washed," she said.

"Yes," he replied without understanding what she was getting at. "I'm thirsty."

She hurried to the kitchen and came back holding a cup with a spout. He took a few sips and jerked his head back, too weak to raise his hand and push the cup away. There was a look of distress in his eyes. He had the feeling that a few drops had fallen onto his chin and remained there, a disgraceful witness to his impotence. She understood. His lips were dry and his chin spotlessly clean, but nevertheless she wiped his delicate face, like the face of an ancient Egyptian, with her hand.

"Who washed you?" she asked nonchalantly, as if in a casual conversation on the balcony of their new apartment.

But he was wary of her, as usual. "They did," he answered vaguely.

"The male nurses or the girls?" she inquired with a sly smile.

"One of the girls," he gave in helplessly, his voice so faint as to be almost inaudible.

"The one with the black curls or the one with the whore's eyebrows?"

He closed his eyes and said in resignation: "The one with the eyebrows." His voice grew even fainter.

Her face reddened. The resentment of years boiled up inside her. She looked over her shoulder and said in a whisper: "Did she put her hand down there too?"

He opened his eyes wide. His fingers picked at the material of the green pyjamas. Suddenly his voice was clear: "No. I washed there myself."

His lids dropped, he didn't have the strength left to move his face muscles. Victoria was filled with gratitude. She knew that with his last flicker of life he wanted to please her. Perhaps it was his last lie, but if so he was lying for her, for her sake alone. For years she had been washing him. After she had peeled off the layers of clothing he would sit where she seated him, a skinny plucked chicken on the white plastic chair in the bathroom. And as she washed him wordlessly his body would submit to her and respond to the touch of her fingers. Even under the warm jet of water in the shower he would shiver, and her heart would brim over with gratification as she gathered him up like an infant into the towel pressed against her breast. His penis was as withered as a dry leaf, and its colour was rusty, almost black, that penis which had inflamed so many women, which had been abandoned to such alien hands. If only they had allowed her to, she would have washed him here in the nursing home too. But between these white walls everything was done according to different rules and rituals. Hefty peasants hoisted the patients in the air, young girls brandished spotless sheets, others unsheathed needles. No, they didn't let her wash him. As if her rights to him had expired. Her throat was full of tears. "Rafael," she whispered, "Rafael."

He sank into a strange sleep. Again she stroked his emaciated shoulder and whispered as if summoning him to come to her aid: "Rafael, they say I have to go now."

A girl in a starched white gown was standing and waiting with the smile of authority. Victoria raised her head in bitter pride. Why not a man? she said to herself. Now too he was being taken from her by a slip of a girl. The lift was out of order. She gripped the banister and walked carefully down the stairs on her swollen, rheumatic legs. A vicious pain split her head. She was afraid to let go of the banister, and ashamed to sit down on the stairs to look for the blood pressure pills in her purse. She might burst into tears, and perhaps she wouldn't be able to get up again. On the ground floor another lone, gleaming corridor stretched out in front of her. A very long corridor.